Succession

STEVEN VEERAPEN

First published in 2020 by Sharpe Books.

CONTENTS

Prologue
Chapters 1 – 30
Epilogue
Author's Note

SUCCESSION

Prologue

Richmond Palace, February 1603

Robert Cecil placed little value on symbolism … normally. It was the job of a secretary to see to the practicalities of state. But this was far from a normal occurrence. The room in which he stood was little more than a closet: a fitting place for a private operation. He placed the gold-fringed cushion on the seat which dominated and stepped back, towards the left-hand wall. Immediately, the arras buffeted his shoulders. His tut was lost to the whispered disputation of the barber-surgeon and the physician, the former small and spare, the latter equally small but overstuffed. Their conference, taking place on the right of the room, was only a few feet from him.

'The flesh is weak,' hissed the learned man, stroking a white beard. 'I know the movement of her Majesty's blood.'

'There will be no blood,' sniffed the barber. 'I have done the like on many men and women and have butchered none. I am as skilled in my labour as you in yours.'

'How many queens?'

'I cannot hold my tools and this.' Candlelight wavered. Held in the barber's hand, it provided the only source of illumination. Some fool underling had forgotten the iron candle-tree.

'It is not the business of a royal physician to carry the candle and light the way of an inferior person.'

'It is today,' snapped the barber, thrusting the candleholder towards him. The flame guttered, leaving a trail of stars. By his tone, the inferior person was enjoying his moment in the sun.

'Enough,' said the secretary. There was no time for petty bickering. The whole affair was to take place in secrecy, lest it get out of the palace, into the streets, and become stained with the darkness of popular premonition. Wrangling the two men had been a challenge in itself. The Privy Council insisted on a physician being present, one having been required to work out the most auspicious day in advance. The barber-surgeon was needed for his skills. 'Take it, Master Physician.' Though Cecil did not raise his voice – he hardly had to in the confined space – the other men froze and turned to him. They put their backs to the opposite wall. Without a word of protest, the physician took the candle and held it at his waist. The three waited.

When the bells outside stopped ringing, their insistent burbling was replaced with the frenzied chatter of dozens of voices and the accompanying padding of feet. The court had finished with the service, and would no doubt be discoursing on the appearance of their sovereign as she retired to her apartments to eat. Minutes passed, taking with them the noises.

And then the closet door opened.

Cecil and his two companions each fell to one knee. The door was swiftly closed from the outside. A grunt bid them rise. Already, Queen Elizabeth was moving heavily towards the seat. She ignored Cecil's proffered arm and settled onto it, roosting like a peacock. It was as well, he thought, that she was not wearing one of the elaborate gowns she donned for portraits and had recently worn for the Venetian ambassador. Not one of them would have left room for the men to stand comfortably. Those dresses, he supposed, she might never wear again. Instead, the day dress – a spangled but otherwise simple affair, more night-gown than anything – made for comfortable and silent passage to her makeshift chair of state.

Two things, thought Cecil, truly betrayed age – and wrinkled flesh was not one of them. The grey hairs she could and did hide, but the carriage, the sluggish movement, was the true herald of impending death. Even a wrinkled old carcass could counterfeit youth if the body was sprightly. Elizabeth, however, had begun to slow, to wobble, to seem to drag herself around.

'Your Majesty,' breathed the physician. He had not fully risen. 'This operation shall give you no pain. If it does,' he added, in the tremulous voice of the lecture hall, 'I pray you cry out and I will put a stop to this …' He trailed off.

She did not look at him, though his candlelight picked out the lines of her face. The hawk-like profile familiar to thousands from its appearance on coins had sagged, the long nose drooping and the cheekbones jutting. Her eyes, charcoal in the dim chamber, were sunken deeper than ever under their prominent upper lids. The vibrant orange wig did not hide her age; it drew attention to it, parodying the woman she had once been. Time, thought Cecil, was a cruel master, seeming to enjoy the changes it forced on people. It was almost sad that so great a queen had come to this. Far better she had died in the full blaze of her pomp, lived on as an image painted in murals, on canvases. A prince ought, he often thought, to die at the height of his or her glory years rather than live to see them recede further and further into the past. This prince had accomplished much and enjoyed the fruits of it, only to succeed at less with each year and watch the vines wither.

Soon, thought Cecil. God willing, soon.

'May I?' asked the barber. Again, she did not respond, but held out her cushioned stick of a left arm. He took it and bent his face over her hand.

That hand, Cecil knew, had, with its mate, been a great source of pride. The fingers, once milky white, were now almost blue. Their slenderness had been lost to swelling fluid until both hands resembled overstuffed bags of flour. One finger on the left was blackening. It was remarkable that she had ignored the pain, determined that the Venetian ambassador would kiss a hand bearing the emblem of England.

Cecil wondered at the agony she must still be in. She had not uttered a word of it to any man. Instead she insisted to her ladies that pain, probably imaginary, troubled only her arms.

'This will not hurt your Majesty,' said the barber. He seemed about to say more, but the queen's silence demanded the like from her servants. Instead, he began flexing the discoloured finger whilst, with his other hand, reaching into a pocket at his belt and producing a little bottle. Silence pressed, broken only by the whistling rattle of her breath. It came from somewhere deep in her flat chest. The scent of lilies filled the room as the barber unstoppered the bottle and began rubbing its contents over her swollen finger. The little vial disappeared and in a wink was replaced with a glint of silver.

With the physician holding the light steady, the barber-surgeon began to saw.

Though Queen Elizabeth gave no sigh or cry of pain, her laboured breathing deepened. It had seemed, over the winter, that she had got over the illness that had plagued her the previous months. But no, Cecil thought, that had been a false hope. Or a false threat. She would have to go soon, and, he thought, she knew it. Today was the proof of her knowledge.

But what else did she know? If only she would die quietly, quickly, before she might discover what he had been forced to do by her lunatic refusal to name an heir.

The sound of snapping bone shot through the air.

'It is done, your Majesty,' said the barber, stepping back. He held out his palm as though showing off a gift. On it, her severed coronation ring – the ring that she had always boasted was the bridal ring signifying her marriage to England – sat like a curling, dead maggot.

Elizabeth looked at it, unblinking, and then theatrically turned her head away, staring into the dim reaches of the room.

What was she thinking? Over the years many men had wondered what secret thoughts lay behind the gowns and jewels, what nature the woman hid behind the majesty. If only they knew what it was: yet more secrecy and sullen silences.

Guessing at Elizabeth's mind, Cecil knew, was a fruitless enterprise. Her thoughts, like her speeches, were labyrinths, though seldom mazes. The endpoint, the meaning, the decision, the opinion itself was usually always there, but the path to it was designed to exhaust and disorientate. Hopefully the next sovereign would prove easier to follow. Or to lead.

'Are you hurt, your Majesty,' asked the physician. He pushed the barber-surgeon back with one ham-like arm and pressed himself on her.

'It was cleanly done, was it not?' insisted the barber. 'A skill of practice you don't get from no *books*.' Rather than answering, she held the finger up to her face. Squinted through failing eyes. She put her hands in her lap and began kneading them. For the first time, she seemed to notice Cecil. With an imperceptible gesture of her head, she gave him his signal.

'Thank you, gentleman,' he said. 'Her Majesty bids you begone and speak to no man of this.'

The pair hovered only a moment before bowing and backing from the room. The barber opened the door and the physician pushed himself ahead and out before him. As darkness again enveloped the queen and her secretary, the muted sound of deferred argument slid under the cracks. Presently it faded.

Only when they were alone did Elizabeth deign to speak. Her disembodied voice was reedy, pettish, dust blown. He thought of ancient tombs being opened up, and ancient air whining out. 'You know what has passed here this day, pygmy?' It seemed to cost her something. He realised, without surprise, that she blamed him for what he felt sure she regarded as the first act of her death. It had been she who had declared that either the ring must go or, if delayed, the finger with it; but, as ever, having made the decision she would hold those she charged with organising the act itself responsible. It was therefore he and not she who had dissolved her marriage to England, and the truth be damned. The tales Queen Elizabeth told herself were their own truths.

Cecil bowed his head, to hide his frown as much as to show right reverence. His father had drummed into him as a child the notion, which he knew to be foolish but could not shake, that she could see in the dark. Another memory boiled up suddenly, as bits of knowledge will, that it was ten years since the count of Wurttemberg had met her and taken her to be eight years older than she then was. If only you could see her now, Count Frederick, he thought. On the heels of that thought came 'better a pygmy than a shrivelled old creature whom time has left behind and whom Death now beckons'.

If thoughts and desires could be proven rebels...

He opened his mouth to speak, but the door opened behind him, and he half-turned to see a lady's silhouette.

'Your Majesty.' The woman curtsied before stepping forward, her voluminous skirts brushing the sides of the doorway. Unlike Cecil, she had to duck as she entered. The Countess of Kildare, Frances Howard. A rotten, intermeddling creature. Yet, he knew, she had been charting the same dangerous waters as he. He had seen her letters to James of Scotland, seen her pathetic little pledges of assurance that she had the power to bring him, Cecil, down, and Raleigh, and any other man the Scottish king might distrust.

The foolish woman, wife to the equally foolish Lord Cobham, ignored him, kneeling instead before the queen. In her hands was a tiny little gilt coffer. 'I received your ring from the barber, madam. And I bring you the other you requested.'

Cecil frowned. This little piece of theatre had not been pre-planned. That was bad. If the countess knew what was passing in the closet, soon her friends would know. He gnawed on the inside of his cheek, where a familiar ulcer throbbed, wishing he might speak, might demand answers of the wretched woman. Instead he watched, as he had been trained to do.

The countess opened the box and drew something out. She had not closed the door behind her and shafts of light speared their way in. Not quite enough to see what she was about, though. Elizabeth held out her hand. 'The goldsmith said that this would fit you right well, as you said, madam.' Lady Kildare slid something onto the puffy digit. And then she added – Cecil realised for his benefit – 'my lord Essex had such big fingers.'

Elizabeth admired her swollen finger with its new decoration and rose, shaking away the countess's arm. The loose flesh of her throat, hanging in two great ropes, quivered. She stepped from the room, her back bent but her gait youthful again. Cecil sent fresh waves of pain through his ulcer at the sight of that sudden burst of energetic movement. Lady Kildare moved to follow. Neither woman acknowledged his presence, but as the queen stood in the doorway, she put a hand on the frame. Gripped it and paused. 'Such changes as age come stealing on … and we shall all be as soon forgot,' she said, loudly but apparently to herself. Her voice then was not pettish but sharp, like knives clicking on a wet plate. As her racking breath faded down the hall outside, he balled his fists once, twice, and then breathed out.

Always, he would be taunted and mocked by the memory of that wretched blunderhead Essex. Essex, Essex, Essex; how he had come to detest the stupid, strutting, fool. Essex had been everything that Cecil was not: tall, incautious, beautiful, beloved – more beloved in death than he had even been in life. In the years since he had died, it seemed he pranced through the great beyond with Robin Hood and King Arthur, only returning as a ghost, in objects and memories, to taunt his old adversary.

Cecil had given much of his life to serving that ungrateful, hateful, barren old spinster, and still her unnatural, decrepit lusts burned for dead men. Never had she shown him warmth or affection – not that he had craved it, he reminded himself. His father had told him that duty and service were their own rewards, and the stability of the state beyond loving words, beyond even jewels and baubles. Being offered perpetual service and trust ought to satisfy a statesman. Soft words and tickled chins were intended only to divert fools not fit for serious labours. Still, it was an unpleasant thing to have something withheld that seemed given so freely to others, whether one wanted it or not. Well, let her reminisce over her charnel house of dead friends and courtly lovers. She would be joining them soon enough. And by now they would be more fitting for her – as bony and colourless as herself.

The image of Essex's smiling, straight-nosed, white-toothed face loomed in his mind. And then it shifted, slightly, like an Ovidian metamorphosis, into a similar, still living face. He breathed deeply again, exhaled the resentment, and let his mind run back to more important matters.

Fair Eliza would be dead – maybe tomorrow, or the day after, or in a month or two at the most. The loss of her ring, rejected by her own ravaged body, could herald nothing else. And when she did die, everything would have to be in readiness. The ship of state must not sink in stormy waters. The loss of a fading captain did not mean the loss of the crew, still less the pilot who, if he could ensure a steady passage, would be feted by the next captain for keeping the vessel afloat. Change could be endured, suffered, or mastered by just such a pilot if he acted with haste and wisdom.

Now, to chase away the storm clouds, and quickly.

1

There is a phrase often uttered in Newgate, the Clink, the Counter, and all gaols that any prisoner will tell you is more loathed than any other.

'What are you in for?'

I could scarcely see the dull wight who asked it, but in doing so he revealed more than he meant. His voice was youthful and his ignorance of the rules of the jail told me this was his first time. 'Nothing',' I said.

How long had I been inside now? Time becomes a thing of no account within those walls. An hour lengths into a day, a day into a year. Sometimes, the crueller gaolers batter on the cell door, announcing the hour with a great belly laugh, reminding us forgotten creatures just how sluggish time had become. But none had bothered this time.

I had been taken in the night, dragged, semi-clothed, through the streets. The men who had lifted me had spat in my face, and I could still feel the sting of it, though I had wiped and scratched and rubbed until my skin was raw. When had that been?

In the usual run of events, I would not have been worried. I would, in fact, have had got myself arrested, secure in the knowledge that my patron would allow me just a few hours to gather information from the unravelling unfortunates of the jail – talk of conspiracy, of Jesuit priests, of secret meetings – before ordering my release. But this had not been a planned arrest. And the Clink prison lay within another jurisdiction from my customary digs in Newgate. I shivered and wiped again at my face, before drawing my shirt tighter around me. Would my master think to have news of the prisoners taken to the Clink?

Yes, I thought. He knew everything, saw everything, heard everything. In London, at any rate. He would get me out before … well, before they did what they did to people like me.

'Me too,' said my fellow. I frowned. I'd forgotten what it was he had asked. 'Nothing that ain't no crime to no honest Englishman.'

Why had no one come for me? How long had I been here? I screwed shut my eyes and tried to think. It might have been five in the morning when they kicked open the door and roused me and led me into the moonlit streets. Dawn had been breaking by the time I was thrown into the cell, my wrists shackled. Then I had been left, left, left. Passing feet on the street outside told me that the day had worn on, that fat old moon returning. Yet it seemed to be morning again. The young man had been thrown in at some point the previous day, ranting then about foreigners and Scots before lapsing into what I took to be a drunken sleep.

The holding cell at the Clink was partially underground. The only light came from cellar-like barred windows high up on the wall, which were open to the street. With the grey light poured sewage and rainwater. I squinted around the room. In addition to myself and the talkative youth were an old man, half-dead, and a couple of foreigners who were mumbling to one another in what appeared to be different languages.

'Shut yer filthy mouths, scum,' snapped the talkative prisoner. 'You're in England, in an English gaol. We don't want to hear no filthy Spanish shit.'

I groaned. 'I think they speak French and … something else.'

'I don't give two shits,' he rasped. 'Foreign, might as well be Spanish, dirty bastards. This is England. It ain't no foreign hole. They should speak English.'

'Or not speak at all,' I offered. A sudden gush of filth ran in through the window. Sometimes people threw in food; sometimes they pissed in on the prisoners. I could not tell what this stream betokened, but as it puddled on the floor, I saw that it was brownish. Reason enough, I thought, to squirm away.

'Ay, it's speaking they've put me here for. For darin' to speak up against bloody foreigners, bloody Scots, coming 'ere and lording it over us decent, honest English.' He looked at his fists. 'Used these all me life and it's *that* they do me for.'

I sat up, my back braced against the wall, and rested my wrists on my knees. I could have paid to be unshackled, but I grudged extra expenditure. It was my own stupid fault I had been arrested, and I intended to suffer any resulting pain and indignity as penance for my own carelessness.

That came in the form of the manacles' true purpose. They prevented prisoners from getting at the small of the back and between the shoulder blades, where fleas itched in their maddening dance. I could suffer it.

Death, I would probably draw the line at.

'Scots?'

'Scots. What did you say you was 'ere for?'

Was there a trace of suspicion in his voice? I grinned. 'I was most abominably accused of seeking to put a good English girl on the throne when the queen was set to marry Spanish Philip, thereby subverting the right succession. Tried to raise Kent in arms, like a fool.'

'What?'

'I was falsely accused of reb–'

'Ha! I saw that play! A good English play, that. Told the truth about the Spaniard. Wyatt, wa'n' it? Good Englishman, standin' up for us, showing that our boys in parliament should 'ave their say. You a player?'

'I am that,' I lied. It is a rule of mine that the truth should only be told when no more entertaining lie can be thought of. 'And I was falsely accused of stealing a play from another company, a scurrilous lie. So here they threw me.'

'Plays is good English things. I like a good one, good bloody one. That one you mention, had heads struck off and carried about, lookin' real as any execution.'

'As do I – the bloodier the part the better it plays. You were saying, though, about those verminous Scots?'

'Ay, the worst of them. Bloody Scotch king. Standin' at our border, waitin' to fill England with 'is lousy pups. Well, my friends'll see the end of 'is designs. We'll have proof enough against 'im. You English?' His words had the inflection of an accusation.

'I am.' The fool, I realised, might well serve my turn. If he was doing any more than running off his mouth, that was. Talk against the Scottish king might one day be treasonous, and my master paid especially well for such talk, the better spiced with gall the better.

'Well, then you ought to join up with us, as any honest Englishman oughta. Show your faith for the Red Cross of England.'

'Who is us?'

Before the young man could speak further, a key rattled in the lock. *Thank God.*

Light spilled in as a gaoler, his nose wrinkled, thrust a torch into the cell. His bulky body followed. I cleared my throat. My best gentlemanly tone seemed appropriate to the occasion. 'Gaoler, I am Edward Savage. I'm waiting for my friends to speak for me. Savage!' I began to clamber up.

Before I could stand, I was pushed back against the stained wall. I slid down, feeling the fabric tear, and cursing for the loss of a good Holland shirt as much as liberty. 'You,' barked the gaoler. He leant down and, with one hand, grasped the young Englishman. 'Peter

Ford?'

'Ay, I'm Ford.'

'Get up. You're out.'

In the torchlight, I could see that Peter Ford was not quite as young as his voice had suggested; he might, in fact, have been a couple of years older than my twenty-something (my own date of birth is no longer recorded, alas – though I do not intend to ever be called older than twenty-three). Short, well-muscled, far from ugly but hard faced. I committed the lineaments of that face to memory. 'You see,' said Ford, brushing down the front of a good-quality doublet, 'my friends watch out for me. You ought to join us.'

'Please, what time is it?' I called. No response.

The gaoler left the cell, Ford at his heels. The latter paused momentarily to aim a kick at the startled foreigners. And then the two were gone, the door closed and a thick clunk signalling that I had been forgotten.

Panic began to set in as my sense of time spun away again. The rush of fetid water had reduced to a subtler, steady plip, plop, plip. Perhaps there had been some mistake; surely it was only I who had friends on the outside with pockets deep enough to secure release? But no. The gaoler had been asked specifically for Ford and no one had asked for me.

Activity began to intensify on the street outside; ankles and boots stamped through mud and voices were raised. The prison lay on the south side of the Thames, in the jurisdiction of the bishop of Winchester. Had I not given in to my own baseness, I would not have found myself in such a place. Again, a sense of my own stupidity threatened to overwhelm me. I tried to calculate the passage of news from the warden of the Clink to the bishop and on to Whitehall. Hardly a great distance, but I did not know if any such passage of information happened. Would the keeper of this fetid place bother to furnish the government with a list of names of prisoners, as did the wardens of the others? Were such reports made daily? Weekly? Monthly? Messengers, go betweens, I thought – and came close to smiling at the irony – might even find themselves behind bars, stymying matters.

I made up my mind to beg, to batter on the cell door until the gaoler came and, loath as I was to even think of it, to offer him money to make enquiries. I would not have enough to effect my own release – I knew from experience that his type expected payment high enough to outweigh the fines they would receive from their own masters for losing a prisoner – but I did have enough hidden in the pouch at my belt for him to carry my name abroad, to some agent or other of my master.

Too public.

Likewise, I might remain here and eventually go to trial, pleading the benefit of clergy. Reciting my neck verse would save me from the noose, to be sure, but again, my name and my shame would be paraded. That was always the way: I'd never known a man hang for such a petty crime, but the public shaming provided a littler death to name and fame. I would be useless to my master, shunned, and, worse, the court would take all I owned. A last resort, I told myself, was all that would be. I must be patient.

But that urge to beat on the door with my bound hands rebelled against reason, and reason had to strike it down.

The dull click of the lock interrupted my thoughts.

'Savage?' growled the gaoler.

'Yes! Yes, Edward Savage. That's me.'

'Up.'

I needed no invitation. I did, however, need a hand, and held it out. No help came; the gaoler, in fact, drew back as though I were leprous. I stumbled up and followed him out into the dripping cavern of a hallway. 'My master, he's sent for me?' I asked. Excitement and relief had called forth the words and I regretted them. Of course, the gaoler would have been told nothing; he would have been given my name and discreetly handed a bulging purse. 'He wouldn't like to hear of me in this fearful place. My God, what a gaol you keep, sir. It's like if Hell had a cellar.'

'Shut your filthy hole.'

'Consider it shut. But know this, by God, trusty gaoler: if you weren't so fucking ugly, I'd kiss you.'

The gaoler raised a hand to strike me. I did not flinch, and he brought down his fists on my wrists, grasping them suddenly and unlocking the manacles. I massaged life back into them as he, without speaking, made a show of wiping the hands that had touched me on his filthy jerkin. 'Friends you might 'ave, you animal, but filth and scum you still are. Should be 'ung. You ever show your pretty face in this place again, I'll see to it you are, and afore any mighty friend sends his minions for ye.'

'I love you too, fair gaoler.'

I looked around the stone chamber. My mighty friend's minion had gone. I returned my attention to my quondam captor. 'Who released the man Ford?'

'Fuck off.'

I bit my tongue and forced my unwilling hand to unloose the purse string at my belt. Drawing out a coin, I held it before him. He took it between thumb and forefinger, barely touching it, and rubbed it on his jerkin. 'Some feller with a red cross sewn on his doublet.' I said nothing. Friend Ford evidently had his own friends. Shrugging, I passed the vomit-streaked entrance counter and put my hand to the door.

'Here,' I said, turning, 'between me and that other fellow, you could leave this rotten place and live high awhile. Perhaps get a new trade in time. I hear they're wanting for big, hairy beasts to fight the dogs in the pit out yonder.'

His curses at my back, I grasped the wooden ring and jerked the door inwards, leaving the Clink and stepping into the grey morning. I drew in the watery air, tilting my face upwards, enjoying the odd spots of rain. It smelt fresh, after the prison – good and clean. I barely had to let my eyes adjust. Winter, after all, only has two times: the full dark of night and the dismal slate of morning and afternoon.

I made to take my leave of Southwark, wanting it behind me. It would be a while before I could rightly show my face about the area again, I suspected. My accuser might have friends waiting for me. It seemed quiet enough, though, as Southwark always was until late in the day, when heavy heads had lightened and revelry again beckoned. Lowering my head, I began churning my way through the mucky street, hoping to spare myself the expense of crossing the river by taking the bridge. Penance, again, for my own errors.

As I passed an alley between two of the white-fronted whorehouses, I sensed movement behind me. Wheeling, my hand a fist, I saw a short figure with his cap pulled low. His face was smeared with dirt. A child: a gong scourer whose job it was to crawl into drains and clean them. I could take him, I supposed, and a cry of 'thief' might at least bring attention if not help.

'Seven-hundred-and-ten?'

I relaxed my fist. 'Yes.' I ought to have known: here was my deliverer in all his nondescript glory. One of my master's little jests. Not a lover of elaborate codes, he preferred assigning numbers to his people. As I bore, so I was continually told, a marked resemblance to the late earl of Essex (in his younger days, I hoped), I was '710': S from the Latin *septem* and X for ten: SX. It seemed fitting. I doubted I ranked highly in the army of people in his employ.

'Go about your business. Be seen to do so. Then go to the hall in the afternoon. He'll not be there nor have time for you until then.' His voice reminded me of one of the boy actors, paid to recite lines they likely did not fully understand.

I nodded, and the boy skipped away into the street without looking back. I had considered asking him if our mutual benefactor was in good spirits, having had to pay my release from the Clink, but thought better of it. It was unlikely he would know, anyway. An older man would have paid the little urchin to do the job and to then forget having done it, and the lad would have no idea who or where 'he' or 'the place' meant.

Personal meetings were rare, with contact usually made only through numbered intermediaries. I might expect a firm rebuke. Or worse.

I crossed my arms and took a look around. The door of the brothel ahead opened, and a large man exited, his thumbs tucked into his belt. I whistled, low and long, and his fleshy face reddened.

No illicit deeds leading that sated fellow to the cells, I thought. No loose-mouthed whores to lull him to sleep and then fetch the constables' men. A chill whistled through my shirt, needling at my back.

As he hurried off, I laughed, and resumed my squelch towards the bridge.

***

My lodgings in Faringdon Without are a poor sort of place, occupying the rump end of a drab tenement building and comprising two rooms whose white clay floors are covered in rush matting. Only the presence of a fireplace speaks of luxury. From the outside it is indistinguishable from its fellow, its outward whitewash flaking and its timber cross-boards splitting. I thought, as I always did, that I must appear a very modest man indeed – a man not worth noting.

Throwing the door wide, I stepped in. I took in the scene at a glance: Faith, my girl, or servant, or, if we were grander people, my ward, was standing by the board of the outer room, a jug in her little white hand. Seated at the board with a wooden mug in front of him was the reedy figure of our landlord, Frere. I shot a look past them, to the door to my inner chamber. Panic flared in a sudden, clawing heat.

'You lied, wench. Not here, eh?' Frere spat. He had a sunken look about him, but his eyes gleamed with malice.

'I … I … You're back, Ned! Thank God.'

'Back, yes. What is this?'

'Mr Frere's here.' As she spoke, she slid across the room to stand behind me.

'I can see that.' I wrenched the jug from her hand and took a swig, feigning an uncaring attitude. 'What can I –'

'You owe me money, Savage. You and your little whore here.'

I took a half-step across the room. I had no objection to his misrepresentation, but I regretted he should say it in front of Faith. 'Mind your tongue, Mr Frere.'

'Hold yours.' Frere unfolded himself from his seat – my seat. 'There are plenty of folks would like to live in a place in London, almost in the city, and would pay for it, too.'

'Mr Frere's come looking for his money,' said Faith. I ignored her.

'And when I arrive for what's mine the little strumpet tells me you're out earning it.'

'Which I was,' I snapped. I regretted the words, as I saw Frere's gaze slide to my belt. He could not have failed to notice my state of undress. 'Yet as you can see I was robbed on the way. Damned thieves and rogues, you know how the city is.'

Frere looked momentarily at a loss, eager to call me a liar but given pause by my appearance. He was not an intelligent man. 'Robbed?' he echoed.

'Robbed. And I have only just reported the matter to the constable.'

'My rent money –'

'Will be with you in a day. At most. I have business to attend to this afternoon, after which I shall be able to give you enough for this month and next, if it please you.'

'Two months?'

'Just so. As you know, my work relies on the good offices of her Majesty's Revels.' I waved a hand airily. 'Sir Edmund is a busy man, but he does not delay paying his men.'

I doubted if Frere knew who Sir Edmund Tilney was, but he was always bowed by fine speech and the mention of knightly connections. Besides, it was true, as far as it went, that I worked for the Revels Office. I had long ago realised that a man must have some honest occupation, at least by day, and I had become a courier of manuscripts between the stage-wrights and the office in Clerkenwell: I would take the acting companies' new plays and their administration payment to the Revels Office, where I and my colleagues would read them and recommend any cuts or edits of slanderous and seditious material, and then I would return them to the players with their license to perform, earning a further fee for my troubles. It was a good pastime, but irregular. Had Frere even the slightest measure of reason, he would have realised long ago that such an occupation could not provide rent money, nor any kind of steady income.

But this was a world alien to my landlord, whom I doubted would have the wit to listen to a whole play. But in its strangeness lay its impressiveness. He swallowed, his Adam's apple quivering. 'Two months. Tomorrow.'

'Certainly tomorrow.' As Frere began to shuffle towards the door, his neck bent to avoid the low ceiling of the shack he rented us, I chanced, 'or the next day. And an apology, Mr Frere, would be a welcome thing. For using language before my dear sister.'

'Sister,' he spat, his jut of a nose preceding him as he pushed his way past Faith. She, I noticed, looked as bemused as he did. 'If you were a man of honour, you'd take her to wife.'

'I am not the marrying kind. Settled in not taking a wife.'

'Hmph,' was his parting shot.

When he had gone, I lowered the interior bar of the door and put my back to it.

'As if I would marry you,' said Faith. Her tone was light.

'You're in luck then that I don't believe in marriage, or I'd give you no choice.'

'Why? Don't you believe in it, I mean?'

'For the same reason I don't believe in creeping to the cross or going into a monastery to learn how to write. I'm not from the bloody dark ages.'

'Marriage isn't old,' she said. 'Everyone gets–'

'Cease harping on marriage. Why did you let him in?' I hissed.

Colour rose in her cheeks. 'I thought it were you.'

'And didn't think to ask? For Christ's own sake, Faith – and feeding him ale? How were you planning on being rid of him if I hadn't come back?'

Tears threatened and her wobbling chin rose. 'I said you were working for our rent and I'd bring it directly you got home. You didn't come home yesterday. I think he'd been watching the house and knew I'd be alone here. Well, I mean, he probably thought he could frighten me more than you into paying up.'

'And he was right.'

'I wasn't frightened. Were you robbed?'

She put a hand on her hip. I sighed, before crossing to the table, replacing the jug, and sitting on the seat Frere had vacated. It retained no heat.

Faith – or, to give her her proper name, Faith Is Our Salvation White – had lived with me for two years. The circumstances of our meeting and my adopting her as a helpmeet must wait – but it is enough at present to say that she provided me with a good character. Her parents, of the Puritan bent, had died, along with two twin siblings, the charmingly named Flee Sin and Praise God; and I judged it fair that mother and father had died for those crimes alone. A younger brother, Dust (whose name I assumed was meant to remind us what we would all come to in the end), had been stolen by Queen Elizabeth's choirmaster and impressed into service, and when I found her I supposed that she might make a life with me or turn to whoredom in one of those white-painted buildings south of the river. I judged her now to be about seventeen, although her frame suggested someone even younger. I fancied we made an odd and unlikely pair, and doubtless Frere's judgment that she was my whore was a common assumption. And a useful one.

Taking my silence for a demurral, she said, 'you were in trouble again.'

'I'm not in trouble now.'

'Will you get us our rent money?'

'Of course.' I took another draught of the ale, wiped my mouth with my grimy sleeve, and stood. 'Of course. You can help me to it.' I drained the jug and held it out to her. 'Fill this with our rainwater.' We should have had plenty, I thought. Ordinarily she sprinkled it around to keep the rush floor green and springy.

'But … I have to do our accounts, Ned.' Her eyes darted to the little book she kept, lying forlorn on her pallet.

'We're poor. There. Done. It's just outside, mouse. He'll be quite gone.' I waited whilst she went outside to our standing water butt and returned with the jug refilled. 'Thank you.' Bells outside chimed. 'Nearly noon. I should have taken a damned wherry. I must change and be off.'

'To get our rent money?'

'Will you quit that?'

'I'm sorry. I don't mean to turn shrew, really I don't. But … it's just that someone has to look after the coin around here. So I can make a good budget – so I know when to put a little aside for if … if you're going to be away somewhere.'

'If I knew when I would be …' I almost said 'detained' and thought better of it. 'Away – then I'd tell you. My business is …'

'It's your own. I know that. I suppose I'll have to start looking at outside work and that.'

I set the jug down, took her face in my hands, and made to kiss her. 'Get out of it,' she snapped. 'You smell like a puddle of puke.' She wriggled away and turned her back on me. The closest she came to insolence was a back-turn.

'Poor and smell of puke, eh? We won't always be poor, though. You know that, don't you?' A little bow of her head. 'And … if I ever go away and don't come back,' I said, forcing a laugh, 'you can have whatever of mine you can sell. And then you can go and buy a great house with it. Just don't sell it in London, mind.'

'I'll do that.' She gave me her profile, short-nosed and pouting. 'At least then I'll see what you keep in there.' It was an unwritten rule that Faith never entered the inner chamber of our two rooms. She kept house, slept, cleaned, and maintained our meagre finances entirely in the outer room. 'Which reminds me,' she added, fishing in a pocket of her apron, 'I went to over to Smithfield yesterday.'

'Smithfield? This is progress, mouse. Not exactly the Exchange, but progress.' Faith had an aversion to leaving the environs of Faringdon Without. Fear of being snatched herself, was my guess. The shops and stalls of Smithfield were hardly far, but farther than the pie seller at the end of our street, which was usually as adventurous as she got.

'I had to.' She shrugged, trying, I thought, to look like it was nothing. 'We needed things. I got this for you.' She produced a little wooden object, with embroidery providing colour on top. As she held it up, I saw something like hope on her face. 'Is that it, Ned? They didn't have many pin pillows, but that one I reckoned was pretty. If it's wrong, it's fine, though.'

'Oh, Faith,' I said, taking the pin cushion and turning it in my hand. 'It's … it's … yes, it's …'

'Not the right thing.'

I bit my lip.

'It's fine, I'll take it back, see if I can sell it. Get something back for it.' She reached out, but I jerked my hand away and held the hideous thing to my heart.

'You *got* it, you said?'

'I paid for it.' She met my eyes. 'We had a bit spare, I thought, after I'd done the counting.'

'Good. I've told you – no shitting in our own backyard.' I winked. 'God's truth, it's perfect. I'll treasure this because a friend bought it for me.' She looked doubtful. Probably she could tell that I barely meant it. Yet there was something pathetically touching in the gesture; she had known for a long time about my desire to procure a very particular pin pillow, as she called it, and had gone out of her way to find one. It was the wrong one, of course, but the gesture was touching. 'Do we have anything to eat?'

'I could go to the pie man and get you something.'

'No. The last time you went to him I found a rat's head in my pie.'

'You did not!' Her mouth fell open.

'A tail, then. It was rodential. I shall eat when I go to work.'

'Work. With those theatrics?' She looked at the ground. Faith disapproved of my honest labours. As a result of Dust's fate, she considered anything to do with theatre, drama, and song borderline criminal. Playwrights, poets, and actors were each pages in the same lurid, obscene, and vulgar jest book.

'What news in the city?' I asked, hoping to draw her away from her memories.

'Oh, that. Nothing much. Not really. There was some folks talking about the queen.'

'Saying what?'

'Nonsense, I thought. Saying some foreigner broke into her chambers and stole the ring right off her finger. Last week or sometime.'

'Nonsense indeed. Though by now I reckon it will be settled truth about the town. Is that all?'

'Well …' She looked into the corner of the room.

'Well?'

'One of the prentice boys said I was saucy. He made to kiss me, like you did just now, and I boxed his ears.'

'That's my girl.' I took a breath. 'And did you say what I told you to say if a lad tried to take liberties? Where he could go and what he was?'

Her cheeks pinkened. 'I … I couldn't say that. Not ever.'

I laughed. 'Look at me, Faith.' She did, her apple cheeks rosy. Carrot coloured hair poked out from beneath her cap. 'Jesus, you have got damned pretty.'

'Don't be soft.' Up flew her hand, covering her mouth.

'You have. Too pretty to roam the ward like a chained monkey. And,' I added, 'I'll thank you to stop it. I prefer to be the pretty one in my own house. Stay away from prentice boys. I need you here, or I shall live in my own filth like the pigs. And I would have to kill the poor prentices on my honour. You don't want that for your old Ned, do you?' She smiled, and I shucked her under the chin. 'Thank you for my gift. Bought with my own money though it is. I love it. You see, I'm taking it into my chamber.'

Before she could speak, I went to my room and slid inside, slamming the door behind me. I opened the wooden shutter to let in some light, which immediately illuminated my extraordinary collection of objects and, more valuable, my several coffers of clothes. Inside those I keep sleeves in every colour, cut, and cloth; fustian doublets and frieze; woollen hose to the thighs and knees. There are laws setting out what a man might and might not wear, of course, but never in my life have I known anyone to be convicted under them. Besides, it is a habit of mine I have not tried seriously to break, this collection of arcana. Mirrors, a brass chamber pot with a false bottom, a comb with most of its ivory teeth in place, clocks and watches of glass and wood – if I see a thing I fancy once, it plays on my mind until I can have it, by any means possible.

Like a magpie, is that boy.

It was my mother's voice, and I clenched my jaw against it.

Objects, after all, are more reliable and trustworthy than people.

I confess that I do not live well, nor grandly; my bed, in fact, is a blanket on top of the largest chest in my little cave. I glanced at my reflection in my polished hand mirror. My hair was a turmoil, and beard growth had set in. That would not do at all. Thrusting aside the blanket, I opened my grandest coffer.

If I was going to go about my business – both the legitimate and the illicit – I would need to select attire that would serve both.

2

A man is known by three things: dress, speech, and manner. A woman too. Imagine yourself walking down a street – the market at Cheapside. A man approaches you. You might take him for a gentleman by the sword swinging at his hip. Ask him how he does.

'I fare well, and God thank you' betrays a gentleman.

'Bugger off' proves that he is not.

At his back follows a woman, her clothes ragged and cheap. She might move aside and keep to the gutter, betraying herself as a common slattern. Yet, she does not. She keeps her course, raises her chin and commands you aside, with 'make way, there!' You have discovered a well-born lady in disguise.

Behind her is another woman, this one bedecked in coloured silks, a mask over her face and a pomander hanging from her girdle. She slops her way through the filth, uncaring of her slippers. To your friendly greeting, she replies, 'I ain't bad, duck, 'ow's about you today?' By that common tongue, she might well be a maid in her mistress' stolen clothes, the pair having swapped.

By changing clothes, adopting a certain carriage, and counterfeiting speech, a man might be anything.

I made my way towards the Mitre tavern, my Revels Office livery – a modified version of that worn by the Yeoman of the Wardrobe – brushed, and my auburn hair swept up and back. With combed hair and clean face, feet and hands, I felt a man again. I looked more than presentable, I fancied; I looked respectable. Nothing like the begrimed, smelly animal who had slunk over London Bridge reeking of crime and punishment.

Partway along Fleet Street, I saw a face I recognised. It was Ford. Peter Ford, I remembered, the prisoner released before I was. He stood just a few feet away from a knot of chatting goodwives and seemed to be shuffling something in his hand. I drew into the shadows of the overhanging eaves and watched.

Ford's arm flew out, and from his hand shot flashes of white. At first I thought he had released a little flock of birds, somehow, like one of the magic pedlars. And then he was gone, darting in the same direction I had been heading. The women, their attention drawn by the sudden activity, stooped.

And then a cry went up. And another, and another, becoming a chorus.

The women fled. Others – merchants, apprentice boys, wealthy men – paused in their stride and turned their heads.

Leaping out of the shadows, I skipped towards the rutted sewer channel, next to which Ford's burden had landed. Stooping, I picked one up.

It was a playing card. A queen. Through the crowned figure's forehead, a nail had been hammered. I turned the card over.

The Queene lies dying & wee are solde to ye Scotch. James of Scotlande is no trew king!

I dropped it as though it were scalding. Yet I retrieved another. On its back was scrawled

The Scotch will have yewr chattels, lande, & women BEWARE!

Down it went too. I swallowed, looking around. A crowd was beginning to form. The women must have begun spreading the word. Libels were a matter for the constables, and I had no intention of meeting, still less aiding, any common lawmen. Nor would I touch seditious written matter. Some things were too hot to handle, and not worth the trouble. The more block-headed constables, of which there were many, would take up even the finders of such things and lock them away, condemning as criminals those who looked at seditious libels simply because the authors were out of reach.

Still, it would be something more to tell my master, who was anything but block-headed.

As I turned my back and resumed my journey towards the Mitre, I considered the implication. Rumours of the queen being assaulted and robbed by a foreigner, and a foreigner-hating English brute freed from gaol and gone straight back to his seditious ways. Freed from gaol, too, by a rich friend. There was something simmering in London, to be sure.

Such information would repay the costs of freeing me: of that I had no doubt.

***

The Mitre was busy, as I suspected it would be. It was a well-appointed tavern, frequented by men of letters who could discourse and drink before their afternoon productions, snug in the heat of a good fire and the comfort of cushioned stools. To proclaim its status as a lettered place, the walls were festooned with cheap printed ballad sheets, mostly about the merits of beer. Tobacco smoke and pennyroyal fought with the earthier smell of woodsmoke – London's signature scent, which clung to all of us – for dominance.

As I suspected, a number of London's lettered men were present. Immediately as I stepped over the threshold, a gap-toothed music-man was at my elbow, plucking and pinching. 'You fancy a song, m'friend? Play for you what you will.' I shook him off, ignoring his spittle-flecked oaths.

The tavern consisted of one large room, but at the far end, some wooden steps led up to an elevated, railed platform with a long table. It was there that the stage-wrights – the actors and writers – would sit. The general throng of drinkers gathered around the base of the little gallery, devouring the scraps of wit that drifted from above.

Always performing, I thought, and the rabble always listening. It was no wonder actors made the mistake of thinking themselves as interesting out of costume as in it.

Present at the table was a crowd of the Lord Chamberlain's Men: their most vocal, the stately Augustine Phillips, was holding court alongside their chief writer, Will Shakespeare, their clown, Armin, a gaggle of young actors, and their seamstress, Mrs Cole.

Only Shakespeare interested me. Though unassuming, portly and balding, his muddy brown eyes were always alert. He was noted an alchemist for turning the leaden readings, arguments, and interpretations of his fellows around a noisy table into golden poesy. Despite his quietness, he was furthermore well liked amongst his company because, unlike some, he did not insist upon his own words being unchanged from page to stage; rather, he welcomed his fellows altering his lines – he was an artisan of shared labour, you might say. It was for that reason that the Revels Office despaired of a new play from the company; we could never be assured that what we read and approved would be precisely what the damned actors spoke before the crowd.

'Mr Savage,' said Phillips, 'you are most welcome to our society.'

I smiled as I folded my way between the tavern's patrons. It was false enough: Phillips' voice was irritatingly bombastic. Actors, even offstage, speak in an accent that was never heard in any honest shire. Rhythmic, loud, and vaguely courtly, it seems to be something they have developed themselves. I call it Theatre English.

'And I thank you. Do you fellows have anything for my master?'

Shakespeare opened his mouth to speak. Phillips prevented him. 'Mr Shakespeare is writing about a wicked slanderer and a Moor of Venice.'

'I say we are all slanderers!' said Armin.

'You slander us by saying so!'

'Hear me,' said the clown, 'do not we all put wicked words in men's mouths, hoping to convince our good patrons that what they see and hear is true?'

I rolled my eyes as a wave of laughter and applause rose from those surrounding me at the foot of the makeshift stage. 'The play is not ready?'

'We have not yet begun to make it.'

'I see.' I knew the working of the Lord Chamberlain's Men. The whole company would read and argue over whichever old book this Venetian Moor lived in, barking ideas and dull jests, and Shakespeare would write. He seized especially on the disputes – if one man thought a character a villain and another a hero, Will Shakespeare would spin lines that offered the hearers of the play both and neither.

I confess, I envied him and all of his trade. I had tried writing once myself – just a little flummery for the stage. An easy thing, I found, to write characters' rich in motive, in hatreds and vices and virtues. It was the rest that eluded me. My dramatic personae thus stood around in my mind, preening and posturing, awaiting an adventurous plot that would not come.

'You shall have no play nor fee this day, my friend,' said Phillips, raising his mug.

'Balls,' I replied, under my breath.

Phillips opened his mouth again, but no words came. His face drained of colour before flushing, and his eyes fixed on something behind me. I turned to see a tall, stocky man bounding into the Mitre. Like the red sea, the crowd parted for him. A bishop might have graced them with his presence.

'Mr Jonson,' said Armin, leaping onto the table as Ben Jonson, England's premier play maker, made for the gallery. 'Friends, friends, see him, hear him, for he now stoops to bear our company.'

Silence fell over the room. Phillips broke it. 'I thought you were gone from London, Mr Jonson.'

'Gone? Gone?! Mr Jonson is our star of England,' said Armin. Jonson looked at him and grunted. 'For we hear that, like the stars, you hang on a knight.'

I tilted my head back. Jonson, so I understood, had sought patronage with a knightly friend and was living in his house and off his table. To aid his writing, I supposed. Hope sparked. Ignoring the laughter that again rose in response to Armin's pun, I stepped over to the playwright. 'Have you finished your Scotch play, Mr Jonson? I can take it to the office now.'

If I could receive Jonson's latest, I could pass it to someone else in the office, earn a cut of the fee, and be on my way. I would not have to read it. A good thing too. Some of Jonson's writing was impenetrable, in love with itself and its rich store of learning. Shakespeare, I knew, had the wit to write what people wanted; Jonson had the wit to write what he thought they should want.

Jonson favoured me with the look of disgust he usually reserved for the actors who mangled his works. 'A play is never finished, sir. It is a child that is ever living and never full grown.' He tilted his head back and narrowed his eyes. 'A man's name, I think, reveals his character, Mr Savage. And you are savage indeed in your greed for a poem.'

Lord, how I detest playmakers and the impenetrable forest of meaningless words they hide in.

'*Robert, King of Scots* is dead,' he barked, putting a fleshy hand over his heart, the thumb disfigured from its branding. Balls, I thought again. 'It was so wanton in its approach to the unities, it would make great Horace blush. I am even now turning to weightier matters. Dead *Robert* will be succeeded. The fall,' he announced, pausing for effect, 'of Sejanus. That corrupt and wicked counsellor of Tiberius, who ruled his sovereign and meddled in the succession. Fitting matter should our peerless Oriana make to leave us.'

My lips twitched. There was a dangerous theme, and one worth reporting. 'When written, it will provide an example for our time and all time. Kindly do not snatch the idea,' said Johnson, inclining his head towards the acting troupe. 'I come here only to consult with yonder noble seamstress on some points of fact about Rome.' He pointed at Mrs Cole: a middle-aged elfin frump whom I knew could talk the legs off a warhorse. She was notorious for spinning tales of time spent in France, Italy, and God-knew-where, and considered herself an expert in foreign languages.

Catcalls. Whistles. The writer was reputed a great seducer of married women – something I doubted, given his expanding girth. Still, he fanned the rumours and I suppose they had acquired the truth of repetition.

Ignoring the tumult, Jonson mounted the shallow steps, leaving me in his wake, and bent his head to the old bird.

I turned my back on the theatricals. A bust, I thought. I would have to use some of my existing hoard to pay my way to Whitehall. It seemed almost unfair, as I considered it a rule that every expense should be met with an equal – or greater – recompense.

It occurred to me that I would be early. As I hadn't eaten, I left the cluster of men who thronged the gallery and purchased a hunk of good London cheat bread and a cup of ale. I did justice to both and let my gaze wander around the rest of the room. It fell upon a thin man with a grizzled beard. He was clutching his own cup in an iron grip, and the candlelight caught at the edges of something protruding from under his jerkin. A packet, I thought, made of shabby leather. The clothes of a traveller, the secretiveness and nerves of a poor spy, and something on his person worth protecting. Maybe something, maybe nothing.

I sauntered towards him, still chewing. 'Good morrow, friend.'

'Good morrow.'

I fought my eyebrow's treacherous desire to rise. 'Here to see our friends before their performance this afternoon?'

'Performance? I ken no performance.'

A Scot.

My rules of assessment failed me when it came to foreigners. I did not know what a gentlemanly Scotch accent was or wasn't. To me, they all sounded like piping Germans, even when speaking English. Travellers of any class, too, were apt to be dirt-splattered and poorly dressed. And even a man of quality might be furtive and secretive in a strange realm. I cursed myself for a cocksure.

'A friend from north of the border. You are welcome to London, I'm sure. I put out my chest, my livery prominent.'

'From Scotland, aye. I … uh … represent our king. Bring tidings from our court of Scotland.' He paused, measuring me. I smiled, and he relaxed. His leather parcel slid a little. 'Sir David Henderson. Ambassador to England.' I wrestled my curiosity, pinning it under that smile.

'An ambassador! Very good. You won't find many great courtly persons here. Theatricals and their hangers-on only.'

'No.'

'You were told that the lights of London gather here, perhaps?'

'Our king is fond of plays.'

'Yes.' I knew that a company of actors had gone to Edinburgh a few years before to entertain the Scotch court. Probably they also carried messages.

Henderson tightened his arms over his scrawny chest. His eyes kept darting downwards. 'I am to go to court myself,' I said. 'Business, you know. I could carry any messages you have.'

'No. No, my king would no' prefer that I hand his greetings over to …' He looked at the livery again. 'To one unknown to him.'

I had gone too far, made him suspicious. 'Perhaps I can buy you a drink. Your cup wanes empty.'

Henderson looked down in surprise, as though he had forgotten he was holding it. 'Aye.'

'With the gracious compliments of the Revels Office. Ale?' He returned a withering look. 'Muscadine?'

'Vernage of Tuscany.'

Son of a bitch.

'Wonderful. Allow me.'

I bowed, conspicuously not looking at his hidden cargo, and went off to find the tapster. I cursed inwardly at the price of the good wine. Still, it might be worth it if I could win the man's confidence. A Scottish ambassador could only be bound for Whitehall, and I might earn a fee by saving him the boat trip. All I needed to do was get him drunk enough and convince him that my business was carrying valuable documents. If it proved to be one, I would be a hero to my master – an asset worth keeping. My passage to the palace would be less noticed, after all, than a skulking Scot's. I parted with my cash, took the wine, which came in a finer horn cup, and gingerly moved back to the stool near the door.

Empty.

Sir David Henderson was gone, and with him his packet. And with them both, the value to my purse of a full measure of Tuscan vernage. I tossed it back myself, enjoying its sting. Being made a fool by a Scotsman, I thought, deserved a burnt throat.

I left the Mitre, bereft of a play, a fee, and a potentially valuable package from a stranger. There was no sign of the fellow in the street outside, and nor was he amongst the pissers who stood with forearms braced against the wall, streams splashing their shins. Neither was there any sign of Peter Ford's libellous playing cards. Instead, two men of the city watch were standing where the things had been thrown, asking questions of the goodwives who had first discovered them. An unproductive day about my usual business, I thought. I had no appetite for scouring the Mermaid or the Three Cranes for the university wits. There was thus no point in going to the office at Clerkenwell. Sir

Edmund Tilney paid me to carry plays, not news of them. Only one man paid for news. The Ford creature and his antics, the rumours about the queen, and the strange Scot would have to be currency enough.

It was time. Plenty of hours had passed since I knew the Privy Council would have met. He would have had enough time to journey down from Richmond.

I turned my head away and made for the wobbly, broken stones of Whitefriars Stairs, where they knew me and would give me a good rate upriver, under a sky that seemed to be brewing a storm.

3

I waited in the narrow, wood-panelled hall. One would not have imagined it leading anywhere of importance: to a closet for holding cleaning materials, perhaps, or dusty, ancient documents better fit for a fire. There were no benches; I sank to the floor and sat, cross-legged, like a child.

Security had been light at Whitehall Palace. It always was when the queen and court were not in residence. It was hardly as if we had a royal family with various branches to house. Our queen had no son and heir, no husband, no brothers or sisters. I almost felt a kinship with the old girl for that. Growing old alone, I knew, would be the unfolding pattern of my own life: an eternally single creature, without family, watching friends marry and produce children, and the new generation doing likewise. A lonely life. Decaying whilst new life burst forth around me. *Her*, I corrected.

I had debarked right at Westminster Stairs, the rag-tag of painted buildings rising in a cluster of uneven rooftops alongside me. Passing through King Street, the riverside royal apartments on my right and the cockpits and tiltyards to my left, I had found only slouching servants and black-robed jurists. Carriages stood in the street, but they were the property of lawyers and judges, being tended to by carters and wheelwrights. Through the two great gates of the palace complex I had strode without check or let, passing the way to the open-fronted riverside Shield Gallery, where visitors from within and without England flocked to see the impresas of the queen's men, painted on pasteboard, nailed to the walls. During other times I had spent many a happy hour there in my bright, courtly silks, singing sad songs beneath the Essex impresas for sweet cakes and sometimes the odd coin. I flattered myself there was nothing to connect the singing mirror of Essex with the royal servant waiting in a side gallery.

Tilting my head back, I looked up towards the low ceiling. Too low, I thought, for the antechamber to the most powerful man in England. But then, I thought, the world was accommodating the new mould of statesmen. Once great halls hung with arrases housed power. Now it was all little rooms and narrow halls. What once took place under the gaze of great men, who wed majesty to politics, now passed in mean rooms out of sight of the world. The remains of majesty were all for show, like gelded stallions running at the tilt. Or like the impresas in the Shield Gallery. Or like me, begging coins dressed as a dead hero.

Creak.

I snapped to attention and sprung to my feet, mindful of the pins in my sleeves. A man I did not know left the room. He jerked his thumb at me and then at the door, before scurrying off. I took a breath, rapped my fingers lightly on the door, and pushed it open.

A small room, the office of a clerk, with a tiny desk, made even smaller by screens hiding the back and right side. Only the chair cried grandness. At that desk and on that chair sat my master, a silver tray of half-eaten bread before him. To no great surprise, I saw that the playing card libels were neatly stacked next to it. His cheek blossomed and fell even as his eyes scanned the document he was holding. 'Mmph,' he said. 'You. Yes. Come in.' His mouthful muffled his mood.

You will have heard much of Sir Robert Cecil: he is Robert the Devil; he is crookbacked to the point of deformity; he is a wicked and corrupt villain. Such were the late Essex's claims. In point of fact, my master has one shoulder raised a little above the other, and a very slight, childlike frame. I knew the old Scotch Queen Mary's Italian secretary had been similarly called a hunchback; so too did it seem that the enemies of Queen Elizabeth's principal secretary enjoyed giving bodily dimensions to what they considered his crookedness. I daresay half the princes of Europe would not recognise the real man if he entered their presence, for they would be expecting a stunted and malformed monster. Instead they would find only a small man with a head vaguely shaped like an hourglass.

'The river was a bit choppy today, Sir Robert. I –'

'To the devil with the river, man.' A bad sign. I swallowed. 'Your name appeared to me on the list of prisoners at the Clink – the Clink – even as I sat in council this morning. And for such a crime, Ned. Such a crime.' I put my hands behind my back and stared at the floor. I could feel embarrassment well up into my cheeks. 'Oh, do not counterfeit shamefacedness with me. I do not judge a man's crimes nor his vices. Show me one without them and I'll show you a man who is of no use to me. A virtuous man has no price.'

'I'm sorry, Sir Robert.' Something lit inside me. 'It's a damned scurrilous lie. Put about by my enemies. My landlord, sir; he's no friend. He probably forced someone to accuse me. Falsely. Lies, sir. Foul and slanderous lies. I have it in my head to sue at the king's bench, if only it would not serve to spread the vile and abominable claims against me.'

Cecil answered first with a bemused look. 'Your landlord is causing trouble. Frere of Faringdon, isn't it?'

'Yes. Wants me out, I think.'

'I see. And for that he might have a fellow make false accusations against you.' My tongue darted over my lips. I shrugged. 'Well, it is in the past now. I would advise you against putting yourself in such positions again. Where false accusations might be made against you, I mean.'

'Yes, sir.' I had already decided against drinking in Southwark again.

'I did not call you here to berate you like an old schoolmaster, Ned.' He drummed his graceful fingers on the table. 'I need eyes in the city. Grave matters have arisen. But first, what news is abroad? The littlest to the broadest.'

We had a system, my master and I. I stood a little straighter. 'Item: the poet Ben Jonson is speaking openly of writing a new play. *Sejanus*. He said, and I quote, "that corrupt and wicked counsellor, who ruled his sovereign and meddled in the succession".'

Cecil gave no visible reaction. I had, in the past, reported far worse words and more directly against his person. He had shown no anger at them either. 'These are whispering times. And that rogue Jonson likes to shout,' was all he offered. 'Keep watch on the writing of this play and we shall see if the fellow shouts himself into another term in prison.'

I nodded. 'Item: the libels now on your desk were cast into the street by a man named Ford. Peter. He spent last night in the Clink for, I think, similar crimes. And he was freed through the offices of a greater man, whose servant bore an English flag on his clothing. Ford spoke to me in that place. Suggested I join with "them".'

This got more of a reaction. 'Peter Ford. Hmm. Yes, I saw that name on the list.'

'The man spoke against foreigners. Spaniards and Scots.'

'Such speeches are becoming common, I fear.'

'Yet with anger, sir. And if there are a crowd of these creatures …'

'Yes. Dangerous times.'

'Item: I saw and spoke with the Scottish ambassador at the sign of the Mitre.'

'What?'

'Sir David Henderson. A cringing man with a leathern package. Of documents, I supposed – it was flat enough and the right size. I regret

I didn't win his trust. He fled me.'

Cecil seemed to sink into his throne-like chair, and his raised shoulder became more pronounced. His jaw worked for a few seconds before he spoke. 'The Scottish ambassador,' he said eventually, 'is called Sir Edward Bruce. 'An ageing, red-haired man with a liver. He was no more supping in a London tavern this morning than he was tripping a measure in the queen's dancing hall in one of her Majesty's dresses.'

'I suspected him for a liar, sir,' I lied. 'A Scotch spy.'

'Or a traitor to the Scottish king.' Cecil let the word dangle. 'Where did he go? Who was he with?'

'I cannot say.' The closest thing I had yet seen to agitation crossed his face. He drew in his cheeks and it passed. 'Finally, sir, there is some rumour abroad about her Majesty.'

'What?' The word shot from him like a blade from a scabbard.

'That her ring was stolen from her finger by a foreigner. I took it to mean …' It was my turn to let implication fill in a blank.

'These rumours, these libels, this angry talk of the Scots and Spaniards,' said Cecil, rubbing at the corner of an eye. His smooth features, I noticed, were giving way a little to weariness. Dark circles protruded beneath both eyes. Overuse, I supposed. 'It is all of a piece with why I called you here.' He held up a finger, as though he had suddenly remembered something, and dove under the desk. His head bobbed back up and he slid aside his meal tray. Onto the space, he placed a small casket, which he unlocked with a key he had produced during his brief disappearance.

'Firstly,' he said, 'I insist that you hold your tongue on all matters, Ned Savage.' I nodded. I had never given him cause to think I would do otherwise. 'Excellent.' He opened the casket and began lifting out books. As he placed each down, one atop the other, he declared the names. '*A Conference About the Next Succession. A Declaration. A Treatise on the Succession. On the Right of the Crown After Her Majesty. An Apology of the Scottish King. The Right of Succession to the Kingdom of England.*'

My throat dried.

Each of these texts, as far as I knew, was illegal. Owning them, reading them, touching them could cost a man his life. Cecil coughed and I looked at him. 'Queen Elizabeth is dying, Ned.' His voice was barely above a whisper.

'Jesus,' I said, hardly more loudly.

'Soon. Very soon, I think.'

'What … what happens then?' In truth, I had no idea. I had never known any other sovereign, nor could I easily name a man or woman who had. What I knew of the succession of crowns I had learned from plays, or the examples of other nations – none of which were heartening. My thoughts flew to my pathetic little rooms on Shoe Lane, my stuff. What would become of it in the midst of riots, of uprisings, looting? If trouble was coming, I would have to get it all out of London and bury it somewhere in the country until peace returned. Or until I could get it, myself, and Faith on a safe boat out of England.

'Order,' said Cecil. 'Order must and will happen.'

'But … who?'

He began stacking the books back into their casket. 'A question that has vexed better men since my father's time.' He turned the lock. The key disappeared into his doublet. 'To make it plain, you might imagine a hare-coursing, with a number of hounds set loose after a crowned hare. Two hounds were bred from Margaret Stewart, eldest sister to Henry VIII. Their names are James VI and Lady Arbella. A slower hound was bred from Mary Tudor, sister to Henry VIII. Its name is Lord Beauchamp – a weaker animal with two lusty little puppies. From Mary comes another hound, a female, Derby. Though she and hers were somewhat muzzled some years back. And then we have a clutch of others, whom no one lays a bet on. Huntingdon, of ancient blood and little mettle but with an heir married to a Derby bitchling. Percies – all of stock long since withered and not fit to be raced. It has even been said some Spanish beasts might be imported, because their canine ancestors were good English coursers.

'You see: England does not lack for heirs but suffers from too many. And not one apparent enough. The weights and measures of each animal are contained in these books,' said Cecil, tapping the casket. 'According, of course, to the wishes of each author.'

My stomach lurched. Still, I was thinking of my property. Of my life, too. These were dangerous waters. Part of me believed it was all fantasy, or a trap, or a plot: that the queen could not die, not really. 'Who does the queen say should succeed?'

A humourless snort. 'That is what cumbers every man of note or not. You deceive yourself if you think she will name any.'

'But … you said James first. The king of the Scots.'

Cecil shrugged. 'I have no opinion. I care only for an orderly succession, that no man might lose his land or his property. That England will not sink in war and blood.' His eyes, I noticed, flicked towards the document he had been reading when I entered. It lay on the desk still, and I could see by the knots of ink along the top that it was a property deed of some kind. For all his confidence, my master was nervous.

'What can I do, sir?'

'Take a walk with me, Ned. You look peaked.' He slid out of his chair, picked up the remains of the bread he had been eating, and began moving towards the folding screen that hid the side and back of the chamber. 'Come.'

I followed, into what became a micro-corridor within the office. 'But … what if someone comes in, steals your casket?'

'Then he will be found and have his hands struck off and his eyes plucked out.' The words sounded obscene in Cecil's soft voice. From behind, he looked every inch a child. I paused mid-step. On the wall to my right reared up a huge portrait. An old man with a double-picked beard, swathed in robes, one knotty hand clutching a staff. 'My father.' Cecil had stopped too, had turned. 'I succeeded him in everything save his titles. A fine man.' He said this without expression. 'Could tell you the names of loyal men hidden in the land of the Turks, and yet he could not leave a room without forgetting his gloves.'

I knew, as everyone did, the reputation of the late secretary, Lord Burghley. 'You favour him, sir. You take after him.'

'Oh no.' Cecil smiled. 'I never forget my gloves.' He turned his back on me and slipped deeper into shadow. I followed, passing another portrait – a smaller one, depicting the queen as a severe, frowning creature, sexless in austere black. Elizabeth the politician, I thought.

We turned a corner where the screen folded, and Cecil opened a door on the far side of the chamber. It had been hidden, and I supposed that if someone broke in that way, they would be prevented by the thick oak screen from stabbing the principal secretary in the back.

One of the small privy gardens which dotted the palace lay ahead. Concentric squares of winter shrubs gave colour, and the air was sweet despite the murky sky. I sucked it in. 'My father held fast to live beyond his natural term. The settling of the succession kept him alive beyond his years, in pain in mind and body. I owe it to his memory to see it settled as he would wish. Observe,' said Cecil, holding up his wedge of bread. Good stuff, I noted, made from fine wheat. He pitched it into the garden.

Immediately, a number of birds burst from trees, from the sky. Each alighted near the morsel and began hopping towards it. A large one, a gull, swooped down, waggled its broad wings, and the robins and rooks cawed but moved away. 'You see how the biggest looks set to take the prize?'

Without waiting for an answer, Cecil stamped into the garden, waving an arm and crying, 'shoo!' The gull returned an answering cry, but it took off. Tentatively, the smaller birds began closing in on the bread. 'You see? How a man might subvert the natural order of things? See how they scrabble and fight, tearing the thing they seek to shreds?'

'What would you have me do, Sir Robert?'

'Watch, my friend. Report on any little men who seek to prevent the noblest bird from taking what God intended for it.' I said nothing. In his demonstration, whether he meant to or not, Cecil had cast himself as God. 'And yet I brought you here so that we might speak even more privily, Ned. For you might do me greater service than that. I fancy that paying for your release from the Clink, from the gallows, warrants a greater return.' I blinked once. Twice. Swallowed. When he spoke again, his voice had lost all hint of humour. 'I have friends tell me that something has been stolen out of Scotland. Some papers touching the inheritance of the king of that realm. Prejudicial to his claims to this realm, in short.'

'What like, sir?'

'I do not know the content.' I could read no deception. Instead, it seemed to me that Cecil was genuinely frustrated, his little brow wrinkling and his jaw taut. 'Only that if these papers fall into corrupt hands, King James will be debarred from having his claim to the crown considered.'

He favours the Scottish king, I thought.

Realisation struck.

'That Scot I saw at the Mitre. His package, so guarded.' No response. 'But … why should a Scot want to hurt his king's right to the …' I shied away from using the word 'succession'. It tasted of treason. That word I said aloud. 'You said a traitor, sir – a traitor to his king … What should I do?'

'Firstly, think. Think on what you have seen already.'

I did. 'Jesus,' I said. 'These men with red crosses of England, their hatred of foreigners. That Ford was outside the same tavern where a Scotch traitor – maybe – was lurking.' It fit. The thieving Scot come to London with some proof against his sovereign, with the aim of selling it to Englishmen bent on preventing that king's succession.

'I suspect we are of the same mind,' said Cecil. 'I have heard of no other visitors from Scotland, certainly no strangers that would falsely claim to be of the Scottish court. These men seek to do as I did. To prevent the natural order. To let the little birds scratch and tear instead.'

'But why?'

'*Cui bono*?'

'Whoever is next after King James.'

'*Qui perdidit*, to be sure. But no, Ned. The one who wins is not only the competitor who takes the throne, but the man who puts him there. The kingmaker. The one who stamps away the great gull and clears a path for whomsoever he wishes.'

'What should I do?' I repeated.

'As I said, Ned. What you do well. Watch and listen. Discover who pays the way of scum like this Ford. These false papers, whatever they are … I should like them to be in my special protection. Not in the hands of whoever leads a rabble of malcontent English fools.'

'False,' I echoed.

'Most certainly. But that hardly matters. If they are seen, if they are printed, they will be believed.'

That was true enough. 'But if they won't have James, if they'll ruin him somehow, whom do they want?'

'That I cannot say. The Stuart girl, Lady Arbella?' He shrugged. 'It is the man who leads them I would have discovered. Then we might find means of drawing his scheme from him. And quickly, Ned.' Hesitation. 'She's going.'

'Someone with money.'

'Without doubt. I suggest you start with Raleigh.'

'What?'

'Sir Walter Raleigh.'

'I know who he is.' I lowered my tone when Cecil's eyebrow rose. 'Sorry, sir. I … I thought you were a friend to Raleigh.'

'I am a friend to every man.' I stood aside as he moved past me, returning to his chamber. He paused in the doorway, half-turning. 'Yet … I regret that my friends do not always favour one another.' A little tut. 'No, indeed. And my especial friend north of the border … well, he does not trust sweet Sir Walter at all.'

'He is a great man. Known, protected by the queen. It is … a dangerous thing.'

'Ah, Ned. Life is dangerous. If this matter is not contained and quickly, we will all be in danger. Perhaps you especially.' I stiffened. 'I fear,' Cecil went on, 'there will be no more escapes from prison if you cannot help kill this business in the womb. I regret the hangman will not be robbed of his quarry again.'

4

'Raleigh wouldn't speak to me. Arrogant prick. His steward wouldn't even let me right inside. Went straight there after casting them libels yesterday, Bartlet.'

Sir Bartlet Everard winced. 'Ah, Peter. You failed to win the papers from that treacherous Scot. And you failed to win Raleigh to our cause.' He tutted. 'This is poor work, my friend.' Rather than showing contrition, the creature frowned, his chest expanding. Bartlet heard his brother cough at his side. 'Ah, well, can't be helped, can it? We will have the Scot's papers by other means.'

'Didn't have the cash to satisfy the greedy prick.'

'Oh, not to worry, not to worry.' Bartlet forced a smile, moving over to a brazier and letting the heat caress his face. 'We have other means than money if the beast will not play fair. And Raleigh … as you say, my friend, more arrogant a man never lived. Why, I daresay he would aim to make himself king, wouldn't you say?' The smile became a clown's grin. Ford visibly relaxed. 'And nevertheless, dear Peter, you've done well in drawing us a good crowd today. All former seamen, are they?'

'Seamen, old soldiers, young lads what can't find work nor food nor money by any honest means. The dock's the only place they can gather safe.'

'And my brother's good warehouse.' He cast an arm around. 'A fine place for talking. Go and walk amongst them, my friend. Give them some tobacco, pipes. My brother here shall join you in a moment.'

'Will do, Bartlet, will do.' With only a brief nod, Peter Ford left the warehouse.

Bartlet turned to his brother. 'For the love of Christ, Gregory, it pains me to have such trash use my Christian name. His words carried condemnation. It had been Gregory's idea. It would make the common rabble warn to him, he said. 'And I do not wish to know how much of my purse has been emptied to provide them with tobacco!'

'It … it … it'll be worth it,' stammered his brother. Bartlet's lip curled, and in response Gregory's balding head seemed to redden.

'It had better be.' He kept his voice low. The warehouse, composed of two floors, had a way of amplifying sound. 'You hear the disgusting clod couldn't get to Raleigh. I told you that was a fool's errand. That arrogant knave will involve himself in no scheme he does not direct.'

'No, brother. I'm sorry. I only thought–'

'Think harder, man.' Bartlet made to strike him, grinning at the resultant flinch. Bastards, he had long supposed, came in two types: the thoroughly cunning, brooding and breeding resentment at their base birth, and the pathetically obsequious, grateful for acknowledgement from their siblings. Gregory Everard was the latter. Pulling his hand back, Bartlet straightened his own collar and smoothed down his doublet.

Gregory coughed. 'No, brother.'

'Hmph. Very well.' He began unloosening the doublet, rumpling it, tugging on one side of the collar. It was bad enough having to leave off his ruff and hat. He had even acceded to his base brother's insistence that they forego the Everard coach and arrive by rented horse at Billingsgate Docks. All to impress upon an ill assorted ragtag of filth that he was on their side, a man of the people, a gentleman to be sure but one who understood their plight and was worth listening to. 'Do I look sufficiently like an animal to meet their demands?'

'You look marvellous, Bart, marvellous.'

'Flatterer. Well, I suppose it is time to speak to them. Tell Ford to bring them in. Then you might go about our other business. This shall not take long, I trust.' He watched as Gregory followed Peter Ford's path out of the warehouse.

A few minutes later, Ford swaggered in at the head of the hilariously named knights of the red cross. In reality, he could see, a sad assortment of discontented cripples, masterless men, and the unemployable. Scraggly, he thought. Unkempt. He would quite happily see them pilloried and whipped through the streets. Some of them already had little red crosses sewn crudely onto their jerkins – a touch, his brother said, that would be mighty cheap but work wonders in giving them a sense of purpose.

Yet, as he had told Gregory, great men might build their names on the backs of lesser ones. Change was in the air, flying towards England like a comet. When it arrived, fortunes would be made. 'My friends,' he said, stamping up a few steps of one of the warehouse's many staircases. He turned to face them. It would be a far cry from making a speech in parliament house – he could hardly address these men publicly, for fear of drawing unwanted attentions to an unlawful assembly – but he would make his point.

Go amongst them, he thought; that is what Gregory had suggested. He made the briefest of moues before stepping back down to their level and into their unwashed, dog-fur stink.

He went to the first group, clapping an old man on the shoulder with his gloved hand. 'A brave soldier from the Spanish wars, are you not?' The man grunted assent. 'Terrible. Terrible what has been done to you and yours. We'll put an end to that, won't we?' He moved on. 'Another brave soldier, eh? Don't you worry, old boy. Will we have our old enemies of Scotland and Spain to lord it over us? No, indeed, no we will not!' He moved on to the next group, humming a companionable jig-tune.

There, he slapped the back of one of the younger men. 'A fine, pretty lad you are. You won't be wishing for your jobs nor your young wenches to be snatched up by lice-ridden Scots, eh?'

'Not bloody likely, Bartlet, not me. Fucking foreigners.'

'No foreigners, boy, we'll put paid to that.'

Surely that was enough. He nodded at Ford – a gracious thanks that the creature had amassed at least thirty men. Enough to spread disaffection. He returned to the staircase and mounted so that he was looking over their heads. By chance, a shaft of light shone in from one of the high, unglazed windows, landing on him. 'I thank you all for coming, my friends. You're all of stout courage. Now I come to our purpose. I am sure the king of the Scots is an honourable man and I shall say nothing of those rumours of his love of wine and things too disgusting to mention.' He mimed glugging from a bottle, threw the invisible vessel away, and tapped his crotch. Laughter rose.

To have to play the clown in front of such people was an exercise in humiliation. Yet it worked. Laughter seemed to draw men to him.

'Filthy, dirty bastard!' shouted one of the men.

'Sodomite!' called another.

'Nor do I say that he is the beggardly king of a beggardly ancient enemy, whose rough people will take your land and your jobs. No, I say only that an Englishman must lead England. That is reasonable, is it not?'

'Reasonable!' cried one youngster, as though it were the first time he'd heard the word.

'I only ask you this. Is it right that honest Englishmen have to eat acorns and grass for want of good food, when our poor queen's parasites swarm the court and feed on her bounty?' No response. The cattle likely did not understand him. 'Our sovereign princess lies dying.' He swallowed. The line had been crossed into treason. 'You all know this. And her desire for an honest English succession is thwarted by wicked counsellors. They, I say, would pass our crown and our liberty into the hands of foreigners. Foreigners who will swarm this nation and this city and take all that you have. Your property? Sold to Scots. Your women? Married to Scots. Or if it is Spain these parasites aim towards, all will go to the Spanish. This is no treason. This is the very opposite of treason. Treason it is to sell your realm to another.'

'He's right,' cried the old man he had patted. 'I didn't fight no Spanish scum across the water to be a slave to 'em now.'

'And my old man didn't fight no Scots all them years back to be slave to a Scotch king. Scotsmen are cannibals and carry the plague, I heard.'

'And you might be right, my boy. What is wrong, I ask, with an Englishman sitting on the throne of England? Would the Spanish suffer to be ruled by anyone but a Spaniard, or the Scots by anyone but a Scotsman? I think not.' Bartlet made a fist of his right hand and began waving it up and down. 'No, no, and again I say no.' Agreement erupted in a chorus. Dangerously loud. He held up a hand. 'Yet what can we do? We are only simple folk. I say that your honest men of parliament – men like myself – must have our say. Only we can protect you from the dishonour of a foreign ruler. England's parliament is confirmed in its ancient liberty. Our sovereign lady herself professed her love for us when last we sat. And now we return the favour by saving her England and ours from being swallowed up by strangers. The time has come when honest men in parliament, men who are friends to you and yours, who are not afraid to come amongst you, advise our ruler. Not self-loving courtly creatures who would sell this nation for the security of their own positions. No, we will have a native king who understands and loves our laws and the constitution of our realm as her Majesty does. None other.

'We'll have no Scotch Church and ranting ministers tearing down our English Church, nor will we be taken back to Rome.' Bartlet's voice petered out, as he read the looks exchanged amongst his audience. Keep off religion, Gregory had said; it frightens them and is a matter they fear to hear discussed. He cursed himself for getting swept up in his own rhetoric, before essaying a vague smile and audible murmur. I'm a little absent minded, it said, but you ought to trust me the more for my honesty. They returned their attention to him.

'And you, my friends, you each have your part to play in supporting us. In saving England. You are England's red cross knights now. You must do as my friend Peter here has done. By subtle and crafty means you must hazard danger and let the caterpillars of the court know that they cannot force a foreigner on us. That we will not stand for it. Go your ways, my friends – write on walls, spread the word that every Englishman who embraces foreign rule is the foulest of traitors. In this you do no wrong, and anyone who says you do is likewise a traitor. Am I not a member of our English parliament?' He had intended at this point to bring Raleigh's name up as another true Englishman. Instead, he said, 'Am I not a knight of the realm, confirmed so by the late Lord Essex? A great man, and an Englishman to the bones of him. Am I not a duly elected fellow, born in our realm and possessed of property here? I tell you it is no offence to save this country by supporting a true succession. And I tell you this: when they come to write the chronicles, when the poets write of that glorious princess Elizabeth giving up her earthly crown for a heavenly one, they will say that the good men of London led the rest of the country in placing that crown on the head of one of their own.'

Applause burst out. Bartlet let it wash over him before holding up his hands for silence. He stepped back down to ground level. 'I must away now. I hazard my own life speaking thus, as the eyes of those wicked counsellors descry all. You know what you each must do. Remember, the ship of state is losing wind. Crack your cheeks and blow. The air of your words will set us at sail again. Friend Peter here will guide you.' As the eyes of assembly turned to Ford, Bartlet added, 'and I promise you this also. Scottish James will fall first. We will this day procure papers which will stand as proof against his claim. Now go, go, with my promise that should any of you face difficulties, my purse and home will be open to you.'

He was eager to be gone before they asked him who he did want on the throne – if their dull minds had even begun to consider it. The fools knew what they didn't want – foreignness – but they had no idea what they did want. He moved towards the door and thrust it open. They left the warehouse in their former small groups and he thanked each one, clapping those he could bear to touch on the shoulder as they exited.

The sheep gone to do as they were bid, he thought. Such power was what he was born to.

***

He slid off his gloves and threw them at Gregory. They hit his brother in the chest and fell to the floor. Without a word, he bent to retrieve them. 'Burn 'em! I'll never have the stink off 'em else. Dear God. To have to mix with the residue of civilisation.'

'But it's working, brother. They hang on you.'

'As a plague boil hangs on the pit of a Southwark trull.' He walked through his combined bedchamber and study, in his own good house in Bishopsgate Street, unbooted feet sinking into the carpet. A shame he had no servants to light the fire and properly warm the place. He would have to have Gregory do it. Standing before it, his back to his brother, he examined the family arms, which were in need of a good polish: a shield with a diagonal bend, surmounted by a lion-headed, goat-backed, snake-tailed chimera. 'And wherever you found that Peter Ford … he might speak their vulgar tongue, but at what cost to my purse?'

'It was I who paid –'

'By Christ, I could drink Spain dry. Have we any of that good Canary left?'

'I've found our –'

'A drink, Gregory. Now!'

His face reddening, his brother fled the study. Bartlet eased off his furred cloak and sat at his desk. On it sat his pride and only abiding interest: a sheaf of papers. On the top was a handwritten title page: *The True Historie of the Noble and Illustre the Late Earle of Essex, His Life*. He touched it reverently. He remembered the real man well enough; he had served under him at Rouen in '91. Been knighted by him there too, back when he was a raw, fresh-faced lad. His only military adventure, thank God. He had, he thought, rubbing a rueful hand over his expanding gut, let himself go since then. Yet in these pages he would be eternally one of the heroes. It would have to be published anonymously, of course, when he had time to finish it. Only when the old queen was dead might the world know that it was born of his mind. There would be other material needing printing too, of course – and that even more explosive. He looked up as the door reopened.

Gregory crossed to him silently, setting down a silver cup and pouring the wine. 'Brother, I have–'

'I spoke to them of Essex. Made the unlettered fools ready for the publishing of my work. Essex, the English hero who would brook no foreigner. Come. Look upon your brother's poor writings.' Gregory picked up the topmost pages and began reading aloud. Bartlet sat back as his words washed over him. 'Well?'

'Well…'

'Will it not send cheer to the hearts of true Englishmen who hang upon such tales?'

'I …' began Gregory, speaking slowly and carefully, 'I think the booksellers and book buyers of London will agree that this is, indeed … a book.'

'Quite. A book for all men to read, if they care to know the knightly ways.' Bartlet grinned. It would manifestly sell. Chivalry had been a long time dying, it was true, and Essex was its last painful gasp; but still the nation was embrewed with the notion of it.

'Uh … forgive me, Bart, but … wasn't Essex a supporter of the king of the Scots?'

'Ha!' barked Bartlet, tapping the pages. 'Not in *my* chronicle history. That Essex will be buried deep by my words. Reborn as a true hero, not a Scot lover. None who read my work could ever think he had traffic with that foreign sodomite. Ah, if only the late earl had bided his time. Waited until the old woman was dying before he rose.'

'His patience must have been running out.'

'His money was running out. Had he been wiser he would have awaited Lady Occasion, not tried to force her hand. Ha! His loss is our gain, my dear brother. What Essex failed by insurrection, we shall manage. No rebellion here because there will soon be no sovereign to rise against. Instead we will place our own man on the throne. Once I decide who that might be.'

'But first the Scottish king,' said Gregory. Bartlet opened his mouth to speak, but Gregory hurried on. 'He's here.'

'Who?'

'Gowrie. The Scot.'

'What?' Bartlet jumped from his chair. 'You fool; you should have told me directly. Has he the papers?'

'He will speak only to you.'

'Where is he? I'll go to him. I … no. No, bring him here. Now, you fool.'

'Yes, yes, brother.'

Bartlet sipped at his Spanish wine as he waited. Within minutes, Gregory returned, pushing a weaselly man lightly ahead of him. 'Geordie Gowrie,' he said. 'He would speak only with you. Shall I leave you?'

'No, Gregory. You are my brother and you are as deep in this matter as I. For the love our father bore you I would have you stay.' Gregory straightened up, smiling. 'Mr Gowrie. Welcome to Everard Place.'

The man did not respond. He looked, thought Bartlet, distinctly unnerved to finally be standing before his purchaser. 'I understand you would not deal honestly with my man Ford.'

'I would not pass anything to a mere nothing, sir.'

'Hard words. Yet you will pass this document to me. Here, have some wine.'

'Tuscan vernage?'

'You have fine tastes,' said Bartlet. He did not add, 'surprising for a Scot.' Instead, he said, 'I regret we have only good Canary. My brother has kept the house up alone. You will understand I had to come up to London in great secrecy, leaving my servants and household stuff in the country. And my wife and son. Hardly wish to advertise my presence in the city. Questions might be asked.' As he spoke, he poured Gowrie wine into his own cup and passed it over. The Scotsman sipped, giving a nod of satisfaction. 'Now, to the matter of our business.'

'You have the money?'

Just like a Scot, thought Bartlet. 'I do.' He nodded at Gregory, the treasurer of the enterprise. 'Yet I am not fool enough to part with it until I inspect the goods. My good brother took up our late father's trade affairs, but I recall that principle.' The word 'trade' he said with scorn. 'Let us see them, then, these mysterious papers.'

Gowrie set down the cup and reached inside his coat, pulling out a leather folder. 'Closed up in Edinburgh town itself.'

'You have read these proofs against King James?'

'No, sir. More than my life is worth. But I was telt that should you read them ye'd never again call him king.'

Bartlet leaned forwards. 'Pray open it, Mr Gowrie.

The Scotsman did so, slowly, untying the thin string that held the leather flap closed. He peeled it back and reached inside. Frowned. Turned the whole thing upside down over the desk and shook it.

Nothing.

'Whit … I witnessed them, checked and put inside again when it wiz steekit to in Edinburgh.' His Scots came on heavy. Rather than anger, disbelief seemed to overwhelm him. Fear followed, his forehead turning scarlet. 'I saw thaim, sir, sealed close intae the pouch, the flap closed and knottit!'

'Where are they?' asked Gregory, reaching for the folder himself. His voice, too, carried rising panic. Gowrie let him take it. 'Some secret compartment inside this thing, perhaps?'

'What manner of trickery is this?' Bartlet's own voice carried a trembling of anger – enough to stop the movement of the other two men. 'What game are you playing with us, Gowrie?'

'They must hae been taken from me, sir, I cannae say where they are. They were in there, I swear by God's truth I saw thaim placed, sealed. I've had this leathern pouch on me from Edinburgh tae Berwick, and so on tae this city, sir, not out of my sight save tae sleep and have a bite tae eat. I had it yesterday at a tavern, sir, the Mitre, I fled a man. He must hae followed me, taken thaim as I slept – no, stolen, I–'

'You're a liar, Gowrie. You said you had these papers yesterday. Containing these great secrets. You are cheating me. You have sold them elsewhere. Where are they?'

'I telt you they have to hae been taken, sir.'

'If you think,' said Bartlet, his voice turned humourless, 'to extract a higher price, then you are mistaken.'

'No, sir. I … that man – the loon who talkit tae me in the tavern, he must've–'

'Take him!'

Gregory, his eyes widening, lunged at Gowrie. The Scot fell forward, his face smashing into the edge of the thick desk. 'His arms,' hissed Bartlet. 'Tie the liar's arms.' He turned to the great tester bed and tore off the sheets, rolling them up and tossing them to his brother.

'I'm sorry,' mumbled Gregory as he bound the man.

'He is owed no sorries, you jelly-livered fool. He means to gull us. To cozen us. I have had my fill of dealing with scum today. Hold him.' As his brother held the dazed Gowrie upright, Bartlet cuffed him across the cheek. 'Where are my papers, you filthy Scotch cunt? Where are they?' Blood gushed from the man's nose. He mumbled something thickly. 'What? Speak, you animal. What is in those papers?'

'I … can't …' murmured Gowrie. 'Must've been stolen. Here. On the road. Been followed.'

'And you will follow them if you lie to me. Where have you hidden them?' Another cuff, harder, across the other cheek. 'You might have left this room a rich man, not a bleeding one. But for your greed.' He took his throat and squeezed it. 'You will answer me.'

'He can't answer you if he's dead!' shouted Gregory.

Bartlet released his grip, surprised by his brother's display of firmness. 'Watch your tongue, you base born milksop.' He moved back to his chair and sat, his shaking hands gripping the edge of the desk. His heart was thrumming: surprise, indeed, at his own loss of control. 'I apologise, brother. You know how much rests on this one document. It was the assurance of these pages that drove us to this enterprise. Without them we have nothing but a rabble of discontented common root-munchers.' He adopted a mock Scottish accent. 'They'll ruin the Scotch king, he promises. Ye'll have them at a right fair price, he promises. And now he dares come before me with this … this nonsense about a fellow stealing the papers when we know – we *know* – he had something on him yesterday. Unless the whole thing is a fantasy, a dream. Perhaps you always had a leather parcel full of *nothing*, you lying scum,' he snapped, leaning forward on the desk.

'What can we do?'

'If those papers exist, I will have them,' said Bartlet. 'If he has to die for us to get them. And if they do not exist … he will die a worse death. Take him away, Gregory. Put him in ward in one of our meaner rooms. Keep him bound. Get what you can out of him. About this tavern man and the contents of those papers. Where he's hidden them, for I will swear by God's truth he has. By any means to hand.'

Gregory gave a tight nod and began dragging the semi-conscious Gowrie out of the study. Before they reached the door, Bartlet called him to a halt. 'If you are milk-livered in your handling of him, Gregory, you will lose my favour by it.' He smiled. 'A rough hand is the only language his abominable race understand. You are a gaoler now. Bring Ford in if you find your liver delicate. Try not to make so poor a job of it. I wish to be left in peace to finish my book … and to hear no more of this matter. Not until we have proof enough to destroy King James or the means to get it.'

5

The round metal thing intrigued me, but it did not ravish with that strange proprietary fever that sometimes comes upon me. It was, I realised, leaning close to study it, a little world all itself, made of brass, like a giant, polished filigree, mounted on four wooden paws. A globe of the earth, with writing carved into the metal. Where, I wondered, was Friesland? A cold and inhospitable place by the sound of it. I considered that one day I might have to run off to just such a place. Cecil's threat of the hangman was worse than a threat, I knew; it was the simple truth. If he lost power through backing the wrong hound, I would not last long. Men with my tastes and weaknesses require a protector who gambles soundly and wins always.

The globe was only one of several strange objects that Raleigh had on display in the large gallery into which I had been shown at Durham House: a gallery almost dominated by an open-fronted wooden cabinet in which musical instruments kept company with scientific objects and oddities. Raleigh liked to show off his treasures, I thought; I preferred to keep mine close.

I had been unable to go the day after meeting Cecil. Finding my stock of clothes out of fashion, I had had to visit Mrs Cole the seamstress, to be outfitted with a broad-brimmed hat, mock velvets and, above all, clean, thin shoes. A cloak was pinned at my shoulder, not with a brooch but a silk rose. Cream hose were tied with silken white ribbons under my knees (chapman-bought but I doubted anyone could tell). Cecil had furnished me with cash enough to have gone to a good tailor and had new stuff made up, real stuff, but I reckoned I might do it meanly and save some of the cash for myself. I had won my way into Raleigh's house on the Strand by tying my feet up in sackcloth on the walk to the wherry docks, only jettisoning the cloths when I reached the river stairs. The steward looked at my clean shoes, as I knew he would, and took me for a true gentleman.

'A marvel, is it not?'

I started. Turned.

'Sir Walter!'

Swisser Swatter chimed laughingly in my head – an old tale from somewhere.

It could be no other. Sir Walter Raleigh was known about town as a man who dressed exquisitely. With a surprisingly soft face for a seaman, only slightly lined by his fifty years of salt and spray, he stood like a peacock. I could see something of what must have fired the queen's lusts in his younger days. His suit was sky blue, the doublet slashed. Silken pink roses bloomed at the breast, and an enormous ruff made his face look like it stood before a painter's canvas. I did not know where he had come from – some secret passage hidden behind an arras in the gallery, I supposed, his shoes and cane sinking silently into the carpet. Nor did I know how long he had been observing me, standing like a bumpkin gawping at his globe. I lowered my eyes, as much to prevent the green beams of envy shining out of them as anything. 'A marvel,' he said.

'Yes. It is.'

'A gift from a friend.' The mingled smells of good tobacco smoke and musk wafted from him, overpowering the beeswax aroma of the gallery.

'Hm.' I was lost, off balance.

'My steward informs me you are a friend.'

'I am that, sir.'

'I count it another marvel and a blessing too that a man should find a friend not known to him.'

'I come to seek news of the Fortune. I am looking to invest.' Cecil had told me that Raleigh was considering outfitting one of his ships for a voyage.

'You have capital?'

'I can get some.'

'Who are you?'

'A friend. William Stanford.' I bowed low, sweeping off my hat and tucking it into my armpit.

Raleigh seemed to digest the name along with my appearance. My suit was that of a modest gentleman, short ruffed, restrained of colour. 'I see.' He regarded me through narrowed eyes, before abruptly turning his back on me and clasping his hands behind it. 'Glyptics,' he announced, showing me his profile.

'Sir?'

'Glyptics.' He jerked his nose at the cabinet. In a dish sat numerous red and greed stones, each one covered in strange carvings. He began strolling along the gallery, leaving me to follow in his wake. He walked, I noticed, with a slight limp, leaning lightly on his cane 'So, you are interested in investing.'

'I am, sir. Yet first I would know a little more of the venture. It seems a hazardous time to invest. If the rumours out of the court are true. I thought you might tell me a little of your plan to go to sea, given what might happen in the coming weeks. I –'

'Mandrake roots. Turned to shrivel.' He had stopped again, swivelling at the hip beside a cluster of displayed brown knots, shaped like bunched-up babies. 'I know not what their true properties are. Yet it is fitting that as we grow older ourselves, we become again as little children, shrivelling and crying and then curling up in the grave. The coming weeks you say?'

'Yes, sir,' I said, resuming my slow pace behind him. 'It's whispered in the streets that the queen …'

'Is eternal. Yes, I know. Our English Diana. A goddess who will reign over us longer than we might endure ourselves. Set above us in the celestial sphere. You see this?' He had stopped again, this time beside some sort of headdress, which looked a little like an old French hood but made of green, yellow, and red waxed feathers. 'Out of the southern Americas. Worn there by the most powerful of tribesmen. Of curious design, don't you think? You are interested in the conquest of Guyana?'

'No.'

'And gold, here, finely wrought as a tiny boat. Spanish gold. My favourite kind.'

'I thought you hated the Spaniard,' I said, giving a little smile.

'Hate? I love the Spaniard. I know of no other enemy worthy of the name. Ah, and here we come to my pride. Black rock from the end of the earth that might be polished to a fine shine to create a mirror of men's souls. Obsidian. Rare indeed.' He picked up a perfect sphere of it and handed it to me. 'Test its weight. Almost nothing.'

'Yes, sir,' I said. I had grown tired of his collection of rarities. 'And I see the perspective glass and the strange staff too. But to the matter of whether a voyage might take place under the present times.'

Raleigh took another few steps forward, passing the end of his cabinet of curios, and halted. This time he fully turned to me, before inclining his head to one side. 'You seem,' he said, 'for a venturous fellow, less intrigued by the fruits of adventure than the intrigues of court and country.'

I cursed myself. He had been tricking me, putting my tale to the test. 'An adventure cannot take place if aught befalls the queen.'

He smiled. Turned his head to the wall. On it hung a large portrait. Queen Elizabeth, her face rounder than it looked whenever I had seen her process through the city, unlined. A stiff ruff, fashioned into points, framed it. From her headdress, a gauzy veil descended down her back, and in her hand was clutched an enormous fan. Eliza the sensual, the patroness of adventurers, steeped in the exotic.

Strange to think of the old tigress gone. She had always been there: Elizabeth of England. Elizabeth was England. Like the moon, as Raleigh had said – always there, glowing above our little world. That she should die – even that she should be old, seemed unthinkable. I thought instead of Kenilworth, and river pageants, and the queen of Scots, and Spanish galleons on fire. Those were the tales that made her immortal. 'It is treason,' said Raleigh, breaking off my sudden thoughts, 'to speak of aught befalling the queen.'

'I …'

'I shall tell you why I had you admitted, Mr … Stanhope?'

'Stanford.'

'I allowed you in because I saw that I would not be quit of you creatures until I told one of you, to his face, mind, that I would have none of your treacherous doings.' He frowned, but my mind turned. *You creatures*. 'Does your master think that if I would not speak to a lowly minion, he might mock me instead by sending a shadow, a ghost from the grave? Shall I blow smoke in your face, boy, and thereby make a hoary false tale green and true?

'No, do not speak. If you think to trap me in immoderate speech, then you are more foolish than Essex ever was. Tell your master that sitting in parliament with a fellow in years past does not make us confederates in anything. There is no parliament now. Whatever his design is, whatever enterprise he ventures, I will have none of it. I care not a whit for the Lady Arbella nor the Spanish nor any of the grasping creatures who look to a dead woman's shoes. Nor do mythical lost papers touching the future interest me.'

'I … I will tell him,' I said.

'Good.'

I bowed to him and began to back away. 'Halt, Mr Stanford.'

'Sir?'

'My obsidian.'

I cursed and returned the black ball to him before leaving.

I had handled Raleigh badly, I knew, unskilfully. Expecting an arrogant man, full of greed and ambition, as he was reputed, I had entered his conversation like a rolling barrel. Such a fellow as I'd imagined would have boasted of his knowledge and leapt upon the chance of investment. Raleigh, however, was cunning. Yet he foresaw less than he thought. Thus, I had scored against him in the end and knew more than hitherto, even if names still wanted filling in. At any rate, I would not blunder so again.

As I returned back down the Thames, a needling, cold rain began. I bent my head against it. My plan had been to draw by gentle speeches any knowledge Raleigh might have had of Peter Ford and his crew of red cross plotters; yet the man had offered it freely, and in the negative. They were led by a man who had sat with him in parliament. Further, he had turned them down. Cecil's distrustful friend in Scotland – a friend who wore a crown, I suspected – would have to look farther and try harder to condemn Sir Walter Raleigh.

With each splash of the oars, snatches of Raleigh's words rose and fell in my mind.

I love the Spaniard…

I care not a whit for the Lady Arbella…

Nor the Spanish…

Nor do mythical lost papers touching the future interest me…

***

I knocked on the door of a man I thought ought to have some knowledge of the late parliament, for his father had sat in it.

No answer.

I pushed the door open and entered anyway.

A long rumple in the cot betrayed his presence, as did the gargantuan feet sticking out of one end and the thatch of curls hanging from the other. Kit Lockhart was my own age and what I suppose you might call one of my few friends. As a law student, Hilary Term ought to have put him in the courts or at a lecture, and yet I had known he would more likely be sleeping off a night carousing in his cell at the Inner Temple. Study did not interest him, and he held it for a truth that the Inns of Court had become mere sporting houses for young men with nothing better to do. It was true enough. He would never make a lawyer – that I had known from the first. But few students were expected to. The great legal training grounds were dumps for spare sons, where they might fritter away a few years and hopefully make connections that would ensure idle futures and plum positions in the state. England looked after its well born young men. Most of their time they spent carousing. We had met, Lockhart and I, through the playhouses, where he went most afternoons. His natural laziness had recently cut even that down.

'Lockhart,' I shouted, disguising my voice. 'Why attend you not to this day's studies, boy?' Then, more naturally. 'Fear not – I'm not one of your creditors come to beat you.' The sudden jerk did not come. Frowning, I crossed the tiny dormitory room and threw back the cover. He lay under it, still wearing what I assumed to be the previous day's clothes. The tang of stale wine soured the air.

'Ugh,' he mumbled, covering his eyes. 'Savage? Get out of it, do.'

'The day marches on, my friend,' I said. My voice, full of cheer, appeared to be doing little for him. 'What are your plans?'

'You are looking at them,' he growled, snatching at the thin bedcover and pulling it back. 'What are you about?' His words, I noticed, still slurred.

'Are you still in drink? It's near noon.'

'Strong wine is a mistress hard to make leave in the morning.'

'No lectures?'

'If I wished to hear old men talk, I should go home.' His voice was as it always sounded: full of old money and boredom.

I laughed, bouncing down onto the bed and jiggling it. 'You don't mind hearing young men guised as old talk. Polonius, Falstaff. Old Lacey and Otley. No play today?'

'There anything new to be heard?'

'No.'

'Then no. What did you come for if we are not for the playhouse?'

'I hoped to delve into that decaying mind of yours.' I jabbed at his curls. 'And I see you've been softening it for me.'

Lockhart sat up, wobbled a second, drew his knees to his neck, and blinked sense into his face. 'That water over there, give me some.' I did. He slurped at it, and then primly dabbed his lips with a napkin produced from God-knew-where before speaking. 'What is it, Savage?'

'It's about the last parliament.'

Confusion. 'What?' I repeated the question; his brow creased and his chin rose. 'It sat in 1601, October to December. The queen spoke to 140 members. Monopolies were the story of the parliament. My father was far from happy about them. The queen promised to end them. Her words were pretty but her deeds–'

'Any talk of the succession?'

'What?' He blinked. Again, I repeated myself. 'No, no, no. That would not have been allowed. It was the old parliaments that dared speak of that. A pair of brothers. Wentworths. And they suffered for it. Now all that talk goes on in our homes. My father hears of it. He knows the troublemakers.'

'Can you find out? Write to him?'

Lockhart whistled. 'Hell of a thing to put to the pen, Savage. Sorry. When I see him next, to be sure. What is all this? What does the Revels Office care for parliament?'

I sighed. Stood up. Walked the meagre length of the room and began picking things off his desk and replacing them: inkwell, pen, book. All covered in a fine layer of dust. I could sense him, behind me, slurping again at his water, but interested.

It has often occurred to me that every man is at war with himself – has, in fact, two selves fighting for control. So it is with me. One self is required to be unknown, secretive. Yet sometimes the other, which wishes to swagger, strut, and boast, overwhelms him. Physicians would say it was some precarious balance of the humours; astrologers that the sun and moon were all at square over my birth. My preening self won, thumbing its nose at its secretive brother - and so I told my friend about my work, omitting only the name of my employer.

Lockhart laughed. 'This is a jest, surely.' I drew in my cheeks. 'You are serious. Jesus, Savage. Why, you are in the service. Who do you work for?' I rolled my eyes. 'Cecil? Raleigh? Cobham? Where did my lord of Essex's men all go … surely it is not truly Cecil?'

'It doesn't matter.'

'Doesn't matter go to the devil,' he snapped, swinging his legs off the cot. He dug around a pile of loose stuff on the floor and produced a little wooden jar. Opening it, he dipped in a finger and began rubbing soot on his teeth. He licked it away and grinned. 'You are a Brainworm! For how long?'

'A Know-well, I prefer. Some years. That doesn't matter either. What does is …' I moved to the door, opened it, and made sure the hall was empty before closing it. I lowered my voice anyway. 'The queen is dying.'

'Jesus. So it is true, then.'

'There's more.' I laid out the tale of the proofs that might bar King James from the throne. 'What do you think of that?' A little pride coloured my voice at being able to impart such secrets.

'Jesus,' he said again. All trace of slur had departed his voice. Only hid red-rimmed eyes remained clouded. 'What is it, this proof, do you think?' I shrugged. 'They say that that king has a fondness for … that he has vices. But,' he said quickly, 'there is no default in a king and no one could prove such fond tales. They did worse than that in Roman days. And he has a wife and family. Pretty Danish queen, so I have heard. A royal lady fit to look upon. That is what England needs, a family man. The nation waxes weary under … at the present time. She,' he said, leaning on the word, 'has done nothing for years. Not to give men honest employment, anyway.' His voice shifted back to thoughtfulness. 'There were other rumours too, were there not?'

'About the king?'

He shrugged. 'Heard them from my father, back in the day. That it was said the Scotch king was not,' he put on a stern voice, 'of his father born. That his mother was a great and notorious whore who took her hunchbacked musician and secretary to her bed and cuckolded the boy king Darnley. King James is the son of that wicked union. A bastard. I bet that is the manner of it, and all has been kept *in secretum*. I'll wager you it is. How much?'

I ignored the bet and considered what he had said instead. I had heard the story and nodded slowly. 'Perhaps it is something to do with that. Maybe the story is less a tale than a truth.'

'In which case King James would be passed over.'

'Yes. Doesn't tell us where the papers are, though, nor who this man who sat with Raleigh in parliament and tried to enlist him is. All we know,' I added, thumping my fist into a palm, 'is that this Peter Ford creature is one of his minions.'

'Cannot your master just arrest the blackguard?'

'My master has no such power,' I parried. 'Besides, if he were arrested and properly interrogated, he would lead us nowhere and his disappearance would send the alarm out to his own master. Where then would they put their proofs? Beyond our reach.'

'Hmph.'

'Will you now write your father?'

'I … I will do you better than that.' I raised an eyebrow. 'I should like in, Savage.' A hard glitter had come into Lockhart's eyes, reminding me of Raleigh's obsidian ball. Fear crept up my back.

'What?' I asked, taking my turn at it.

'Please, let me join in.' He had the wheedling tone of a child. He even looked like one, with his froggy eyes and big mouth – ill-fitting on such a large body. 'You don't need to tell me anything you don't want. Jesus, but my life is so dull. The whole country has turned dull, waiting for something to happen. For change.' He punched his pillow. 'By God, to be useful to the realm. Come on, let me aid you. Help you track down this Ford brute, these parliament men. The treacherous Scot!' He threw the pillow in the air and again punched it. Tiny feathers burst forth and fluttered languidly. 'Come on, give me purpose! I can help you in the arts *sub rosa*.'

'I … I will speak to my master.'

'When? Do I meet him? Are there some secret rites? Jesus, it is like a play, Savage. A play about the games of kings. He will have me, will he not? I bet you he will – a pound says he will.'

'I …'

'Alright, a half-crown then.'

'I'll speak to him. I promise you nothing. But … meet me on the morrow.'

'At your lodgings? Shall I come to your lodgings?' Slyness crept into his voice. 'I own I have a mind to see this pretty mopsy you've taken up with.'

'No,' I said. I have a strange aversion to my friends intermingling. I suppose I am selfish by nature, and cannot bear the thought of them liking one another, meeting one another, perhaps preferring one another to me. Better, I always find, to keep them apart and have each wholly to myself when it pleases me. Besides, I doubted Faith would like to be considered a mopsy, and I knew she would dislike a man leering at her. 'By the Globe.'

I left his chamber, and the dormitory building, and made my way back to Chancery Lane. A pretty pass, I thought. I was less worried about what Cecil might say about my bringing someone into the affair than about the dangers I might be leading my friend into. Though I do not believe in omens, the sudden darkening of the sky warned me that if I had made an error, if something happened to Kit Lockhart, it would be another sin added to my ledger.

Still, I did as I'd said. Cecil had safe houses dotted about London, one of them not far from my lodging in Shoe Lane. There I could write a short message, leaving it with one of his messengers – rarely was it the same man twice, and occasionally it was a woman – and pick up any messages marked '710'. I simply wrote '710 for 10', the latter being Cecil's own chosen signifier. He had, before I last left him, instructed me to keep in regular contact, the matter being so pressing.

She's going …

That done, I took myself home. As I passed into Shoe Lane, I brushed past a group of loitering men led by a bull-like leader but paid them little attention. 'Mind yourself, lad,' one snarled. I said nothing. Such sights were becoming ever more common in the city – idle men spoiling for a fight for lack of other occupation. Keeping my head down and straightening my good hat, I marched straight for our pathetic little ground floor tenement.

Faith was inside, as usual, sitting at the stool, her small pink tongue darting out as she tended to her precious account books. It was a thing I encouraged, her mastery of numbers over literacy, though I warned her that I would have no books of calculation in the house. Too close to conjuring, I thought, and ripe to attract accusations of witchcraft. 'I return,' I announced, smiling. 'How has your day been? You've been out?' I listened awhile as she fixed me some bread and cheese, fussing over the state my clothes had got into. Watched her, too. In the past, I had tried to drum religion out of her, teaching her the art of taking from those who could afford to lose – the merchant with his huge stock who wouldn't miss one small trinket; the overfed wife who flaunted her jewels so amorally. She had understood the practical nature of it but retained that hard shell of Christian morality her mad parents had cursed her with. It was all a wasted effort, anyway, on someone who had a terror of being too long out of or too far distant from the house.

'They were so pretty, fresh on this morning.'

'So was I,' I said, chewing. 'And I mean to be again. I think a shave might be in order, mouse. Have we cash enough for–'

Bang. Bang-bang-thump!

'Who is it?' cried Faith. Her face whitened, the freckles that tickled a pattern over her cheeks standing out.

'I don't know. Stay back.' I got up from the stool and crossed to the door, where the furious tattoo had begun again.

I opened it.

6

The corpse was sprawled on the floor. Blood painted the wall in streaking lines. Bartlet's first instinct was to cry out in rage. And in fear.

Gregory's screams had drawn him from his study, through the house to his half-brother's chamber. There he had found the simpering fool screeching like a woman, Peter Ford shaking him. Geordie Gowrie, Bartlet knew, had been imprisoned in the little oratory leading off Gregory's chamber.

It was in that small space that his body lay.

'Silence,' hissed Bartlet. Gregory's keening softened to a whimper. 'What is this? Who has done this?' He kicked at the corpse. As he did so, the scene began to resolve itself. In Gowrie's clasped hand was a knife, and the blood had issued from his throat, spraying one wooden wall of the oratory red. Before Ford or Gregory could speak, Bartlet spun in the doorway. 'Who gave this fool a knife?!'

'Not me,' said Ford, who had been acting as the chief inquisitor, visiting the man every few hours.

'Nor me,' sniffed Gregory. 'I gave him bread but no means to cut it. I only unbound him to let him eat.'

'You searched him? When you put him in ward here, you searched him?'

'I did, brother. Nothing in the pockets at his belt and nothing in his coat nor doublet.'

Bartlet closed his eyes, reached up, and dug his nails into his forehead. 'His hat,' he said, surprised at the levelness of his voice. 'Scotsmen conceal their knives in their hats.'

Gregory's mouth fell open. 'How could I know that, Bart? You never told me that.'

'You do trade with Scots. You heard of this knave from them.'

'But I don't know their habits. He was … I didn't think he'd do this. Why would he? What would drive him to such an act?' His eyes slid to Ford, Bartlet noticed. 'What did you say to him, Ford?'

Peter Ford's chest rose on its usual bellows of truculence. 'I did what you feared to do, Mr Everard.'

'You laid hands upon him?' asked Bartlet.

'No, sir.' He cracked his knuckles. 'Threatened to, to be sure. Let 'im know what was waiting for him if he didn't start talkin'. Showed him a couple of tools I might make light of 'im with – things that break the thumbs and pop the eyes and that. Didn't touch 'im. Heh – said I'd deliver what was left of 'im to his barbarian king to chop up for firewood.'

'I … after Ford here threatened him – each time after, I spoke with him,' said Gregory. 'Wrote down his answers.'

'What do you mean "threatened", Everard?'

Gregory found that the rising tide of his own rage was quelled by the storm brewing between his brother and the rough-mannered puppet. 'Be silent, both of you.' He took a deep breath. 'There are no servants in the house. Mr Ford, do you know how best to be quit of this mouldering Scotch filth?'

'Me and a few of the boys surely can do it.' He shrugged. 'I'll fetch 'em.'

'Go your way, then.'

'Will do, Bartlet.' Ford sauntered from the chamber.

'Scum,' said Bartlet under his breath when the man had gone. 'Putting bricks through the windows of Flemish merchants and Moors and ridding us of dead Scots, that is the measure of his worth.' He closed the door, hiding Gowrie's body. 'Crazed serving maids and dishonourable Scotch curs. The only type to cut themselves off in so vulgar a manner.' He shook his head slowly. The sensation of matters slipping ever faster into dangerous waters swept over him. Ordering around common gutter-crawlers, being cheered and adored, even the thought of gaining and printing matter that would sway the future of the country: all seemed the stuff of political games. That was the stuff to which he had been born – it was his right and his privilege. Even having those who sought to gull him threatened and beaten was his absolute right as a knight. Death in his own house, however – a body that would now have to be got rid of – verged on the dangerous.

It was a good thing the government of England was presently in turmoil, he thought. A good thing that Elizabeth of England was keeping them busy dying and all London tensed with it, knowing without knowing, suspecting with saying.

'But why?' asked Gregory.

Bartlet shrugged. 'Fear of Ford's tortures?'

'He feared that worse than … worse than damnation? I'll … I'll sleep no more in this room.'

'Sleep where you wish. Christ Jesus, what a mess.'

'I should not have left Ford alone with him. The man is a mad dog.'

'Your mad dog, Gregory. You found him.'

'I thought him broad-mouthed, only. An orphaned young brute with a grudge. His parents starved to death, he told me, the food taken from their mouths by foreigners. I thought it would be a charity to have him with us.'

'Foreigners. Bad harvests and sloth, more likely,' sneered Bartlet.

'The blood …'

'I do not speak of the blood, you fool. You ask what drove the Scot to do himself to death? I'll tell you. Despair. Despair at losing his fortune. His only hope of advancement and favour. He would not have done it if he had sold those papers elsewhere. This death … it speaks of the truth of his claims.' He considered. 'It is either that or … or he had indeed sold them elsewhere and Ford frightened him so that he thought never to return to his hidden gold … and cut his own life short rather than letting us do it.'

'We wouldn't have killed him, surely?'

'What did he write?'

'What?'

'You said you noted down his answers when you questioned him. Let me see them.'

'Oh,' said Gregory, brightening. 'Yes, brother. Come.'

Gregory's chamber was the centre of his trading business. His modest bedframe and flock mattress lay obscured under piles of account books, inkwells, and the little woollen flag patches he doled out to new recruits for their women to sew onto their jerkins. Against one wall, something lay hidden under a sheet. 'What is that?'

'Ah.' This time Gregory smiled, a little shyly. 'That is a surprise for you, brother.' At Bartlet's raised eyebrow, he went on. 'Remove the sheet. Yes, so. And voila!'

'What is …' Bartlet trailed off as his eyes roved over the odd, boxy collection of wooden and metal instruments. 'Why it is …'

'A moveable printing press. I got it in parts. Assembled it. It's for your book. I thought that no um … no honest printer would take a book about the late earl. And it would cost a lot to get a dishonest one to print the document when we have it.'

A rush of affection towards his half-brother rose up in Bartlet, surprising him. He had never liked the fellow – born of a serving whore who had died in childbirth yet acknowledged by their father and raised in his household. Throughout their childhood, he had taken great delight in treating the boy as a slave and, for his part, Gregory had seemed to welcome it. It had been almost a regret when the base-born son inherited one of their father's businesses whilst he went off to Cambridge and then the wars. 'My book,' he said, taking him in an embrace. 'That was a kindly thing.' Gregory slid from his grasp, waving the gesture away.

'Oh, go on.'

'When this matter comes to fruition, when we are recognised by the new king as having cleared his path to the throne. Then, then I will see that you are respected, brother.' He meant it. As their father had lain dying, the old man had extracted the promise from them that together they would protect and promote the name Everard by any means to hand. The legitimate means was parliament. The illegitimate was business. Both had worked together in matters of state, with Gregory learning of the document from Scottish sailors who sold south and Bartlet learning of the queen's decline from his friends in politics. 'I mean it. This scheme is for us and our family. You are brother to a knight, and I do not doubt to a noble lord when we save the crown from the Scot.' Gregory nodded, his eyes shining. 'And this,' added Bartlet, patting the printing press with an avuncular air, 'this will have fitter matter even than my little book to occupy it. When we have this mysterious document. This beast shall then spew forth quartos enough to land in every man's hand, to be nailed to every door. If we can find it.'

The press was tiny in comparison to a great oak desk that made Bartlet's own seem mean. Gregory stepped over to it. 'We'll find it. I've already started looking. Here,' he said, turning over leaves of paper marked in a regular italic hand.

Bartlet peered down, his eyes rolling from side to side. 'Hmph. He never moves from his tale. He saw those papers placed in their pouch in Edinburgh. Never read them himself but knew that their contents were likely to shock and amaze the world. That they would utterly debar James from his false title of king.' He broke off from the papers and turned to Gregory. 'I've heard it said that the old queen of Scots willed her claim to England to the Spanish. Could that be the nature of it all?' Without waiting for an answer, he looked down again. 'He says he never once opened the leather case from Edinburgh to Berwick or from there to London. Bloody fool. And he maintains it for truth that a man in livery approached him in the Mitre tavern and tried to cozen him.

'For the love of Christ, anyone might have emptied his pouch along four-hundred miles of road, in any inn or tavern. Likely he was drunk as a lord in every one. Still yet he might have visited one of the Scotch king's competitors and sold – or tried to sell – it for a better price.'

'What do we do?'

'Hmph. We search.'

'It would be as well searching the whole route northwards. Ford–'

'Ford. Yes, Ford will follow the man's route north. Dispatch him forthwith, with a couple of our stouter boys. Younger ones, good hire-hacks. Ha! Tell him to guise himself as a printer looking for work – those creatures are always travelling. He can threaten his way up the spine of England, seeking whispers of a secretive Scot who lately travelled south. That Stuart whore, whatever her name is … Arbella, Arabella … she would gain if James fell, for all they say she's a crooked-minded woman-child.'

'If he's going north, Ford can–'

'Ford can attend on her on his way to Edinburgh or back. She will not say no to the chance of printing these pages, I think. If she has them. Yet if the papers were stolen in London, then we must find the man. Whether he is the thief or Gowrie hid the paper in lodgings here, we scour the city –'

'That, brother – I've dealt with that.'

'What?' His surprise was more at Gregory cutting him off than his brother's words.

'Well, you said you wished to be left in peace.' Gregory's chest rose in approximation of Ford's. 'So when Gowrie repeated that tale about the liveried man – he repeated it again and again – I sent out a hunt for him. One of our boys might have found him by now. And if he stole our property, they'll get it from him. By any means to hand, you said.'

7

I stared into the face of the man whom I had jetted past on my way home – the big one who was loitering at the head of a rough-looking crew. The others were not there.

'Seven-ten?'

I breathed out, unaware that I'd been holding my breath. Yet here was no thoughtless gong-scouring boy messenger. My heart thumped irregularly. 'Yes.'

'You're wanted at the master's house. On the morrow. After dinner.'

I nodded, holding the door so that Faith could not see him. Reason swelled. My message could not have reached Cecil yet, never mind have done so and allowed him to send out a party of messengers that reached Shoe Lane before I did. And why such a party? I swallowed, my grip on the door tightening. The stranger saved me from questioning. 'Master gives his fanks. And says not to worry no more 'bout–'

A scream.

I started, instinct driving me back from the door. The scream was cut off. Shuffling, punching sounds rumbled up Shoe Lane. Doors slammed shut.

'– rent money.' My visitor gave a gap-toothed grin, putting a hand to his cap. 'Tomorrow.' He shrugged. 'Midday, I reckon.'

He turned on his heel and walked away. I stood, irresolute, as I heard him bark commands out in the street. Laughter followed, some jeers, and then the pounding of feet making their way towards Fleet Street.

'Uaghh … uaghhhhh…'

'Is he gone?' Again, I started. Faith was at my elbow, her face wan. I thrust my arm out to hold her back from the door.

'Yes. Stay here.'

Sliding outside, I blinked. Sunlight had brightened the sky, though spots of rain still shot downwards. Unnatural, I thought. Looking towards the source of the moaning, I spotted a brown-coloured bundle. It was moving, but only barely.

'Christ,' I said, skipping over the sludge towards it. I leant down, moving a muddy-coloured arm from a face.

Frere.

My landlord had been beaten. Savagely, beyond reason. I judged his nose to be broken, possibly also his ribs and at least one leg. Blood soaked into the muck around him. He winced, crying out, trying again to hide his face. 'Mr Frere? It is me, Ned Savage.'

'Uaghh!' He tried to roll. Away from me, I realised. He was frightened of me.

'Let me get you home, sir.' Frere lived by the print shop near St Bride's, just off Fleet Street. A few minutes' walk away, even with a cripple. The word sent a shiver tingling up my spine. They had likely crippled him.

'No,' said Frere, thickly. 'Please, leave me. I'll not … never come by again. Sorry. Let me know … when you don't need … the house … yours … till then.'

I bit at my lip. 'Let me get you home.' My voice, in my own ears, sounded as though it came from somewhere far away.

'What happened?'

'Faith!' I turned. She was standing behind me, her hand over her mouth. 'Mr Frere here has had an accident.'

'Will … will I get the constable, watchmen?'

'No!' The word erupted from my lips and Frere's in unison. 'Just go back inside, mouse. Forget you saw anything.' She looked from me to Frere and back. Something hard came into her face, something I didn't like. But she did as she was bid, disappearing into the house.

I helped the reluctant Frere home under a rainbow which arced across cold and mottled blue. No one accosted us. People, in fact, made way, looking the other way as we passed. At the house by St Bride's, a servant fetched Mrs Frere – a flinty woman whose face melted when she saw her husband. Confusion, running for water and bandages, calls for the barber surgeons. And for the constables, of course, which Frere refused. When Mrs Frere began to thank me for my tending to the man, shame demanded I make my excuses and leave. 'God bless you, sonny,' she said. 'It's a good thing, if you ask me, that even in these troubled times, no one wanting to help no one, that there are still some right kind young folks.' I took my hat off and accepted a kiss on what I felt to be a blazing cheek.

Above all, I tried to stifle the voice in my head. *You have a free house. You and Faith have a free house*. It paid to work for Mr Secretary Sir Robert Cecil.

When I returned home, I found Faith sitting at the desk. She was not at her books, but had her hands clasped in front of her. 'Is he well?'

'Oh,' I said, feigning a casual air I didn't feel, 'he will be. We're outside the city walls, after all. These things happen.'

'Who were they?'

My eyes rose, partly in response to the strength that edged her voice in comparison to the brittle cheer of mine. 'I don't know.'

'It's not my business, Ned, I know. But … I live here. And I thought we were friends.'

'We are!'

'Then … surely I have a right to know what it is you do. Were those men … were they with the theatres, the stage men? Something like that? I know they're a rough lot.'

'Faith,' I said, almost laughing. 'No. Nothing like that.'

'Then … what then? What is it you're in?' Her bright green eyes bored into me.

'I should call you fox, not mouse.'

'Ned.'

I sighed, crossing the room and kneeling before her. Lie upon lie paraded through my mind. Any one might do, I thought – to protect her. She did not blink, and I looked away. 'I am in the service of a man of state,' I said.

'Is that why you go away sometimes?'

'Sometimes.'

'Is it dangerous, your work?'

'No.' I chanced a glance at her again. 'It might be.'

'What's going on, Ned? Men half-killing Frere and you going away all the time.'

'You know the queen?' I licked my lips and lowered my voice. Confusion broke her solemnity and her brow wrinkled. 'She's dying.'

'Eh?'

'Queen Elizabeth is dying.'

'Don't jest, Ned. I'm only after the truth, if you'll share it.'

'That is the truth.' I stood up. Her reaction knit my own brow: she laughed. 'Not a laughing matter, I'd have thought.'

'You're at it.' She shook her head, the laughter subsiding. 'She can't die. She's the queen.'

'Everyone dies, Faith. She's … the queen is old. Very old. A good age.'

'But … but she's the queen of England.'

'Even queens of England. Death caught her mother and her sister – you think it won't catch her?'

'Queen Elizabeth is different.' She began knotting and unknotting her hands, shaking her head slowly and frowning. 'My parents told me. When they were … they said she was a specially blessed queen. Like Methuselah.' She announced each syllable like it deserved attention. 'In the Bible. Said he got to be near a thousand. And our queen is like that. Our Eliza, they called her. Specially blessed.'

'It's not Biblical times.' I crossed my arms, frowning a little myself. Her sudden cry cut down my growing frustration. Tears stood out in her eyes. 'What is it?'

'I'm sad. If you're not lying.' Still a hint of accusation. 'Aren't *you*?'

I wasn't, particularly. I had never spoken with the queen, nor yet been given anything by her famous white hands. I shrugged. 'My parents, they loved her,' Faith continued. 'Said she was a new Deborah, saving our souls. Loved her like she loves her people.' I fought the urge to roll my eyes, instead offering her a handkerchief. I had seen plays enough to know that sovereigns loved themselves and their crowns, not their people. That was just ornamented rhetoric and we, the people, were the enraptured audience. The old lady had a certain style, I would admit, in her magical clothes and her fiery wig, and the tales of her boxing her younger maids for their insolence delighted me – but I could not say I loved her. 'And Queen Elizabeth … she's a woman not scared of nothing. Not scared of going out, not scared of no men.'

I nodded the truth of this, at least. Faith blew her sniffles into my handkerchief. 'You might keep that,' I said. 'But you know, don't you, that with this terrible business, this news, there is work that keeps men occupied? It will all be over soon enough. And we needn't worry about rent money again.' I bit my lips and closed my eyes. 'Forget that.'

'What?' When I didn't reply, she wiped her eyes. 'This person you work for, Ned – he sent those men out there?'

'I said forget it, Faith. By God, you're like a wife, sometimes. Come, let us not sit upon the ground nor tell sad stories about the death of kings.' I moved towards the door of my bedchamber, expecting a barrage of questions. None came. To avoid deflating entirely, I said, 'my hope is to keep us both safe. From bad men. Better to be on their side than set our faces against them.' She was staring at me as though I were suddenly deformed. 'I mean only to keep you safe. And myself. There is no danger.'

***

Slamming the door of my bedchamber, I left Faith in the outer room with the door of our house barred. She had set the stool against it too. We would do without supper, I supposed – or I would. Well done, Ned, I thought: if the girl was reclusive before, frightened of the dangers of the street, she will be doubly so now. Terrified too of the danger that lurked under the same roof as her, inviting rough men's company.

I began picking up my things. My mirror, but I could not stand to look upon myself. My little glazed jug, empty. Nothing gave me pleasure, no matter how pretty or how hard it had been to come by.

Instead, absurdly, I felt angry tears sting. My mind, despite my will, kept returning to the circumstances by which I had met and adopted my troublesome little conscience of a friend. Curious, when I thought on it, how intertwined it was with the beginning of my association with Cecil. I picked up the mirror again and forced myself to look.

Everyone says I look like a dead man.

The past rushed upon me in a distortion of memory and colour.

I tensed for the scream, for the slap. It didn't come. It was April of 1601 and I stood in a crowd at St Paul's Cross. The great yard, paved with stones from the old abbey buildings, was always packed, as people met in the shadow of the crumbling brown cathedral with its blunted, spire-less roof. They made for easy pickings, then as now. The florid woman with the painted face had not noticed the ring I had slipped from her finger as she let me clutch her hands. 'Bless you, my lady,' I said. A blush crept into her cheeks.

'Are you truly kin to the late earl?' she asked. I looked skyward, imitating heartache. My silence, I hoped, would answer her question. 'Cor, but you don't half look like he did in his youth. Saw him riding out, I did, many a time before the troubles.' I tightened my grip on her hands again, squeezing.

'You are a good woman to hazard letting a stranger kiss you.' This time I smirked.

'If my husband should find out…' A feather, sticking stupidly up from the brim of her black hat – a persistent fashion I rather like, city wives wearing mannish brimmed hats – fluttered as she giggled.

'Then I hope he will treasure you all the more as a prize worth having.'

'Oh, go on.' Her chins wobbled with delight and she thrust forward her bosom, her kirtle straining. I pressed her hands down towards her waist before letting go. I was eager myself to be gone. Pulling a handkerchief from my courtly guise, I tucked it into her generous bosom. 'Oh, I say – I–'

The crowd in the cross fell silent.

I tensed.

A whole rainbow of colourfully dressed men was cutting a path through the jumble of merchants, booksellers, buyers, foreigners, goodwives, and pickpockets. Accompanying them was a small detachment of soldiers. City alderman, I realised, with the mayor, draped in scarlet, and the sheriff. The soldiers fanned out around the covered pulpit whilst the mayor and sheriff mounted the steps.

'Good Christian people,' began the mayor. 'Hearken unto the queen's presence.'

The silence deepened. Only the pickpockets, I saw, were slinking through the people, heads down. I ought, I thought, to be following them. The sheriff raised his hands, before taking a paper from the mayor. He cleared his throat, before bellowing, 'hear the words of our gracious sovereign lady, the most high and mighty princess, Elizabeth, queen of England, Ireland, and France, defender of the faith. These her words:

Whereas divers traitorous and slanderous libels have of late been dispersed in divers parts of our city of London and places near thereunto adjoining by some lewd and ungodly persons, tending to the slander of our royal person and state, and stirring up of rebellion and sedition within this our realm, and to the end such wicked persons may be discovered and known.

My blood froze in my veins. At my elbow, my mark – the richly dressed woman with the painted face – whispered, 'what's the cause of it?' I ignored her. The sheriff continued.

These shall be to signify to all manner of person and persons that whosoever shall in any sort either openly or secretly discover and make known to our Privy Council, or to the Lord Mayor of our said city, the name of any of the authors, writers, or dispersers of any of the said libels, whereby the offenders therein may be known and taken, shall presently have and receive for their pains therein the sum of £100 of current money paid and delivered unto him by the Lord Mayor of our said city.

The said mayor stepped forward again, holding up a purse.

Under the breast of my doublet, papers crinkled. The soldiers began to move out, pushing their way into the crowd, grabbing at people's sleeves.

Searching.

All at once a hundred voices rose in agitation, fear, anger, confusion.

I had on my person several tracts relating to the late earl of Essex. They could fetch a good price, in those days – he had only been dead since the February and people were hungry for scandalous written material relating to his rising, his fall, his strange relationship with the queen. I had made quite a habit of collecting the libels that were cast about the streets, before the constables could retrieve them, and had several interested parties. Above that, I had a stolen ring and several other hot purses concealed on my person.

Without a word to my female companion, I turned on my heel. She called after me, and I quickened my pace, my head lowered as I moved to left and right through the people. Her cry became a scream.

'Thief! Stop! I'm robbed! Thievery!'

I ran.

People clutched at my sleeves, at my back – and why not? I was now worth £100. From the eruption of voices, I could tell that the soldiers had gained my lady's attention too. I was marked.

From St Paul's, I escaped into Paternoster Row, where the booksellers kept their shops and stalls. I paused for a second, looking up and down. People in every direction. I might lose myself amongst them. Better yet, I might disappear into one of the myriad alleys which snaked off the main streets. Taking off towards Cheapside, I turned to see a soldier stumble into the Row and, as I had done, look up and down. He spotted me. Pointed. Shouted something.

Again, I fled, my shoes clattering on the cobbles. I ducked left around a tight bend, and into the first of a warren of little streets. My clothes, I thought – I must be rid of them, with the papers celebrating Essex and calling the queen a tyrant too.

As I flew, I realised that in losing my pursuers I was getting lost myself and had no sense of when I was turning left nor right. I leapt over something in the gutter – a man, I thought, and stopped, whirling.

'You,' I cried, falling to my knees. 'How would you like a good doublet, man?' Already I was removing the thing.

'Eh?' It was an old fellow, I realised, only partly aware of himself. Drunk.

'Here. Keep out the chill.' I slid out of my doublet. The papers folded inside fell to the ground at the drunkard's side. 'Get that mouldy coat off.' Without waiting for a response, I roughly jerked him forward and tore his coat from him.

'Wha'? Wha'?'

'Easy now.' I draped my doublet around his shoulders, not bothering to fasten it on. 'Go back to sleep.' I took off his cap and replaced it with my feathered hat, pulling the thing down over my eyes. I strode away down the alley, letting my shoes soak into the dampness and mud, tightening the foul coat over my chest. Only then did I realise I still had the woman's stolen ring clutched in my other hand. Over my finger it went, and into my breeches went my hands as I tugged out the padding and cast it into the gutter. A regular jack I was then.

The searchers might, I realised, take the old man up for a libeller if they found him. More likely still, he might be reported by someone hoping to claim the reward. That was not my concern. Even the stupidest constable would realise what had happened and likely the old fellow would get away with a charge of drunkenness, and that deserved. Or he might be hanged as an example.

I turned.

Returning to my insensible saviour, and cursing myself for a fool, I picked up the papers and stuffed them under my new coat. I could throw them in the river. The important thing was that I was disguised.

Thus attired, I modified my run into a careful slouch – the carriage of a ne'er-do-well looking for work. I made my way back towards Cheapside, crossing it and turning right. In the unlikely event that I was still being followed, I hoped to make my way back to Shoe Lane by a circuitous route, skirting St Paul's along the south side towards Ludgate and the Fleet Bridge. I was making good progress, my heart slowing and regret building for the loss of my best doublet when I heard the screams. They came from a lane just off Ludgate.

Ignore it. Go home. Hide.

I had taken a few steps past the lane when something compelled me to stop. I might now think it fortune, but then it was a needling feeling of curiosity. I knew that, were I to continue on my way, I should change and return anyway, urged by a desire to know what had happened.

I had only taken a few steps into the darkness of the lane when I saw the pair, and I took in the scene at once. A girl was on the ground, screeching still, whilst a fat, red-faced man was striking at her. His breeches, I noticed with disgust, were unloosed. 'You!' I shouted. 'Get away from my sister!'

'Fuck off,' he shouted, turning. His leer twisted into anger, his face a side of boiled meat.

'I said leave off my sister, you fat fuck.' I reached to my waist and pulled free a small poniard, the libellous papers sliding to the ground. It was more ornament than use, but I trusted it to make my point. The man stood back, fiddling at his breeches.

'Sister my arse. You think to cozen me with that old game, eh? Don't think I'll pay *you* for being trapped so. She's a whore, living on the streets.'

I stepped towards him and he began backing away. The girl's cries died to sniffling moans. His back thumped against the wall. 'I'll go for a constable,' he said. His hands began to ball. Before he could strike, I thrust my forehead onto the bridge of his nose. Silence. Then he screamed. Before it could grow too loud, I stuck him with my fist. The back of his head hit the wall and he went down.

I bent and retrieved the brown-flecked papers, tucking most under his coat and folding one between his fingers.

Turning, I held out my hand to the girl. She didn't take it. 'You're safe enough with me. What's your name?' She turned away and began crawling towards Ludgate. 'I skipped ahead of her, smiling. 'I said you're safe, girl. Do you understand me? What's your name?'

'Faith Is My Salvation.'

'Quote no verses at me, child. I'm a friend, not a priest.' I held out my hand again and this time she grasped it and got to her feet.

'That's my name.'

'Christ.' I put her at about fourteen or fifteen. Painfully thin, red-haired. 'Your parents are cruel masters.'

'They're dead,' she said, fire kindling in her eyes.

I held up my hands. 'And you out on the streets?' She began moving away. 'Let me give you a meal. I promise, you're quite safe. My name is Ned. Ned Savage.' And I supposed it was by then. 'And I'm in need of an honest friend and servant.'

We stood awhile, as I used gentle speech to persuade her to come. Why? I might say that I wished to stop a poor wretch being forced into whoredom just to escape Death. I had, after all, just decided to give one over to his bony clutches and might pay for that by saving another. Yet the truth was that I thought she might have her uses. And so began my friendship with Faith, as I led her out onto Ludgate and took her home – pausing only to inform some men passing by that her tormenter was lying in the alley and might have wicked papers against the queen about him. Evidently, they had heard about the proclamation, for they ran off to find authorities and, I trusted, the man would find himself on the end of a rope, protesting that the libels had been placed upon him by a cozener.

You might imagine how proud I was feeling about my trickery. For the price of a coat, I had gained a ring, a serving girl, and some pouches of coin. No common thief was I. I deposited Faith at Shoe Lane, changed, and went off to buy us both some food. When I returned, I found her sitting at my table, and made to engage her in conversation, to learn something about her and make formal my proposal of service. Shyly, she pointed to the door of my inner chamber. 'Gentleman to see you … Ned.'

I dropped the pies, my throat constricting as they bounced at my feet.

As she scrabbled to pick up our feast, I opened the door and went in. There stood a young man I did not know. He was holding a jewelled bracelet I had stolen long before, turning it over in his hands. I said nothing. 'Mr Savage?' I gave a slight nod. 'Do not fear. My master has been watching you for some time. You have skill. It was a fine escape you made today. And having that brute discovered with those papers…' He tutted. 'A pretty piece of trickery. Oh, do not fret. My master knows all that passes in London. He'll hang, you know.' My eyes darted to the bracelet and he set it down. 'My master would engage you in more valuable service, Savage. He will like you. You will like him.' He waved a hand around the room. 'I think it will be profitable.'

I had no choice, of course. There were enough stolen goods – mixed in amongst many honestly come by, I should add – to hang me several times over. I agreed, and the man disappeared. I never saw him again, though many similar have made my acquaintance since.

And so my work for Sir Robert Cecil began on the same day that I adopted Faith. It was strange how things worked out. Perhaps there was a designer behind it all. Which meant that there was a reason for why I was the way I was – that that too came from God.

I stood and began digging through my things for that old bracelet, wanting to hold it, to feel the past. Finding it, I slid it over my wrist and jangled it about. It had its own memories attached, which I did not choose to unlock. Taking it off, I reburied it alongside the pin cushion Faith had bought me as a little token of the friendship she bore me – of the love that I was risking. Some men say that the mind is a kingdom, through which we can stroll, looking upon palaces of memory. I say it is a prison, in which we are locked and tormented by cruel and taunting gaolers. And I know my prisons.

I had told Faith that I meant to keep her safe as well as myself, as I had promised her the day we met. I had said there was no danger.

I did not know what awaited me the following day.

8

I had only a light dinner with a silent and sullen Faith, who clattered about, casting water over the rush matting and wielding her mop like a pike to do the walls. Occasionally she threw a handful of herbs over the little pot of coals kept over the fire, and even that she managed to make an act of sizzling aggression. When the bells called noon, I gratefully made my way to the Whitefriars Stairs, which descended to the great inland sea of the Thames.

My mind was elsewhere: running ahead of me, in fact. As I scuffed down the steps, crushing the weeds that sprang from between the stones, it was mapping the route from the Strand stairs up towards Cecil's waterfront house. I should not debark at his own little port, I thought, so as not to attract attention, but at the main steps, and thereafter go along the street and in by another entrance. Thoughts of secrecy occupied me. So it was that I did not at first hear the man call to me, nor what he said. I was waving to the wherryman, signalling the direction upriver I meant to travel.

'Oi! That's my boat.'

The words cut through and I turned, my mouth twisting in irritation. 'What do you–'

I got no further. The punch came hard and low. Direct to my gut. I folded at the waist, eyes bulging. The air seemed to be pressed from me.

A heavy young man, dirty, rough. I blinked stupidly at the red cross patch stuck to the front of his coat.

Heavy, stupid, like a bull.

My attacker pulled his meaty hand back, preparing it for a heavier blow.

Go low or go high.

I went high, pulling myself up, aiming for his face, his eyes. My fingers jabbed at them. There was no strength behind my strike – surprise and the gut-punch had weakened me. But he was weak too, I thought – weak because he thought he had won already.

He put his hand to his face, protecting himself from another blow. I was right: untrained, clumsy. Strong, but stupid. I punched low, hitting at his groin. He was confused then, spinning. But quickly recovered.

I had done no damage; I had sparked anger. I raised my fist as though to hit out again, and he raised his own, barrelling towards me. I hopped to the side. His momentum carried him forward and I stuck out my leg. He tripped, stumbled, didn't fall. Turned and roared.

The steps, I thought wildly: they're wet, use them, stop him. He was coming at me again. Thinking, or trying to – working out whether I would run or fight. I ran, darting up the steps two at a time. Loose stones crumbled downwards in a dusty cascade. He followed, and I leapt off, down the moss-veined side, and onto the riverbank below.

The wherrymen had spotted us and began shouting, calling out: to each of us, cheers and encouragement; to each other, bets.

'You're dead,' bellowed the bull. He was looking down on me. His boots thundered on the steps. I drew level, reached out, grabbed his ankle and pulled. He tumbled headfirst down the remaining slimy stairs. I didn't wait to see if he would get up; I leapt towards the river, towards the wherry that had drawn level.

'Get on,' snapped the boatman. He was a friend – a man who had ferried me up and down many times, at any rate. His craft wobbled and bobbed as I jumped aboard. Making a poor landing, I fell and smacked my face on a wooden strut. I felt nothing, rolling over immediately to see how close by was the red cross man. In the process of getting up, I saw: bent at one knee like a genuflecting knight. I shouted a stream of swear words, born more of shock than anger. Gripping the oar alongside my saviour, I wrenched it from his hands, and, on shaky legs, I whirled the thing from side to side, pushing the craft away and into the current even as I wielded it as a potential weapon. It was too long, too unwieldy to do any damage, but it made my point – and he did not try and grab at it.

'Gi' me that, Savage,' snapped the wherryman. I let go, collapsing to the floor as we launched.

I grinned, idiotically. The smile froze on my face as I saw, at the top of the water steps, a number of other men appear. No travellers, these, but compatriots of the villain, now rushing to help him.

How many of them were there? I wondered.

***

A strange kind of lightness had overcome me as I pounded along the Strand. It was the same sense of exhilaration that I had after stealing something and getting clean away. Survival. I knew from experience that it would not last. As the grand mansions stood in judgment, I considered what I now knew. These men of the red cross, these plotters, must know I worked for Cecil – they might have a spy amongst his many agents, and they had now marked me as a person worth being rid of. Had I not fought back, had I let the young bull overcome me, I knew I would have ended up beaten senseless and tossed in the river to drown. The wherrymen would not have saved me, not even those who knew me. Nor would they have reported anything they saw. Too much trouble.

On the heels of the thought came another: how dare they try and hurt me? Dirty, filthy scum. It must be that they had the document relating to the king of Scots and were now looking to silence those who knew of them.

To my surprise, Cecil himself was standing outside his mansion, which stood not far from Raleigh's more imposing Durham House. Like a little boy in his father's clothes, he was muffled, staring up at the red and white bricks, which were surmounted by onion-like domes, sharp against the dirty fleece sky. Two female servants were at work scrubbing them. I followed their progress. On the wall was written 'TOAD' in white chalk, and it was this they were attacking. Cecil's face, I saw as I drew closer, had a look of deep sadness. A crowd was standing well back, the folk whispering amongst themselves.

I walked along the side of the house. I had dressed not in livery or my counterfeit court attire, but as a labourer. That, I realised, not having thought of it before, meant that the red cross plotters must have been hunting me. How else might they know me now not by my clothing but my countenance? Worse, they might know where I lived.

I moved alongside the muffled Cecil, putting my hand to my cap. He turned to me. Stiffened slightly. Jerked his head to the side of the house and then, without a word, he walked through the main door.

Rather than do as he silently bid immediately, I tarried about the Strand awhile, asking folk if their homes needed work. It was a broad street, fringed on either side by rival palaces competing for glory. Towers, cupolas and gilded weathervanes fought for the attention of the well-heeled strollers and scurrying servants below. Thankfully, my offers received only disgusted looks and demurrals. When I judged that I had been myself judged worthless, I wound my way around the mansion, past a walled bowling green, and found a small service doorway. I was passed from servant to servant and room to room, each time saying only to carry '710' upwards. With each room I passed the place grew more opulent, clean but bare surfaces giving way to rooms covered floor to ceiling in wooden panelling and tapestries and bearing cupboards of plate and tables with dangling fringed cloths.

Eventually, I was prodded into a small gaming room containing only two cushioned curule chairs and a chess table, a scatter of block-printed cards incongruously littering it. Cecil was sitting in one of them, regarding the nails on his smooth white hand.

'I haven't much time today. Ireland, Spain … Scotland.' He swallowed, before narrowing his eyes. 'What happened to your face, Ned?'

I put my hand up and winced, my cheek stinging at the touch. 'Attacked, sir. By a man with a red cross on his breast. He had friends.'

'Where?' I told him. 'Do they know of your connection to me?'

'I can't say.' I thought. 'But I've been careful. And to attack at Whitefriars … they knew who I was and where. Not where I was going.' I hoped that was true.

'As long as you are unhurt. A crowd of them. But why you?'

'They must know I met the Scot.'

He put his fingers to his chin and began pulling at his beard. 'Yes. It must be so. And so they have the document. Are silencing those they think might know of them, or trying to, or …' He gave himself a little shake. 'My mind moves too quickly.' A little tap on the side of his chair. 'Tell me of Raleigh. You have seen him?'

I smiled, in spite of myself. My cheek nipped again. 'You are a great man, Sir Robert. Ireland and Spain and Scotland. Me, if I had a surfeit of cares, I'd buzz from one to the other like a bee to flowers. And gain nothing. It's a wise man can sort these cares with ease and attend to each according to its value.'

Cecil returned a tight little smile of his own. 'I see you can still gloss and glaver. The troubles are not Ireland, Scotland or Spain, but England. This city, and what is being said and done and hidden in it. Raleigh.' He tapped his chair again.

I told him everything that had passed in Durham House. He interrupted only once, to issue a spluttering, 'parliament? A den of ravening wolves! And harder to herd, even when garbed in furs as leader of the House.'

When I had finished, he lapsed into what I took to be simmering contemplation. 'He said he loves the Spanish?' he asked at length.

'Yes, sir.'

'That was poorly done of him.'

'But I think he knows nothing of these red crosses, or at least isn't meddling with them. Save his knowledge that a man of parliament leads them. I've tried to discover who myself, sir, but no luck yet. I thought you might know.'

'There are hundreds of men in parliament. I nominated over thirty of them and swore the whole pack in myself. The house was in a great stir.' He looked up at the carved ceiling and, I supposed, into the past. 'Buckhurst was trouble. Hoby too.' Tap, tap, tap. 'I shall have a list made of all who attended who might now be in London.'

'I regret,' I said, 'that I haven't been able to find the Scotsman.'

'I have. He lodged at the sign of the Tabard. Called himself Henderson there too. He left some days ago and has not returned. I have a man in the place. It seems he took his papers with him. There is nothing hidden in the inn that my man could find.'

'Someone shielding him.'

'No one,' said Cecil, his voice cold, 'can be shielded in this city for long. Not from me. I intend that London shall be pulled down brick by brick and reassembled if needs must.' I looked at him. For the first time, I thought I glimpsed real nervousness manifested as a show of strength. He meant what he said.

'And these bastards on the street,' I said, swept up, 'pardon me, these red cross plotters. You can have them taken up, arrested, thrown in gaol. They advertise, sir, advertise their sedition.' I patted my breast.

Cecil looked at me and seemed to settle in his seat, his own passion cooling. He closed his eyes. 'No. Even the search must be done privily. By gentle means. If they think they are discovered, that we know of what has been brought from Scotland, their masters will be alerted. The document will disappear with the big fish whilst the little fish writhe in the net. And … and too great a tumult will reach the queen. Sick she might be. Careless of England she is not.'

'How fares the queen?' I tried to speak as airily as I could.

'Her Majesty eats less than usual. Closets herself in her bedchamber each day reading. Talking much that I fear is nonsense. She has no interest even in entertainments and cries hard words on every man who comes near her presence. Ned, I think there is little time left. She might linger weeks, a month yet, perhaps, if she is persuaded to eat. I must have that Scotsman and his damned papers. If they are in these wretched men's hands there will be turmoil after … when … well, you might imagine. Disorders and riots, every man proclaiming his favourite creature king or queen.' His tap of the chair became a punch, delivered with his little white fist. 'If I knew what was in these damned papers! If I knew what fire I am expected to fight!

Christ Jesus, otherwise it will burn down both the king and m- and his friends.'

'What can I do, sir? Search London …' Doubt crept into my voice.

'No. If they know you, if they suspect you, you are no use to me here. I mean, you are in danger too, of course.' I fell silent. Cecil gripped the sides of his chair and stood. I jumped up. 'I have other business for you. Unless the playmakers have magic pens, I think our friend the Revels Master will have no need of you yet awhile.'

'As you wish, sir.'

'Business out of London. Several things. I would have you go to Scotland. As quickly as you can and return as quickly. King James must be assured that I will get these papers – that everything in this city is in hand.'

'I speak no Scots, sir.'

'Hm,' smiled Cecil. 'King James holds that there is no Scots language, nor no English either. Only British. You will please him.' His eyes lingered on my face and I looked at the carpet. 'I think you will please him greatly, Ned.'

The urge, absurdly, to cover myself washed over me. I felt like Cecil was looking at me as though I were naked. 'I have a tale prepared to smooth your passage north. You will announce that you serve her Majesty's Revels Office. That you carry an offer to the king of another visit by one of the London companies.' I smiled. It had been done before, though I had never had any part in it; I recalled the year this time – it had been in 1599 that a company of actors and, I presumed, spies, had been dispatched from London to Edinburgh to play before the king. 'It will appear innocent enough. Cast about, by subtle means, you understand, of rumours in that city of the matter contained in this damned document.' A maggoty little vein pulsed in his temple. 'I hear only wild bruits of his mother's doings and his … tastes. Trash. Nothing in my father's papers casts any light.' A little sniff. 'Some tedious and obscure legal ruling, perhaps. Something that must be countered. I also,' he said, 'wish to know how quickly the journey between London and Scotland can be made. That there are good posts along the way speeding the route.' His finger jabbed the air. 'But if you find anything in Edinburgh that might help crush and bury this madness swiftly, return by the fastest ship out of Leith.'

He pulled at his beard again, holding it between his first and middle fingers. 'Oh, yes. And the Lady Arbella writes me. No end of letters. I would have you deliver a message on the way. Out of your own mouth, nothing written.'

'You wish me to investigate her, sir?'

'No, no, no. I wish you to quieten her.' My mouth fell open. 'Not in that manner, you devil. She writes demanding a special envoy visit her, Sir Henry Brounker. A man,' he said, with a meaningful look, 'of sufficient quality to investigate a royal lady. That odd bird sets greater store by such trifles than her kingly cousin, who is fed well enough on a pretty face and reassuring words. Tell her I will dispatch him forthwith. That he will follow you. You might have a care about her surroundings, her condition, but no more. I trust your eyes, Ned. I think the woman quite mad. I doubt that these red cross men will want her anywhere near the throne any more than they want King James.'

'Whom do they want, sir, do you think?'

'That I cannot say. All I can is that they will have nothing, they will subvert nothing. This city will be searched by my men. Hard men. The time for charm has passed.' I shivered, thinking of Frere, and considered mentioning it. Cecil seemed to read my mind. 'Your landlord was mishandled?' I shrugged. 'I regret that fellows on the street can be overbold at times.'

'Where does this Lady Arbella live?'

'Derbyshire. She is at present at her grandmother's house of Hardwick there, though the old woman begs permission to move her. It will be easy enough to stop on the road north, and … what is it?'

I stood rooted to the spot.

Derbyshire.

'I … sir, I think, I regret I can't go.' His eyebrows rose in something like amusement. Their hard, unblinking sheen told me that he wasn't making a request. 'I … I … my friend, my servant – Faith her name is. She won't be safe.'

'Your girl will be safer without you here than with you, I think, if it is you these men seek.'

'And my work at the Revels Office … I'll be fined if I miss church.' With effort, I stilled my rambling tongue. Already it had stirred suspicion. That might easily lead to curiosity, and I had no desire for Sir Robert Cecil to know more about Edward Savage than he knew already. 'A weak stomach, sir.' I forced a smile. 'Fear for a moment. Of course I will go. On the morrow, at daybreak.'

I bowed my way from Cecil's presence and left by the trade door, after being handed another bulging purse. For once, it scarcely interested me. What, I wondered, were the odds that I would run into someone to trouble me in that shire?

I knew the answer. Small indeed. It was my own inability to prevent myself seeking out trouble that worried me.

***

It was only after I left Cecil and began to gather my wits that I realised I had promised to ask him if Kit Lockhart might join his service. Further, I had said I would meet with Lockhart. I decided to keep our appointment and to lie about Cecil's opinion.

I waited for him outside the Globe, feeling conspicuous, my head bowed low. My last experience south of the river was yet fresh upon me. I had remained outside as the daily crowds, eager and chattering, wound their way in: apprentices and merchants, housewives and milkmaids, prostitutes in their striped petticoats and pedlars with packs and bells. Even a few Inns of Court students strolled by me, ribbing one another and generally making nuisances of themselves, though Lockhart was not amongst their company. A poor crowd, I thought – no ripple of bright colours or tinkle of horses' harnesses signalled the arrival of nobility deigning to pay for the playhouse's seats. 'Groundlings', Mr Shakespeare had called the penny-payers, after the little fish. It was an insult, meant in good sort, that the playwright was desperately trying to make catch on as a popular term. It wasn't working. I still called them pennyworths and was myself often enough in amongst them.

The flag was up to announce the performance, but the placards nailed around the curving plastered walls of the building were sagging and worn. It was an old play. By the time Lockhart arrived, I had my back against the wall of the theatre and was quite alone, one hand tucked into my coat for warmth. Dimly, I could hear the muffled speeches of the actors, punctuated occasionally with louder, raucous laughter from a thousand throats.

My friend had, I noticed immediately, undergone a change. For one, he was entirely sober. For another, he was freshly dressed. 'You are here, Savage! What happened to your face? Why are you dressed like that – is it a disguise, part of the service?'

'Ho, there,' I said, putting up my palms and launching myself off the Globe. 'I came not to keep our meeting but … um … to say farewell. I am being sent on a journey.'

'Oh? Will it end in lovers meeting?'

'It will end back here. In London.'

All humour left Lockhart's voice. 'Is it for himself? For the service?'

I inclined my head, frowning. He did not need to ask the question. His eyes did that. I sighed, trying to frame an answer as I looked at him, dressed and clean and thrumming with life. Even his unruly mop of blonde curls was brushed back and dressed. Behind me, a chorus of hissing boos rose from the open roof of the theatre. 'You're in,' I said.

Lockhart whooped, punching the air.

'If,' I added, 'you can get yourself spurred, booted, and ready to go to Edinburgh on the morrow.'

'Edin … Scotland?'

'I know of no other. It is no great worry if you can't.' My words began tumbling. 'If your studies here, or rules, or whatever might keep you. I can go alone.'

'No, no! Scotland. Is my name not born of Scotland?' He leapt forward, thrusting an invisible sword. 'Lockhart of … somewhere in Scotland. My ancestors are said to have been Scotch nobles, who turned traitor and joined the ranks of the evil English. It will be a homecoming of blood, what? I just – give me time to buy things for the road.'

'You're really for this, Kit?'

'For it? I have not been for anything else in longer than I can remember. When do I meet our master?'

'You don't.' He frowned. Opened his mouth to speak. I held up a finger. 'Not yet. That's not how this business works. You … you go to him when called. Speak through others.' I took his arm and began leading him away over the flattened, dead grass that surrounded the Globe.

'Right. Yes. I understand.'

'And …' I bit at my lip. I already regretted my decision. It is a failing of mine that I cannot refuse anyone anything, especially friends. 'This is – well, it is not like you see in the plays. This thing, this whole matter, it is bigger than us.' I craned my neck to gaze up at the stupid, excited look on his face. 'Well, at any rate, it's bigger than me. It's not all creeping about emperor's palaces and standing in corners talking of secret plans.' Pride rose up, fighting reason. 'Though we might see a king.'

Lockhart's eyes widened. 'Christ, Savage. I am for this, by God's own truth. Hang my creditors, they won't see me about this damned city for dust. You wait till you see what I can buy that will help us look every inch the spies.'

My heart sank.

9

Candlelight shone on the first page of the papers taken from the Scot who called himself Henderson and Gowrie. The reader's lips moved silently along the words, translating them into English:

In great fear and trembling of the Lord I subscribe my hand to this the confession of my manifold wicked and detestable sins and errors &c not in the like manner of the papists but for the better cleansing of my soul. By recounting of the state of the realm at this time and the great and terrible calamities that have been the cause of my doings, I pray they might be better known and understood and forgiven &c. I do not mean this document to be read in the manner of a CHRONICLE history but to preserve the light of TRUTH in all that has passed and for better avoidance of the evil that might fall if this King James lives longer to rule over men. For it will be by my own grievous fault that the grace of God will be denied this island of Britain and misrule be unchained. From the cruel and unnatural subversion of nature in the man all disorders will flow, as a tree will bend and sicken with the engrafting of a diseased branch.

In this our time and for many years past, the reign of that unfortunate princess Marie, sometimes our queen, whom some call a murderess and a tyrant and others a gracious sovereign lady, has brought upon our heads mighty broils fit to shake any nation. Of her true nature I shall say nothing, for the love my wife bore her. We have done our best and also with our own person to guide the realm into the light of understanding. And if we have committed errors, we humbly crave pardon and the reason of pure intentions.

The nature of the present wickedness which might infect the realm of England in time to come was begun in glory. To return to the celebrated birth of that most high and mighty prince, James, of the ancient race of Stewarts. He was born in June in the year 1566 in the fortress castle of Edinburgh attended by goodwife Margaret Asteane his midwife. The baby was born with a caul or some small skin over his face which was read as a sign of good fortune and long life and he was in nowise a sickly child but rather the best in health and bonny. We did not know which he might grow up to be, yet the stars proclaimed he would be no tyrant.

The infant prince was well beloved of his mother and his people and he grew fat and lusty. But in the course of events, the monstrous storms that swept over this our realm would utterly alter and subvert the nature of this smiling and well-formed little man and of this I will say more.

10

The executioner dug into the man's guts. Bartlet felt Gregory waver at his side. He shared his brother's disgust. It was not the sight of the bowels drawn out in a red string that sickened him, but the twitching arms and that initial digging in – big hands thrust in between sharp shards of broken rib bone. The bowels were held up, droplets of blood falling to the boards. The crowd cheered.

Bartlet wondered if the priest, who had called himself Anderson but was really a Richardson, would be the last papist to die the death under Queen Elizabeth. He did not as a rule attend such entertainments; they were the stuff of common delight. Far more pleasant, when in London and in full view, to visit the theatre or the bear baiting, where naked flesh was hidden by costumes and fur.

'A ghastly way to go.'

'A fitting end,' mumbled Bartlet, turning to his brother, who was looking somewhat jaundiced. 'And you need not complain about the gore. It was you who drew us to this thing.' He grinned. 'Drew. Marvellous. Drawn to a quartering, eh?' No response. He pouted. 'What became of that wretched Scot's corpse?'

If anything, Gregory's colouring deepened. 'Ford took him to one of our older fellows. He … said he was trained as a butcher in his youth. That he could … disarticulate him and feed the parts to the Thames and the pigs.'

'Did he now?'

'Well, he didn't say "disarticulate". Split up right good and proper, he said, and feed the bowels to the beasts and the trash to the river.'

Bartlet felt his own colour drain and gave himself a shake. 'He was dead by his own hand anyway. A fitting end for such a cowardly deed. Besides,' he added, gesturing to the heaving mass of bloodthirsty people, 'it was better done than this. And Gowrie had no mean folks making merry at seeing it done. It … it was a necessary act.'

'Necessary. Yes, see the crowd, Bart.'

He did, scanning the cheap caps and dull beiges. There were plenty of women, too, being passed around and groped, as many as there were vendors selling nuts and ale. 'Rich pickings.' They had come all the way to Tyburn for two reasons: the great crowd allowed people to mingle and therefore to be recruited; and in such a crowd he might speak to his rabble of malcontents freely and easily, in the guise of one of many come to see and discuss the show. 'Ho, here's one of our creatures now.' He grinned, clapping a beefy young red cross on the shoulder. 'Greetings, my boy.'

'Good morrow, sir – Bartlet.'

'What news?' He kept his voice low but maintained his smile.

'Bad, sir.' The lad gestured a little way off from the main crowd, who were punching the air as the executioner set about carving up the unfortunate Father Richardson, the saw glinting in the light. Thankfully the wetness of it biting into flesh and snagging on bone was muffled by the excited chattering and jeering. Some folk, Bartlet saw, were getting too close to the low scaffold, trying to collect blood. If there were government agents mixing amongst the spectators, their eyes would be on such pathetic idiots.

'Tell us.'

'We found the man what met with the Scot in the Mitre. Name of Edward Savage. A music man at the place saw him enter an' told us he spent time flappin' his gums with the Scotch cur. Took a bit of persuasion, but.' He regarded his balled fists.

'Savage?'

'Works for the man what makes the queen's entertainments. As a messenger, like, for that ol' gent. In the tavern a lot, the music-man said. Known, like.'

'Tilney? A messenger for that old duffer? Gregory, what do you make of it?'

Gregory shrugged. 'A fool who stumbled into something.' Then his eyes narrowed. 'Or he has some other master, perhaps.' Bartlet silenced him with a look. The sheep should not know or hear too much.

'We set upon him at the water stairs. Whitefriars. Got away but, he did, sir. He's … he was cunning, fast. A man of training, like, you might say. A gentleman, like, but not. We meant to try again, wait for 'is guard to be down, but … 'e run off.'

'Run off?'

'Near as we can tell, sir.' He scratched at an eyebrow that a scar had left partially denuded. 'Lef' London.'

'Flown,' Gregory mumbled.

'Where?'

The red cross lad removed his cap and began turning it. 'Dunno yet, sir.'

'Put that back on,' hissed Bartlet. He had dressed himself as a ground-crawler and did not want another to be seen deferring to him. Turning to his brother, he said, 'Flown north, I should not wonder. Well this proves it. This Savage has the document on him. Got it from the Scot and now plans to return it to that king and kingdom.' He looked again at his acolyte. 'The searches of London have turned up nothing?'

'No, sir. The Scot had dealings with no one else. Asked around lots, we have, like. Can we do anything else, sir?'

'Hmph? Oh.' His mind had moved elsewhere. 'Yes, yes. Go amongst these people. Ask them if they wish such creatures as that torn carcass to rule them. James of Scotland is soft on priests and his queen, I hear, is turned papist. Tell them that true Englishmen who love their country will have no stranger for their lord and master, will bend the knee to no filthy foreigner. No need to have them join us if they are suspicious. Enough that they listen and learn to hate the foreign yoke. Have a care. Use subtle means.' The ox blinked stupidly, evidently unsure what 'subtle' meant, but he crunched his way over the litter of oyster and nut shells, back towards the crowd. 'Dear God,' said Bartlet, watching him blunder his way amongst them. 'I never thought it possible that a man's *arms* could be bow-legged. Still, his simple honesty will appeal to them.' When people's blood was up about traitors to England, they would listen to any whispering voice that spoke against foreigners. 'You know, I believe we ought to give them some phrase that will appeal to them and to other dull ears. For England and St George, do you think?'

'Mm. Or the English crown in English hands.'

'Kings don't wear crowns on their hands, Gregory. We must press the word England, make it simple.'

'I see,' said his brother, with a wan smile, 'you believe our rhetoric now.'

'What, what? It's the principle of the thing.' Bartlet brushed the side of his face with the back of his hand. 'Why should we not have an Englishman for our king, and why should the Everards not be the ones to ensure it? I …' Bartlet noticed that his brother was frowning, nibbling on a finger. 'Oh, what is it? Mmph. Don't say it, Gregory – I know. No religion. Well, it can hardly be entirely avoided at such a scene as this. Come, let us return to the city in our poor weeds and have a play or a gamble.'

'I wasn't going to say that.'

'I hear the priest was a Welshman.' He gave a last look at the scaffold, its indulgent slaughter, and its braying audience. 'Better off dead, then. Can't trust a Welshman any more than a Scot or a wild Irish. And taught his false doctrine in France and Spain.'

'I wasn't going to say anything about your mentioning religion,' said Gregory, a little more emphatically.

'Oh? Then why the sheep's eyes?'

'I was thinking of Ford. He's gone north too. I sent him off just the other day, as you said, to follow Gowrie's footsteps and cast about for news of the lost papers. He might cross paths with this Savage.'

'Let us hope,' said Bartlet, 'that he does. If Ford finds any man on the road carrying papers relating to Scotland, I doubt such a fellow will have possession of them for long. Or of his life, either.'

11

You might laugh or think me a clay-brained moon man, but I can smell Derbyshire. If your eyes do roll, consider the smells of your own childhood, whether of city or house or mansion – and whether, when you enter into some new places, smells hit you that conjure the images of your youth. For me, the shire has its own style of manure, of hay, of grass, and mud, and farmstead. It was a welcome stop on the long journey northwards and seemed to me more welcoming than the inns at which we rested each night, every one smelling like the road and looking the same. Travel is a wearying and painful business, and after the first night I was thirsty for the highway of the Thames.

You are a city boy now, I thought.

They accept your ways in the city, even if they prefer not to look at them.

Our destination was Owlcotes. The people of the country had informed us that it was the present home of Lady Arbella Stuart, who stood to succeed to England's throne if King James were removed from the line of succession. Her carriage and luggage train had been quite a sight leaving for it from nearby Hardwick Hall only a few days before we arrived in Derbyshire. We reached it in the morning, having spent the night at Sutton-in-Ashfield. It was a fine, new house – not large, but neat and even, with tall mullioned windows. Wide and pretty but not deep. It reminded me of an ornamental box, of the type sometimes brought in from the eastern reaches of the world. If it could be shrunk down, I had thought as I'd drunk it in, I should have liked to put it in my pocket and take it away – a pretty little puzzle box for hiding tiny treasures.

On the road out of London I had given Kit Lockhart everything that has passed save Cecil's name, though I suspect he had guessed who his uncomprehending new master was. He had listened with care – more care than I imagined he ever gave to his lecturers at the Inner Temple – and we had worked out our plan of action as the land around us grew more untamed and dangerous. A sign, I should perhaps have realised. At the time, though, I had no notion of what was to come. On leaving the spires and sprawl of the great city, I noted only that the land became flat and featureless, with little wrought by the hand of man to excite the mind or eye. It was as though the metropolis had sucked in the surrounding life.

We had both of us heard of the owner and builder of the house we had ridden up to. The countess of Shrewsbury, known throughout England as Bess, was a living remnant of a bygone age. You would scarcely know it, however, to look upon her. The woman into whose chamber we were eventually given access, after thorough interrogations from her staff, was shrunken with the weight of her years. The squat little figure was swathed in black velvet, a white ruff circling her waggling throat, and a string of pearls dangling down to her waist. She did not rise to greet us but stared through squinting eyes. We each fell upon one knee.

'News out of London?' Even her voice was crinkled. 'Tell it me.'

I chanced a look at Lockhart before speaking. He gave a minute shrug. 'We are come to speak with the Lady Arbella.'

'My granddaughter is not well. She sees no one.'

'We are sorry to hear of it, my lady. Yet we are commanded by one greater than us to give advance warning of a reply to her late request to London.'

'Himself, eh?' Bess coughed after speaking, a knotted fist rising to her lips. 'I know of her letters south.' A little note of defensiveness crept in. 'We are allowed to be here. It's safe here, safer than Hardwick. I had leave to bring her here for her health. You are gentlemen?' Her careful gaze again swept us. At the last stop, I had adopted the courtly clothes I had worn to visit Raleigh, which I'd packed along with an array of other costumes in my saddle pack. Lockhart had fine clothes of his own, made ridiculous only by the expensive sable riding cloak with a silver hood he had brought from the city, insisting that it was just the thing for a fellow engaged in spiery.

'We are,' I said.

A satisfied little grunt. 'You were given no special instructions for me?'

'No, my lady.'

'I see. You will have seen that there is no trouble about this place. My granddaughter is protected well here.' It was true, I thought. Bess was evidently the final and sturdiest defence against those who would look at or speak with the mysterious Lady Arbella. 'Nor no trouble hereabouts neither.' Her accent was of the old school of nobility, still roughened by the dialect of her region. I heard my childhood in it.

'No, my lady,' I said again. There had, perhaps, been a larger number of men lodging in the villages and hamlets than I would have thought, but none seemed particularly dangerous. None were wearing red crosses either. And, I supposed, it might simply be that the county had grown busier since I had last set foot in it. If there were any trouble brewing, it was doing so quietly and was in any case the problem of the man Cecil was sending at the lady's request.

'Well,' she said, rising and straightening her cap. White hair still flecked with russet peeped out. 'I won't have it be said I'm not a lady of hospitality. Nor one who don't trust the queen and her government. Come.' Without turning to see if we did, she swept from the room like a rolling black marble, no sign of age in her movements.

We went through a series of galleries and chambers. At each, I noticed, Bess drew up a key from a chain heavy with them that hung at her belt, unlocking and then relocking the doors as we went. If there were a fire, I thought, the Lady Arbella would suffer the worse for it. Eventually, the old countess drew up short. 'My granddaughter resides within.' She unlocked the door and stepped in ahead of us.

My eyes were drawn first to the frenzy of activity coming from a desk in a corner of the room. The lady was seated at it, her arm moving back and forth furiously, the quill in her hand racing across the page. She did not acknowledge the intrusion until she realised her grandmother had not come alone. As she looked up, she started and, as she rose, she knocked an inkpot over. A pool of black formed on the floorboards.

Lady Arbella Stuart looked, as Cecil had suggested, to be a strange bird. She was thin – painfully thin – her gown hanging on a flat-breasted frame so childish it made the queen's principal secretary look like Hercules. Her face, however, was aged by it, making it difficult to place her. I judged her to be around thirty. What I noticed immediately were her eyes, which were made enormous by the drawn cast of her face. Her teeth were likewise made prominent by the tightness of the skin around her mouth. Pity swelled within me. There was something wrong here, I thought, though I couldn't put my finger on it.

Just as we had with the countess, Lockhart and I made our obeisance, removing our hats, lining carefully kept inward, and each making a leg for her. The act of bowing and cap doffing was useful, I always found. As those I deferred to were judging my deference, I might judge their appearance from behind my lowering hat. The lady stuttered, stammered, knocked at her breast, and then bid us rise. 'Who are you?' Regaining my feet, I noticed that her big eyes were focused on me, the pupils huge. I wondered if, perhaps, she was on some physic that made them so.

'Friends, my lady,' began Lockhart.

'We come from London to warn you of a visit from Sir Henry Brounker. We understand you have asked for him.'

'Yes. Letters. I've written letters to the secretary. He is coming?'

'He is, my lady.'

'Grandmother,' she said, shifting her attention from us. 'I am very hungry. Please bring me food. Now, please, when my stomach calls for it.'

Bess, who had been standing to one side, furrowed her brow, bit at her lip, and left the room without a word, closing the door partly behind her. Silence ticked for a few seconds, and then Arbella moved towards me and took my hand in her own bony ones. 'I know you,' she said under her breath. She barked her next words, making me jump: 'I am glad you have brought me this news. It pleases me.' I realised immediately that she spoke for the benefit of the old woman she supposed to be waiting just outside. 'Tell the queen I am imprisoned,' she whispered. 'Watched all the time.'

At a loss, I said nothing. 'You know one another?' asked Lockhart, looking at us.

Arbella released my hand from her inky grip. Squinted. 'No. You looked like another. From a long time ago, it seems. I was confused. I have not been well. Is Brounker truly coming? Is he taking me to court?'

'I cannot say, my lady. I know only that he comes at your command.' To investigate you, I thought.

'My servants taken, dead, imprisoned. I have done nothing. And yet still the world suspects me. I must see the queen. The queen must hear me. The queen will see me married and out of this place.' She began pacing the room in a circle, speaking more to herself than anyone. Her chamber was a treasure trove, I saw, as full of trinkets and baubles as my own, albeit better organised. Yet I could tell just from looking that most of the things were childish. Dolls sat like well-trained children on shelves. Vases and carved puzzle boxes sat in rows. Little glass carvings were arranged with care. All pretty, mostly cheap. The exception was her collection of miniatures which covered several wooden panels, with the rest spilling out onto a table. Most of the people I did not recognise, but some of those on the table depicted Queen Elizabeth. I edged my way towards them for a better look, whilst the lady continued to move around, her face to the floor. With a coy glance I took in the nearest. It showed Elizabeth the sneering, whose leonine head almost seemed to burst from the flat surface to surreptitiously watch all that passed in Arbella's room.

Every courtier in England, I thought, must have their own image of the queen, each limned according to how they viewed her. A hundred, a thousand little mirrors not of the queen, but of their owners' loves and fears and hatreds.

Abruptly, she stopped. Looked at Lockhart, and then again at me. Lashes fluttered over her enormous eyes. She ran a hand through the cloud of hair that fell in a frizzy cascade under her peaked headdress. 'I must be saved,' she said. Her voice had lost its abrupt staccato and grown silken. With an inward wince, I realised that she was endeavouring to be flirtatious, and in the same moment I realised that her only instructions in the art had probably come from books. 'I am utterly at the mercy of that old woman,' she whispered, before pouting.

I opened my mouth to speak, but she must have read my reaction, for suddenly the display was gone. Again, the regal lady took over, her chin atilt and a hand poised over her lower bodice. 'My cousin the king of Scotland will save me if the queen of England won't.' Her flat chest rose. 'When I called him my lover, I meant only that he loved me as a friend.'

'What?' barked Lockhart in a half laugh.

I gave him a warning look. 'We know nothing of that, my lady.' I wished very much to be gone from her strange presence. As I spoke, I moved again, this time towards the papers she had been writing. She had lapsed into sullen silence, watching me, her breath shallow. I glimpsed downwards.

Scribbles. Ravings. Pleas. Nonsense.

A shiver ran through me. It called to mind the times I had heard the Hamlet plays read at the theatre. When watching and afterwards, I had never been able to make up my mind whether the prince of Denmark was truly mad or only feigning madness. So it was with the Lady Arbella Stuart.

We were prevented from further discourse by the return of Bess, who led a servant carrying a tray of food. The old woman looked at Arbella, who drew herself up to her full, modest height, and backed against a wall, bumping it and exclaiming. 'You have given her your message?' Bess said. 'You see? You see what I have to put up with' said her expression.

'We have, my lady,' I said, echoed by Lockhart.

We fled the room, the countess and servant following us. The latter disappeared, and the old woman locked the door. As we made our way back towards the front of the house, repeating the ceremony of incarceration, Bess spoke quite frankly to us, of what she called 'the child's' wilfulness, her obstinacy, her constant complaints, her 'tanters and tantrums'. I did not know which of the noble women to feel sorrier for: the captive or the gaoler.

When we came to the entrance hall of the house, Bess said, 'are you for London? I have messages of my own for my friends there.'

'Alas, no, my lady.'

'We're for Edinburgh!' announced Lockhart. I closed my eyes and held them tight for a second.

'To King James?!' Excitement sharpened her words.

'To the Scottish court,' I admitted. Anything else would be an obvious lie.

'How is the queen?' I heard suspicion in her voice – and again that edge of excitement.

'She is as well as ever, thank God.' I touched my hat.

'I see. Well, when you return to London, if you do, tell your master that the girl is well protected. She has seen no one but you. No, not even that group of ruffians calling themselves printers who tried to get in. Peddling good English poesy that might entice my granddaughter and offering their services as printers. Gave them short shrift, my people did.'

'Printers?' asked Lockhart.

'How many men?' I put in.

'Three. Three men. Led by a hard-faced lout with a look of the streets about him. Printer my eye, I said, when I saw them out the window. They stood out there looking up to her chamber. Trying to signal, I wouldn't wonder. Sent my strongest men out, so I did, and chased them off my land. Printers! Wearing badges bearing red crosses on their breasts – not any printing guild I've ever heard of.'

Before Lockhart could speak, I bowed and thanked her for admitting us, assuring her that her news would be relayed faithfully and honestly. We left Owlcotes as we had entered it, and stood on the gravel path, waiting for our horses to be fetched.

'Three men, claiming to be printers,' I said. 'Looking to sell their secret document to the lady, is my guess. With an offer to print it too, if she would pay.'

'So they have it!' said Lockhart, grinning and tightening his ridiculous sable cloak about his shoulders. 'We are on their trail, to be sure. Do you reckon they sold it to her upstairs? She is mad, to be sure.

Did you see how she moved? Destined for the bedlam when her cousin takes the throne.'

I bit my lips, wondering. It seemed unlikely Bess was lying as to their being prohibited access to Arbella. 'What's that?' asked Lockhart, breaking into my thoughts. 'It is her! She signals us!'

Turning to him, I saw that he was looking up at the white-walled front of the house. I followed his gaze. Up above, from the window of her chamber, the lady was throwing something. My heart leapt. Both Lockhart and I darted about the gravel, following the arc of her throws. Letters, I thought. Lockhart reached one of the things before me, stooping to pick it up. 'What the devil?'

I looked at the thing in his hand. A chunk of manchet. Arbella was throwing away the food she had begged from her grandmother. 'Does she fear poisoning by means *sub rosa*?' asked Lockhart.

'I cannot say.' In truth, I suspected that fear of poison was an excuse. From the lady's appearance, I judged she had developed a passion for starving herself.

Her Majesty eats less than usual.

Cecil's words echoed. Perhaps, I thought, Arbella Stuart thought to make herself more like her cousin the queen.

Or perhaps she just loathes herself as you do.

That poor woman, I thought. She needs help and love and will likely get neither.

At any rate, she would never be tolerated as sovereign, nor would any woman, not even if the red cross plotters found means to bar King James's accession. The rain of bread and cheese stopped, and a click above us said the window had been closed.

Our horses were brought, and we mounted. 'Until Berwick then,' I said, touching the brim of my hat. On the first leg of our trip north, we had arranged that we would separate. I had dispatched Kit Lockhart – and fancy my power to dispatch anyone anywhere – to his father's estates near Mansfield, to enquire of the old man the names of any parliamentary troublemakers. Where he had been reluctant to do so before, he was eager now to show his commitment to what he called 'the service', eager to show his worth and ability as an intelligencer. Further, we agreed that we could make a fuller judgment of the condition of the country by splitting up and covering more of it, even if it would add time to the journey.

I watched the dust fly off behind him. When it had settled, I began to make my own way in Derbyshire. As I had known from the start it would, something called to me. Even then, standing outside the pretty prison of Owlcotes, where the Scottish king's cousin was kept for her own protection, I told myself that it would be a simple matter. I might slip onto the land and take the thing I wanted and be gone again. As if as proof of my own abilities, I grasped the purse at my belt with a gloved hand. Even through the layers of material, I could feel the small oval shape. A fine miniature of the queen, lifted from the table of Arbella Stuart. It would be worth a great deal after Elizabeth died. Not that I would part with it.

Don't do it. Don't be a fool. Go straight to Berwick.

I batted the voice away as though it were a wasp.

***

It was not a great distance to ride, but the weather turned against me. If I were a smarter man, I might have taken the sudden onslaught of rain as a warning to turn back and forget the adventure.

I dismounted by a fencepost – unfamiliar, new – which enclosed partially flooded fields, and took off on foot. Those fields I knew. Once they had been the home of the raised mound of the archery butts at which I'd practiced every day as a boy, becoming quite the expert. The trail I also knew well, even though it was partially underwater and sinking deeper. I thanked God I had changed into my workman's clothes for my twilit raid and asked Him also to smooth my path. Entering upon the woods, I saw trees I remembered.

Into the woods, at the base of the big oak. You should be able to see the house from there.

I followed the old, familiar path of my childhood, and for a moment I wondered what the little me would make of the creature that haunted the place now. Disgust, I supposed. Horror, revulsion, shock. At six years old, we imagine ourselves heroes. I slopped on. In my memory I had buried the thing in summer, when things always looked brighter and happier. It was always summer and the sun always shone in memories of childhood.

Coming to the largest oak, I fell to my knees. The ground was dry here, the sheet of rain not quite making its way through the overhead tangle. I removed a small sliver of metal from my belt and began digging. When I had cleared a good chunk of the slime and rotting vegetation, I thrust my hands into the damp earth beneath. Carving. Digging. Scratching. My nails, which I had always taken pride in, were soon ruined by half-moons of black. Still I drew up the earth, tossing handfuls of it to the side.

Thump.

My fingertips tingled as they hit flat metal, the delightful pain shooting up and through my hands for only a second. After all these years, it was still there, and I had found it. I eased my fingers around the edge of the casket, waggling it until I could get a grip and slide it out. Overhead, the rain intensified. Pulling it free, I hugged it to my breast, before scrabbling at the catch. The thing wouldn't give. After years of interment, it was rusted shut. I tutted, shook it, and began clattering it against the trunk of the oak. 'Come on, give!' I shouted.

To my horror, someone answered.

I froze.

'Put your hands on your head and stand.'

I sighed. Had I not known this would happen? Had I not feared it? Had I not, in truth, wanted it? Keeping the casket in one hand, I got up from my knees and stood, turning. The figure standing before me, robed in good woollens and a heavy riding cloak, raised his sword. The tip wavered towards my neck. The years began to merge, falling in on themselves like a house of cards.

Let's go and play at buried treasure.

You stole that!

No, it's treasure. See, if we bury it by the oaken, it becomes buried treasure and then men hunt it one day and, and we fight them to keep it hided. Be a man, Thomas. Not a baby.

I'm not a baby. You're a baby.

When he spoke again, the command had fled his voice. Irritation had replaced it, and something like fear. 'What in the devil's name are you doing here, Adam?'

12

'Adam is dead,' I said. 'And I never cared for the name.'

'Then what are you calling yourself?' He removed his hat, tipped water from it, and replaced it.

'Edward. Edward Savage.'

He appeared to consider this before speaking. 'You look like an animal. I found your horse as I was riding the estate to see the flooding. A poor sort of beast. Rented or stolen? You look like you've turned thief.'

'And you look prosperous, Thomas. Or should I call you Squire Norton, now? The beard becomes you. One can hardly tell you lack a chin. Are you become the gentleman of the manor yet?'

'Father is still alive. But … he is not in his right mind all the time.'

'I didn't know he ever was.'

'You're angry, Adam,' said Thomas, stroking his neck. 'As father's successor, I am running the estates. Why did you come back?' He looked at the box I was still clutching. 'What is that?'

'You don't remember, brother? We buried it out here when we were playing as boys.'

Confusion reigned. 'I … no, I cannot remember.'

'It was mother's. Is she–'

'She's dead, Adam.'

My mouth fell open. I closed it quickly. When I spoke, my voice sounded distant in my ears, dry. 'Did she ask for–'

Thomas looked at the ground and began fussing with his hands in a gesture I remembered. 'No. She said only that…'

'Yes?'

He cleared his throat. 'She said only that she regretted the death of her first son. And the substitution of so unnatural and twisted a monster in her little boy's place.'

Something inside me shrivelled. I thought of the bracelet I kept in my lodgings in London. It was an imitation of one I remembered my mother owning. One of many sad little remnants of childhood I had taken possession of to recreate the past in my shabbier present. Suddenly I wanted to ride back to London and cast the thing into the gutter. 'I did not know.'

'I thought,' said Thomas, 'you must have heard.'

'No. I listened for the news out of the county for a year or two. Then I stopped. I live in London now.'

'London, is it? Heh. Father says London is a leviathan, swallowing up all around it, and, as is the way of things, leaving a noisome wake of shit.'

'He was always a man of charm and subtlety.'

'You came all the way back here for that?' Thomas pointed at the box. I held it up, turned, and smashed it against the tree. It fell open, and I caught the object that escaped from it. 'What is it?'

I held it up in the fading light. It was a pin cushion, made of wood fashioned into the shape of an imperial crown, the pin bed made of faded silk stuffed with horsehair. 'Only this,' I said.

'What the…' Thomas moved towards me, his sword sheathed. 'That. I remember that. I remember. We stole it out of the house. Buried it as treasure. It was a game. How the hell did you ever remember that foolish toy?'

'Foolish toy,' I said. 'Yes. Trash.' But it was a piece of trash that had haunted my dreams for years. I needed to possess it more than I had as a child, when owning pretty objects was a game.

'Is that truly what you came for?' Suspicion, I noticed, tinged his question.

'Yes. Don't fear, Thomas. You can succeed him. I am dead.'

He relaxed. I looked a little more closely at him. My years in London, I fancied, had sat lightly on me; his in Derbyshire had made an older-looking younger man of him. 'Come, then. Don't let's stand in the rain and dark.' Hesitation. 'Do you wish to look upon the house?'

'No. I hardly think it welcomes ghosts.'

'It has none to haunt it. The old hall is gone.'

'What?'

'Pulled down.' A rush of feeling struck me. Gone, I thought. The halls and walls and turrets and casements I had made lost idols of were all crushed and smashed into rubble. 'We have a new Norfield. In the new style. Father wanted it for mother. She didn't live to see it finished, but … uh … when he goes to his reward, it'll do well enough for me and Ann.'

I smiled, shaking my head. 'You married her, then. Last I heard you'd been betrothed.'

'I did, Adam, what you would not.'

I swear he enjoyed using the name I had let moulder after casting it away. 'I'm glad,' I said, and meant it. I had refused to marry the girl who had been a childhood friend. Refused to condemn her to a chaste and childless marriage. It had been that refusal and the reasoning behind it that had led to my death, to the inking over of my name in the parish records. As far as Norfield went, I was less than a corpse: I had never been. 'I know she'll make a good wife.'

'I have never cause to beat or strike her,' he said without expression.

'I should hope not.'

He cleared his throat, a frown crossing his face. 'You … ah … you might look upon the place. I don't think it would be right if you came in. You understand …' A little smirk flared, blotting the apparent discomfort. 'Though you always did enjoy entering places you shouldn't.'

My colour rose. 'You think you have a country wit now, don't you?'

'Do you wish to see the place or not?'

No, no, no.

'Yes. Let's have a look. It doesn't matter to me.'

My brother led us out of the woods and back to the trail where the moon shone like a torch, as it can only in the countryside, and our horses were each tethered. We did not ride but walked the beasts through the estate until lights twinkled ahead. I tried not to look at the scarred and pitted ground where the old house had stood. There lay the traces of my childhood. Somewhere on that blank space the ghost of the child I had been frolicked. Looked for his lost horn book. Evaded tutors, whose own phantom voices cried, 'That Adam is a wicked boy and there is no remedy but the stick'. My mother's embroideries and the smell of the brewhouse and the first feel of a pen in my small and clumsy hand: all gone.

Next to the vacant land, built of what appeared to be the scavenged stones of the house I remembered, stood the new place: a three-storey affair with pretensions, its outside whitewashed, western and eastern wings protruding on either side of a recessed central entrance. The windows were all glazed, proclaiming their value in those shining lights within.

'Norfield Manor,' he announced, before calling for grooms. I could hear in his voice the pride in both the place itself and the fact that he had taken it from me – the twisted monster. I pulled my hand and the reins in it away from the young groom, shaking my head. Our altercation was interrupted, however, by the front door opening. Out from under a stone arch and down the short steps skipped Ann, little changed from the days in which I'd known her. Save, I noticed, from her swollen belly. The succession to Norfield looked to be assured, and she every inch its lady in her pearled cap.

'Tom,' she called, her eyes on the ground and her skirts held up as she moved. 'Tom, your busy child stirred and gave me such a kick, I…'

'Good evening, Mrs Norton. My lady of Norfield,' I said.

Her mouth fell open. She gave a slight shake of her head, looked back towards the house in doubt, and then turned to me. A smile split her face. 'Adam. Oh, Adam.' Her hands flew out and I took them, bowing. 'I thought – we thought…'

'You look blooming, Ann. Jesus, can you be the lass I ran through fields with? The one who tripped and danced and wondered what the bumps rising on her chest were?'

'Oh, Adam.' Her cheeks rose in twin apples. I thought of Faith, still young. 'Why are you come?'

'He had one piece of property here only. He has retrieved it.'

I nodded. I had stowed the crown in my saddlebag, stuffing it in with my rag-tag jumble of clothes. 'I didn't mean to trouble you. Either of you,' I added, arching an eyebrow towards Thomas. 'May I be the last to congratulate you on your marriage. Both sets of parents must have been well pleased.'

'They were,' said Thomas. 'We knew our duty.'

'Duty,' said Ann, laughing. 'I hope it was no duty. Come.' She began dragging me by the hand towards the house. Thomas objected, spluttering loudly, torn between stopping us and preventing the groom from making off with my horse. He lost both battles.

Ann led me into a large entrance hall, covered in wood panelling with wall sconces guttering happily and thick carpets on the floor. Before Thomas could reach us, she whispered, 'I'm sorry about your mother.' I noticed, as she spoke, that her head inclined to one wall, where an indifferent painting of the old woman hung. Again, that strange shrivelling of the innards wrenched me.

'He cannot stay,' hissed Thomas. 'I'm sorry, Adam, but you …'

'Of course he can stay. He's … he's a friend.'

'I don't want to be an inconvenience to anyone. Perhaps just to dry off, to have my clothes a little brushed up.'

'Lower your voice, man,' my brother snapped.

It was too late. Down the staircase stomped my squat, elderly father, a steward and chamberlain clutching at his elbows. 'All this shouting, what? Won't be locked in me own damned rooms.' As the countess of Shrewsbury's had been, my father's accent was riddled with earthy Derbyshire. The vestiges of command strengthened it. 'Weren't no good shutting me up if you weren't going to watch me, ha! Ha! Ha!' His head twisted on his shoulders. 'What's this? Who's this?' His clothes, I noticed, were patched and worn. Having succeeded him, I supposed, Thomas must have seen no point in dressing him grandly. 'See?' He turned to the grooms. 'I told you I weren't hearing no voices, not this time. There are people walk the walls at night, what? Who are you? Who? This is my house.'

I turned pleading and, I will admit, fearful eyes on my brother and his wife. Both stood rooted. I swallowed, trying to think of a lie. I was a tradesman, a workman. I was not Adam. My father's frog-like eyes rolled over me. Confusion drew further lines in his forehead. He blinked stupidly and a line of spittle started from the corner of his mouth. And, I noticed with surprise, a tear rolled down one cheek. 'I am no one, sir,' I began.

'You. I know you.' He spat. Looked into the corner, apparently too ashamed to admit that he did not know me. And then he turned back, the prominent eyes sharp and glinting. 'You,' he said again, with more certainty. 'I told you yesterday to get gone from my house. Gone! Go! You are dead.' His squawking voice began to deepen, to rumble with anger. 'Unnatural knave! Monster! You diseased, shameful sodomite!'

'Get him upstairs,' Thomas said to the servants. The tone of his voice suggested that their job was a familiar one. 'Tie him down to the bed if need be.' Anne put a hand on my arm, apology in her eyes, as they began dragging the old man away.

'Would rather seek pleasures with other men than marry where he's told, what! Sodomite! Deformed inwardly, what? Killed his mother for shame, I've not forgotten! Don't touch me, you rotten slaves, I am your master!'

'I apologise for father,' said Thomas when the scene was over. His voice remained flat, but he removed a handkerchief from his sleeve and mopped his brow. 'I would have hoped he would have been secured before now.' He turned semi-accusing eyes on Ann.

'Won't you stay the night at least, Adam?'

'My name's not Adam. It's Edward. Edward Savage.' I addressed myself more to my brother than her, though I took her hand and squeezed it.

'Edward, Adam, whatever you call yourself,' he said. 'You … we might find you a space for the night in the kitchen closet. If you're gone before father rises.'

'The closet?' Ann cried. 'Thomas, you can't be –'

'That is my will, wife.'

'To hell with your will, brother,' I snapped, finding my voice. 'I would rather sleep in a ditch than under that mad creature's roof. Or yours, or whoever calls himself master here. This is no house for me, nor ever was.'

'Oh, Adam, please don't go. It's so wet!'

'Fare you well, Ann. Marrying into this family. I say the name Norton is a curse and one I'm glad to see the back of. And Norfield Hall or Manor or whatever this place is now too. I at least spared you the monstrous farce of a marriage with me.' Her hands flew to her cheeks. I turned on my heel, prepared to sweep from the hall. Yet my blood was still up. 'You, you might remember and know,' I said, eager to rant and rave before the tears burst from my eyes, 'that if I am … am *inwardly deformed*, if I'm a monster in nature, then it's a visitation of God's wrath on my parents. That creature up there must have made me as I am. His wife too. I hope your son doesn't succeed to it.'

Relishing the look of anguish that crossed his pompous face and ignoring the punctured sound Ann made, I stomped from the house and into the pouring rain, calling for the surely bewildered groom.

What else did you expect? Love?

I did not look back and the rain washed the angry tears from my face.

13

Pen and pages flew as the reader translated.

Notwithstanding the birth of the high and mighty prince, he who was christened Charles JAMES, I must here note that the beginning of that princely infant was made in all sin. His mother, the queen, Marie, of the house of Stewart and first of that name, returned to us from her life as consort to the king of France, Francis of the Valois, of good memory and fame, the said Francis having departed this life in A.D. 1560.

On her return to rule over us she proved herself a wise and virtuous princess and sovereign lady and at her hands the true Kirk prospered notwithstanding her affection and practice of the false and abominable doctrine of the kirk of Rome. And yet it is noted in many goodly CHRONICLES that the falling into wickedness of the prince acts as it were as a fountain, the poison trickling downwards. In the year 1565 A.D. the said Queen Marie did become swept and utterly carried away by unnatural lusts and entered into a carnal marriage with the Master of Lennox, called in England Henrie the Lord Darnley, the said Darnley being set above us as our king and becoming father to the said Prince James. Of the nature of this King Henrie I say nothing.

Yet to return to this matter of the poisoning of the realm, I can vouchsafe for its pure truth. For when the queen gave in to her lusts it fell out that a number of the men of the ancient blood of Scotland did so too, though it is not for me to accuse any other man of anything (see what disorders fell out in the reading of the CHRONICLES O unhappy nation!) and that it was bruited that foul practices of witchcraft had enticed the said Marie into her marriage. Even I, who had never before looked upon a woman carnally other than my true wedded wife, who is named Minnie, felt the wicked burning and passions and did sometimes lie with a serving girl in the household, the fault thereof lies entirely in the example set by our queen and the devilry which did then attend upon our ancient realm. For the said serving girl, who was called Bessie, did use sundry sortileges and charms and privy speeches to bewitch me into kissing her, her tongue in my mouth and mine in hers, and so to lie with her against my will.

Such witchcraft and devilry and all such filthy practices &C aforementioned I decry utterly and speak of only because it was then spake of that in Edinburgh at the birth of the said Prince James, that his midwife, the said Margaret Asteane, did invite and solicit &C witchcraft to ease the sore pains of his mother, Queen Marie her labour, in bringing him into this world. And in this way, I say that devilry did infect and does infect the realm and did cause the wickedness that would fall out and of which I was art and part, and for which I hope surely to render my account to him that stands above all princes. The evidences and shows of this monstrous and abominable devilry thus shewed themselves even before the birth of the said Prince James and will further explain, though they shall not excuse wholly, the terrible truth of that prince's diseased nature.

14

Cries and screams rose up from Bishopsgate Street, waking Bartlet before the lightening of the sky had a chance to intrude on his dreams. Muttering, he threw back the coverlet, put his feet to the chilly carpet, and stood. His head was still swimming, the noise still hammering at him, when the door opened.

'What the devil?'

'We've lost control of our boys, brother!'

'What? What?'

'It's all over, Bart.' Gregory's voice wavered somewhere on the edge of tears. 'She's dead. The news is all about London. People are going mad, locking their doors. The boys are out on the streets crying hellfire on James of Scotland. But it'll be too late. And still no word from Ford from up north.'

Bartlet swallowed, trying to clear his throat of the syrupy taste of morning. 'Queen Elizabeth is dead?'

'Yes, yes, or so it's rumoured. The news has blown into London from Richmond. The people are–'

'Then to hell with this. Pack my things. We're undone without that paper. Leave the boys to hang and be buried with their red crosses as they wish. I'm going west. Go and fetch fresh horses, if you can find 'em.'

Gregory fled.

Bartlet ran a hand through his hair before staggering over to the window. The plan for the succession, for the subversion of King James, was at an end; it was stillborn, killed by the loss of that damned Scotsman's much-vaunted secret proofs. Still, his life need not end with it. No one knew he was in London nor that he led the red cross knights. The fools would go to the hangman without naming him, surely. They might even be pardoned by the new king as rambunctious and unlettered dolts. Better, though, that they hang and quickly, lest any of them brabble.

As he opened the window, the street sounds grew louder, carried in on a blast icier than he had felt in weeks. Looking down, he saw hats bob as men ran back and forth, sharing news. Though he couldn't see her, he heard a woman screaming. The scream was cut short but plaintive wailing succeeded it. More men ran down the street, joining a cluster at the far end. Each seemed to be flinging his arms high, arguing, shouting. All in a passion, thought Bartlet, for the death of a woman whose reign had ended in a staggering whimper.

Strange, though, that there were no church bells, no peals sent heavenward as heralds of Elizabeth's soul.

He bit his lip, closed the window, and began gathering things and dumping them into the heavy travelling chest at the side of his bed. With luck, he would be on the road out of London before the city gates were closed. No one need ever know he had been in the city.

Bartlet jumped as the door opened and he wheeled, a gauzy ruff in his hand. His brother was panting, his large forehead slick. 'What the – Gregory – the horses are ready?'

'Brother, I've been out in the streets and–'

'Hang the streets! I must be away before they are shut up, stuffed with officers of the watch and Christ knows what other scum! That hunchbacked little freak Cecil will have an army of men out now, spreading thistles to welcome the Scots and snare men like us!'

'Be silent!'

'What?' The shock of Gregory's words sent Bartlet reeling back a few steps, his naked feet nearly catching on the carpet. He held the ruff over his chest protectively and then, realising the primness of the gesture, he dropped it. 'How dare you, you base born–'

'Be quiet, Bart.'

In response, and still in shock, he meekly acceded to his brother's wishes, sitting down on the bed. 'What is it?'

'I've been out on the streets. Pulled in some of our men, the ones I could find. Closed their mouths.'

'But why, if the queen–'

'The queen is not dead. It's a false rumour.' Relief seemed to pour from Gregory in a long sigh after he'd spoken. 'It is some mingle-mangle. One of her ladies has died. Some other old woman. The countess of Nottingham. At Arundel House down by the Strand, not Richmond.'

'Catherine Carey,' said Bartlet, thinking. In contemplating his knowledge of the nobility, some of his strength returned. He stood. 'Wife to the queen's cousin and mother of the member of the House for Surrey. Do not, Gregory, presume to speak to me like a superior person again. You are in point of fact my inferior, as our late father understood and made clear. You bring woollens from inferior nations into this realm and I stand as a member of its ancient parliament.'

Gregory hung his head. 'I apologise, brother.'

'It is by my grace now and out of respect to my father that I let you call me that. Ah, now, come. All is forgiven. So the queen yet lives?'

'She does.' Gregory raised his head. 'When word reached the city that a great lady had died, the tale grew arms and legs in the telling and caused nearly a riot.'

'And the only riots we wish, of course, are those that rise up against the foreign yoke. You said you have herded some of our sheep?'

'Some of our boys, yes. I fear … I fear many were excited by the news. Went off like badly loaded muskets. I've pulled in those I've found.'

'Into this house?'

'By privy means.'

'Hmph. Well, it will be a treat for them to stand on carpets for the first time in their miserable lives. Yet we cannot have this, we cannot have the creatures running loose every time some piece of false news burns through the city. Go and round them up, man. I will be down directly.'

Once Gregory had gone, Bartlet dressed himself, whistling as he did so. It seemed to him that the false news had been a warning – a warning to move matters along. But how, without the document? Inactivity, the weariness of waiting for news, was death to a plot. Nothing had been found of the Scot Gowrie's papers in London, and so that avenue would have to wait until the brute Ford rode back along it with firm information.

Until then, though, something would have to be done to keep the sheep fed.

Once dressed, he went downstairs, rumpling his clothes, and found the men standing in the broad gallery. He frowned. Gregory ought to have known better and kept them in the hall outside. Here they were rubbing old wall hangings between their hands, smoking pipes, catching the carpets on their filthy, nailed boots. A hazy blue fug hung over the pack of them and through it Bartlet thought he saw fleas dance. 'My friends, my friends,' he said, spreading his palms and moving towards them. 'My brave knights of the red cross. You are welcome to my home.' An excited murmur rose. 'I understand you heard the news out of the city.' He tutted. 'Let it be a warning to us all, eh? You see how easily it can fall out that a life is lost. Imagine it had indeed been the poor queen. Where would we be now? Where would you be?'

The murmur turned to confusion. Gregory appeared at his side and whispered to him. 'Don't frighten them, brother. They think they're safe from the law and gaols by our purse, like Ford was.'

Knitting his eyebrows, Bartlet said, 'it was only the old lady of Nottingham who went to meet her maker. Come, lads, you know as well as I do that the queen is at Richmond. You saw her people carry her chattels and goods and boxes out of London, as I did.' He wagged a finger then winked. 'But remember: the next time they move her Majesty, they'll only need one box.' Laughter rippled, more slowly amongst the goats too stupid to understand the joke. But he had won them.

'Good old Bartlet,' one muttered, none too quietly. 'He'll speak right bold and witty of anybody, by Christ.'

'And we must be ready for it. For the death of that lady who's of no mingled blood of Scot or stranger, but true-born English, born here among us. And who'll go to good English earth in the end. And whose crown will fall upon a man of like blood and birth. Now then, now then, we'll have no more open shouting or crying in the streets, boys. Subtlety, remember. By subtle means we must let them in Whitehall and Richmond and all about know that we'll have no king save one your parliament approves of. One who's English born and agreed by us, not them.'

'Who, Bartlet?' This came, he saw, from the stocky youth who had been at the execution. 'Who'll be our new king, but?'

'Which Englishman?' added another, raising a finger, picking his ear, and flicking the result on the floor.

Damn, thought Gregory. The fools had begun to ask the question he had thus far managed to avoid. 'That,' he said, 'will be a matter for England's own parliament, where you have friends like me to lead the way.'

'But whose name do we cry for?' persisted the ear-picker.

'I … I will tell you, my friend, when the time is right. When we have ensured that James of Scotland is not banging down your doors and threatening your property and your women.'

'Property,' barked one of them, laughing.

Bartlet joined in the laughter. Out of the corner of his mouth he whispered, 'get them out of my house.' Gregory gave a small nod and moved out amongst them, handing out more tobacco and guiding them in small groups towards the door.

When they had gone, his brother returned. 'We are losing control of them. They're getting restless, not enough to do but moan and decry Scotland and the Scots to folk in the taverns and streets. They want more.'

'Then we shall give them more.' Bartlet put his hands on his hips and strode into the centre of the gallery, nudging the soiled parts of the carpet with his foot. 'And thereby buy a little more time. Time for Ford to capture this Savage and cut his throat for the document against James of Scotland. To keep the peace until then we must give that rabble a name. A king. If they'll no longer be fed with nay, nay, nay, we will give them a yea.'

'Who?'

'The best Englishman.' Looking into his brother's wide eyes, Bartlet said, 'you have friends enough in the dock trading business, I warrant. Men who know how to get hold of things that the queen and her minions would have kept secret. Like that press of yours.' He raised a finger. 'I wish us to have a book on the succession. One of those things the queen prohibited. Whichever is the newest and will furnish us with the names and claims and titles of the candidates to the throne. Then,' he added, 'I will decide which poor creature will wear the crown of England at my command and on a wave of support from my flock.'

15

Hoby. Bacon. Everard. Finch. Donhault. The names on the list Lockhart had procured from his father repeated in my head, keeping pace with the hoofbeats of my latest horse. Some I recognised, some I did not. Cecil might have had better luck discovering the dealings and plots of members of parliament. The list was probably meaningless, but it gave me something to focus on other than my own curiosity and the stupidity it too often brought about. Besides, I needed more than anything to feel a sense of purpose. We had lost the trail of the red cross plotters when we passed into the north country. To Yorkshiremen we were southerners and our money, even if we pleased to part with it, couldn't open their proud mouths. That, however, seemed a small matter; I judged that after their abortive visit to Lady Arbella, they would have skulked off to try and entice other English heirs.

The hilly, bracken-strewn countryside of Scotland gave way to the peaty smoke of Edinburgh. Before we curved around a large hill and saw the city, we could see the issue of its many chimneys, then the treetops of the palace's park, and then, ultimately, the grey-brown sprawl of the place as it climbed another steep east-west hill crowned by the dank and forbidding castle.

At each town in both countries we had made our presence as travelling players' men known, and we separated and reined in as we saw Edinburgh. 'What a foul place,' was Lockhart's assessment. 'Grey as a … a…'

'It's two towns,' I said, saving him the embarrassment of not knowing how to finish a simile. 'You go into Edinburgh and see if you can find lodgings. I'll try the Canongate.'

He nodded. 'I will find us a good place where we might lodge *sub rosa*.'

'Would you stop saying that,' I said with asperity. 'I don't know that means. Just find a damn inn.'

His mouth puckered. 'Very well. A barber at least.' I raised my hand to my face. Both his and mine were buried in thatch. It was my turn to nod. Lockhart gave a half-salute and rode away. In truth, I think he was glad to be quit of me. I had been largely silent since we met in Berwick, and not a scrap as eager and pleased about his procurement of the list as he seemed to expect. It was only with a conscious effort that I could smile and jest, and I was not inclined to make the effort. To excuse myself, I had pleaded urgency, not only of our mission, but of beating the weather. Winter had sharpened its fangs for one last bite

We separated, Lockhart riding uphill, his foolish sable cloak billowing, as I scouted the east. On the road, we had elected not to try immediately for the palace. To do so would be to alert too many people to our arrival and, if there were any about who had knowledge of the missing document, they might take fright and flight. King James could wait until we had gathered intelligence in the unsuspecting city.

The little burgh of Canongate abutted the royal palace of Holyroodhouse. If Edinburgh was the seat of the Scottish kings, the palace was the seat of the capital. Keeping to the side of the broad main street, I surveyed the crop of densely packed buildings. Here, I knew, sat the townhouses of the nobility, whose piles would usefully be within a short walk of the court. As I rode past them in the direction of Holyrood, turning at the end of the street to make my way back up the other side, it was hard not to compare them with their peers' townhouses on the Strand. Here were no fresh-minted palaces, but small-windowed, grey-faced fortified manses that even a modest gentleman in London wouldn't see himself entombed in. These noble houses did not sit haughtily, secure in their own majesty, but huddled, hard, cold, and suspicious along the cramped Canongate. Edinburgh, I thought, as my horse carried me past the last of them, appeared triply unfortunate. It lacked space, men skilled in the art of building, and money to pay them.

Where are the inns?

I had passed none of the cheerful, painted wooden signs on my ride down towards the palace. Nor did I see any riding away from it. The occasional board proclaimed the shop of an apothecary; a bare butcher's wooden block announced its owner (as well as lamenting Lent); there was even what looked like a tailor's shop, outside which hung, disconcertingly, miniature dummy people clothed in black. Still at a loss, I dismounted, feeling the tightness in my thighs and hardness flare up through my stomach. The latter growled. It had been years since I had done any sustained riding and I had almost forgotten the thrill and feel of it. My belly, at any rate, would have become a fine furnace for concoction, I thought – if I could find a place to eat and rest. I began walking the horse by the reins slowly over crusts of ice towards the arched gateway that led almost seamlessly from the smaller burgh into the city proper.

I drew up just shy of it. Hanging on a rusty hook above was the arm and part of the breast of a man, the entire chunk of flesh tarred. The blackened hand appeared to beckon visitors inside. I had seen such things before, of course, in the wake of the Essex rising in London. Still, it was, as it was intended to be, a daunting and unpleasant sight. Ignoring it, I passed under the archway and into the small gatehouse.

Inside, a sentry slouched. I wetted the inside of my cheeks, judging how I might affect a neutral accent, but he seemed disinterested. 'No' a papist, are ye?' I gave one hard shake of my head. 'Huv tae ask,' he said, holding out an open palm. Quickly I placed in it a Scottish coin I had picked up in Berwick and was able to move into Edinburgh unmolested. I had not got far up the street when Lockhart approached. Like me, he was leading his horse, boldly stamping his way through the scattered crowds of people.

And what a people, I thought. In England the reformation had been largely confined to the churches. In Scotland it had spilled into the streets. The women marched in lockstep, arm in arm, almost fully covered, their collective gaze directed at the ground. Every man was in black or grey and likewise silent, their noses and cheeks glowing with cold rather than good cheer. There was no singing as the people went about their work, no ribaldry. Looking up, around and behind Lockhart's horse, I spotted what could only be a preacher, swathed in black with a skull cap resting on the crown of his head. He stood, arms clasped behind him, chin in the air, looking down his long nose approvingly at the city of heaven-bound souls. Occasionally he barked something, and heads bowed a little lower, steps shuffled a little more modestly. The buildings on either side of the street seemed equally as cheerless; far up the hill, on the left side, the spire of a great church, a cathedral perhaps, craned its vulture-like head and neck above them. Inwardly I shuddered. There, I thought, but for Queen Elizabeth's love of life – and her fraying thread of it – might go London.

My religious views, in as much as they exist, are not deep. Perhaps that's because neither Protestants nor Papists can explain nor stomach me. Though I have no liking for the hypocrisy of Romish priests, I do think that the dry religion of England and the drier one of Scotland missed a trick in their insistence that private communication with God and His word answered all. As I see it, it is plain superstition to think, as the Catholics do, that a priest might intercede with the supreme being on their behalf. Yet the unburdening of the mind to someone who listens is surely a balm – perhaps even stronger a balm if the listening priest is dim and disinterested. Keeping your troubles to yourself and speaking only to God, in prayer, alone, is apt to pile care upon care, especially if you receive no divine answer. The reformation of religion took away our listeners, forcing us all to be inward. It is all one to me, of course; I learned by the universal hatred of my vices to reveal my shameful thoughts to no one, Catholic or Protestant. I had been inward since the first hairs sprouted over my lips.

The shiver moved from within to without and I shook. I had cooled from the overheated ride and rapidly. The Scottish air felt like shards of glass sprinkled down my throat and up my nostrils. 'Any luck?'

'None.' Lockhart stamped his boots on the frozen ground. 'Not a damned inn in sight. No signs, nothing. This is a strange city.'

'Lower your voice,' I hissed.

'What – my tongue offends?'

'No, I …' I bit my lip and jerked my head behind me. The low city wall sprung from either side of the great archway leading to the Canongate, and on one side of it sat what I first took to be a child. I was conscious of him staring at us, head cocked to one side. The image of the gong-scourers of London rose in my mind: Cecil's spies. Perhaps King James or one of his ministers employed similar tricks.

Abruptly, Lockhart laughed. He shook his head at my frown. 'It's only a cripple,' he said. My grimace deepened. 'A dwarf. A half-man.'

I turned fully and saw that he was right. We were being watched not by a child but a dwarf, who sat on the walls, legs dangling. His handsome face, a jarring contrast to the malformed body, was slack. Drool led down from a corner of his mouth. 'Only a …'

The look of dull incomprehension vanished. The man winked. Slackness returned. A player, I thought.

I gestured to Lockhart to stay put and moved towards the city wall, taking a seat next to him. A chill immediately clutched at my backside. 'What news, friend? Might you tell us where we can find an inn?'

'Ye're no fae here then, is it?'

'I … what?'

'English, are ye?' He kept his voice low, I noticed, and occasionally glanced up the high street.

I swallowed. 'Yes.'

'Do … you … speak … ENGLISH?' I jumped at the intrusion, before turning a furious look on Lockhart, who had sauntered over. The little man looked at him, then at me, shaking his head with a look of amused contempt.

'Bloody gowks,' he said.

'An inn,' I persisted. 'Do you know of one?'

He slid down off the wall and adjusted his frieze jerkin before straightening his flat-topped cap. Loudly, he said, 'Cauld, cauld, cauld. Mr Francis Mowbray's a-hung up oan thon gatehouse, an'll never come back nae mer,' in the whiny tones of a witless oaf. Then, giving a shrug, he whispered, 'follow. Wait awhile first.' Then he marched out through the city gate, back in the direction from which I had come.

'Should we trust a half-man? He had the look of a fool,' said Lockhart.

'He had the look of one feigning it. I doubt he's leading us to the slaughter.'

We stood around awhile, rubbing our hands and breathing into them before, as casually as we could, following the dwarf into the Canongate. 'Where is he?' Lockhart cried.

'Will you please stop talking so loudly? If we … ho! There he is.'

About a third of the way down the long street, the man was slouching before an open archway on the right-hand side. He removed his cap and gave a brief wave. 'I say,' said Lockhart, 'this is spiery to be sure. Meeting with strange creatures in a strange city.' I did not bother to silence his nonsense, moving instead in the direction of our new friend.

As we drew close to the archway, our horses with us, he disappeared under it. I shrugged at Lockhart and went first. Through the archway lay a small, cobbled courtyard or garden, a well-maintained stable at the back. The dwarf leant against its wall. 'Fur yer beasts,' he said, rapping the building. 'Gang, noo. Auntie'll feed an' watter thaim.'

After stabling our mounts, we returned to the garden, where our saviour stood under a skeletal tree, watching with sharp eyes. 'We thank you,' I said, rushing to speak before Lockhart could put his foot in his mouth. 'Mr …?'

'Andro,' he said. 'Honest Andro Allardyce o' Edinburgh.'

'Andrew - Andro,' I said. 'Do you speak English?'

'Ken I micht be persuatit tae tak o' thon tongue.'

'What?' asked Lockhart, folding his arms.

Rolling his eyes, Andro rubbed his fingers together. Matching his eye-roll, I handed over some coins. 'Aye, that'll do,' he said, turning them over in his fingers. 'A magic set o' coins, these, that make me fit to know your own tongue.' I started at the polish in his change of language. He grinned. 'The city has become a right busy place for Englishmen over the years. It pays to have a smooth tongue.' Again, he straightened his jerkin and cap.

'What are you?' I asked. 'Are you an innkeeper?'

'What am I?' He removed his cap and ran a hand through his hair. 'I'm by the way o' things and as it were a linguist. A keen looker on o' the fallen and corrupt condition of man, you might say. A true philosopher.'

'You talk enough for one,' observed Lockhart. Andro Allardyce essayed a bow.

'No innkeeper then. There's no sign on this place.'

'An inn sign you're after, are you? You'll find none around Edinburgh. The Kirk has no liking for them.' His sigh curled white through the air. 'Our dear fathers in Christ reckon that inn signs invite drinking. Gambling. Invite secret papists into the burghs and give them shelter. Reckon that if there are no inns, strangers will have to ask around, advertise their presence, you ken – you know? Here, looking at you boys I think they're right.'

'Is this true?' Lockhart asked, before laughing. 'Inns are evil now? I should not like your churchmen to look upon London.'

'Nor should they like to see it, I reckon. But if it's a place to eat, sleep, and piss, Honest Andro'll see you right. Come, come, my arse is frozen through from that wall.' He moved away from the tree and towards the building that glared over the courtyard – a tall, grey edifice much like all the others in the burgh.

'So you *are* an innkeeper?' I asked.

He paused, looking over his shoulder. 'Me? No, no, no. This is my aunt's house. I'm a simple idiot.' He looked at Lockhart. 'A dwarf. A half-man.' I felt colour tingle in my cheeks and began stammering. 'Don't fash yourself,' he said. 'It's a fine thing to be thought a fool. If I weren't, I might be put to some more or less honest occupation by the city.' He winked again and moved into the porch, throwing open the door. 'It's nothing rich to your London tastes, but there are worse places, I reckon.' He disappeared inside. After a moment's hesitation we followed, packs tucked under our arms.

The doorway led into a decently sized kitchen. A gaunt woman stood stirring a pot over a fire, and Andro spoke rapidly to her in Scots. She seemed to put up an argument before sagging, and he turned his winning smile on us again. 'Auld Auntie Peg says you might stay a few nights if it pleases you.'

'Thank you, madam,' I said, taking off my cap. She said nothing, returning to her pot. I looked around the room. A large table and chairs stood in the centre – old, but sturdy. The walls were unpanelled stone and the floor, though it was aged, was spotless.

'Not a bad wee place,' said Andro, scraping out a stool and clambering onto it. 'Sit.' We did. 'Aye, this old house used to belong to an Englishman like yourselves, so the story goes. With a French wife who lay pregnant when your queen's old da burnt Edinburgh and all around to the ground. House was only spared because the old boy was English. So the story goes, anyway.'

'That's very interesting,' I lied.

'So you're English, eh?' He clapped his hands together and sucked air over his teeth, making a 'fssshhaw' sound. '… What's … uh … Francis Drake like?'

I laughed. 'A long time dead.'

'Ah well, that's a wee shame right enough. What brings you lads to Scotland?'

'We represent touring players,' I said, resting my forearms on the table. The good smell of peat lay heavy in the air and the room was warm, pleasant after the chill of the streets.

'Is that so? Ha. That'll please the king. And the queen too. I've entertained Queen Anne myself. Tumblit a pretty turn for her, when I was a small boy.' Lockhart snorted and I clenched my teeth. 'A smaller boy,' said Andro, apparently not offended. 'Aye, Queen Anne likes a tumble, or so the stories go.'

Without our asking, the old woman, Peg, began dishing her fishy Lenten stew into wooden bowls and served us each some coarse dredge bread, not unlike the jannock of the north of England. 'Come, let's have a bite and we'll have a good talk after,' said Andro, raising a cup. I chewed and slurped gratefully, along with our host, whilst Lockhart carefully sipped, his napkin spread over a shoulder. He had kept up the same custom in every tavern and inn on the road, as though the rules of communal eating picked up at the Inns of Court had become ingrained. My friend, I had already decided, would never make an agent of the state. He simply could not be other than himself: a gentleman's son with not enough to do. He could not adopt the manners and customs of any other company, could not shift his fashion or speech to put other men at ease. When we returned to London, I would call on his services no more – tell him, perhaps, that I had been released from service myself. Then we might return to being simple friends in leisure (a true thing, I realised, that friendships of leisure are tested in work and travel).

After our supper, Andro showed us to our room upstairs: a surprisingly large chamber with painted cloths adorning the walls and, bizarrely, a billiard table strewn with musical instruments lying next to a flock bed on a rope frame. 'You'll have a fine sleep here. Make sure the windows are right well shuttered if you care to make music, though, will ye?'

'I thought your church would have banned music,' said Lockhart, stepping around the table and making directly for the bed.

'Ha! And you'd be right, more or less. Yet every other house in Scotland has its music and dance. Only behind locked doors and shuttered windows these days. Well, you must have seen how it is out there, the Kirk's godly men on the peep for any naughtiness. It's getting so a man can't tumble an honest whore for fear his neighbour'll brabble to the preacher. But the gospel-spouts can't see what we get up to behind our own doors.' He tapped the thick wood. 'Not yet, anyway. There's nothing so sweet as a forbidden pleasure, don't you know.'

I ran a hand over the lawn surface of the billiard table whilst Lockhart began tightening the ropes on the bedframe. 'Oh, I know. Thank you, Andro,' I said. 'It was good fortune we met you, to be sure.'

'Call it what you will,' he said, hooking his thumbs into his belt. 'No fortune. There's no better place to get the old girl downstairs custom than the city wall.'

'You're a shrewd one,' Lockhart called up from the floor. 'I misjudged you.'

Andro shrugged. 'Judgment's an odd thing, I reckon. Now, see, I'd not have taken either of you for players' men.' He tilted his head up to look at me. Lockhart and I had both stopped what we were doing and exchanged glances. 'No, no, I'd have taken you for English gentlemen at a glance. English gentlemen on a wee turn of business, I'd reckon. And I'm seldom wrong.'

I sighed. We were, after all, in the city to gather information. It seemed unlikely that a dwarf who was reduced to touting for custom on a city wall was in league with anyone dangerous. 'In truth,' I said, 'we have come to see the king.'

Andro registered no surprise. 'You'd not be the first. Your queen dead then, is she?'

'No, her Majesty is not,' said Lockhart, getting off his knees and gingerly sitting on the bed, his chin rising.

'Ah. King James will be right sore to hear that. Reckon he'll not have a merrier day in his life than when he's told "Elizabeth is dead, and James owns England".'

'King James,' I echoed, 'might also be sore to hear about the rumours in London.' Andro raised an eyebrow. 'Some tales about a document taken from Scotland that will prevent him from ever wearing England's crown.' I watched Andro Allardyce carefully. His face betrayed no hint of surprise. A slight quiver at the corner of his mouth might even have suggested amusement. 'You wouldn't have heard anything about that, would you?'

Andro took a deep breath, before turning away from us and closing the door firmly behind him. 'Who in Edinburgh hasn't heard tales about that?'

Excitement threatened, and I took a few slow breaths. There is an art to extracting information, especially when it is dangerous. Be too forceful, push too hard, and you might frighten people into sealing their lips. 'We are here only to learn the truth about this document,' I said, forcing a yawn. 'Queen Elizabeth and her government would like to know that her heir is fit to sit on her throne.'

'I'll bet she would.'

'Can you tell us what you know of it?'

'Where is it?' asked Lockhart, jumping from the bed.

'It's in London, of course,' I said, balling my fists. 'As far as we know. We are not charged with finding where it is but where it came from.'

'And what it says, I'd wager,' said Andro.

'You know?' asked Lockhart. 'You know its contents?'

Andro didn't answer. Instead, he skirted the table and bent over the small grate, tutting until a fire caught. As cheerful light burst across the chamber, he turned and tugged at the mattress. Lockhart stood, and the little man began arranging the bed stuff around the floor so that we might all have a seat. As soon as we were comfortable, he produced a pipe and made a show of filling and lighting it, blowing smoke up to the ceiling before passing it to me. I took it; I was not averse to tobacco, and it was surprisingly good stuff. 'Another thing the Kirk doesn't like,' he said. 'Nor the king either. But by God, I do like a puff.'

I let the smoke trickle out of my nostrils. 'We'll pay you, of course,' I said. Clenching the stem between my teeth, I produced another few coins and passed them over. 'Now, tell us what you know, my friend.' I passed the pipe to Lockhart as Andro stretched and settled onto his mattress. When we were sprawled out like eastern princes, enjoying our tobacco and cushioned floor, he took up his tale.

'I've been my whole life in this burgh. Heard it all. Heard all about the king's mother and father, about what beautiful folk they were. Beautiful, so the story goes, but without too much wit to burden them. The father, anyway. Well, you must ken that the old Queen Mary ran off to England and died the death at your queen's hands.' A little edge of accusation coloured the last. 'So King James, whom you say you'll be meeting, was a cradle king, more or less. Raised to reign from before he could wipe his own arse. And there have ay been tales told of him.'

'What tales?' asked Lockhart.

'Ugh, the usual. He's mad, he's bad, he's a bastard, he's a sodomite, he's a drunkard. And the latest I've heard – that as a bairn he did something very abominable and wicked and sought to bury the truth of it deep within a castle where even God couldnae find it.'

Keeping my tone light, I asked, 'is any of this proven by this document? Or are these fantasies?'

'Can I tell my tale without interruption?' Andro reached out for the pipe. Lockhart took one quick draw before letting him have it. Neither of us spoke. 'Where was I? Aye, the king became king when he was a babe in arms. Not his mammy's arms, though – she was fled. And not his da's arms – he was dead. No, the wee kinglet was raised at Stirling by the earl of Mar. And that good old man, he became our regent. Until he died after supping with the wicked earl of Morton.' I listened but could see nothing useful in the history lesson. Until Andro's next words.

'Now Morton, he was a right bastard, you know? A cunning man, but nasty with it. Now it's said that he made it his business to learn things about the king – about the whole royal family – when he got wee King James in his clutches. And he kept all the proof of his findings in a secret leathern pouch. Not unlike the secret casket he found that had lodged in it all he needed to destroy Queen Mary. As I said: a right bastard.

'Morton, he must have thought he was set up for his lifetime, I reckon. He was the regent of Scotland. He had the young king in his power. And he had a document hidden safe in a pouch that could destroy the Stuarts. A mighty thing to hold over a king, I reckon. Everyone knew what he was about, but when Morton ruled Scotland, so my auntie tells me – I was a babe myself, mind – people whispered about what he might know, about what he might do – but they held their wheeshes. But then it all went a wee thing sour for the old pig. He was forced out of power, and that pouch with its naughty document disappeared. The king, I reckon, would have been about ten or eleven.'

'And then where did it go?' pressed Lockhart, snatching the pipe. Before he could use it, I tore it from him and puffed life back into it, nodding apology to Andro.

'Well, there were fights, struggles. No one knows. Not for a while anyway. But Morton didn't get it back. After the boy king had announced himself fit to rule by himself, he sent his old captor and regent straight to hell. Lost his head on the maiden, so he did. Snip.' He drew a hand across his throat.

'So King James found the pouch,' I said, more to myself than to Andro.

'Not so, no, no, no. Scotland had its own king in sole charge, more or less. But I reckon the boy didn't find that pouch amongst Morton's things. It next turned up in the care of the earl of Gowrie.'

'Who?' asked Lockhart.

Ignoring him, Andro went on, 'that good earl had also in his possession the casket letters of the king's mother, and it's said he collected a right good library of stuff that would damage his sovereign. What we call in Scotland the blackmail. Tried to make use of it too, by kidnapping him back in … let me see … '84. Yet he failed. And he went to the block. Snip.

'And before you ask, no – the pouch still didn't fall into the king's hands. Not for want of trying, right enough. That mysterious document remained, so they say, in the possession of Gowrie's sons.'

Something chimed in the recesses of my mind. 'Gowrie,' I said.

'You've heard of what happened?' I shook my head. 'Well it seems that King James sweated like a blacksmith's arse crack awhile after Gowrie lost his head. He knew the rumours, like we all did, of a secret letter or paper that would ruin him – one that had been floating around Scotland in its leathern pouch since Morton's day. He had hacked at noble necks for it and it continued to hide from him. By Christ, he must have lived – still live – all a-tremble. So, a couple or three years ago, he visited with Gowrie's sons. A strange affair, that was.'

I took up the story, the memory of it going around the London taverns suddenly flowering. 'I remember. King James went to Gowrie house and spent time alone with the dead earl's two sons. And suddenly he cried treason, and his men rushed into the place and killed them both.' It had been quite a scandal. The popular gloss had been that James had thrust his hand into the handsome young earl's codpiece and, on being rebuffed, had had the man and his brother swiftly silenced.

'That's just so. The king said he'd been lured there with a promise of hidden treasure. After being closeted with the new earl awhile, he cried murder, and the earl and his brother were slain. Not so much a snip as a fury of stabbing that time. Yet it's said that another man was in the room too. Someone was named – a man called Henderson – but no one truly believes it was he.'

I pictured the man in the Mitre. Sir David Henderson, he had called himself. Whether he was the same one who had been in Gowrie house that bloody day or was simply an opportunist retainer of the slain earl, one who had borrowed the name to aid him in selling the document south, hardly mattered. He now had a connection to a noble house: Gowrie.

'What happened to the pouch, then? The document? King James got it?' Lockhart looked puzzled. Smoking had brought colour into his face.

'No one knows. The story runs that the king was cheated of it. All he found were his mother's hoary old casket letters – the ones that condemned her. Forgeries and fiddle-faddle, all of them, and probably went straight into the fire. But they were not what he sought. The paper spelling out the wicked and black secret of his youth was. So that's four men he had had killed all to procure this bloody document, and he never did get his hands on it. Five if you count ... Did you note the body of Francis Mowbray, hung up on the Netherbow Port?'

'The what?' asked Lockhart.

'I did,' I said.

'Mowbray was sent up from London a prisoner only a month or two back. By your queen's secretary, Cecil.' A shiver ran through me. 'It's said he'd been intriguing there against the king and Cecil beat what he could out of him then sent him back here. He was locked up in the castle. Escaped, so he did, but fell and managed to break his neck. If you can believe that.' Again, Andro drew a hand across his throat. 'Crack. It's said he knew something about where this document was headed. And that's been the rumour up here, anyway. Behind every door in this town and the next I reckon folk are clappering their tongues about the king's black secret. That it went by some hand or other to London, to be sold to his enemies.'

'Cecil,' I breathed, my mind still on the blackened hand.

'As eager to get his hands on it as King James, I'd bet. It's said up here that Robert Cecil is everything in England. Rules the queen like a man might have rule of a doting father.' I said nothing, disliking that comparison. Yet I wondered what lengths Cecil and the king of Scots might go to yet to secure ownership of the thing. If Elizabeth was dying, there was little time to lose. If the red cross plotters produced it as the proclamation of James's succession was read out, there would be rioting. Sudden fear came over me that that might happen whilst I was out of the country, my stuff unprotected, Faith alone. 'Aye, if you ask me, it went to London with some flea-bitten servant of the Gowries. That's the rumour, since thon creepit corpse Mowbray's dying breath blew life into the old tales. And so, for every man the king has killed for it, it's managed to slip right through the royal fingers every time. And now every Englishman wants to know the truth of a tale our king would have none know. I warn you lads, though, if it's true you're bent on meeting our king … well, that's the manner of man he is. He'll kill anyone who threatens his royal estate. I would bet that he'll see you, right enough.'

'I'll take that bet,' said Lockhart. 'A shilling?'

Andro narrowed his eyes. 'Whit?'

'Ignore him,' I sighed.

'Anyway,' said our host turning his look of bemusement from Lockhart, 'that's all I know.'

'You haven't,' said Lockhart, 'told us what's in it.'

'Now that I daren't say.'

'You mean you don't know,' I said.

'Only those who have read it know for sure. And,' he added, putting his knuckles to the floor and easing himself up with a grunt, 'as it's meant death to every man who did know, I'd as soon not, thank you very much. My pipe, please.'

Andro made to leave the room, pausing in the doorway. 'Rest easy, lads. I'm sure as soon as the king hears where you've come from, he'll be eager to welcome you to Scotland properly.'

'Good day to yo–'

'Just one thing,' I called, cutting Lockhart off. 'I only wondered … do you wish your king to succeed to Queen Elizabeth's throne?'

'Me?' Andro gave a smirk. 'What do I care?' He scratched at his square chin. 'Can't say that I've a care either way, I don't reckon. No, I don't mind if he goes – but only if he promises to take the Kirk's ministers with him. He won't, right enough. Be glad to see the back of them.'

'A fair point.' I had not before considered whether the Scottish people might wish to retain their king, by fair means or foul. Perhaps some of them would be willing to pay a higher price to cut off James' path to England than any English heir might. Yet that depended on whether the document destroyed his English dreams alone, or knocked him off both British thrones. I bit at my lip. 'Good day, Andro Allardyce.'

The door banged shut behind him.

Immediately, Lockhart began talking. 'Not a bad mind for a misshapen half-man, that one! Christ, but I do wish he had left us that pipe. Just like a Scot to be mean. What a bloody tale, fit for the stage.' I barely heard him, preferring to nod only when it seemed appropriate. In my head, I was tracing the journey of this paper, from hand to hand, inside its battered leather pouch, from Scotland to England, from a man in the tavern to the red cross brutes and whoever led them. We knew now where it had come from; we knew, or thought we knew, where it had gone and by what means; but we did not know its contents nor how to come by it without its being made public. If the thing had been around since the Regent Morton's time, it must pertain to something the king had done in his youth.

Better than nothing. But not by much.

And there was something else. Something Andro had said, something that hinted at danger, danced around just out of reach of my racing thoughts. 'We'll go to the king tomorrow, I said,' cutting Lockhart off. 'It's getting dark. I'd have some sleep.'

'Sleep! Are you ill? Should we not wait until full dark and then … and then break into somewhere – the castle or somewhere – and find news?' He stood, putting one hand on his hip. 'In disguise, perhaps, as servants?'

'I think not. Is it not enough that we see a king tomorrow?'

'Tsk.' His arm relaxed. 'I suppose. Yes. We will mine a king's secrets. Uh … do you wish to take the bed?'

'I thought we'd share it.'

'Is it not … is it not somewhat small?'

'Suit yourself,' I snapped. 'Take the floor.'

I slid between two padded mattresses, pulling the uppermost directly over my head – the better to drown out Lockhart's by-rote prayers. Sleep did not come easily at first. My mind's eye kept conjuring a blackened first; a blackened arm; the sharpened point of a hook slicing through dead flesh. Eventually the images faded and I passed out into a sweet and dreamless void. Likely I would not have done had I known that we had been spotted coming into Edinburgh and would not spend another peaceful night there.

And now every Englishman wants to know the truth of a tale our king would have none know.

Every Englishman.

16

Early the next morning, we scrubbed at our hands and feet, combed our hair, and dressed ourselves in our remaining clean underwear and the best of our clothing. On went my court clothes, and Lockhart brushed down his sable until it shone. I talked him out of dragging us to a barber, arguing that it was a courtly enough thing for men to be bearded. We ate a light breakfast of unsweetened pancakes provided by Andro's Auntie Peg – the little man himself was nowhere to be seen, and our hostess offered us no explanation – and decided to put matters off no longer.

It was time to meet the man who had executed a regent, an earl, and cried out for the sudden and secret murder of two sprigs of that earl's noble house. It was easy enough, I thought, to believe that such a king might have had black secrets.

The palace of Holyroodhouse was a small but rather elegant affair, more sedate than the gaudy new buildings going up in London yet easier on the eyes than the rambling piles of Whitehall. The sentry at the gate had given us no trouble; indeed, he had flushed with excitement when he heard that we were English. Only when he had ascertained that no, we did not carry urgent news out of London, did he seem to deflate. Thereafter he lapsed into business, alerting what he called 'the big hoose' to our presence. He led us then across the wide, open courtyard, towards the building – a stone facade with a pair of towers on the left-hand side. The double entrance doors stood in the main block which stretched off to the right.

Inside, we were compelled to wait on a wooden bench whilst, I assumed, further discussions were had about us. The entrance hall of the palace was narrow – so narrow, in fact, that I supposed it must front an internal courtyard. The arrases and tapestries on the walls, however, were as good as any I had seen in Cecil's house. Glittering wall sconces made up for the small windows, illuminating the sparkling gold and silver thread of the arrases. What was most noticeable, though, was the noise. Unlike in the silent town, the palace servants went about their business singing, humming, drumming their fingers. All who passed gave us neat little bows and curtsies, doffing their caps and smiling.

'A cheerful place,' whispered Lockhart. I nodded, leaning back on the bench until my back rested on a wall hanging.

Eventually, a steward emerged from the direction of the towers, a stout, red-faced man of middle age at his back. The steward inclined his head towards us and then backed against the far wall, melting into insignificance before his superior. 'The gentlemen who are come fae – from the Queen of England's Revels Master?' He spoke slowly, deliberately. On seeing his approach, Lockhart and I had sprung to our feet, and we made low bows, removing our hats. Glancing up, I saw the fellow's smug grin as I did so. A man not entirely used to polished manners, I thought. 'It's welcome you are to the royal court of Scotland. And pleased we are to have you in our service. My men telt – told – me that a party had arrived in the city some days since. We have waited your coming yet awhile. You are only two?' I began to speak, but he snapped his fingers at the usher, who began leading us off in the direction from which they'd come – straight into the tower rooms. Over his shoulder, the superior said, 'his Majesty can spare you a wee bit of time. He wishes to hunt before dinner.'

We were halted first in a square chamber, in which a group of men were throwing dice at a table, laughing and cursing in incomprehensible Scots. All were booted and spurred to ride, and I judged them the king's hunting companions. Carved wooden chairs lined the walls, which were as richly decorated as those in the entrance hall. Seeing our party, one of them called out, 'ho, Bruce, ye were a muckle while gone there.' It drew laughter. Our noble – for I assumed he was noble – leader turned to us, his face redder and nostrils flaring. 'I am Lord Kinloss.'

'Now ye are,' cried one of the gamblers. 'M'*lord*.'

There was a pause in our conversation as we were searched for weapons by one of the men, who, patting us down, found nothing. Even our hats were removed and felt, inside and out.

'Have either of you gentlemen paid court in France?' asked Kinloss. We shook our heads. Lockhart mirrored my look of bafflement. 'King James favours the court manners of France. We're a right open and free court. As these loons will attest. Yet only we of the noble blood have free attendance, yea, and into the king's very bedchamber. As is the court in France.'

'And welcome to it, so ye are,' shouted the mouthier gamester.

Without knocking, the usher opened the door into a larger room painted in blue and gold, with hunting scenes covering every available surface. The air smelt heavy: unwashed clothing was being combatted by burning herbs from a large fireplace. It was, from what I could see, an audience chamber – the type of royal room in which courtiers of sufficient rank might linger awaiting the king's appearance. As if proof were needed, a gaggle of men better dressed than the gambling gamesters stood in tight knots, their arms folded. The nobility of Scotland, it seemed, were a different beast from the swaggering peacocks of England. Rather than bedecking themselves in all the colours of the rainbow picked out in thin, gauzy satins and silks, these fellows displayed their wealth in deep blacks and heavy crimsons. The ruffs at their throats were smaller and flatter, crushed almost by the rich, elegant furs that circled their throats and cuffs. It was, I thought, a different kind of nobility.

The usher stood back whilst the nobleman turned left, making directly for a small door. He opened it without a word and stepped inside, looking over a furred shoulder laced with silver thread to cry out, 'Revels Men, come. His Majesty is at home to you.'

We passed from the blue room into one whose main feature was an enormous tester bed. We were, I judged, within the confines of the tower itself. If you have never been in a king's rooms, I will share with you how they differ from those in which the rest of us live. It is in the fineness of detail, the sharpness of every fitting, hanging, and carving. Gold glints from every roundel and ridge; dull edges and corners are moulded with exquisite precision, as though tiny master craftsmen had set to work. Hunger burned within me: to touch, to treasure, to take.

Our hats were off again, though I noticed Kinloss's remained firmly on his head.

'Is this thaim?' The voice was petulant, thin, and reedy.

'Aye, your Majesty.'

'Good man, Edward.' Kinloss cleared his throat. I kept my eyes on the floor and could sense Lockhart doing the same. The king laughed – a brittle, nasty sound. 'Oh, we do forget, don't we? Forgive us. And you forgive us, gentlemen. We did *forget* that we have only recently made a lord of auld Sir Edward here, for the manifold services he has done us. Get out.'

My head shot up.

'Get out, Kinloss. We will speak to our sister of England's subjects alone. *Out*! And steek the door man; see that it is chekit to. We would no' have busy ears burning at it, heh?'

Kinloss backed from the room, bowing at the waist.

'There, we are better rid of thon auld gowk.' He shouted the words at the closed door, presumably hoping his ennobled servant would hear him. 'Step forward, laddies,' said King James, patting his thighs through a pair of padded breeches. 'We heard there were Englishmen come to our realm. We have awaited you some days. Come, let us have a look at you.'

We did, each sliding down to one knee. A little pride, it is true, burrowed into my sinews as I dipped. Whatever my oafish and proud brother or my scatter-witted father or even my dead mother thought of me, there I was: being received by a king in his bedchamber in a princely palace. But … what a king. As James studied us, his eyes, I thought, lingering on me longer than Lockhart, I studied him.

He sat on a carved and gilded chair by the bed. His clothing was plain but of excellent quality, silvery white in colour; his small selection of jewellery was well placed about his person, with a brooch at his breast, one ring per hand, and a cameo pinned to his hat. The problem was that the clothing all seemed ill-fitting. He was, to be plain, wearing the clothes of a fat man, when his stockinged legs were thin and the neck and head that emerged from the ballooning doublet were likewise as scrawny as a half-drowned chicken's. He peered at us from sad eyes set in a sad face, a lizard tongue occasionally darting out to moisten fleshy lips. His nose was rounded at the tip and flecked with broken veins. A drinker, I thought. The firelight, usually so forgiving, picked out overfilled coin purses bulging below eyes that shared the heavy lids of his cousin Elizabeth.

I thought too, though you might think me hard, that he was unattractive without being offensively ugly and ill-proportioned. It was said by all, as Andro had noted, that the king's mother had been the most beautiful princess in Europe, the famous Mary Queen of Scots whom even Elizabeth envied. The father had been a wastrel and a nincompoop, but he had had the good grace to be a pretty one. It was an unfortunate corruption of nature that two such paragons should have created such a plain and worn-out looking fellow. Some crueller wits said that virgins like Queen Elizabeth were fated to lead apes in hell after death. It would be a sad day for England when it found itself losing a queen and led by a dressed ape.

'I see you see fit to call upon me after ten?' He asked. The reedy, mocking whine he had used in Kinloss's presence was gone, replaced with a softer voice. 'One of you speak to us. You.' He clicked the fingers of his left hand at me.

'10 has sent us,' I said, taking the hint.

'Your mistress lives yet, I hear.'

'She does, your Majesty.'

King James took a long, deep breath. 'Then why are you come?'

I swallowed. 'Her Majesty is dying.'

'We have heard that before. Ken she will gang as long as sun or moon. We hear, indeed, that she takes to her bed. That she is cured of her love of grand robes and gowns. That they weigh heavily on her bent back.' I slid a glance over to Lockhart but said nothing, suspecting that the king had yet more to say. He began fussing at his shirtfront, his lips pursing. 'It is our belief that only weak sovereigns must trick the eye of the common people with vulgar display. We true, true kings shun such trashes.' His head flicked up. 'Well?'

'Sir – 10 sends us with words for only your ears. Regarding … a certain document that was stolen out of Scotland.' I waited, unsure of how he might react. I suppose I expected anger, denials.

'False and seditious, slanderous goddamned thing.' Greyness suddenly mottled his face. 'Does your master have it?'

'He is even now hunting it, your Majesty.'

'Then he does not.' James banged a fist on the arm of his chair. 'Must I be plagued by these lies and imputations all my life? Christ, give me a drink!' I rose from my knee, twisting my head towards Lockhart in confusion. We both froze as a lad of about fifteen in a livery appeared from around the other side of the bed and hurried towards the king, a silver jug in one hand and goblet in the other. He poured and proffered the goblet, which James took and drained. That done, he passed it back to the servant, who returned to his hiding place down the side of the royal bed.

James sucked in his cheeks, and again licked his lips. 'You,' he said. 'Come closer, that I might see you better.' I slid across the carpet, my soft court shoes sinking. 'Closer.' I was on my knees before him. A sour smell wafted towards me. Old soap. His right hand flew out, making me jump as it grasped me under the chin and tilted my face upwards. 'You have an evil mind,' he said.

'Your Majesty?'

He squeezed once, hard, before releasing me. The needlepoints of my beard stabbed at my crushed cheeks and I fought the urge to rub them. On my knees, I backed away a few steps. King James jerked his head towards the bed. 'You think that because I have faithful friends still in their first flush of youth that the king of Scots is a Zeus playing upon his Ganymede, do you? His minions, heh?'

'I thought no such thing.'

'And you – the lang ane.' He jabbed a finger at Lockhart. 'What do you think?'

'I … d-d … umm … your Majest-tes … umm.'

My heart broke for Lockhart. A failure in debates at his Inn and a failure as a public speaker before the king. I could almost feel the heat rising in waves from him.

'Pah! Thick tongue chekit your chops, lang ane?' James threw his own head back and laughed the shrill laugh he had directed at Kinloss, banging the chair arm once more.

Then Lockhart made a foolish error. He joined in the king's laughter, offering a nervous giggle. Abruptly James stopped, as though his throat had been cut. 'Is your sovereign lady's sickness then a matter fit for laughter, lang ane?'

Lockhart turned white and began stuttering. 'N-no-n-no, I–'

'No? Then it is apparent you have no love of laughter. Nor thanks that your wearied realm, your neglected nobility, will soon be tended by such a physician as we are.'

Defeated, utterly lost, Lockhart closed his mouth, evidently aware that he could not say the right thing. It was apparent that King James enjoyed making others uncomfortable – enjoyed the sense of power over them that it gave him knowing that lowly mortals, which for a king meant nearly all mortals, could not argue back. I suspected that the wine he had just swallowed was not his first of the day. 'We are a good father to all our subjects and the youngest need the most direction. And affection. It disgusts us and saddens us that men will read evil when we mean only good. That they will read a twisting of nature when we mean only the friendship demanded by the Bible.' He tutted. 'This world is a twisted and disgusting place, peopled by twisted and disgusting creatures wi' twisted and disgusting minds. Such foul slanders and glosses are poured into every man's ear, and so often that they are falsely gilded with truth.' He bowed his head, lowering it into his hands. 'Is your master truly a friend to me?' He asked at last, the serious, solemn voice returning.

'Yes, your Majesty.' I fought to keep the dislike out of my voice.

'Then we are sorry, yes, sorry, that we have treated you thus. Do you hear me, boy? You have the solemn apology of a prince of Christendom.'

'I thank your Majesty.'

'Aye. Aye. Is this all you have come for? To tell me that this damned paper is lost in England but will be found?'

'My master asks only that I assure you that … the queen will be dead within weeks, sir. And you are the true and rightful heir.' I had likely gone beyond my commission. Something about the man inspired sympathy as well as disgust. 'Even now a route is being secured between here and London, that your Majesty will be the first to know when you are proclaimed England's sovereign.'

'When I am proclaimed sovereign over this whole isle of Great Britain,' he said, looking up and flitting his gaze between Lockhart and me. 'For we are of one language, are we not?' He spoke slowly, as if to emphasise his point. I thought of his earlier words – steek and chekit – and wrestled down the urge to laugh in his face. 'One island knit in perfect harmony, to be ruled by us. God's will. Peace within a British realm. Peace with all the nations of the world. An end to wars.' Coloured silks tangled in my mind with warm furs; fortified manor houses turned granite faces towards pretty pleasure palaces; literary wits like Ben Jonson raised meaty fists against the bellowing cries of Presbyterian preachers. 'So it will be, howsoever the rabble grumble.' He tutted. 'You give the common man year upon year of peace, of wisdom and stable rule, and you get naught but contempt and slander. My cousin Elizabeth – if she is dying at last – has she named me her heir as God's law and man's demand she should?'

'I cannot … I do not know, sir. Yet my master, he–'

'My master,' he mimicked, clearly reading the doubt on my face, in my voice. 'If he can do as he promises he will be rewarded, aye, and more richly than he receives by the hand of his present mistress, my good and honourable cousin.' James's face twisted into a mask of loathing. His voice dropped so that I had to strain to hear it. 'Dead at last. Your sovereign lady, gentlemen, is a cunt.'

I looked up, my eyes wide and my mouth falling open. At my side, I could just see Lockhart's hand slide to his belt, where normally a sword might hang. I looked directly at King James and could barely read the expression on his face. Anger, perhaps, as decades of caged frustration suddenly burst forth. But something else was there. Excitement, I thought – excitement at the shock he could cause and the knowledge that he might cause it without consequence. For when would either of us dare to repeat those words to anyone? Even thinking them was dangerous. 'Elizabeth is dying, and James will own England' might well have blazed forth from those spaniel eyes.

I had heard it said that the queen had always refused to name her successor for fear that the common people would turn their eyes towards the future, leaving her in the past. King James had afforded me the rare privilege – or horror – of seeing what being the rising sun looked like to the successor. It looked like excitement at the prospect of death and hatred of those who took too long about it.

To distract the king from Lockhart's stiff back, I offered him a man-to-man smirk, judging it best fitted to indulge him.

He merely waggled his fingers in response.

Tired of us. Wishes to go out and play with more sporting prey.

'Get out. Both of you. *Out*. Return to your master and pray that he finds that cursed slander and burns it. For if he does not, this whole island will sink in blood and fire.'

***

'England is cursed,' said Lockhart. He was walking in circles around the billiard table in our lodging house. After leaving Holyroodhouse, we had walked on jellied legs about the Canongate, drinking wherever we could purchase wine. Neither of us were drunk on it. Shock and disgust had been driven in too deeply. 'What hope for our nation, if it is to be that … that *knave* who rules us?'

'He has a son,' I offered, 'that might well be raised a good Englishman.'

'And if not him, who – that crazed wench we saw in Derbyshire?' He had ignored me entirely, and so I lapsed into silence and let him rave. There was something in the character of so many English gentlemen, I knew, that encouraged them to tiresome displays of honour whenever they felt themselves or their rulers debased by a foreigner. I was almost sorry to see Kit Lockhart revert to the form. 'England ruled by a man who uses such language of our queen that would get him hanged for a traitor at Tyburn.' He mimicked James' accent. 'My good and honourable cousin. And then … *that*.'

'Aye,' I said. 'He's double-tongued alright. He had better watch or it'll grow too big for his mouth.'

'Ha! Well you can be sure that I shall tell any man who asks that the Scottish king has a monstrous tongue. Too big and too doubled and forked like a snake. By God, no Englishman will bear his rule.'

'Be careful,' I said. Then a little more loudly, 'be careful, Lockhart, and hold your tongue. What, are you turned republican now? Would you fancy the people choose their king rather than God in His wisdom and through His law?' I cocked an eyebrow at him. He stopped mid step and leant over the billiard table, hands whitening as he gripped the edges.

'Me? No, I … of course not – it is only that I …'

'We are subjects ' I sighed. 'You have guessed who our master is, I take it?'

'Cecil. I bet you it was Cecil and I was right, by God. Still, whoever stands behind that man … even a king cannot just say or do whatever he likes.'

'Well,' I shrugged. 'Maybe that king thinks he can.'

'Pshhh. And the master secretary, does he know this? Surely … surely Sir Robert Cecil of all men living cannot know *that* man's nature.'

'Sir Robert Cecil knows everything. He knows that King James is next in line to England's throne and if we think anything otherwise then … then we're akin to the red cross men who stir up trouble. Who set their faces against England's own government.'

He banged the table. 'So that is it, is it? We accept either the rule of a vile-tongued buffoon or we are ourselves traitors to the crown?' One of his fingers went up in the air. 'An abyss in front, and wolves behind. When someone is hard pressed on both sides by two great evils, so that whichever he falls into, he is bound to be lost.'

'And I thought you never listened in lectures.' Lockhart looked at me, the seconds crawling by. And then his laughter burst forth – hearty, rich, and needed after the tension of the day. I joined him. When we had recovered, I said, 'well, Erasmus knew politics. And that is politics. You and I, we're not supposed to like or hate it. We just have to be on the side that wins. So, sometimes we find ourselves on a side led by a mule in a stuffed doublet. Better that than be on the side of bloody malcontents out to stir up hatred and violence.'

'The lesser of two evils, indeed.' Lockhart finally slipped out of his sable cloak. 'I see how the land lies.'

'I don't think that king is evil,' I said. 'Just … unpleasant. Not, as they might say, a man who is good with people.'

'Then it is a damned shame that he is set to be given hundreds of thousands more of them. I thought…' He trailed off and I raised my eyebrows. He did not meet my gaze, suddenly finding something interesting in the dust caught between the flagstones. 'I thought,' he said, worrying at it with the tip of his shoe, 'there was something womanish in his manner. In his voice. Didn't you?'

I felt my stomach lighten, something within fluttering for release. 'No.'

'Perhaps not. Only I shrink from the thought of being touched by him as you were.'

I shrugged. 'Forget about him. Like I said, he has a son. He will know soon enough what Queen Elizabeth has known all her life. That England looks towards the future, not the past. Christ, I've never known any king of England who came to the throne to find his people already looking over his shoulder at the next in line. Is it any wonder he's such a sour apple? At worst he and Cecil will bring us a few years of dull rule whilst his young princeling is reared up to take his place. Besides, I thought you were tired of an old woman's governance.'

'I … well … it is one thing to be eager to see the old dame pass the crown to someone. It is another to see her called such vile names.'

'I heard her called worse in London when there was nothing to eat a few years back, whilst the royal court feasted on cartloads of – what's that?'

'Hm? What is what?'

A heavy, clunking tread. Downstairs.

'New guests? Unless Mr Andro Allardyce has grown apace today. Is there any wine left in that–' I silenced Lockhart with a hand, and crept across the room, past the billiard table to the door. Opening it, I tilted my head out.

Voices. Muffled. But English. Punctuated occasionally by the higher pitch of Andro's lyrically accented English. I stepped out. The narrow hall outside led directly to curving, steep stone steps. I descended a few, my eyes adjusting to the dimness. The meagre light rising from downstairs was blotted suddenly by greater gloom. A man, thickset, lurched onto the staircase. In a second, I registered the drawn dagger in his hand. Another followed behind him.

Every Englishman wants to know the truth…

A party had arrived in the city some days since…

'Andro, you little shit,' I cried over the men's heads as I backed up. 'What have you done?'

His voice drifted up. 'Call me a misshapen half-man!? May hell mend ye both, pair o' piss squeaks, ye!'

17

I slammed the door shut and put my back to it, my heart beginning a wild, haphazard drumbeat. 'What is it?' I ignored Lockhart's question, throwing myself towards the billiard table and gripping it. No good. I swung around the side and began pushing the thing.

'Help me!'

Lockhart did, and we got the thing across the floor, upending it against the door even as it began to screech inwards. Musical instruments and the heavy billiard maces clattered. 'Who are they? What is it?'

'We're betrayed,' I said, my eyes scanning the room. One window, set deep in the wall, not big enough even for a child to escape. Fire grate too small. We would have to fight our way out. 'That little bastard Andro. Sold us to two men, two at least, that have a hard-shaft for killing us.'

Colour drained from Lockhart's face. His eyes looked huge. 'Oh, dear God. The window, we must flee!'

Bump. Bang. Bump. The sideways table wobbled but didn't give. Yet.

'We must fight.'

'Fight! I have no sword.'

Nor did I. Both of us carried only the smallest poniards for protection on the road. 'We don't have to fight as gentleman,' I said.

'Oh God, Savage. Oh God. There is no escape. Do not let them kill us!'

Coward, I thought. What did he think that service to the state was? I did not answer him. Instead, my eyes rolled around the room. A plan formed – or half formed. 'Your dagger,' I hissed. 'And take up the poker.'

Lockhart half tripped across the room, pulling his dagger from his pack. Then he jerked the poker up in a flurry of ashes. As he did so, I pulled down one of the painted cloths, its painted unicorns and does turning their dull eyes on me. I stationed myself at one side of the door, which opened inward an inch, its barrier sliding across the flagstones. Lockhart stood irresolute, his face blanched. I pointed at the other side of the door and he made for it.

Taking two edges of the thick cloth, I shook it out and threw the other end towards Lockhart. He took my meaning, dropping the poker, putting his dagger into his belt, and taking the other ends. We pulled it taut between us and raised it over our heads. It formed a canopy just over the doorframe, higher on his side.

'On three, we kick away the table.' My voice was barely above a whisper. Outside, I could hear a murmured conference. The banging had ceased. They were, I suspected, preparing for a combined assault. Lockhart nodded slightly and I counted in heavier ones.

As one, we booted the billiard table into the room. It landed with a protesting thud. At the same time, the door flew open, the canopy above us wobbling as it nearly hit Lockhart. He managed to recover, keeping it stretched tight. Into the room flew a barrage of darkness. 'Now!'

We brought down the heavy cloth. The descent stopped and startled the two men, who were barred already by the table. They collapsed to the floor and I leapt onto the back of the one in the lead – transformed now into a writhing mass of cloth.

'Get the other–'

'Arghhhh!'

I looked up to see Lockhart, his dagger in one hand and the poker in the other, stabbing wildly into the cloth. Terror was etched in the wideness of his eyes and the round O of his mouth. Muffled grunts of pain rumbled from beneath the cloth as he murdered one of our assailants.

'Lockhart,' I cried, bucking as my own captive tried to roll. 'Lockhart! Kit! Stop! Be calm! Stop!'

He had thrown away the poker and was stabbing through the cloth like a man possessed, mewling. The cries from beneath him ceased and so did he. He held the bloody dagger in the air. His hand, I noticed, was shaking; he was shaking all over. 'I did it,' he said, as though in disbelief. 'I did it, Savage, I killed him! Killed him like Hamlet!'

Tightening my thighs to stop my own prisoner from moving, I said nothing. The fool had deprived us of someone who might be made to talk. But it was no time for censure.

Certain that my weight pinned down my own man's arms, I pulled back the painted cloth to reveal his head. It was facing the ground and a small pool of blood had formed from, I assumed, a burst nose.

'Who do you work with?' I asked, only then pulling out my own dagger. There was no response.

'Kill him!' shouted Lockhart.

'Be quiet!' I took the man's lank, greasy hair in my fingers and banged his face on the stone. Then, keeping his body tight under the cloth, I rolled him over.

He was young, I thought, but hardened. I repeated my question.

'Fuck you,' he choked.

'I think not. Let's try another question. Why have you followed us here? Why are you in Edinburgh?' The lad tried to spit but failed. 'Your friend is dead. You'll join him if you don't tell us.'

'Ford … Ford'll get ya.'

I looked at Lockhart in confusion, before remembering the name. '*Peter* Ford?'

'Even if you've given it to the Scotch king, Ford'll get it back.'

'Given it …' My eyes widened. 'You …'

'Given what?' asked Lockhart. I shook my head at him, trying to think. 'You were in Scotland trying to sell the document to King James's Scotch enemies, were you not, you wretched common dog!?'

'Wha'?' asked the man on the floor.

'Quiet, both of you.' I banged the fellow's head on the floor again. 'We … we … you,' I said, looking down, my hair falling over my face, 'you think that we have this goddamned paper? That's what you think, you and your fucking red cross friends?'

The lad looked at me in dull, uncomprehending confusion. I threw my head back and laughed. 'For Christ's sake, Lockhart – we thought they had it. And they thought we had it. We've been chasing each other a merry dance. They've not been trying to sell it – they've been trying to find it.'

'What?' Lockhart was on his knees, wiping bloody hands on the edge of the cloth. I repeated myself. 'So … these men do not even have the thing? Then where is it?'

'You bastards … you have it … Ford said so. Liars.' My prisoner spoke calmly. Too calmly. It was only then I noticed that his weight had shifted beneath me. His arm was snaking out from under the cloth. The blade of his dagger jutted from his fist.

Without thought, I lunged forward, burying my poniard to the hilt in the soft flesh of his throat. He blinked at me stupidly. Once. Twice. And then he stilled. Blood began to pour more thickly from his nostrils, from his lips. 'Not clever,' I said.

Lockhart stood, putting a hand against the wall to steady himself. I lifted myself off the cloth, folding it over the staring face. 'But Savage … if they seek it from us and we from them … where is the damned thing?'

'I don't know.'

'What do we do?'

'With two dead men? In a foreign city? We run.' Lockhart began to mutter inarticulately. 'Do you wish to be hanged in Edinburgh for murder?'

'But they were going to kill us!'

'And? We must get back to Cecil.' A faint hope rose in my mind that perhaps the document had never left London – that perhaps the queen's secretary had had better luck in his searches of the capital.

'Whit in – oh, shit!'

We turned as one. Standing in the doorway behind the bloody cloth was Andro Allardyce. He swallowed and began to turn, a hand at his throat. 'No you don't!' I lunged towards him, catching him by the sleeve and giving a hard yank.

'Unhh!'

I pulled the man back into room, spinning him as easily as a doll. Then, taking him by the front of his jerkin, I raised him off his feet and held him against the bare wall. Putting my face close to his, I said, 'you tried to have us killed, you bastard.' He twisted his head from side to side. I braced one forearm against his chest and pulled back my other fist, eager suddenly to spread his features across his face.

'No!' cried Lockhart. We both of us swivelled our heads in his directions. 'You cannot strike a dwarf, Savage. It is bad luck!'

Andro made a gurgling noise in this throat, cleared it, and said, 'he's right there – right, he is, master. You've done murder in my auntie's hoose. You'll not want no more bad luck.'

I relaxed my fist and instead took a firm grip of his jerkin. Turning on the spot, I threw him to the floor. His fall was cushioned by the corpses. Before he could recover, I fell on him. As he wriggled and moaned, I grasped around under the cloth. 'What are you doing?' asked Lockhart.

'Go and saddle the horses. We're getting out of this city tonight. Now.' He hesitated and then, seeing the look on my face – I fancy it must have looked insane – he fled.

'It'll do you no good to kill me,' said Andro.

My hands were stained with gore. Slowly, I began spreading it on our host's face, on his clothes. 'I'm no killer,' I said. 'You're the killer, you little prick.' I held him fast, bloody on his bed of death. 'You knew these men, did you? I will kill you if you don't speak the truth.' His wriggling ceased.

'They … they came to Edinburgh a few days ago. Didn't let them stay here when they arrived at the gate, same as you did. Rough looking buggers. Took 'em tae a nuncle o' mine up in the city.'

'Three of them? A man called Ford is their leader?'

'Three, aye, aye.'

'Where is he?'

'Ford? He … in my nuncle's, I'd guess. No, I remember, I remember. They said he'd gone to the docks up at Leith. Goes there a lot, looking to see if a friend's ship is come into port.'

'Did you fetch these lads to kill us?'

He swallowed. I reached for my dagger. Then the words spilled over one another. 'They were like you, sir, askin' all about the pouch's secret papers when they came into the city. So I told 'em, like I told you. The whole sorry tale. They said to send 'em word if I heard anythin' about it, said I'd be rewarded for it, right well enough. And then you lads appeared with the same questions. And your friend there bein' a long streak of piss with a nasty tongue, I did take word. That's all I did. When you went up to the king today, I went up there. Ford, he said you boys must have something o' theirs and they just wanted it back, that's all. Ford, the hard one, he sent these boys to get it whilst he went tae the docks.'

'What's he been doing?'

'Lookin', is all. Hear he's been lookin' about the city for news o' the paper. His lot must be as lost as yours about it. Dunno if it truly got to London or is up here somewhere. Your lot and his, both after the same bloody thing.'

My anger, all the tension and excitement and horror of the previous half hour, washed out of me. I sagged, releasing my grip. 'You're a bastard,' I said.

'Aye, I am that.' I stood. 'What are you going to do to me?'

'I'm going to leave you, Andro. I'm going to leave you to your king's justice.'

'I've no' done nothin'!'

'You have a merry time explaining all that to your justices, if Scotland has any. Explain the two corpses on your aunt's chamber floor. Explain why you're covered in their blood.' As I spoke, I gathered Lockhart's and my own pack, throwing things in.

Turning on my heel, I left the room, banging the door shut behind me. I pounded down the stone steps and through the kitchen, which bore no sign of the hapless Auntie Peg. In the small courtyard, Lockhart was leading out my horse, scuffing a mounting block along the ground ahead of him.

A misty rain had started up as we saddled up. It did not seem to fall but rather hung in the air. Lockhart secured his sable over his shoulders. 'Let's be gone from here before that little devil can persuade the watchmen to give chase,' I said.

From behind, Lockhart called out in a tone I might almost have pitied, 'did I do well?'

I was saved from answering him. As we emerged from under the stone archway onto the Canongate's high street, a dark shape detached itself from under the overhanging roof opposite. It began moving towards us.

In the dying light, I could just make out a face I recognised: one I had last seen in the underground cell of the Clink. 'It's Ford,' I cried. Lockhart barked his confusion. 'Go! Ride!'

Spurring the horse, I jerked in the saddle as it jolted forward. I turned my head in time to see the man twisting his between us and where we had come from. It would not be long before he discovered what we had done to his comrades. And then he would come for us.

Our horses' hooves drew sparks from the cobblestones as we thundered out of the town, losing ourselves by design amidst dark, tumbling hills draped in torn and dirty sheets of snow.

***

The flames licked higher, sending fat, choking plumes of smoke to be sucked upwards and out of the building. Outside, dawn was breaking in orange-streaked tongues of grey. Over English soil.

We had arrived back in Berwick ahead of Ford – ahead of any pursuers. Our horses had devoured the miles and I confess we did not spare their slavering. Too early in the morning to bother the officials with our papers, we had claimed asylum in an inn, rousing the host from his slumber.

I put my feet up on a firedog in the parlour, my hands tight around a mug of sour beer. Memory struck me, and I set it down and dug into the inside of my coat. Smiling without humour, I produced the pipe I had stolen from Andro Allardyce as I'd held him against the wall of his aunt's room.

'I killed a man,' said Lockhart. Excitement danced in his words. 'I did it – I really killed a scoundrel.'

'Yes.' The pipe was empty. I frowned, sliding it away.

'Will you tell Cecil? Will I?'

'I doubt he will care.'

'But … it was an enemy of the crown.'

'Who gave us nothing. We're no closer to handing him that paper than we were when our dead friends still breathed.'

Lockhart lapsed into silence – a sullen silence, I thought. It did not last. 'So we shall discover it in London, or on the road south.'

I considered this, trying to envision the thing. As I had done a hundred times. I could almost see it, though, irritatingly, I could not see any words on it. A sheaf of papers, secure in the pouch in which they had lived, being passed from hand to hand for years. That pouch in the hands of a man calling himself Henderson, servant to the last owners, who were murdered by a king who wanted it. And the man then doing as we were now doing: riding from Edinburgh, bound for England. The road would have taken him, as it had taken us, to Berwick. Perhaps he had even lain in the same inn.

And then there was a hideous blank. He had arranged with the leader of the red cross faction to sell them the contents. How? By letter? Did he have friends in London, or who travelled to London in trade or on business? With the arrangement made, he must have kept riding, on the road we were about to take. There were only so many ways to the capital, but upwards of three-hundred miles of inns, of taverns, of footpads, of punks, of filchers and anglers. The fool might have hidden his loot or been unwittingly relieved of it, carrying only the pouch and hoping to trick his buyers. That would be a laugh, I thought – if the leather pouch I had seen that day in the Mitre contained nothing but dust. And then he had gone to ground himself, as invisible as the men who did business with him. It was not hard to imagine why. The mysterious Scot had to be hiding out in London, waiting until he might exact the highest possible price from Ford's master or some other buyer. Cecil's men would find him. In my mind's eye I could see the rogues who had beaten my landlord forcing their way into private dwellings, searching up chimneys, tearing up floorboards.

If they don't have it and we don't have it, where is it?

It was useless to speculate. And it was not my business. Cecil had ordered me to assure King James that all was in order ahead of the queen's death and to cast about for the history and origin of the document. That I had done. Only the content still eluded me, and that could only be guessed at. It was the secretary's job now to determine what must happen next.

Idly, I thought about the blood that had been spilt already. One little paper had sent a regent and a nobleman of Scotland to the block, had caused men to be stabbed to death by a suspicious and grasping king, had set a man's corpse up on the gate to Edinburgh, and had now brought about the deaths of two London lads in the service of someone who sat in the English parliament.

What could it possibly have to say?

I dozed a little, getting up only when the grey day shared its meagre light with the innyard. To London, I thought. We might at least measure the speed at which the journey could be made, free now of the need to ride about the countryside.

As we spurred our way out of Berwick and into another dreary spring day, I did not know that the true horrors of our journey were yet to come.

18

And so it fell out that in the weeks following the nuptial feast of the said Prince James his parents, his nuncle the earl of Moray did rise in open rebellion of arms against his natural sister, the said Queen Marie, and her husband King Henrie, and thereafter Scotland was in war and civil blood like to be spent. We the ancient blood of this realm did foresee great tumults such as I think were never seen in our time in any Christian commonwealth, as the sister and the brother chased one another and were all at squares. It is an unclean thing that natural siblings should thus conduct themselves. Yet it is true that the unnatural state of Scotland did infect us all, as I have said, as I continued my lustful life, nightly lying with the said Bessie, my sweet Minnies own serving lady, who thereafter did bear me a baseborn son, a thing seen much in Scotland and always to be condemned by the Kirk, for the corrupt and vile increasing of bastards is a thing as shameful to the community as to the drabs that bear them.

Yet God saw aright and cast the said Moray into England, wherein he did visit with the Queen Elizabeth, who spoke hard words against him, as an example to all men who rebel against their sovereigns. And so our realm of Scotland seemed to be at peace and the news did jet about the nation that Queen Marie and King Henrie were to be blessed then with issue, the which we prayed daily would be a fair and healthy son and not a twisted and unnatural monster (for, in the troublous times, it was reported about the realm that poor women had been delivered of misshapen lumps of flesh and in Fife a calf with two heads was born and did speak vile and wicked words before witnesses before it were slain).

The benisons of marriage did not enrich our nation nor our king and queen, for a storm blew in on the heels of the earl of Morays unnatural rebellion and such troubles were not done with us. It was at this time that King Henrie conceived a great jealousy of the said Queen Maries private secretary in the French tongue, one David Riccio, an ITALIAN of no great or ancient fame in our land. The said Riccio had been grown from nothing by our queen and yet he was like a dandelion grown in blossom and bringing an itch to the nose of the king. Proud weed indeed! and the said king determined that he must be utterly cut off and drawn from the queens side.

King Henrie alone did beget and plot a means of ridding Scotland of Riccio, the which he determined should be taken from his wifes presence chamber and without stabbed to death. Of his fellows in this plot I know nothing and accuse no man and forbear to say no more than that the plotters were all commanded by the king alone and cannot be blamed for nothing therein. The dark and shameful deed was in its form a manner of justice against the proud secretary in the way of the old ROMANS of ancient times. In the undertaking of the business it is said that the queen did try and protect the said Riccio and for his part he did cling most shamefacedly to her skirts crying upon her that she might save and spare his poor life. King Henrie would allow no mercy and in the tumult a pistol was pressed against the queen her belly, the which did then carry within it Prince James, and I think that the sharpness of the cold metal might have turned the bairn in her royal womb and thereafter cast a portent that his life would see cruelty and misfortune &C. Yet in truth at the time I stood so amazed by the conduct of our king and queen and divers of our nobility and lairds that I looked only through my fingers and wondered like one stark mute at what the world should think of our affairs.

Once the secretary was slain and lay bleeding with the said King Henrie his dagger in his belly, the king and queen both did find themselves greatly troubled in their minds and did ride off to Dunbar for a spell, and thereafter they did return to Edinburgh. At this time, as natural husband and wife and yoked together by God (and let no man pull such asunder!) and with the princeling yet safe and growing in her womb, Queen Marie and King Henrie ought in truth to have been happy, but that the spells and enchantments between them had been broken. More wicked than carnal love is the great hatred that does follow, and Scotland was like to be swallowed up in the gall and black hatred that did spread like poison in a glass between our king and queen, the which would bring King Henrie to death, Queen Marie to disgrace, and might in time yet bring us all to ruin.

19

The wooden shutter of the shopfront fell inward under the onslaught. Screams pierced the air. Within seconds, the door was thrown open and the owner emerged, waving a studded metal rasp.

Bartlet's gang of men had fighting-wit enough to know that a single man with a short weapon is easily swarmed and overpowered. From across Saint Martin's Lane, he watched, a mask over his face, as they forced the shoemaker to the ground. The rasp fell too and was immediately trampled into the mud. The unfortunate man, a Scot, cried louder as blows rained down on him.

'They go too far,' said Gregory. Bartlet ignored him. Typical of the man to set things in motion, to prod actions into being, and then to shy away from the outcome. What did he expect? Thin-blooded, that was Gregory: the result, doubtless, of the watering down of stout Everard blood with the weak strain of a worthless whore. 'I shall try and stop this. They were to attack the shop only.' He began clumping across the street but darted back at the sudden irruption of a sharp voice.

'What the bloody hell?'

An old man, his white beard trailing, had stepped out from a doorway on Bartlet and Gregory's side of Saint Martin's, leaning on a stick. He began stumping over to the commotion. 'Goodman Shanks,' he called out, waving it in the air, 'what is this? You, foul draw-latches! I'll call the constables, I will, I'll see you in chains, see you hanged!'

The old man stood a little apart from the group of red cross plotters. One of them moved away from the stricken Goodman Shanks, spitting on the ground as he made his plodding, flat-footed way towards the would-be champion of the Scot. 'You protect foreigners, you old prick?'

'How dare you! I – I'll call the constables!'

'Get yourself to–'

'We're no' Scots anymore!' A ruddy-faced woman appeared in the doorway of the shoemaker's shop, an infant on her hip. With her free hand she held up a sheaf of papers. 'Ma husband has his papers, we have our letters, denizens, we're denizens.'

'You're a Scotch whore,' shouted one of the plotters, aiming a kick at Shanks.

'I'll call the constables directly, Goodwife Shanks. You get inside.' The old man's thin voice was full of authority and he emphasised it by waving his stick in the air again. The red cross who had bandied words with him – Bartlet did not know his name, but he was one of the older men – stepped closer. With a hard push, he sent the old fellow sprawling on his backside into the central gutter. He sat there, dazed, amidst the ordure. A cloud of insects that made the foul mists of the sewer channels their home buzzed around him.

'Get back in your house or I'll rip your arms off, you old bastard.' The attacker leant down and grabbed the fallen man by the beard, hoisting him to his feet. With another shove, he sent him hurtling back in the direction from which he'd come.

Bartlet and Gregory drew back under the crooked eaves, watching as the abortive hero slumped into his house, head bent. Above, the sound of closing shutters began: a series of hurried bangs. Beneath that could be heard chains as doors and windows were fixed in place. No one would be going for help. Every man would be looking instead to secure his own property.

It must have seemed to all, thought Bartlet, that the queen had died and the rioting had begun. The rumours of the past week had been that, since her friend the old countess had died, she had refused food entirely and listened daily for Death's hollow footsteps.

Gregory stepped across the street, calling low, 'enough, lads, enough. It's the place to be broken up, not the folks.'

Lily-livered.

Bartlet's men ignored him, and continued their attack on Shanks, who lay bloody before his shop. His wife tried to reach him. 'Get inside with your child,' said Gregory. She looked at him, confused and white-faced, protesting in Scots. But she did so. 'Leave the Scot. Destroy his shop.'

Bartlet breathed in the brisk morning air as his men poured through the broken shopfront. A hail of items followed their path in the opposite direction: shoes, tools, wooden fixtures. Hammering and the splintering of wood filled the air. He had told them that they might fill their pockets and get reshod at their will once they had made an example of the Scotch leech. It had been an easy enough thing to convince them; the story in every man's mouth across the city was that James of Scotland stood on the borders at the head of an army of 10,000 savages – or was it 12,000, or 14,000, or 20,000? – and that the Scots living across England were only waiting to rise up and slaughter true Englishmen and women in their beds. Already they had begun poisoning wells.

Mopping his brow with his hat, Gregory rejoined him. 'Your plan worked well, brother,' said Bartlet, enjoying the resulting wince.

'I told you they were eager to show their worth.'

'Indeed. Now I would be gone from here. See that they're scattered in case the constables do come.'

With that, he began walking away from the destruction, whistling to himself. It was a pretty place, Saint Martin's Lane, full of modest, white-washed shops and houses crowding it. Too good a place for interloping foreign scum.

His presence had not been necessary – it was perhaps even dangerous – but he had grown bored of his days locked up in the great, empty house on Bishopsgate Street. Well-disguised and with his blond beard thick, neither his wife nor son would have known him. Besides, until they had secured the missing document, his only other task was reading. He took his time returning through the city streets.

A change had come upon London. The city almost seemed to be holding its breath. Still merchants, pedlars and pie-sellers touted their wares, but they seemed to be doing so in lower voices. No man stopped him to ask him news. People appeared only to be speaking to their neighbours or people they knew; the sensible lot, those who could afford it, kept their properties locked up. The wealthiest had left the city: the nobility to be near Richmond, the gentry with moveable goods out to homes in the country. It was a pleasant thing, seeing the place so quiet.

After letting himself in the side door of the Bishopsgate mansion, Bartlet quickly tore off the ugly tradesman's weeds and put his good woollen dressing gown over his shoulders. Sighing, he set himself to his task.

On his desk were not his pages telling of his part in the life of the earl of Essex, but a series of tiresome books listing and comparing the claims of Queen Elizabeth's heirs. Helpfully, Gregory had arranged them in the order of their publication, the oldest, a yellowed manuscript volume by one John Hales titled *A Declaration* on the left, the newest, *A Pithie Exhortation* by Peter Wentworth and the poet Constable's *Discovery of a Counterfeit Conference* on the right. It had taken some time for his base-born brother to find them: he had had to lean heavily on the rogues and brutes who trafficked in such things, smuggling them in and out of the ports at Billingsgate and Queenhithe. A waste, possibly; Bartlet had no intention of spending his precious time reading through the damn things. Still, he ran a finger over the cover of the first. Even to own them, to possess such naughty goods, was a thrill. If Cecil's men raided the house, they would hang him.

That thrill tickled its way through him. What power it was to order an army of poor men to destroy a house; to return to one's mansion and gaze at the secret documents that made a sovereign and her legion of bishops and ministers tremble.

He pushed most of the books across the desk, where they bumped against his own papers and inkwells, and opened the first. Scanning it, he saw that it was an artless defence of the descendants of the Grey girls, themselves descended from Henry VIII's younger sister. Both of whom, he smiled, were dead, but one of whose sons had sons of his own. Yet there was some dispute about the Grey girls' marriages – or pretended marriages. The descendants were Seymours, and none of that clan had any right to be anywhere near a throne again; they were too political by half. The kingmaker who set a Seymour on the English throne could expect nothing by it.

Idly, he began leafing through the pages of the older books, ignoring the names of the dead, ignoring the attacks on the long-dead Mary Queen of Scots. One name, though, stuck in his mind.

Huntingdon.

Bartlet tilted his head back and thought. The earl of Huntingdon, at one time considered a match for the queen due to his Yorkist blood. If the old books spoke true, then the old man had once been considered a good heir should the queen die of some sickness she had suffered in the past. Huntingdon had himself died some years before – Bartlet thought perhaps around the time Drake and Hawkins had sailed away to their deaths – but the line had not died out. No, his brother had succeeded to the title, all legally and correctly. And that brother had had issue.

Quickly, Bartlet turned to the more recent books, flipping over pages, his eyes hungry. No, there was no mention of Huntingdon. All eyes had turned towards James of Scotland, towards the Spanish, towards the crazed Stuart girl and the Beauchamp offspring of the Grey sisters. All had been looking, really, at the descendants of Henry VII. The descendants of the Yorkist kings, the last good run of kings, had been lost to the pages of history.

It could not be more perfect. Tired of an old woman's rule, the people would embrace the idea of a forgotten true heir – a lost prince rediscovered and set upon the throne. The idea might be less attractive when that lost prince was an old man, but if he had children, grandchildren, then his star would ascend. England would have a kindly, fertile grandfather rather than a dying spinster.

Bartlet scraped back his chair and, excitement rising, turned his back on the succession books. He turned his attention instead to the sheaves of papers and documents he had collected to ensure the truth and accuracy of Essex's lineage.

The day was dying out by the time Gregory returned home. By then, Bartlet was in bed, surrounded by documents. He sprang out.

'Brother,' said Gregory, 'I have news.'

'Silence! I have it. I have our new king – the man whom all England will fall behind after we see off that foul Scot.'

'But I–'

'Listen, you fool!' Excitement had built with each new page and Bartlet imagined himself declaring his day's findings in parliament. 'Huntingdon. George, fourth earl of. Of the ancient and noble house of Hastings. An old man, to be sure, past sixty, and his eldest son is dead; but his grandson by that heir lives. A lad of sixteen, married already – to a girl descended from the sister of Henry VIII. Mary Tudor, Gregory.'

'That's … good?'

Bartlet padded across the room and shook his brother by the shoulders. 'Don't you see? I have done it. I have found the man we shall make king. And he is come from the Yorkist kings, and his heir has married himself to Tudor blood. And no one has seen this – no one has cared but I.' He pointed at the succession tracts he had brought into the chamber with him. 'All are looking to James. When we take him away from them, ruin him, they will be all at sea. Until we declare for Huntingdon.'

'Does … does he want it?'

'Want it? Want the crown of England?'

'Does he? I've … I've never heard of him.'

'Well of course *you* haven't. You're in trade.'

'But if none of the books speak of him either, I …'

'I hope he doesn't want it. I hope he has neither dreamed nor thought of it, not like the grasping Stuart wench and the Seymours. Why, a man who has never thought of or hoped for the throne is the man best suited to it. He will fall into it in a swoon. It will seem like a gift from heaven. Yet it will come from me.' Finally, Bartlet released Gregory's shoulders and began walking in short circles around the room, almost overwhelmed. He had expected to find some candidate named in the latest books; he had not expected to find one for himself in the fustiest. It was an almost religious experience. 'And when his name is declared in the streets, the Privy Council will have to take note. They will be already in the doldrums having lost their filthy Scotch pet. I will present Huntingdon to them as a gift from above. And when the new king needs counsellors, I shall offer my services. And you, you, my brother, shall have a monopoly on anything you fancy.'

'I think it is a fine thing, brother. I am amazed. Amazed that you have found this man.'

'Ha! Did you doubt me? It was I inherited our father's brains.' He reached down for a cup of wine he had left on the floor, rising with it already at his lips. 'You … said you had news?'

'Yes. I have been to the docks. There is news from Ford in Edinburgh.'

'He has found it? He has it?'

'No. It is not in Edinburgh, Bart. The message he gave to the crew of my ship was that all is quiet in that city. No sign of anyone having the thing in their possession. Nor could he see any trace of it on the road northward.'

'God damn it.' Bartlet clutched at the bedpost and kicked at the coffer which lay at the foot. It fell to the carpet, disgorging a muddle of sheets and a whiff of lavender. 'We ought to have let that blasted Gowrie travel from Scotland on your ship rather than have him ride south.'

'The customs men search the ships out of Leith and into Billingsgate, Bart. I can't bribe them to overlook a man. Books and things, but not a man.'

'Hmph. Well, if the cur missed a journey over the sea then, his damnable bones will be seeing it well enough now.'

'There is more.' Bartlet turned his head up sharply, away from the upturned coffer. 'The man Savage has been in Edinburgh.' He held up a hand. 'No, he does not have the document. We were wrong. Ford learnt from a dwarf that Savage and another man were as eager to find the thing as we. Thought that Ford and our men had it, in fact.'

'A *dwarf*?'

Gregory shrugged. 'They fled Edinburgh after killing two of our boys.' Bartlet stiffened at this, and his brother hurried on. 'But Ford is giving them chase. He'll find out what they know and silence them afterwards. And then take another route south. If that Scot hid his paper anywhere between here and Edinburgh, Ford will discover it. And if not, then it is somewhere in this city. We'll find it. We could put the men to work searching. Booksellers and the like, men who might know.'

'Do it.'

'They … they're becoming harder to control, Bart. We have a wolf by the ears and … and our hands are slipping. They killed him.'

'Who?'

'The Scotsman, Shanks. The shoemaker.'

'No great loss. I cannot rein in turbulent spirits, Gregory.'

'And the wife – I had to stop them from … from raping her. She got away with a bloody nose, the babe in her arms. Their shop is ruined.'

'Good. She got away with the babe, and so there is no harm done. And no justices stuck in their noses?' Gregory shook his head. Bartlet frowned at him. There was something brewing in the soft bastard. Something like resistance. Base-born brothers, like servants or horses, could only be pushed so far before they started to buck. 'I will give them the name.' He cut the air with a dismissive hand. 'That will keep them soft, give them something to chant. Someone to follow, whose name can fill their cheeks, that's all any rabble of malcontent cattle want. Tell them that they are red cross knights for Huntingdon, the true prince of England, who will soon claim his throne. Put out foreigners. Restore sweet England's pride. Tell them that they will see the reward of it, if they can find the Scotsman's document.'

'And I thought … only…'

'What did you think?' sighed Bartlet.

'Well, I had thought to give them weapons, more than just clubs. I can get them easily enough, but now I think … it might be a danger to arm them.'

'By all means, give them things that befit their station. Bows, daggers, go to, treble-fold in the double. They must be seen to be men of some purpose when the Privy Council hears that Huntingdon is claimed king. This will not be the rising against Queen Mary by the young pretender Jane Grey. There will be no king or queens for our arms to be set against. Only a king for them to be raised for.'

'Yes, brother. Yes.'

'No king for them to set arms against,' Bartlet repeated, ice frosting his words, 'if the fools can find our document. Forget attacking Scots for the nonce. They must start raiding taverns.'

'They'll find it.'

'You had better hope they do. This … this whole matter started with that goddamned corpse Gowrie looking for a buyer for his document through the crew of your ship. If we fail now, if we cannot bar King

James, then we are sunk.' Gregory began tidying the papers and books that littered the floor, his large forehead turning pink. Bartlet picked up one of the succession tracts and launched it at him. As always, he bent to dutifully retrieve it. 'And if this enterprise sinks, remember that it is you have who ranged about London, living in this house, commanding an army of scum. Not me.'

20

Marshy ground sucked at the horses' hooves, compelling us to dismount. Gravel and stone paved the road, and yet it was patchy, overtaken here and there by encroaching bog and grass. Around us, the country had turned flat, but it was wild with trees. Still, it was the main road out of Darlington. And still we were following the Great North Road: a route that didn't pass through Bedale and Richmond, as my journey north had.

I called a halt, seeing a narrow expanse of grey cutting through the flat green vista ahead. The River Wiske, we had been told at our last stop, was one of many streams which stitched the country thereabout. It had to be forded. I looked over my shoulder. Lockhart held up a hand in salute. Go ahead, it said. Behind him and to the left I thought I spotted something to the side of the track.

A deer?

I watched for a few seconds, shaking my head. We had seen nothing to trouble us on the journey south, though impassable roads, heavy rains, and even snow flurries had holed us up in inns for more than one night. If the queen were to die suddenly in the midst of such a dreadful spring, I could only report to Cecil that any man carrying news to James of Scotland had better have Hermes' sandals to hand (or to foot, rather).

Nevertheless, I had slept poorly at every rest stop, had distrusted every horse trader and suspected that he might betray us to any man who asked later who had passed through and exchanged tired mounts for poorer but fresh ones.

On our side of the riverbank – which was simply a tangle of bracken forming a fringe by the narrow river – stood a pair of weather-beaten posts. From them were strung ropes, which met a matching pair on the other side. The set up was crude, ancient, and, I hoped, effective. We clumped over ground beaten flat until we were at the Wiske's edge.

My dappled mare tested the languid, brackish water with her hooves. And then, all at once, she sank forward, the grey becoming turbid as it met us, as it rose up her flanks and attacked my boots. Wakes passed off on either side of us, and one began behind as I took hold of a ropeway with one hand and gently guided her onwards.

A scream rent the air.

I turned in the saddle, and felt the horse's legs grow skittish, stall. She dipped, and the lazy current threw a wave up over us, soaking into my russet coat and only repelled by my cheap canvas doublet. I could see enough. A group of bandits had emerged from the scattered woodlands behind us and surrounded Lockhart. Over the rush of water, I could hear his pleas: 'Oh God, oh dear God, for the love of God, please do not kill me! I will do anything, please!'

Not so hard a man when the enemy isn't trapped under cloth.

Laughter rippled through the crowd.

I hesitated, not sure what to do. I could leave Lockhart to his fate and make for the other side of the river. It was not far. I could return and be robbed or murdered too.

I turned ahead, tightening my grip on the rope. And began to tighten my knee on the horse's flank, beginning the delicate manoeuvre of reaching the shallower far bank and turning her. As we splashed forward, the jeering behind us increasing, I pulled up short.

The far side of the river was no safer.

A matching band of the highwaymen had emerged. A neat trick, I thought. Hide out on either side of a river that has to be forded and fall upon unsuspecting fools as they bunch together at it. We had as good as bound and gagged ourselves and lain upon the ground with a note bearing the inscription, 'enjoy our goods, with our compliments'.

My heart sinking, I held up my hand in submission. If we were clever, we might get out of the thing alive, if poorer. But Lockhart, I suspected, would not be clever. Either his cowardliness would get their backs up or his superior airs would raise their hackles. I made a show of controlling my horse, needing time to think. Eventually, the horse's front legs clambered into the shallows and I got her turned. My hand remained up. The bandits on the far side had arranged themselves in a semicircle, all mounted themselves, and each one pointing a weapon directly at me. A veritable armoury, I thought, of stolen blades.

I returned to the other side of the river, aware that Lockhart's cries had lessened. I chanced a glance up. A sword was being held to his throat.

Don't do anything stupid.

Something fell before my view of him and, as I gained the riverbank, water streaming from my boots, I jolted in surprise. One of the bandits, the leader I assumed, sat easily in his saddle a few yards from me. In a rapid movement, he drew out a fine rapier – a deadly weapon in skilled hands. So trained was I on the sword, the point of which was aimed at my chest, that I did not at first understand his words.

'It's never the young Ned Savage! It's pretty Savage, my rascals! Lads, stand down.'

His rapier lowered, and was slid away. What, I thought. Then I looked into his face.

'Jesus Christ,' I said. I felt laughter burbling within, and it tore out in jagged gusts. 'Ratsey!'

The bandit chief was a handsome fellow, clean shaven and hatless, his fair hair an artful tangle. 'A long time, Savage. What brings you from London?'

'A desire to see the world,' I said. 'And you? I thought you went to Ireland.' The last time I had seen him he had enlisted to join Essex's company in that wild land, the better to escape charges in the city.

'Ireland's a shit-pit and soldiering there worse in crimes than thievery. Came back to London months ago. Desire fell upon me not long after to get out again.' He laughed. It was a carefree, musical sound, like his bouncing accent, which seemed to blend the north, London, and a lilting Irish twang. 'A desire to escape the hot blood o' London scaffold-wrights and the lash o' the whips o' York.' I looked around at his crew. Lockhart was no longer being held at sword-point, but riders were still hard by him. One of them, I saw, was a woman in men's clothing, her dark hair tumbling about her soft face. I did not recognise any of them. Evidently Ratsey, the terror of the roads out of London, had not brought his old comrades in the criminal arts north with him. That made sense. He could travel more quickly alone and a man of his charm would take swift charge of any rag-tag of cut-purses, reivers, and wild-riders he cared to command.

He smiled at me again. 'You've turned to some honest work, have you?'

I laughed. 'Don't know the meaning of the words, friend.'

It had, as he'd said, been a long time. Yet when I had first fled Norfield and made my way to London, in the years of the great dearth, I had quickly discovered that I would have to steal if I wished to live. Thus it was that I had found my way easily into the small and friendly fraternity of criminals which used Whitefriars, in Faringdon Without, as a refuge. Living amongst fortune tellers and cutpurses, I had drunk in their cozening and cheating ways and found them a great deal more honest amongst one another than the wealthier and more moral of the city. They had never become family to me, though I reckoned that they considered me so. And, though I would not have said it to them, I found their dealings small and somewhat grubby. Ratsey, when he had arrived in the city a year or so before my association with Cecil, had been different, and I confess I had developed something of a soft spot for the reckless fool, knowing that he was too merry in his ways to live a long life. I had supposed him dead in an Irish bog. 'It's a good thing to see you again,' he said, clapping his horse's neck.

I looked again between him and his people, and then between the woman and him. 'There's a pretty fellow,' I said. The woman turned blazing eyes on me. It was true, though; her sharp chin and rounded nose made her quite remarkable. Beauty in a man, I thought, measuring up Ratsey, is bland perfection of form and feature. Beauty in a woman is slight imperfection.

'Nell is both wife and brother to me,' he said, saluting her. I smiled without mirth, recalling that the fellow's tastes had always run in either direction, and he might as readily be found in a sweat-soaked muddle with a pretty tavern wench as with a groom. Envy stirred, though of what I could not exactly say. That he possessed a gift for doing right as well as wrong, likely.

Wind rustled through the trees, lifting branches only just budding with new life and rippling growing grass. I gave my head a little shake, and began to say, 'I hope you'll be letting us go on …' I narrowed my eyes. 'Ratsey?'

'I am he!' Laughter from his men.

'How long have you been working this road?'

Suspicion glinted in his eyes. 'A while, friend.'

'Did a Scot pass this way? A good while back, I can't say when.'

'A Scot?' He made a show of stroking his bare chin. 'Perhaps. Might be.'

'A quivering wretch, thin, alone I should think. Carrying on him a black leathern pouch like it was a new-born babe.'

Ratsey stared at me. For too long, I thought. He regarded his fellows again, before fetching a sigh. 'Aye, I recall us having a friendly meeting with such a one. Good while ago now. Called himself Gowrie.'

My heart began to speed. 'We're seeking him, my friend and I.' He knew better than to ask questions. 'The man got to London, but we lost him after. It might be he said something.'

'Ha. Aye, I remember the creature. What you mean, dearest Savage of London, is did I relieve him o' his worldly goods and send him south lighter.' I did not respond. 'Your man passed by north o' here. And yes, we came upon him. Your friend there put me in mind of him.

He mimicked, "don't kill me".' Laughter. I did not look at Lockhart. 'Said he had friends in London would pay us if he was left alone.'

'Did he say who?' I nearly added, 'please, Ratsey', but did not wish to appear too desperate.

'His letters did, in a manner o' speaking.'

Dryness dusted my throat, so that my voice came out a croak. 'Letters? You took the letters from his pouch?'

'No, we took nothing o' that little pouch o' his. Looked like he'd have kittens at the thought. But his talk o' friends intrigued me. So we took his pack, his sword.' He shrugged. 'A lousy haul. Some spoons and knives, rotten bread. Trash. Let the little shit keep his pouch. Oh, yes, and letters from someone inviting him to London, telling him the road to travel, where to go. A house in London.'

'Do you have them?'

'You desire them bad, don't you?' Ratsey began stroking his horse's mane. 'I'm sorry then, Savage. Letters are no good to me. I tossed the things in the fire.'

Hope withered. Fate seemed to be mocking me and it was with a deal of will that I prevented my head from slumping. 'I don't suppose you recall the name of the writer? Or the house in London, even, the street, the ward, anything?'

'I do not. Barely read 'em.'

'Hold!'

I looked up. The woman, Nell, was sliding down from her horse. In her heavy men's boots she trod her way over. 'My dearest?' asked Ratsey, reaching a gloved hand down. She took it and pressed it to her face.

'I saw them letters.'

'Dear Nell,' said Ratsey, stroking her hair, 'you can't read.'

'Saw them pictures on them. I got eyes, don't I?'

'Pic … ah, the seals?'

I hardly dared hope. 'Seals?'

'Pictures,' Nell insisted. 'That monster with all heads.'

'What was it?' I asked.

'Ah, yes,' said Ratsey. 'Your friend's friends were masters o' the monsters. Their seal was a freak. I recall it. Pressed in wax, it was. A lion with a goat's head on its back and a snake dangling between its legs like a great big yard-shaft.' He shrugged. 'That's the arms of your friend's friends. You can thank Nell for that.'

Chimera.

'Thank you,' I said. Simple words, but I trusted that the relief and gratitude I felt inside would prove their honesty.

'Now, we've been too long in the open like a right troupe o' proud players.' Ratsey clapped his hands together soundlessly. 'Come, away, my rascals. We'll have better sport than these poor fellows today. We let them pass.'

If there was disappointment or dissension amongst the team, I never saw it. 'Fare you well, old friend,' I said.

'And you, Savage.' He raised his fingers to his forehead, touching a cap that wasn't there, and turned his horse around. Over his shoulder, he said to me softly, 'A word, Savage. Carrying a well-fed princess the likes o' that lad won't get you to your business any quicker. More like'll get you killed. Or him.' I did not answer that but cast a sad look over at Lockhart. More loudly, he said, 'the devil keep you, my friend,' before rearing in his saddle, ever the gallant, and riding off into the trees. His company followed, none in exactly the same direction.

'How do you know such … such low creatures?' asked Lockhart when they had gone. His voice was coarse with shame. I shrugged, not willing to be a balm to him, not willing to listen.

'Let's go. We have something for Cecil now. A chimera. A seal bearing the arms of the chimera.' Already I could see myself riding into London, directly making for the College of Arms between the river and St Paul's.

We forded the Wiske. On the other side, all sign of the other half of Ratsey's raiders had gone. Yet, as we rode, I could feel eyes on us from amongst the trees. I paid them no mind. I had then the foolish lack of sense to be exhilarated, to be hopeful.

***

Another inn, this time in Northallerton. Thus far on the road south, all had been orderly. Post-horses were ready at every stop and every ostler seemed to have received payment already from Cecil to keep back their fastest mounts for the day that all knew was coming. I was more alert than ever, not to the chance of our being followed by the rogue Ford – whom I hoped might be killed on the road, by Ratsey or others – but of time passing. Our going to Edinburgh had taken too long, even if our time there had been brief. Our return was proving just as long. Every new day brought the queen's death closer. The woman had to be about a hundred. As we passed our horses to the innyard ostler, stars twinkling between scattered clouds above us, I wondered if the very old saw time as the rest of us did. Did it race by for them at a terrific gallop, the fear of death hastening it? Or did it slow to a crawl, as they sought to make the most of their last days?

As befitting a busy market town, the downstairs taproom of the inn was crowded, full of ploughmen and traders enjoying a drink and a smoke at the close of their day. To my surprise, there was also entertainment, in the form of a balladeer, who was playing odd notes on a shawm as we entered: a tall, good-looking fellow about my own age. I watched him as I procured us a lonely spot on the single communal bench, whilst Lockhart went to fetch us beer and secure us a room for the night.

'Only ale,' he said.

'Hmm?'

'Only ale in this rotten place. Did not even have their own cups – I had to use ours. He has given us the room upstairs. It is as cheerless as this swill. The packs are up top.'

I turned to him. Since our flight from Ratsey and his company, Lockhart had remained sullen, and I was in no mood for his bad one. I reached out and took the small, scuffed wooden cup that had lain in his pack. As I sipped, he drained his in one gulp.

'Vile stuff,' was his assessment. 'I shall see if they have anything stronger.' He slid up and returned to the tapster.

The balladeer had put down his shawm, picked up a lute, and begun stamping his feet for silence. 'A tale, a tale,' one of the ploughmen cried. 'Give us a tale.'

'A tale you'll have,' he replied. 'A tale of old. A tale of the noted and famous king, Arthur, king of Great Britain, who will rise again to unite the realms.' I sucked in my cheeks, wondering who was paying him to soften up the English yokels to the idea of a single sovereign of the two British nations: King James or Cecil. My guess was that we shared masters. In a clear voice, he began,

When Uther passed away, the realm
  Fell in great jeopardy,
For many wended to be king
  Through might and bravery.

Lockhart returned with two drinks: his cup and a wineskin. He gulped the ale down again. 'I have mine still,' I said.

'The other is for me too.' He started slurping at it, staring moodily at the wall behind me. 'I do wish that wretched fairy would cease his prattling.'

'I like entertainment.'

'Like him, do you?' Lockhart snorted.

I pursed my lips and knocked back my own beer, before pushing myself up. The crowd were mostly standing, congregating around the musician. I took more drink from the tapster, who tried to foist expensive wine from a fresh skin on me, apparently reading us for two lads out to make a night of it. I indulged him. If Lockhart was going to be an ass, I could match him. It was not unpleasant stuff, the Northallerton wine. From the first gulp, I could feel it burning down into my gut and the vapours rising pleasantly to my head, reminding me that that neither Lockhart or I had eaten, and making the fact seem merry indeed.

Returning to the bench, I belched. 'I see strong drink will bring you courage, if nothing else.'

Redness flooded his cheeks, which seemed to glow in the firelight of the tavern. 'To hell with you. I'm going out to piss.'

I will confess that when drink is of a mind to hit me quickly, it tends to sharpen my tongue. To sharpen and unsheathe, I should say. It is not something I'm proud of. 'Ha! I thought you had done your share of that today, pissing your breeches at the sight of a team of bandits.'

Lockhart turned a furious glare on me. With one swing of his hands, he knocked the cup from mine. Across the room, the balladeer faltered. A number of the patrons hissed in disappointment; but I could see expectant eyes turn on us. Eyes that danced at the prospect of a fight. 'You go to hell. Rather piss my breeches at bandits,' he spat, 'than be a notorious bum bandit. You are a sick man, sick on the inside. Too much fish has made a woman of you. No, worse! A – a werewolf, turning beast at night with animal lusts. Your - your hairy inward evil coming out in your shaft at night! And I do not care who knows it! I shall never speak to you again.' With that, Lockhart turned his back on me, cutting a path through the crowd and banging the door to the innyard as he departed.

I have wondered a thousand times since if his words struck me at the time as having the ring of prophecy. Wondered if either of us had any inkling about the grim fate that awaited him. But in truth, I think there was nothing but rancour between us then.

I swallowed. Still, I could feel the crowd watching me. Laughing inwardly, perhaps, or feeling tendrils of revulsion. I hoped that they might think the outburst simply an insult, a slander, and slouched on the bench, spreading my legs wide and scowling.

And down on bended knee they fell
  To pay him homage due;
And thus he won Excalibur
  And all fair England too.

Soon Scotland, and the North, and Wales,
  To him obeisance made,
Won by prowess of his knights
  And of his trusty blade.

The balladeer's return to his song saved me from the unwanted attention. He was, I noticed, looking back at me, the firelight glinting on his curls. I smiled thanks. He returned a wink.

The evening wore on, involving more drinking than it ought to. Anger and shame seemed best withstood by it. If I wondered anymore about the whereabouts of my friend, the concerns were swept away by the music and fog of wine. It is all somewhat of a blur. The crowd thinned, the lights dimmed, and somehow I found myself trying out the musician's shawm. And then we were jigging about the taproom like players on the stage, until the yawning tapster announced he was going to bed and put the bar of the door down. Probably he laughed at us behind his hands. I did not care. I was young, and carefree, and felt as handsome as only strong drink can make one feel. Up to the sleeping chamber I went with my new friend, and so to bed.

Different drinks, I find, work different courses on men. Some dull the wits. Others stir the blood. To mix them in the gut, as I did that night, is to court folly. Yet this is to make excuses. In truth, in that moment, I wanted to do something and so I did it. I confess I am no angel. But nor I think am I a devil.

In the morning, he was gone, and I felt the familiar rush of satisfaction and shame. I half expected men to come bursting into the room and from there to convey me to prison. I checked my clothing and my pack: all present and correct. My bed-mate had not robbed me, which was a relief – and he had the sense to leave before he could be seen. But had anyone seen us go upstairs? I thought not.

On the floor, I saw that Lockhart's pack was undisturbed. I frowned, remembering.

Found some other tavern to skulk in.

Probably he felt as ashamed at his conduct at I did, albeit for different reasons. Shame is infectious and there is always plenty to go round. Today, I decided, we would make a clean breast of it and be on the road quickly – before the shakes could set in. If we managed a good breakfast, the ride would blow any foul vapours clean out of us.

Once dressed, I tucked a rolled-up pack under each arm and left the chamber as clean as I'd found it, slipping down the shallow wooden staircase into stale smoke and soured beer. I could taste the cloying bitterness of the smoke on my tongue and recalled begging tobacco off of strangers to refill my new pipe. The rings of light around the closed window shutters told me it was still early. Finding the door unlocked, I slipped out and roused the ostler from his pallet in a chamber off the stables. The reek of manure hit me like a battering ram. I was glad to escape it, leading my own horse out.

The screams sliced through my head.

Outside the innyard.

'Murder! Murder!'

'What?' I said aloud. 'Who?'

You know who it is. You let him go out alone into the night.

Like one asleep, I staggered out of the innyard. A maidservant, her skirts kirtled up and her sleeves rolled, had her back to me. Her pail lay on its side, milk washing white over the mud. She was standing in the street, the other side of which was a fenced farmer's field. Shaggy cows filled it. A chorus of birdsong rose and fell gaily. I walked over on leaden feet and looked past her.

There, face down in the drainage ditch which ran around the edges of the field, was a long, stretched form. The sable cloak of which he'd been so proud was crudely stretched over as if to hide the body. The back of his head was a bloody pulp, from which broken bone and brains spilled, staining the dry mud. The weapon used to do the deed lay proud beside it. I knew it. It was one of the thick wooden billiard maces from the house in the Canongate. A clear punishment. A clear warning. A clear threat.

I dropped the packs and hunched double, emptying the contents of my stomach.

'Murder!'

The maidservant's cries were drawing attention. I turned on the spot and saw only suspicious faces. The tapster and the ostler were coming up behind me; the inn's side of the street held also a long line of shops and houses. 'Jesus Christ,' shouted the tapster. 'Your friend, ain't he, mister? Here, lad,' he turned to the ostler and spoke low. 'Go and fetch the town watch. Anyone you can find.'

I turned and began walking quickly back towards the inn, my mouth putrid. No one tried to stop me. I should like to say that revenge was on my mind – that I determined to hunt down Lockhart's murderer

Ford

but in truth terror had eclipsed anger, had blotted out even shock.

The whole tavern had seen us fight, had seen him storm off.

A lover's quarrel. Jealousy.

The musician might be searched for. I did not even recall his name.

Amoral pervert.

Our night together would then be aired publicly.

Shame.

I was a stranger in a strange town with strange tastes and a man now murdered had been in my company.

Because you left the door barred against him in the night.

I took my horse and I ran.

Coward.

21

Sometimes I have heard it said that a man on the run might sleep anywhere in England unknown, live off the land, steal what he can to get by. Not so. It is a fearful life. Every scrap of the country, brown, green, or blue, is owned and jealously guarded by someone. Fields are secured, woodlands are coppiced, even rivers have officers on the lookout for those who would poach fish. People guard their land more than the possessions they carry about their persons, the memory of the dearth years still fresh.

I sped away from Northallerton, it is true, but thereafter made slow progress, walking the horse often. I did not dare to visit towns or cities. Officials there would ask questions, demand papers – and officials could be bribed or threatened by a violent man and would give me away instantly to any justices who might have taken it in mind to put out a hue and cry. Nor did I trust trading horses.

In all, I was like a small creature who felt himself hunted by ravening wolves. The only remedy for that was to shelter beneath the belly of a more powerful lion. My king of the beasts was Sir Robert Cecil, and I knew only that I must reach his protection quickly, and yet could only safely do so slowly.

That nightmare journey is a daze of sleeping in ditches, hiding with my horse below stone-arched bridges, and paying to share maggot-ridden meals with the lowest creatures I could find. I must have made the right speeches to people, behaved mechanically. I think I might have pretended to be a travelling merchant, and perhaps I sounded convincing, but my thoughts were elsewhere.

You got your friend killed.

Eventually, I reached Ware, and knew I was getting close to London. I cleaned myself in a horse trough. And so on to Cheshunt.

He has an older brother and a father and a mother yet living.

I rode on until I entered the built-up sprawl of the city I loved. The first thing I noticed – it has always been there, but only now did it seem ominous – was the huge mound of Bonehill. It was grassy, the hill, and a windmill lent it a good, functional air; but all London knew that it was an artificial thing, the earth only raised by an enormous quantity of skeletons exhumed from the cemeteries of the city when they had swallowed their fill of the dead and begun to spit the corpses back out.

I sold the horse in the city – a drover's price for it, but I didn't barter – and made my way home. Inside my rooms at Shoe Lane, Faith fell upon me, her arms circling my neck. The packs fell to the floor. I squeezed back, hard, before looking into her freckled face, her keen green eyes. 'You look terrible,' was her assessment. 'Are you well, Ned?'

I managed a smile. 'Of course. A little tired is all.' With effort, I made some cheer. 'It's only I've missed your pretty face.' She wriggled from my grip.

'Leave off!'

'Have you been out?'

'Had to,' she shrugged.

'Far?'

'Far enough.' A little moue.

'Good. Good.'

'I'll fetch you water. You can clean up. You're all road dust and … dust.'

I smiled and retreated to my chamber. She had not been in; nothing had been disturbed. No sight had ever been sweeter than the pathetic little room I had thought never to see again. I began emptying my pack. The miniature of Elizabeth, stolen from Arbella Stuart, was hidden away with my new pipe and the pin cushion crown. The last I had always hoped to display somewhere I might see it before I slept at night, might touch it whenever the mood struck me. Instead, I cast it deep into a coffer and pressed it under clothing. I dug out the one Faith had bought me and put that out instead. Better to value what I had, not what I had lost.

She knocked on the door and I retrieved our jug and began washing myself, before napping on my makeshift bed. That done, I rose and dressed in my livery. Throughout, I was, I knew, attempting to delay what I must do: look through my dead friend's things. My things now.

A comb, his cutlery, his clothing (too big for me, but I wanted to own and look after it, not alter and wear it). And his list of names. I hardly needed that.

Hoby. Bacon. Everard. Finch. Donhault.

I returned to the outer chamber, where Faith was at her account books, humming contentedly to herself. Pleased to have me back, I thought, with a rush of affection. 'Are we still poor?'

She didn't answer that but looked up in dismay. 'You're not going out, Ned? I can go get you a pie.'

'I won't be long. Just one thing I have to do today.'

'The playhouse?'

'Not there, no.'

'Your business. I've missed you.'

I crossed to the chair and gave her arm a squeeze before leaving without a word. As I made my way through the city, bound for Baynard's Castle ward, south of St Paul's and Knightrider Street, I stepped easily. Focusing on a task, even a simple task, seemed to push away darker thoughts.

But only a little.

As I walked, I noticed something I hadn't seen before. Instead of the usual hucksters selling their assortment of trinkets and beads and ribbons from stalls were men selling chains and ropes.

'Secure your goods!'

'Lock up your homes!'

'Protect your wife and daughters, mister!'

The usual crowds, the plodding men up from the country and the gossiping wives and preachers, were absent. Instead, pairs of men were patrolling. Not constables, but hard-faced rogues. Cecil's men, I thought, out on the search for the missing document and its Scotch owner, the elusive Henderson-cum-Gowrie.

As I passed lanes and narrow alleys, I could see also small clusters of faces that I knew, or just-about-knew: filchers and vagabonds who usually confined themselves to the sanctuaries in daylight hours. Now they were unloosed, rat-faces peering out and judging whether passers-by were worth robbing. And why not? It was well enough known that a new sovereign issued a general pardon for just about everything except murder. Thankfully, my livery made me too dangerous a prey. I doubted they knew it marked me as a Revels man, but any livery spelt the backing of someone powerful who would not take well to being slighted.

Strange, really, that I felt safer amongst the den of thieves that was a dying queen's capital than I had on all the long road out of the north. I was no better than they.

Worse. The petty thieves and cutpurses look after their own.

As the city sloped gently to the river, the wall of great buildings rose above the irregular rooftops of Doctors' Commons. Ahead of me and to my left stood the turrets and octagonal towers of Baynard's Castle, seeming to sprout reed-like from the water. As though in competition, the wide sprawl of the College of Arms stood directly ahead, on the slight mound of St Bennet's Hill.

The College had formerly been Derby House, the seat of the Stanley family. Over time, however, it had been altered, enlarged, and so changed that, with its grey stone and the smoke billowing from multiple chimneys, it resembled what I imagined the great Catholic monastic complexes of the old world to have been.

The main building was entered from the river, and so I felt very much like I was sneaking in by the postern gate. Entering through the tradesman's archway, I found myself in a huge rectangular courtyard of rough stone. Activity abounded, but what caught my eye were not the servants with scrubbing brushes and pans, but the college staff. Young men, on the whole, they lounged around against the walls, wearing black hats with the brims pulled down rakishly low at the front. Some were chewing on straws, others flipping coins in the air one-handed.

No wonder the place is known as the state's own Whitefriars.

I kept my head up, showing no fear as I marched across the open yard in the direction of the main building. One of the black hats was at my side before I had got halfway. 'What's yer business, friend, need to see the Garter, needin' yer family's arms, workin' fer yer master? I can get yer in whatever. Name's Mark, mate, I can get yer in.'

I paused in midstride. Drawing authority into my voice, I said, 'I am a servant of the queen's Revels Master, Sir Edmund Tilney. The queen commands a performance of the old *Chronicle History of Henry V*. We must revisit the arms for the costuming of the players.'

'Queen wanting plays, ye say? Not what me an' the lads has been 'earin'.'

I made a show of digging out a coin and holding it up. 'You say you can get me in?'

He grinned. 'I can get yer in, mate.'

We passed into the building and the enterprising Mark disappeared. The place was orderly within. The entrance hall in which I stood was tall, and at regular intervals long, colourful banners portrayed noble arms – I supposed all the nobility of England were represented. An empty desk stood before me and I went to lean against it. No doors separated the room from the ones adjoining it on either side, and from them I could hear dozens of voices. As time passed, I began to think that I had been tricked into giving away my penny. But to my surprise, Mark actually returned.

'Yeah, mate, no fear. Come with me.' He crooked a finger. I followed him off to the left, through a huge chamber filled with desks set on irregular legs so that they provided sloping drawing surfaces.

People milled about between them, and at some artists were at work making up their clients' armorial designs.

Out the other side, we passed through damp-smelling rooms full of lined bookshelves and stuffy offices for smaller groups of men, until I lost count and my sense of direction dulled. We stopped before a tall oaken door and Mark knocked before opening it.

Inside an airier chamber, a beefy old man with trailing white moustaches and a forked beard was speaking quietly to another of the youthful runners. 'You tell him he ain't getting his shitty no-name family nothing. You tell him, if he gives you a rough tongue, I'll pay him a visit meself.' He paused, seeing us and raising an eyebrow at my livery. 'No. In fact, you tell don't tell him nothing. You take some of the lads round and *show* him he ain't getting no coat of nothing.'

The younger man grinned, nodding. 'Ay, sir. You won't hear nothing from him no more.' He left the room.

'Mark, m'boy,' said the stout man. 'This our friend over from Revels, is it?'

'Ay, sir.'

'Capital. You can get gone, lad.'

I felt my heart sink as Mark left. He was an overdressed urchin, to be sure, but the half hour I had known him made him perforce an ally in the strange and black-reputed place. 'Sir William Dethick,' announced the old man, stepping over and clapping me. 'Who am I doing business with?'

'Edward Savage, sir.'

'Capital. Get you sat down.'

There was no desk in the room, but several large chairs. I tentatively perched on the edge of one. Dethick lounged on another, sticking his booted feet out before him and regarding them. He hunched forward and began jigging one leg up and down, patting his knee as he did. 'You ain't come to press me for a coat, 'ave you? 'ere, you don't 'alf look like that rascally traitor Essex.'

'I came, sir, on orders to discover a name. A name that has its coat of arms already.'

'Oh? Is that so? Palace intrigue, eh? I thought the queen was past … Sir Edmund looking for favours already, is he?'

I shifted on my seat and began fumbling at my purse. It would take more than a penny to buy Sir William Dethick's cooperation – everything I'd got for the dappled mare, I guessed. But it was well enough known that the Garter king was one of the most corrupt men and offices in the city. The more moral of the queen's officials had been trying to boot him out for years. When he had taken the money without a word of thanks or acknowledgement, he said, 'what are these arms?'

'A chimera, sir. And there's a chance it belongs to one of these names.' I passed him Lockhart's list and he frowned over it, his mottled lips moving as he appeared to chew on nothing.

'You wait here, lad.'

With the list in his hand, he moved to the door, opened it, and began barking at someone outside. The thuds of running feet. He turned and gave me an old man's smile. He shouted again, and I regarded my hands in my lap, turning them over.

'Ah,' he said. I looked up. Through the door, someone passed him something. Some jest or other must have passed between them; he hacked out an old man's wheezing laughter, it sounding only like a desperate struggle for breath. He closed it. Returning to me, he gave me back my list. As I folded it away, he held out something else, just out of my reach, smiling as I grasped for it. 'Chimera. Don't see too many of them. No call for the old beasts. People want signs of their trade, they do.' I swallowed. 'Here.' Taking the paper, I saw that it displayed exactly what Ratsey's girl, Nell, had suggested: a rampant lion, facing the interior left of a shield, a goat's head emerging from its back and facing the same way, and, for a tail, a snake curling beneath the back legs and body.

'Whose is it?' I whispered.

'Name of Everard. Sir Bartlet Everard the present knight. Old family.'

'Thank you,' I said, my tongue feeling thick.

'No skin off my nose. This Everard, he done something?'

'Not my business, sir.'

He shrugged and sat down in his seat. 'Capital. Good man. You keep that. See yourself out. Ever need anything, you come to Sir William Dethick.'

Thank you, Lockhart.

I could feel his paper crinkling against my breast alongside the chimera and made to return home. I had only one thing left to do. Dropping in at one of Cecil's safe houses, I gave the nameless new agent there a message: '710 is returned and has urgent news'. No need to say what it concerned: Arbella Stuart, King James, Edinburgh, Everard. Cecil would want to know it all. Whether or not I should share with him Lockhart's fate – the fact that I had even taken Lockhart with me – I would sleep on.

Either way, it was time to see my master.

22

To no great surprise, I found a new face at the safe house early the next morning alongside a message to see Cecil at Whitehall in a couple of hours, not in his chamber but in the Shield Gallery where he would be fresh off the boat from council. I had risen far too early, so that I might leave Faith still sleeping.

Thereafter, I went a wander before dropping down to the Mermaid tavern, hoping to catch up on the London news. The streets outside were barren of even their usual early morning traffic but one could always rely on an alehouse to have custom.

With a beer in my hand, I sat down at a table – a more elegant place, the Mermaid, than the rough, benched beer halls and inns of the north. I listened carefully to my neighbours.

'But if she got well again, mebbe she won't die.'

'If … if … can't trust no word coming out of them physicians.'

'Invasion it'll be, then?'

'I'd say Scotch rather than Spanish.'

'Unless this Huntingdon is the man they're shouting 'e is.'

Murmurs, slurping, tutting.

I finished my beer, wiping my lips with the back of my hand, and began to rise from the table. Suddenly, more animated chat from the men paused me in mid-air and I gently lowered myself back down, grasping the empty cup and staring into it.

'Speaking of Scotch, did you hear about that wench over in … I think it were over somewhere in Westminster. Where all them shoemakers keep shop.' A grunt of incomprehension. 'Woman got ravaged, right in front of her babe. Husband killed. Whole shop set to ruins.'

The speaker's fellow gave a sharp intake of breath before speaking. 'That's what the Scotch get, if they've got this army readied up and fit to march on us.'

'But raped in front of her babe. Don't no one deserve that.'

'Ay, a bad business that. Better she were done to death like the husband. You know what I heard about these wild lads?'

'No?'

'Me barber's brother's cousin – works out of Smithfield market he does – he told his cousin that these lads in the red crosses said yesterday that they're meeting tonight at the place what they meet. Heard it out of their own mouths at the market. Me barber reckons it's some rich lord what keeps them and gives them shelter. Has to be this Huntingdon they cry St George about.'

I must have made a noise. The men ceased their talking and I could feel their eyes on my back. I made no great show of being busy; to have overdone it would have been obvious. Instead, I sniffed at my drink. They must have judged me harmless, for the other man went on. 'Not what I heard. Me wife's sister heard they meet in some stew-house other side of the river. Who cares? Nothing to do with me. Reckon the whole city's turned rotten.' Greedy slurping. 'These roaring boys running wild against Scotch invasion and the Scotch king. The queen … searches everywhere. Heard an old boy in Cheapside had his house torn inside out just cos he'd once been accused of 'aving said that the queen shouldn't marry no foreigner way back when. Got on some kind of list, he must have – folk worth watching. It's run mad, you ask me. No liberty 'cept if you're a bloody criminal.' The thud of a horn cup on wood. 'I'm for leaving. Had enough. Might as well be done to death on the road than be torn apart in me own city when …when it all falls down.'

I gazed into the gloom of the tavern as my neighbours parted, my eyes tracing the pamphlets and ballad sheets that decorated the wooden walls. One of them, I noticed, was a ballad on the earl of Essex. The Mermaid had always been known for its salacious clients. It was on the round of the players' favoured drinking dens – at least until Jonson had pronounced that it was becoming too popular to be seen in.

A Scotswoman raped. Men in red crosses. Searches. A meeting tonight.

London doesn't look so safe a haven now.

I left the tavern and found that the sun was out, though a cold wind still prowled the streets. Whitehall beckoned.

***

Sir Robert Cecil was a man I never thought to see nervous. It occurred to me that he had chosen the Shield Gallery because it gave him a place to pace, and I struggled to keep up with his light tread. Royal guards stood at either end of the gallery, barring the public from using it as a thoroughfare and gawping place. I say 'gallery' as is it known by that name, but it is truly a terrace, the palace-side a stout wall bearing the arms and impresas, and the other side bearing only a waist-high wall, its marble pillars set at intervals to support the tiled roof.

Sunlight streamed in on us through the waterside columns, heating the sludgy, fishy scent of the river, as I poured out my story. I included Lockhart: he would have found out anyway, somehow, and then I should have been judged an unreliable liar.

Only then did I say, 'and I have the name and seal of the man who commands the men of the red cross.' Though the knowledge had been boiling over in my mind, craving release, I had saved it up, hoping to end my long tale on a note of dazzling discovery.

'Sir Bartlet Everard,' said Cecil without expression, pausing mid-step. 'I know.'

I felt like I had been punched in the stomach. 'How?'

'One of the gong-scourers who somehow find their way into my service. He reported that more than one fellow was living in a house on Bishopsgate Street. I set a fellow to watch and Sir Bartlet Everard was noted, when only his base-born brother should be there. One Gregory Everard, a merchant.'

All for nothing. Lockhart dead for nothing.

Cecil sighed, reaching out a hand that got only to my elbow. 'This friend of yours, Savage, did not die in vain. I have reduced the searches of the city, imagining that Everard must have the thing, or this man Ford he sent north. Yet you tell me they do not.'

'They did not. They might now, sir. I have seen nothing of Ford since…'

Cecil stepped to the wall. Beside him reared the colourful painted arms of the long-dead Sir Philip Sidney: a porcupine and a lion standing on either side of a crowned shield. Around it were arranged the lost hero's pasteboard impresas, which he had given to the queen after each Accession Day tilt. Almost absently, her secretary raised a finger and traced the painted image on one of the lower ones. It depicted a ploughman's harrow. In golden letters under it were written the words 'nechabent occulta sepulchra'.

'Graves have no secrets,' I said. I thought of Bonehill, and its army of skeletons shifting the earth.

Cecil turned curious eyes up to me. 'Clever boy. No day-worn Latin, that.' He moved along, drawing his hands together and releasing them, again and again. 'The little lad says only two men are resident in the Everard house. My men tell me it is so: Sir Bartlet, who seldom leaves – and then in disguise – and his bastard brother, Gregory. The damned Scotsman who started this whole business, he is not there, there is no sign of him, vanished, gone, disappeared.' Cecil's voice rose in pitch and he stopped again, crossing his arms.

I had never seen such frustration. It hit me suddenly: how my poor master must have prayed for the queen's death all these years, so that he might manage it. And now that it was at hand, how he shrunk from it, feared it, wished to delay it. If she should die whilst this document was at large, all his fine plans and schemes might crumble.

And his friends and servants with them.

He turned his back to the wall and leant against it. His head rolled back, his hat bouncing again an impresa depicting an earth sitting between a rising sun and falling moon ('hasta quan' ran its motto: the meaning was lost on me).

Dead men's offerings to a dying queen.

'I have set men to watch Everard's house in the country – he has a wife and son there. I have set a man to watch his brother's ship and warehouse at Billingsgate. My eyes in the customs house say the fellow has procured weapons lately, crates of them. I did not stop their passage. As far as I can, I have let Sir Bartlet and his brother, their minions too, think themselves untouchable, unsuspected.' A snort of laughter. 'So it was in my father's time, and his friend Walsingham's. Together they let the most evil plots advance, biding their time until the wretches had all but hanged themselves.'

'Should … should we allow them to arm these red cross beasts? I heard in the tavern a woman was raped, a man murdered, a Scot.'

'I heard about the Scot. Yes, Ned. Let them bear arms. When the time comes it will give us reason to arrest them all.'

When the time comes…

'Why not just raid them, sir, raid the house? They might not have the document, but at least we might crush the men who wish to use it.'

Cecil began walking back along the gallery, then abruptly changed his mind, turned, and went to a gap in the columns. I rushed to follow his crazy passage. Together we looked out over the wide expanse of the Thames. Boats and wherries bobbed in the white-capped waters, churned by the wind. On the opposite side, the sun picked out the sparkle of distant windows. Immediately below us was a narrow stretch of grass ornamented with bushes, a path cutting through the middle and leading to a marble staircase and private landing stage. I wondered, dimly, how to get there from where we stood. 'I considered a raid,' said Cecil, interrupting my thoughts. 'When you were abroad, I did consider it often.' He took a breath. 'As soon as I heard the name

Everard, I have burned to know what the creature and his base-born brother know. I supposed they might be sheltering this man, this Henderson or Gowrie or whoever he is, and that the risk of alerting the world to him and his paper by having armed men smash down those doors would be worth it.

'And yet, not knowing where the Scot or his papers are, I have been forced to step forward like a creeping, crawling babe. Whilst they have thumbed their noses at true authority and advanced their wicked plans. And now you tell me they did not even gain the thing. That it is lost somewhere.'

'A raid, it might still help. They might know more than they told the weak-minded fools they sent north. Or might have learnt more since.'

Cecil gave a mirthless laugh. 'Yes. We have sought to discover this thing and they have sought to discover it. Perhaps they have had better luck. In some days, it will all be over. We might see King James proclaimed and not know who might step forward to ruin us.'

'Queen Elizabeth,' I said softly. 'I heard that her physicians said she was doing better.'

'Lies. Wishes. She has days – I doubt even a week. To tell God's truth I am amazed she has lasted this long. Since the countess of Nottingham died, she has withered on the vine like a rotting fruit. She refuses food. Her throat swells so that she can say little.' That laugh again. 'Daily she cries through the pain on the perfidy of man, the falseness. Her ladies do not even dare to try and dress her. And keeps to her chamber, reading and writing, not sleeping, rarely sitting. I think she hates any person who will dare to live to see the sun rise over a single day that she will not. There is nothing for her now but death. Her mind is gone, her reason and wits. The body will follow.'

An idea was forming in my mind. It been since the tavern.

'Forget a raid,' I said.

He released his grip on the low wall and turned to me. Tears stood in the corner of his eyes, though whether born of sorrow or fear I could not say. 'What?'

'I go in. I heard the plotters are meeting tonight. Might not be true, but I heard it. I go into this Sir Bartlet Everard's house. Alone. Find out what secrets might lie within their walls.'

'… to find secrets. You harbour no idea of wild revenge, do you?'

'No, sir. I only wish to see an end to this.' *To see your future assured so that mine might be too.*

'They might know you.'

'I will be disguised.'

Cecil took a deep breath, before rubbing his throat. 'It might be dangerous.'

'Perhaps you could station some of your men outside. In case I should need … help. In case of trouble.'

He shook his head, doubt drawing his brows together. Then the tension drained, his forehead smoothing. A sudden gust threatened his hat, and he raised his hand to steady it. 'Yes, I can have some lads outside. But in unmarked clothing. Stuff that cannot be traced. If it becomes necessary to save you from something, you can arrange with them some signal or other. But I would not wish the hens to know the colour of the fox that chases them. When will you engage in this … this subterfuge?'

I shrugged, turning my gaze out over the water. 'It's early yet. Tonight.'

23

The process of encrypting had begun, the rambling confession speeding towards the heart of its secrets:

The foul hatred and manner of suspicion between the king and queen did breed such faction and disaffection that I stood again as one amazed. Her majestie Queen Marie went forth into the country on a progress and King Henrie did follow yet no man shewed him proper honour or affection and so it was bruited that he did conceive manifold plots and secret acts &C. And of these I know nothing.

The queen was delivered of the high and mighty James, Prince of Scotland, as is known in the year 1565 A.D. and yet the joyous news which at the said birth did spread across this our realm and across the world did not repair nor restore the royal marriage unto its former state and our sovereign lord and lady did thus continue in their abominable and unnatural hatred. The royal imp was thus delivered into my care with all due ceremony and according to the customs of this land and we were then at the castle of Stirling where he might in time learn his letters beside my own sons by my lawful wife Minnie and my base son by my said wifes serving woman, Bessie.

The Prince was bonny and lusty and gave every appearance at that time of being a good and noble king, as I have said, but the state of the realm of SCOTLAND was troubled. The queen did hope that this troublous time could be as it were covered over and mended and so her Majestie did begin to prepare the baptism or christening of the said prince and it took place in December of the same year at the castle of which we were keepers at Stirling.

I think that there never was such a display of majesty seen in any kingdom of Europe. The gentler sort of nobility of many realms were in attendance and we did require the great hall to be painted again in gold and many fine foods and stuffs procured. The prince was named Charles JAMES and as his gossip stood the queen of England her proxy. And he was to be known thenceforth as James of the noble race of Jameses of our ancient house of Stewart.

The glister of majesty was but a show. Queen Marie did assure that the prince was baptised into the ancient and false harlot of ROME and thereby it was apparent to all men of the true and pure religion of

CALVIN that she did intend that in time this our realm should return to the popes dominion and tyranny. As you will understand, by this revealing as it were of her hand in the game of cards, the queen did make many enemies who set forth to ruin her and thereafter they did plot the means to be rid of her by her utter destruction and shame and to seize the prince my charge before her papist arrows could hit their mark. Of the names of these plotters I know none but Bothwell, the wicked earl.

At the baptism there were such things as powder set ablaze in the sky in the manner of artificial comets. It is a thing well known that comets in the sky foretell the deaths of great ones. That being so, it seems to be a matter of pure reason that such comets as are made by the artifice of man foretell death by the hands of man. And so it proved to be, for in the time following the Roman baptism of the said Prince James, there fell out a matter that would so slander and manifestly ruin our queen that it did shame and dishonour the nation, and thereby I think set a pattern for the unnatural state of the present age and the twisted and unnatural creature who leads it.

24

Hair drifted over the woollen cloth tied tight about my neck. With a trembling of my knees, it fell to the floor, where it clumped in russet patches.

'Stay still!'

The scissors met again in a tinny clash. More hair fell. Of all the places in the world, I was sitting on a stool in the tiring room of the Globe playhouse, which stood otherwise empty, the players and audience having recently departed following the afternoon performance. The seamstress, the old woman who attended to the costumes, Mrs Cole, was fussing about my hair. Knowing how well the players can counterfeit various guises, even in the same play, I had guessed that my best means of affecting a new face lay in stagecraft.

Her first assessment on hearing my request was that hair and beard had to go, utterly and fully. The hair I was sorry for – my reddish-brown locks had a good wave to them and sat well when combed back, away from my face and over my head, adding height. When she had done with the scissors, out came the razor again.

'There,' she announced. 'I'm no barber, but I don't think any barber could have done better. Your own mother wouldn't recognise you.' I did not respond, but perhaps something in my face spoke, for she immediately looked away, muttering gibberish as she fussed about, looking for something in an open coffer. 'Ah, here are we are.' She held up a battered glass.

Hideous.

My head looked like one of those odd, lumpy potatoes. I had lost all manly maturity, too, for she had shaved my beard and moustaches already. Looking back at me was an awkward, dull-witted lad of fifteen. His cheeks were hollow; I had had lost weight on the road. 'Dear God.'

And farewell, pale shadow of Essex.

She had no need to interpret my meaning; my face must have betrayed me again. 'Oh, hush your mouth. You lads today, you're worse than the girls, fussing about your hair and your looks. You look grand, Mr Savage, like a proper man, not some courtly popinjay.'

I set the mirror down on the heavy, all-purpose desk that held the players' cosmetics. Blinked away the image of the me who wasn't me.

'Are you needing any clothing again? We've had a bit of a gift here.' She skipped across the carpeted floorboards – the cheap rug, I assumed, was to muffle the thuds and chattering of those backstage during performances – to a large trunk with several locks. Her hand drifted down to the keys hanging from her waist. 'When old Lady Nottingham died, she gifted some of her gowns to her servants. As though a servant would be able to dance around a hall in a great padded gown.' She laughed, seemingly finding her own joke a good one. 'Though I've seen the day … Anyway, they sold them to us, and so our boys will be right proper ladies from now on.'

I untied the woollen smock from around my neck. 'No, thank you.' Under it, I was wearing the mud-spattered canvas doublet and jacket that had clung to my back all the way from Northallerton. I had not even asked Faith to clean it. All that protected me from its foulness was a clean, cheap shirt beneath. For added effect, I had had the seamstress crudely sew a small St George's cross onto the front of the doublet.

'I thought,' said the Cole woman, 'you just wore that for your chop.'

'No.'

She folded her arms and stepped nearer one of the fat tallow candles that stood about the room, making the air heavy and rank. As the light and shadow conspired to mask the lines on her face, I realised that she must have been a fair-looking woman in her day. Nothing special, perhaps, but unremarkably pretty. 'You're in service to someone aren't you?'

Nosy old cow.

'Don't think I'm being nosy,' she said, and I almost jumped from the stool at her perception. She shrugged. 'I don't care. I did a little spying myself, back in my young day.' Sure you did, I thought. She was well known amongst the playing lot as a noted tale teller and crack-brain. 'Believe me or not, as you will. But I know when someone is setting about a disguise and not for the stage.'

'I have to go. Thank you for your work. How much do I owe you?'

'Nothing, lad. Forget it.' I bounced up; I was not going to argue that point. 'Only a word of warning.'

Always the same with old people.

'Yes?'

'Get out of it as soon as you can, whatever it is you're in. You'll never get away otherwise. Once you do good service, they have you then. And masters, you can't ever trust them. Throw you to the wolves as soon as look at you. Just be sure to get what you can out of them before you leave their service. Be careful, lad.'

I smiled at her. 'Do you take me for a low born nothing?'

'Walk. Up and down here, walk.'

I obliged her. No fool I, I essayed the rolling gait of a demobbed sailor. For once I was glad I was not tall.

Like Lockhart.

The tall stand out as well as they stand up. I was, further, able to lose a further few inches by means of an artificial stoop. 'Good, good, don't overdo it. But you're a little too clean in the face and hands. Tell me, Mr Savage, did you ever hear about the man called Babington?' I shrugged, halfway to the costume trunk. She moved away and took my vacated stool. 'I can't remember his other name. It was the great news a long time ago. Twenty years nearly, I suppose. He plotted for the Scottish queen. I met her you know, Mary of Scotland.'

And I've met her son – who cares?

'Anyway, this Babington, he was caught by my old master Walsingham. And he fled London, like a thief in the night. Went to hide in St John's Wood. He was a knight, a sir. Anthony, that was it, Sir Anthony Babington. So he's out in the woods, and he's changed his clothes, I guess, and you know what he does? To look like a poor man, he dipped his face in walnut juice. Browned his face up good and proper – just white teeth showing in a brown mask. Do you know what he looked like?'

I considered. 'A knight in borrowed clothes with walnut juice on his face?'

'Exactly so. And so he stood out, and they caught him, and they tore his guts out and chopped his balls off.'

'I had intended,' I said, putting a hand on my hip, 'to begrime myself.'

'Don't forget the teeth. And the nails. Be careful.'

I nodded, before giving her a smile and leaving the tiring room. Rather than exiting through the back, I pulled back the curtain leading to the stage and stepped through.

The Globe rose around me, its circular walls and stands climbing, seeming to lean in. There is nothing, I thought, quite so unsettling as an empty theatre; it seems somehow far bigger than when it is filled, and yet also far smaller – it is difficult to believe that upwards of a thousand folk can fill it. Then, in that state, it seemed to me a great hollow skull, the stage its expressive tongue. The genius of the playwrights who laboured where I had come from, they were its hidden mind.

My footsteps echoed across the boards that stood in for Caesar's Rome, for Hamlet's Elsinore, for Sogliardo's Italian countryside. How it must feel to be someone else, convincing over a thousand people that you were not yourself! I scuffed past the chalked crosses that marked the players' positions, reaching the far end of the stage, where gentlemen often perched during performances. There I sat, my legs dangling over the side. Putting my palms on the edge of the boards, I lowered myself down to the yard, where the penny-payers stood. My heavy, tattered boots crunched into the leavings of hundreds of men and women. Seafood and hazelnut shells were embedded in the hard-packed floor, alongside orange rinds and apple cores. Damp patches sat about, inviting speculation. I closed my eyes and threw myself onto it, keeping my mouth shut too.

There, on the yard of the empty Globe, I rolled around in other people's filth, digging my hands in, scratching. A shard of shell cut my palm, and I let the shallow wound bleed until muck staunched it. Then, horror of horrors, I took a handful of dusty grit and put it in my mouth, holding my breath as I chewed, sucked, and spat.

I was by then no walnut-flavoured knight, but an animal. I began walking in my awkward, rolling fashion towards the main entrance, stopping at a sudden cacophony behind me. Old Mrs Cole had come out to see what I was about, and stood centre stage, applauding, whistling, laughing. From the ground, I took a bow, grinning my hideous, brown-toothed grin.

What a reversal the Globe saw that day!

I was ready.

***

I found the house on Bishopsgate Street. Three of Cecil's men were concealed in the place opposite, but I should have known it even without the secretary's direction: men, some in small groups and some alone, were entering it. Boldly, I thought – by the front door.

The place was nothing compared to the palaces of the Strand, but it was a respectable dwelling. Built of dressed grey stone, it had no turrets or towers, but boasted straight lines. In the countryside it would have been a grand manse; in the city, it was a dwarfed but neat building fit for a knight of no courtly connections.

I rolled up to the main double doors, one of which sat open. 'Ho, friend.' The man just inside was a good few years older than me: not old, though his hair was receding. He did not study me, but I let my coat fall open anyway. Instead, he said, in a bored voice with a border of contempt, 'we subjects true unto our queen.'

The words rang a bell. They came from one of the oldest ballads in London, pasted in fading letters on yellowing paper on every tavern wall in the city. Forcing a roughness into my voice, I quoted the next words: 'the foreign yoke defy.'

'Good man.' He yawned. 'In. Take a weapon.'

I slipped past him and into an entrance hall. It was not wide, but it fell far back into the house, ending in a staircase leading up. A large chandelier hung from the ceiling – one of the old-fashioned ones, made of a two crossed planks with candles set along each. The walls were free of hangings, as though most of the household stuff were missing, the place not fully habited. Halfway down the hall, on the left, a large door opened into what I supposed to be a main hall. Voices drifted from it. A table beside the doorway was covered in daggers and bows. I breathed out my relief in a fetid wave; I had come unarmed in case I were searched.

I took a bow and, from a tall jar, a single arrow, clutching all to my chest, and entered the hall. It was packed with men like myself – or, rather, like the man I pretended to be. Old sailors and young masterless men slouched around on stretches of second-best carpet, their Monmouth caps still on their heads. At the far end of the room, to my right, a higher section of floor marked the master of the house's space. It was lost in shadow. On the wall to my left, facing the street, were tall glazed windows, and a huge fireplace opposite me cast a festive glow on proceedings. The flames illuminated, too, the glazed chimera carved and painted above.

I remained standing near the door, my back to the wall, and listened.

'You ever hear tell of this Huntingdon?'

'They say he's like ol' King Arthur, been waitin' for ter take 'is place.'

''e's English, proper English. Think on that – an English king after all these years of a bloody woman.'

'Ho! 'ere comes good ol' Sir Barty. 'e'll know what's what.'

Conversation dimmed as, at the far end of the room, a double-chinned man in his thirties emerged from another entrance. He held up his hands and waved, all rather informally, and cleared his throat. He made a show of shading his eyes and peering across the assembled men, as though astounded to see so many. 'My, friends, what a lot of us there are this evening. You shall each have a copy of my book, to read or be read to you. A life of our great English hero, my lord of Essex. I was his firmest friend, chief amongst them all, and gave him wise counsel. Though he did not please to take it at the end. When the Scotch- and Spanish-lovers broke him.' He patted a low table on the stage, which was piled with loose pages. 'You have heard now that our next king is announced. The good English earl of Huntingdon. King George. And his heir, soon to be Prince Henry.'

A cheer went up. I joined in. 'Good name that,' someone said. 'George. Henry too. Proper English.'

'We're building a new England, my friends. A better England for you and yours.'

'Brother!'

Heads turned towards the door I had come through, as the younger, balding man tumbled through it. 'Ford is back!'

I looked towards the far end of the room and saw Sir Bartlet frown in confusion. He stepped down from the shallow, raised area and began to move through the crowd, ignoring the hands that reached out to clap his back. I tried to melt into the wall, heat prickling up on my shorn scalp.

In the wake of the brother – Gregory, Cecil had said, Gregory Everard, an acknowledged bastard who thrived in trade – strode a man I recognised. Peter Ford, sporting a deep cut which ran from the corner of his eye to the edge of his mouth. In his hand was a poniard. 'He has brought us a new man, Bart. A man with news of the slave Savage. Who has bent his mind to our service.'

Ford tucked away his blade and stood with his hands on his hips, his chin high. The red cross plotters made a wide circle around him. 'Evening, Bart.'

As Sir Bartlet went to him, taking his hand, I could tell by the tight smile on the knight's face that he resented the familiarity of his hardened inferior. 'What news? Do you have it?'

'Not yet. But I've got us news of Savage. Right from the lips of his friend. No fear, Bart – they ain't got it neither.' He put his fingers to his lips and whistled. More movement at the entrance to my right. A tall figure dipped and entered the room, walking on unsteady legs, hat turning in his hands.

Kit Lockhart. Hale and hearty and wearing a freshly turned coat.

25

I think I might have made a noise – some inarticulate, strangled choking sound deep in my throat. Thankfully, it was lost amidst the general hubbub that broke out in the hall.

How?

'My dear, dear Peter,' said Bartlet. From his unctuous tone, it was clear Ford was anything but. Clearer still was his surprise and alarm. 'Perhaps we should speak in private, hear your news.'

'We are all friends here, brother,' said the other one, Gregory. Even from a distance I could see a secret message pass between them, hear the warning in the man's tone.

'Yes. Yes, of course. We're none of your courtly intriguers, hiding our affairs from our friends, from our people. Come, Peter, share your news with us.' Then, evidently unable to resist. 'Have you found the document?'

'Not yet, I said.' Ford beckoned to Lockhart, who stepped forward. I slid against the wall, to be nearer the door, but also for a better look.

Very much alive, Lockhart had only a black eye. 'I-I-I …'

It's him alright.

'Found this bastard outside an inn up north,' said Ford. 'He was in league with one Edward Savage. Been trying to ruin us, Bart. For weeks now. Met the man in gaol. That ain't no coincidence, I don't reckon.'

'Do they have it?'

'No, sir. They're as lost as we is. Threatened to knock this one's brain's out and 'e sang like a parrot. Betrayed 'is mate for his life. Didn't you, rat?' He shook Lockhart's arm.

'I-I … I've told him everything. S-S-Savage made me go. Cecil! He works for S'Robert Cecil.'

God forgive you, Lockhart, I thought; for I never will.

Murmurs and gasps went like a tide through the crowd. Even Bartlet Everard seemed to quake. 'Cecil.'

'He knows nothing!' cried Lockhart. 'Savage knew nothing, we discovered nothing, and so you are safe.'

'Tell them about the document, rat.'

'Now, Peter,' said Bartlet. 'If Mr…?'

'L-Lockhart.'

'If Mr Lockhart here has been good enough to join us, we can be good enough to welcome him.' He turned a smile on my former friend. 'Tell us what you know of the document.'

Lockhart cleared his throat and, twisting his hat throughout, he provided the entire company with a watery, confusing rendition of the tale Andro Allardyce had given us. Then he revealed a version of our meeting in which I, an infamous pervert, had tried to seduce him and when that failed had forced him to join him in a mission on behalf of the crooked hunchback Cecil. He had the grace to falter more than usual on those lies.

When he had finished, Ford said, 'and I chased him and Savage out of that filthy city. Chased 'em right into England.' He put a hand to the livid red welt that ran down his face. 'Was near robbed by bandits for my troubles. Only managed to get away by running down a woman in man's weeds with me 'orse.' He chuckled. 'Broke her head like an egg. Found this one takin' a piss outside an inn and he near shat himself.' Laughter. 'Begged me to spare him. Begged to join us instead and tell us all he knew. So we fixed it up so he looked like one dead. The man Savage had a lover. A musician.' He paused for effect, looking around the group. 'A man.' More laughter. Groans of disgust. 'Tall, like this rat – sorry, Bart – like our new friend 'ere. Well, there's one less of *them* filthy creatures in the world.'

I inched closer to the door. No relief trickled through me, but disgust. I had still got a man killed; and a better man than Lockhart, it seemed. The craven, weak-willed coward. He stammered, barely loud enough to be heard. 'I-I-I am with you. I hate the Scotch king too, as – as you do.'

Ignoring him, Bartlet asked, 'And you know no more? About the lost papers?'

Ford shrugged. 'Dwarf told me the same story, me and Ralphie and Rowland.'

''ere, where *is* Ralphie and Rowland?' This from one of the older men who made up the gaggle of malcontents.

'Dead.'

Shouts and cries. Anger. 'They was only lads,' I heard.

'Rat 'ere killed them,' said Ford, his voice rising above theirs. 'I reckon that warrants justice, don't it?'

'W-w-wha'? It was Savage, I told you, S-S- he lives in Shoe Lane! You'll find him in Shoe Lane with his whore!' Ford approached him, head lowered. 'But you said – you said–'

The fool had trusted Ford over me. Because Ford is more a man and less a werewolf.

It all happened quickly. Sir Bartlet Everard and his brother made some attempt to calm the horde, their arms waving, but it was a futile one and it did not last. The brothers hustled quickly away from the crowd, back to the raised platform, and disappeared into the shadows.

Lockhart disappeared too, under a small hillock of fury. Weapons were raised. Fell. Cries of bloodlust mingled anger and glee. His screams heightened in pitch. Even Peter Ford backed away from the madness.

Some foolish thing inside me pushed up and out. 'Stop it! You fucking animals!'

At first, it seemed that I had been lucky – that no one had heard me.

And then Ford shouted for silence. He was staring at me, his face working in confusion, eyebrows dancing and jaw chewing. Trying to place me. And then he had it. 'That's 'im! That's Savage! 'e's here!' The tip of his poniard pointed in my direction. A head bobbed up from the mass of writhing killers, teeth bared. And then another. And another. Their blood was up now.

I ran.

Through the door, pulling it closed behind me. At the same time I did, I heard the windows in the great hall shatter.

Cecil's men.

I had told them to watch, and to come in if there were any disturbance. They would buy me time to escape. To my right, I saw that the door to the house was barred. Barred and, I presumed, locked. No time to wrestle with it. I turned left, and ran for the staircase, my boots pounding on bare wood.

The noise behind me increased in volume. They were out. And after me.

I turned as I reached the staircase, realising only then that I still had my bow and arrow. A single shot.

There were three of them, Ford in the lead. Perhaps if I could take Ford out, the others would take fright long enough for Cecil's men to get to them.

My pursuers paused at the sight of the arrow. And then they bunched together, moving slowly. A demonic grin split Ford's face, and his arms spread wide from his muscular frame, as if inviting me to take a shot.

Just a few more steps.

Taking the arrow, I raised my bow and pulled back. The sight of it stopped them in their tracks. Perhaps they thought I had more than one. I squinted. It had been years since I had spent every day practising, competing with Thomas at the butts outside Norfield Hall. Biting the inside of my cheek, I called upon the memory that lodged in my sinews. And I fired.

The men behind Ford flinched, though he remained still. And then, as one, they began laughing. The arrow had gone high, far too high.

My breathing deepened.

And then they realised their mistake.

A crack from the ceiling drew their attention. Their hands flew up. My arrow had, as I'd intended it should, buried itself not in flesh, but in the wooden latch that secured the chandelier to the overheard ceiling beam. It was old, the wood rotted and splitting anyway.

The whole thing lurched. Pitched to one side. Flames danced crazily. Some of them went out; more of them flared wide. Freed of its restraint, it fell, cutting a brightly lit path through the air. I did not stop to see if the flames caught and grew but turned and raced up the stairs, throwing the bow behind me.

The landing at the top ran left to right. I went left, running down the hall. There were doors on either side. I kicked at the first on the right and burst in, closing it behind me. It was an office of some sort, though it had a cot as well as a desk. Papers and books lay everywhere, amidst jumbles of inkwells and quills. String was tied about the ceiling in a bizarre criss-cross, wooden pegs still dotting it. Against one wall, smelling of fresh wood and the blood-like tang of metal and ink, was a bizarre contraption that only dimly made sense for a moment.

Printing press in miniature.

I ignored it, my eyes fixing instead on what I sought. A window. A window which must lead to the back of the house.

Too small.

I might make it with careful wriggling. Another door led off the room and I moved to it. Inside was a smaller room, an oratory with an ancient wooden prayer stool. It was not somewhere I cared to be trapped, and so I decided upon the window. Picking up an inkwell, I raised it and made to throw.

'You ain't going nowhere.'

The door was open, and Ford stood framed in it.

I threw the inkwell at him instead and it bounced pitifully off his chest. He threw his head back and laughed. It was all I needed. I dived at him, scrabbling for his wrist. He had been unprepared for the sudden move, expecting me to run. Perhaps even to cower and beg, as Lockhart must have.

I put all my weight into bending his wrist, and he grunted, releasing the poniard. Stupidly, I scrabbled for it, my mind untuned. He seized the advantage of my distraction, and I felt his fist connect with my belly. Unsuspecting, I had left it soft and yielding, and pain rippled from his punch.

I got to my knees, using the door for strength. Breathing shallowly, I said, 'you can't … get away.'

It has always been my strategy in a fight to keep the other man talking, to attack when his mind is busy framing his words. 'Nah, but I can kill you.'

An opportunity missed.

Ford was on his feet too, and we measured each other. He was shorter but undoubtedly more powerful. He seemed to make the same judgment, and he lowered his head and moved towards me. I skipped back, and began guiding him away from the poniard, which lay forgotten on the floor. Around the desk we went. Neither of us spoke again. Neither of us, I realised, was a fool.

With the desk on my left, I darted out my arm and swept books from it. They scattered in front of him. He ignored them. I could feel the back of the room, where the oratory lay, rearing up behind me. I saw him make a fist. Relax it. Clasp his hands together into one underhand mace. And I lunged at him, shortening the distance between us. With no room to swing, his blow was useless.

But so too was my weaker body against the relentless freight of his. I might as well have battled a brick wall.

Brick walls lack eyes.

He was complacent in his brute strength. My hand flew up, and I jabbed at his eyes with my filthy nails, before tearing them down the healing wound on his face. Blood started up and he yelped. The yelp became a roar as he raised one hand to his face. The other, in a flash, collided with the side of my head. My vision blurred and sound dimmed.

I had enraged the beast. I thrust my knee into his crotch, and he howled again. As I made to run, to move, his fist hit me in the face, and I reeled backwards. Again, pain blasted me in meteor showers. Moving backwards seemed to relight the dull fires of it that had burned since he got me in the stomach.

He's coming now.

Before I could turn, he was on top of me, and I fell to the floor. He punched me again, this time on the side of the face. Before the shock of it could wear off, I returned his blow, catching him underneath the chin and sending his head rocking backwards. Weakly, I dug again at his bleeding face, even as I could taste the syrupy blood forming behind my nose, in my mouth.

There was no coming back, I realised. Once a man has you pinned to the floor, in a confined space, a fight is over. From his leering, blood-soaked expression, I could tell that Ford knew it too. The weight of his body was crushing the breath from me, so that even the shallow sips I could manage were becoming impossible.

He opened his mouth to speak, but my hearing was still weak.

I did not understand what happened next.

The hard face above me, secure in its victory and wild in its anger and pain, seemed to vanish. Light seared the room, filling my vision with bursting comets. And then my mouth, my nose, my eyes, were filled with redness. As he had prepared to make an end of me, to pummel me out of existence and leave me a broken corpse

Like Lockhart

Like the musician

Like Nell the bandit with her sweet face and men's clothes

his head had explored in a starburst of blood and gore.

26

In the after-months of the papist baptism there were cast about this realm dark practises so that no man trusted the other and all was rumour and dark talk. I confess now that then I did hide at Stirling, where the puissant prince was brought for to be kept safe and raised in all majestie and it was then said that the king did plot to steal him clean away and that the queen did also plot to steal him from our care.

At this time it is said that Queen Marie did also conceive of a passion for Bothwell and was again made prey to evil charms that did entice her to his embraces and that together they did plainly compass the most wicked and abominable murder of the said Henrie, king of Scots. And in the doing of this plan the said queen did convey her sick husband, who was then safe in the care of his father in the town of GLASGOW, to a house in Edinburgh at the kirk o'field by the Blackfriars (luring him it is said with sundry kisses and caresses and the counterfeiting of a love new-made after its former fashion). And the said house was then mined under with powder and the poor king his corpse then discovered in the orchard, cruelly slain.

This wicked murder was the great shame to Scotland such as like has never been witnessed in the history of any nation and we of the ancient blood did then cry out that the queen must avenge it, we not knowing that she did have foreknowledge of and did carnally know the murderer, the said earl of Bothwell. This we knew only when the said queen married that earl in a Protestant marriage, the better to trick men of the true faith and undo her revealing of her papist plans by the princes idolatrous baptism.

All men of any wit and learning in the CHRONICLES know what then did follow. The queen was disgraced, the nation dishonoured, and the earl of Moray did by gentle speeches and cares remove Queen Maries burden of the state by putting her away in the keeping of his mother in the house of Lochleven. In this state of unmajestie did the said queen utterly renounce her royal estate and abdicate her sovereign lordship of this our realm of SCOTLAND. The said Prince James was crowned with the ancient honours of our realm and the better part of the nobility and all done in accordance with our ancient laws and customs &C and it is for this reason he was said to be as it were a king from the cradle.

Queen Marie did then leave her protection at the house of Lochleven and raise an army, the which was put down and the said queen removing to the realm of her cousin and sister queen, the sovereign lady Elizabeth of England, the protection of whom she lives under yet. Never again did she see her bonny son.

Scotland ought then to have been at peace under King James, the sixth of that name, though he was a bairn, for his nuncle, the said earl of Moray, of good fame and memorie, was made regent and tutor to him. The dark plague that had befallen our polity did not depart with Queen Marie. Instead, wicked men remained to fight in her name and did call themselves the queens partie. And those who fought for the new king and an end to wars were then the kings partie. In this manner there was a state of CIVIL WAR that did cost lives and bring great disturbances to our people so that no Scot could lift his head in any foreign country without feeling shame at the name as foreigners laughed into their sleeves at the infamy of our realm.

The ancient fame of Scotland might only be restored to its former state if the child king could grow old and wise and show before the world that our policies were going aright and that God had not forsaken this our realm. And now I come to the matter of this confession (and pray you forgive that I am tedious in the casting of these hoary memories), in the hope now that you will understand what I did and judge the best of it, knowing the weary and dangerous state of this realm at the time I was then compelled by the weak nature of this king to bear witness to so evil and grievous a thing.

27

The name 'Cecil' repeated in Bartlet's head as he and Gregory hurried through the night. Roberto Diablo. Robert the devil. The most powerful man in England. He had found them out before they could rob him of his pet king.

They had left the house on Bishopsgate Street by the trade and service entrance at the back and found themselves darting through the shadows of the empty streets. It was too early for the watch, but who knew who might haunt the city in the queen's dying days. What had seemed so pleasant to Bartlet as he had strolled home from Saint Martin's Lane and the Scottish shoemaker's shop had become threatening. The crooked buildings seemed to loom over them, ready to reach down, pluck them up, and cast them towards Tyburn. People above leant from their windows to snuff lights.

For as long as he lived, he would never again think well of the city, and nor would he remember with any clarity that journey towards Billingsgate. And he might not live long, he thought, if Cecil managed to give the odious Scotch king an English crown.

They drew into the darkness of a shuttered shop front as a troupe of link boys lit the way home for a well-dressed husband and wife. 'Make way, make way,' bounced in a self-important squeak between overhanding roofs, and the brothers drew deeper into shadow until the procession passed.

'Where are we going?' Bartlet detested the fear and panic in his own voice. For once, he was content to let Gregory lead. The whole affair was, after all, his idea and, if it should collapse, that would be his fault. 'We must leave London! Now! You must get me out! My God, I knew we should never have had them in the house so brazenly – I told you. That was a *gentleman* Ford brought, a *gentlemen* they set upon, by my faith. If Cecil is watching us and we lack the document–'

'Shut your mouth.' Gregory's voice had changed. Contempt lapped at it. 'Do what you will.' He began moving off again into the night.

Bartlet followed in his wake, puffing and gasping.

Through the warren of streets and alleys they went, the night growing darker. The moon appeared weak, offering little light from behind its bank of clouds. It seemed that the area grew rougher, more dangerous, as they passed from the wider thoroughfares. Eventually they came to a small lane. The words 'Shoe Lane' echoed in Bartlet's mind – amongst the last words of the man Lockhart before Ford's party of madmen had fallen upon him.

'Gregory?'

No response. Instead, his brother slid through the street to a door on the ground floor at the end of a tenement block and, with two hard kicks, blasted it inward. Bartlet put his hands over his ears. A scream emerged from the place. Not a man's, but a girl's. The light that had filled the open door dimmed as Gregory's figure blocked it. Bartlet moved closer.

His brother had his thin arm around the throat of a struggling woman or girl, her legs kicking wildly. As he tried to remove her from the building, her hands gripped at the doorway and her screams heightened. She would, he thought, wake the entire neighbourhood. As if in confirmation, the click-bang of shutters opening above drifted down. But no one called out to ask what was happening. They were softly closed again. Bolts slid home.

Gregory seemed to tire of his quarry's struggles. Bartlet could not see what he did – they were simply two writhing black silhouettes – but he heard a dull thump and then the skirted figure fell limply. His brother picked her up and slung her over his scrawny shoulder as easily as he might a doll.

With his victim secured, he stepped out into Shoe Lane and began moving off. At a loss, Bartlet followed. 'Who is she?' Again, no response. He plucked at his brother's shoulder, something of his old hauteur returning. 'Answer me, you fool. Who is she?'

Gregory stopped. Took a deep breath. The girl muttered in her induced sleep. With clear effort, he said, 'I assume this is Savage's whore. If he'll dally with musicians, why not little girls?'

'What use is she?'

'If Savage is Cecil's man, we must have something the crookback's creature will not wish harmed. Or do you not wish to get out of this? Remember, brother, even the queen's secretary is nothing without the document.'

'But it is lost.' Even saying it out loud tore at his guts. All his dreams, his chance at power, unravelling. The only possible way out was securing the lost papers and destroying Cecil and James with them; even bargaining with the secretary would be futile, finding the thing and selling it to him. Such deeds came back to get you eventually.

Gregory began moving away again.

They were heading towards Billingsgate. 'Wait here. Take her.' Bartlet accepted the girl's weight without question. His faith now, such as it was, had fallen upon his brother. Bastards were like rats – they could escape sinking ships. The image conjured up the ship his brother owned. Escape, he thought. Yes, the fellow must have some plan or other.

He crouched down, the girl against his shoulder, and waited.

Footsteps. He started to rise and fell back down. Not Gregory. Another man, all in black and muffled, hurried by and disappeared in the direction from which they'd come – back towards the city. He had gone from sight when Gregory reappeared. 'One man,' he said. 'Only one.'

'City watch?' Panic threatened again in Bartlet's voice.

'No. Come.'

Gregory led his brother and their captive not to the docks, where his ship formed a black hulk against the lighter gloom of the sky, but to his warehouse. 'Is it safe?' In response, Gregory threw open the door.

'Take her in.'

Once they were inside, Bartlet placed the girl on the floor, where she began stirring. Gregory produced a tinderbox and began lighting torches and braziers. Crates burst into life; the wooden staircase with its rotting bannister; the dusty earthen floor. The smell of sawdust, dry and burning, filled the air.

'Who was that man?' He forced command into his voice.

'One of Cecil's. Watching.'

'How did you get rid of him?'

'Cecil wants the document. I told him where it is. And that I've hidden copies enough to ruin him if he doesn't come to terms.'

'A lie.' Bartlet crossed his arms across his paunch before straightening his hat. 'A lie will not get us far.'

Gregory grinned. An unusual sight, thought Bartlet, and an ugly one. 'In part.'

'What?'

'I had no time to make copies.'

Confusion dropped Bartlet's jaw. 'What?' he asked again.

Rather than answering, Gregory drew out a weapon – one of the poniards with which he had provided the red cross knights. In a darting motion, he thrust it deep into his brother's belly.

Bartlet gasped. He could not at first comprehend it. He felt as though he had been punched, and his hands pressed against his gut. Wetness enveloped them. Then the pain sharpened and seemed to spread in all directions through his innards. The image of the priest at Tyburn shot through his mind, the guts being torn out. He opened his mouth to speak and instead collapsed to his knees beside the fallen girl. 'G… G…'

Gregory laughed. Had he pushed his brother too far, finally? Turned him?

'You fat idiot,' he hissed, his face a badly carved mask. 'I have the Scot's fucking paper. He didn't cut his throat. I did it for him.'

Bartlet's chin dropped to his chest. His blood, staining the front of his doublet, looked like ink. 'But … you're good.' His voice sounded like it was coming from someone else's mouth. 'You … tried to stop … the men.'

'Fool. It was I who planned this whole enterprise from the beginning. You were my tool, you fat ass. It was I who encouraged them. It was I who held down the fat Scottish bitch and ravaged her the other day. It is I who carry the secrets of James of Scotland and who'll profit by them. You stupid oaf. Nothing has come out of your empty head save an abortion of a book.'

'You have the document? You always had it?'

'Have it, had it, read it. Put it in cipher. And a glorious end it has too. Gowrie made his deal with me, not you. And together we set out to cozen you, my dear Bart. But I had no desire to let him live after that. Can't trust a Scot. We'll see how badly Cecil wants it now, the hunchback. I shall make a deal with him. A *trade*. If he wants the Scotch ape on the throne, he can have it. For a price. And when he sends someone to parley, he shall see I have a pretty little piece of collateral.'

'But … brother.'

'Don't "brother" me.' Bartlet murmured something. And again, more loudly. 'What? Have a care, fool. Your breath is leaking out of your fat gut.' He giggled.

'Bastard. Bastard!' Blood bubbled up at the corner of his lips, as Gregory aimed a kick at him. He took it on the side and collapsed in a shower of dust. His eyes flickered, locking on those of the freckled girl who lay at his side. He saw terror in them. 'I'm sorry.'

Gregory had begun whistling. He removed his coat and threw it to the ground, before leaning down and fishing in it. He pulled out the black leather pouch that had once belonged to Gowrie and folded back the seal, removing several yellowed pages. 'All here. Would you like to know what it says?'

'Go … to hell,' said Bartlet. Gregory laughed again, before replacing the pages and sliding the pouch underneath his doublet. Then he moved off into the warehouse, whistling again. 'Run,' he mouthed to the girl. His strength was ebbing. He recalled hearing, in his few soldiering days, that blows to the belly were always lethal – there was no remedy for them – but that they were slow and painful in their manner. Looking into the face of the stolen girl, he thought of the son he barely knew, the wife he didn't care for. 'Run now.'

The girl rolled to her side, her face away from him. She landed on Gregory's dropped coat and the thump brought the bastard back out of the shadows. The girl got to her knees and began crawling, but he was upon her, ropes in his hand. She fell to the ground. 'What do you say, Bart – should I see if this one is as unwilling as the shoemaker's wife?'

Summoning up strength, Bartlet grabbed a handful of earth and threw it at his brother's face. 'Bastard,' he hissed again.

Gregory quivered. Wiped his face. And then he began binding the girl's hands. Then her feet. 'Perhaps later, pretty one. Your owner might not desire you anymore if you've been sullied by another.'

As life and consciousness drained from him, Bartlet considered asking why. But he knew. A lifetime of his taunting, of his hatred, of his superiority had made his brother a bastard – not his birth.

28

Warmth spread up and through me. Comfort too. I was in bed. I stretched, and the sudden pain in my stomach, in my head, sharpened to needlepoints. 'Oh, you are awake?' Whose voice was that? Turning on the pillow, which was unaccountably causing an ache in my neck, I saw my brother, his face bearing its usual imperious stamp, looking, as it always did, older than his years. Yet there was concern on it now.

'Thomas?'

What was he doing here?

'Shhh. Rest easy. You're not dead yet.' He put a hand to my forehead. It was pale and clammy. 'You took a fair beating.'

'You are looking after me?'

'Of course. You are family.' That feeling of warmth again. 'I could not leave you to die in London amongst strangers and criminals. They'll find our treasure. Dig it up. Mother will tend to you.'

'Mother? Mother is dead, Thomas.' I frowned. His hand pressed down harder, and fresh waves of pain pounded.

'She wants her crown back. Father is dying too, Adam. The house is mine. Ann is mine. The archery butts are mine. The crown is mine. You are a twisted creature.'

Thomas. *Thomas*. 'Thomas!'

My eyes opened wider.

'Becalm yourself. Who is Thomas?' My brother was not in the room. Of course he wasn't. It had only been a phantom; brought about by I knew not what. In his place stood Sir Robert Cecil. Worry creased his brow, but I did not fool myself that it was for me.

Ignoring his question, I tried to sit. The pain was still there, and my head swam. My ribs, I could feel, had been bound tight. 'Where am I?' I looked past him. In the rosy dawn light, I saw the desk, the printing press across the room, the lines strung back and forth across the ceiling. Memory rushed back. 'Ford!'

'Dead. One of my men took him out of the world. With a snap-chance pistol. One of a number of bodies, I'm afraid. No help for it.'

Lockhart, I thought.

'Where are they? Everard, the brother?'

Cecil did not answer immediately. Instead, he moved off across the room. Other noises came to me: snapping, hammering, shouting. He returned and I gave a more measured judgment. The secretary was angry, but I could see excitement dance there too. And perhaps fear accounted for the unusually unkempt hair standing in jagged waves under his hat. 'Everard has the document. Had it all along. His slave of a brother brought him to their warehouse last night. My man was there watching it. The brother told him to send me word that they had it. Had made copies and would have them on every street in London if I do not come to terms.' He looked over towards the press.

'They lie,' I said, shifting position on the cot. 'They lie to escape.'

'Perhaps.' Cecil made fists of his pale hands, whitening them further. 'A risk. They have been using that press. To print pages from some pathetic scribbles about the late earl of Essex.'

'What do we do? Fall upon the warehouse, burn it?'

Cecil smiled at the word 'we'. Then he said, 'there is too much danger that way. We do not know if there are indeed copies of the thing, if they truly do have it. Or where those copies might lie. The house is being searched. Nothing thus far.'

'But … copies,' I said. 'Printed pages. If the thing itself is in the warehouse, what use are they?'

He frowned, etching deep lines from the sides of his nose to his lips. 'Print. Still, print has a certain power. People believe what they see in print. Even if we could burn the warehouse with those fools in it, if the thing is in print…'

'Did he say what was in the document? About King James?'

'No.' His fists made another appearance.

'They spoke of Huntingdon. Of making Huntingdon king – a King George.'

A snort. 'Yes. They have chanted his name and title for some weeks now. Huntingdon. That old man. His health little better than the queen's. I would not have that good old fellow dragged into this foolery. Those red cross creatures will make no one nothing. Those that did not resist have been taken away. They will not be seen again.'

'To prison?' Newgate, the Clink, the Counter, each greyer and more hopeless than the last.

'No.' He began twisting a ring. 'Now only the brothers remain. And might well have what we seek.'

'I … I could…'

'You could rest, Ned.' He rubbed a hand across his forehead. 'And then … perhaps then you might visit that warehouse. I have men watching to see they do not leave. From a distance. But I cannot say how long that pair will remain there in quietness without hearing from me.'

'Today, sir. I'll go today. I'll get it from them.' I thought of Lockhart, turned, tricked, killed. 'I'll wring the truth from their necks.'

He smiled. 'You understand, I hope, that these men cannot be allowed to live. They must give up their secrets and then be got rid of. Without fanfare. Without trial.'

'I…' Faltering, I tried to summon up my dead friend's image again. 'I'm no hire-hack, sir. But I understand.'

'Good. I must go. This nonsense has taken me away from court too long today. I cannot be so long away from the council. Nor the queen.'

'She is…'

'Being carried to her bed. She has not spoken now in … I cannot say. Her voice is gone. You know what happens once someone in such a condition is at the last taken to bed.'

'I know.'

He gave a nod. 'We have no choice. We must wait on events.' The words were edged with frustration, bitterness. My master, I knew, was one who prided himself on shaping events, not waiting on them. Without another word, he moved towards the door, kicking away the inkwells and account books I had upset during the fight with Ford.

For a time, I lay on the bed, at a loss. A wave of tiredness overcame me, and I slid back down.

Wretched pillow.

Rubbing at my stiff neck, I sat up and lifted the thing. Feathers escaped it and drifted on the currents of the air. 'What the?' I said aloud. Tucked beneath the pillow was a small book. I opened it to the title page, moths darting about my stomach. *A Pithie Exhortation to her Maiestie for Establishing her Successor to the Crowne* by Peter Wentworth. Hideous title. Turning the pages of the slim volume quickly, I searched for marks, for signs of some kind of encrypted message. It was clean. Just a plain old illegal text on the succession.

Why this book?

I considered racing after Cecil but decided against it on so slim a discovery. I did, however, get out of the bed. Ford's body was gone, but dark streaks on the floorboards remained a testament to our fight and its gory end. As I left the room, a man in black entered. 'Safe to lift the floorboards now, mate?' I nodded, leaving him to his destruction. The book, still in my hand, went under my tattered coat. On the threshold, I spotted the poniard that had drawn no blood. A good thrusting weapon. I plucked it up, with a stab of pain in my side, and tucked it into my boot.

I went downstairs, through the quiet former battleground of the house. The chandelier lay where I had shot it down: a mass of broken wood and spent candles. I stepped over it, wincing slightly, and looked into the great hall. More of Cecil's black coated men were at work. They were ranged around the blazing fire, a pile of papers at their feet. Dutifully, they were reading each page, laughing and turning them over before feeding them to the fire. Looking to see if the printed pages of Everard's book on Essex had, hidden amongst them, anything worth saving.

I cleared my throat. Heads turned. 'Was a tall man found here last night? Wounded?'

'Ay,' said one, crumpling a paper in his hands. 'Wounded? That's pretty. More holes in him than a pin cushion.' At the words, numbness overtook my own battered body. I said nothing, leaving them to their work.

'Christ, listen to this,' I heard one of the men say as I left the room. 'The big man would have been better wiping his arse with these pages than writing such tripe.'

I traipsed through the city towards home, seeing nothing, paying attention to nothing. Nor did the city seem to notice me. In the periphery of my mind, I realised that it was emptier than ever, the buildings shuttered and quiet. When had I last even heard church bells ring out?

It was not until I reached Shoe Lane that I found activity, and that squalid. My landlord, if landlord he still was, Mr Frere was making his laborious way down the street. He moved leaning on sticks, one braced under each arm. Even then, he stuck close to the tenement building. Flakes of plaster rained down on him, looking like dandruff on his grey hair. He saw me and stopped, panting. 'Good morrow,' I said.

He squinted at me, failing to recognise me at first. Then he froze. Looked away in fear. And then back. 'Begging your pardon, Mr Savage, I … I…'

'What is it?'

'I don't know if you know. Wasn't my business. Isn't. Only … your maid, your girl.'

My spine stiffened. 'Faith.'

'She … I heard she–'

Before he could finish, I threw myself at the house, my bones protesting. The door fell inward. Her pallet was empty, the woollen cover on the floor. She never left it lying so; as soon as she woke, she folded it neatly and stowed it away. Nor was she in my room. My throat ran dry and my arms fell to my side. The book I'd taken from the Everard cot fell at my feet.

Back out in the street, I caught Frere. 'Where is she? What did you see? What happened?' The questions tripped over one another in my haste to have answers. I realised I was shaking him as one stick hit the ground with a crack. Shaking myself, I retrieved it. How I must have looked to him, shaven-headed and -faced, dressed like a grubbing vagabond. Probably he thought I had escaped a gaol.

'It was them upstairs, sir,' he spluttered. 'Saw last night. Man broke in and took your wench. Carried her off. With another man.'

'And no one stopped them?' I looked up at the closed wooden windows above. 'You cowards!'

'Thought you'd want to know, sir.'

I left him, running out on to the eerie emptiness of Fleet Street. Once there, I forced myself to take in deep breaths. The air was clean, purified by the lack of people and business about. Fear seemed to be acting as a cleanser in the city. With the air, reason wafted up into my mind. The Everard brothers. They had taken her. Thankfully Ford would not be joining them. They were gentlemen, after a fashion. Besides, if they took her, it was for a reason. What had been the word Andro Allardyce had used?

Blackmail.

No. Worse than that. She was a hostage. They knew, then, that I was Cecil's man and hoped to raise the stakes in their attempts at bartering with him for the document.

To hell with the document. And Cecil, and King James. Get her back.

My multitude of pains became a memory as I took off at a shambling run for Billingsgate.

***

I found the docks as quiet as the rest of the city. As I made my way around them, around coiled lengths of rope and slimy, stinking crates, I was startled by another man whom I took to be in Cecil's employ. He looked at me with narrowed, suspicious eyes. 'I work for him,' I said. 'I am 710.'

He nodded. 'I ain't touched the place. No one been in or out since first light. It's that one.' He pointed at a featureless wooden building on two floors. Beyond it, I could see a small merchantman cargo ship.

'Ain't no one in the ship neither. All quiet.'

'How many ways in and out of the place?'

'Front door. Back door. Windows. Stairs at the back.'

'You have men around them all?'

'Men? There's just me here now.'

'What?'

'The lad inside said he has a friend of the secretary's prisoner. A woman. Says she'll die if he don't get sent one man direct from the master. I thought you was the man.'

'I am.'

'Said last night when they come down that if he thinks we're trapping him, if he thinks he's getting "played false", he said, then the girl dies and all London knows the king's secret. What'd he mean by that, d'you think?'

'I have no idea.'

I left the unnumbered agent standing on the docks and walked towards the door of the warehouse. In truth, I should like to say there was something heroic in my manner: that I burst through the door in a blaze of fury.

I walked up to it and knocked. It opened at my touch.

Despite the dismal daylight, the inside of the warehouse was dim. Small pools of light around wall-mounted torches sent wavering shadows around. I made my way inside. 'Sir Bartlet Everard? I come from the queen's secretary. I come alone.'

Movement. Upstairs.

I took slow, steady steps into the room. It is a rule of entering a dangerous place that one must never bluster or race: not if the ground is unfamiliar but known to an enemy. I held up my hands, suspecting I might be being watched.

I had not gone far when my boots bumped against something on the floor. I bent. My eyes, adjusting to the weak light, just made out the shape of a body. My breath stopped. Lying on his back, his skin greyish white, was Sir Bartlet Everard.

What on earth?

I ran my hand over him until it came away sticky and black. The bumping sound came again. 'I'm here, Faith. Ned's here.'

A rickety wooden staircase led to the next floor and I climbed it, keeping my tread heavy. At the top, I moved down a hall, one hand steadying my way along the wall. The wall met a door. Again, I knocked. Pushed it open.

Inside, light blazed. Every wooden blind was open. I cursed, throwing up a hand to shade my eyes. Another door was built into the back of the room, leading outside. To a ladder or the external stairs, I guessed.

'Ned!' Her cry was cut off.

'Faith.' Gregory Everard was holding her in front of him like a human shield. A knife was at her throat and her hands were bound. Her ankles too, I supposed, though her nightdress covered those.

'You're Savage?'

'I am.'

'Cecil's man?'

'He sent me to speak with you.'

'You know then what I have?'

I knew I must keep him talking, at least until I could formulate some plan. 'Yes. You have the matter written against the Scotch king. Brought into the city by one Gowrie. Where is he?'

'Dead. I killed him.'

'Right.'

'I've made copies. Printed copies. A slow beginning for readers but the ending will heat their blood.'

I swallowed. 'Where are they?'

He laughed. 'You have a choice, Savage. You can try and take me and my document, or you can have the girl.' The knife wavered away.

I sighed. 'I only want her. You can go. Make your own deal with Cecil.' I meant it. The secretary could deal with the madman and his document. I did not care. I would not see another friend killed due to my involvement with the government.

'Trust him? Trust you?'

'How do you see this ending, Mr Everard? What do you seek out of this?'

'I seek only what–'

'Go to hell, you pigfucker!'

Gregory and I both jerked as Faith's voice tore across the room with the force of a thunder clap.

You know what to say when a lad tries to take liberties?

At the same time, she jerked her elbow, catching him in the stomach. His knife fell and she hopped towards me, tottering and falling. My arm flew out, circling and dragging her to me. Pushing her behind my back, I fumbled at my boot, ripping out the poniard.

Gregory Everard was gone, more sunshine spilling in through the door.

I used the blade instead to slice through Faith's bindings. 'Did he hurt you?'

'No,' she said, and I hugged her.

'Thank God.'

'I'm not hurt. And I'm not frightened of that … that *pigfucker* or any like him.'

'Steady now, mouse, you've said it now, it's out there. No need to wear it out.' There were some small crates lying about the room, and I guided her to one. She resisted sitting down. 'For me, please.' We both sat, and I willed my heart to stop its merciless beat. As it did, the pain began its now familiar drumbeat.

'Aren't we going after him?'

'No. I work for the queen's secretary. Let him catch him.'

'I robbed him, Ned.'

At first her words did not register. She repeated them. 'What?'

'From his coat, downstairs. I took this.' From the deep pockets sewn into her nightdress, she produced something. Hope flared within me. It was a book. The hope dwindled. Not a document. She opened it and began reading. A frown caught at her lips.

'What is it? Anything about the Scotch king?'

'What? No, it's … it's accounts. Like mine at home. But…'

My heart sank, but not by much; the hope hadn't had time to take root. Instead the word 'home' caught me. 'Let's go. Perhaps the fellow outside gave the creature chase.'

29

Back at Shoe Lane, Faith forced me to lie down on her pallet. Cecil's man was absent from outside the warehouse, and I supposed he must indeed have given chase. At any rate, we did not wait around for him or any other. She spoke breathlessly, excitedly, about what had happened. About how she was not afraid of anyone, about how she wanted to go out to the Exchange that day. I suppose I must have dozed, for she shook me awake. I was alert instantly. Pain does that.

'Ned!'

'What is it?' I reached towards my boot. 'Is he come?'

'No one's come. It's … I've been looking through his book.'

'Accounts?'

'Yes, but. Well – I do your accounts.' I grinned at this. 'Well, I try. And this looks like how I would do them, see?' She held up the book, open at the first page. Neatly formed lines of numbers were formed in a column, and against each were what I thought must be in-goings and out-goings, in pounds, shillings and pence. I shrugged. 'No, look.'

'Faith, I don't understand numbers.' It was true. I was no idiot – I knew that one plus one equalled two, and I could buy and sell at a good price. But keeping detailed accounts was woman's work.

'They don't make sense, none of them. There's so many, but none make sense. And the list of numbers on the left there, it's all a-scatter. The numbers jump about between one and two-hundred.'

'And that's bad?'

Ignoring me, she continued. 'And £3, 5s, 1d minus £6, 5s, 9d doesn't make £1, 4s, 8d.'

I sat up. 'So he can't count.' But she was right. There was something here. 'Is it a code?'

She shrugged. 'Maybe.'

'No, not a code. A cipher.' The difference, I knew, was that a code meant a simple message did not really mean what it said. Thus '710 arrives at the hall' would mean 'Ned Savage arrives at Whitehall'. A cipher took the words of a message or a book

or a document

and replaced the letters with something else. Like numbers. I beat back hope for the second time that day. 'Could those numbers stand for something? Like letters?'

'Letters?' She moved over to the stool and sat, taking the book with her and examining it. 'Maybe. If we knew where to find the letters.'

I sprung up from the bed and into my inner chamber. The book I'd taken from under Gregory Everard's pillow was where I had dropped it, forgotten on the floor. Plucking it up, I took it to her. Excitement sang in my voice despite myself. 'This, mouse, this – could this be the key? Could you turn that jumble of numbers into letters? Into words?'

Doubt passed her face as she reached out for it. 'I … if it is just adding and subtracting and that. Then I think I could. I'm not some stupid pigfucker.'

'That's enough,' I laughed, wishing I'd never taught her the word. I patted her hair. 'If you can, I swear by Christ I'll marry you.'

'It'll take some time to see if I can.'

'Take it! Take all you need, you angel.' I leant down and kissed her.

'Get out of it.'

My sore body forgotten, I left the house, locking the door behind me, and sought around for food to bring her, and ale. As everywhere seemed to be closed, I was reduced to going over to Frere's house, where his wife gave me all I wanted, still grateful that I had brought him home after what she called his accident. Laden with loot, I returned. 'Have you cracked it?'

'Oh Ned!' She was still hunched over the table, both books open. She had torn blank pages from one of her own account books and some ink was marked along the top of one. 'I've got it. It's so easy.' Her freckles were livid, her cheeks pink, and red hair tumbling about her face. Her cap she had untied, torn off, and thrown away. I looked at her page. Some random letters were written, and she had drawn a line through them. Farther down the page was written, 'In great fear and trembling'. I read it aloud.

'Words,' I said, careless of how stupid I sounded.

'It's so easy,' she said again. 'The first column of numbers tells me which page to go to. Then the stuff that looks like sums – if you just pretend it's not sums, not pounds and shillings and pence, and just look at the numbers – each number is which letter on the page you look at. I thought it was harder, like the alphabet was made numbers, but it's not. It's just like: 2 means go to page two. £3 means go to the third letter on that page. 5 shillings, go to the fifth letter. It's the easiest thing in the world. I can do the whole lot in a few hours.'

'Jesus,' I said. 'He was not a master cipher-maker.'

'Maybe he had to do it quickly.' She smiled. 'But it is clever, Ned.

Clever because it's so easy.' Her cheeks glowed a darker red. 'I mean, a child could do it if he had the book, like you got for me, and knew that that book was the key. But the cleverest man in the world couldn't break it even if he knew how but didn't know which book he needed. Or at least it would take him a long time.'

'I couldn't do it, even with the book. I would lose count. Please, mouse – do it.'

I left Faith working, fetching her food and ale and fresh ink whenever she needed it. I even did a little tidying, discarding her wastepaper. I thought of the Globe, and the seamstress applauding at the yard whilst I bowed from it.

As she worked, she passed me the blotted sheets and I read, following the rambling deathbed confession of a tedious old man who had apparently been of the nobility of Scotland in the king's mother's time, and who moaned endlessly about the state of the country, interspersing his history with pathetic excuses for betraying his wife. It was only when she had deciphered the final pages that the full horror of what I was reading, and what it meant for the succession, became clear. Most of the words I did not understand well. Realising they were in Scots, I did what I could to translate them in my head:

Whilst I was given the care and charge and education &C of the said Prince James, the state of Scotland did grow dolorous still. With the fallen queen in her rest in England the governance of the realm did fall to her brother, the earl of Moray, who was then cruelly murdered, and there following to the said king's grandfather, the earl of Lennox, who was in the same wise murdered by his divers enemies, and so in time it fell to me as the kings guardian and the which sore burden I did much regret. Now for too long have I beaten about the bush and so I come to the matter.

Under my authoritie I was sometimes called to Edinburgh and the king remained within our walls at Stirling. In the year of our Lord A.D. 1571, I had word in my chambers that the king was with fever and that though it were but a little fever he should be tended and so I did ride to visit with him in the nursery at Stirling. Upon my arrival I found that the said King James of Scotland had succumbed to his fever even as I rode hard up the wynd and into the castle and I did find that his poor corpse was still warm and none save his nurse, who was the same Bessie, serving woman to my wife and with whom I had sometime lain and by whom I did sometime bear a son. At that time, it must be understood that the wars in Scotland were still being fought in the name of the fallen queen and I so recent made governor of the realm and with the death of the said king who knew what might fall out.

It was thus not for the sake of vanity nor vainglory of myself that I did conspire with the said Bessie, but for the good of the peace in Scotland that we did remove the king his poor body from his cradle, he having been at his death under the age of five, and in his place did place the sleeping body of my own base-born infant, also called James.

Bessie did then wrap the body of the sickened and dead king in cloths of wool and take them to the castle at Edinburgh which was then in the hands of the queens partie and did gain admittance there in the false weeds of a washerwoman and therein she did place and conceal the poor bones of that dead king. I judged it the best that a noble imp of such ancient and royal blood should best lie there and though it were dangerous to do so I judged that none of the queens partie should know the face of the dead infant even should Bessie fail in her task.

Since that day there has been no James king of Scots but only the counterfeit James, that is to say the base-born son of Mar and Bessie, who by my own wicked deed is so named as our lord and sovereign that he bears no knowledge or understanding of his own mean birth and believes himself in truth to be the king. I pray God and the saints to believe that I did think only that my false and wicked deception of placing a corrupted youth of base blood in the place of a king might for a time prevent bloodier wars. Placing my trust in God I did choose to believe that the matter would be revealed at the right time and order restored to this our realm, whether by the truth of this confession being made known or by the death of that abominable bastard my spurious son. What other path might I have chosen? The death of the little king being so commonly known, our realm would have been torn asunder, the queens partie rampant, the apostolic see at once on our shores with armies in the name of Queen Marie and the said queen like to be killed by her English cousin before she might be released by the said Catholic armies, and stones rising from the ground and such other disorders of nature.

And to this time none have known of our false kings true nature and all have believed that wickedly got creature born in sin to be truly King James, son of Queen Marie and King Henrie, though he be not their child but my bastard. As I make to depart this life I seek to unburden my soul of this matter. And also to the matter of our crown falling one day into perfect unity with the crown of England, I pray that Queen

Elizabeth of England does make her marriage with the French duke, of whom we hear daily, the tragedy of St Bartholomew notwithstanding, and by the which produce issue of her own body. For if it should come to pass that this matter is kept privily it will be a false wretch draped in kings clothing which will be made king of England too, and so the disease and corruption which I began though my own grievous fault will infect this whole island and at such a dark thought I shrink and tremble, as should all Christian men. So disordered and unnatural a world cannot be nor can I count myself amongst the ELECT if I were to have been the instrument of such wicked devilry as this matter given let to continue unknown.

And these pages I give into the hand of my friend the good and noble earl of Morton at this my last supper with him, trusting in God and him that he will judge it best to make use of them on this the xxvi of October in what is commonly said (but falsely!) to be the fifth year of the reign of our sovereign lord James, the sext of that name, A.D. 1572.

John Erskine, earl of Mar&C, REGENT and governor of SCOTLAND, this his seal.

I lay on the cot, feeling nothing. The scandals of crowned people interested me, as they interested most people, but this was something wilder and more dangerous than anything I had heard of. The man I had met in Edinburgh, the man whom the world knew as James, king of Scots, was nothing but a changeling: a base-born son of the true king's guardian, slipped into the cradle when that king died in childhood.

Could it be true?

'What does it all mean?' asked Faith. Writing, deciphering, she must have not have kept track of the words, written as the original had been in confusing Scots.

'Nothing.' I gathered up the papers and account book, feeling giddy and light and shocked, and disappeared into my inner chamber. There I dressed, putting on sword, shoes, and my finest Holland shirt and counterfeit court clothes. I emerged, feeling better now that I was wearing garments that held me together tightly, and swept over to her. Before she could ask, I said, 'I must go to court.' It was something I had always wished to say, though not in such bizarre and discomfiting circumstances. It was fewer than ten miles to Richmond but convincing a boatman to take me upriver at such an hour would take all my powers of persuasion. 'Madam, a kiss.'

'Leave off, you pi-'

'Don't even think it. Here.' I gave her the poniard. 'If anyone comes, don't use that new-minted rough tongue. Use that.'

With the papers sanded and dry, I left our tenement and stepped into the cold evening. Daylight lingered. Already a pleasant, pale moon loomed large in the moody sky, although rag-ends of clouds drifted past it. They were dark, I noticed, threatening rain.

I locked the door.

A jingling tinkle rang up the lane. At the junction with Fleet Street, I saw him. Gregory Everard. Come for his book, I didn't doubt. Like me, he had undergone a change, donned a disguise since the morning. Probably he had the same destination in mind. On his head was a tall hat, velvet black, and his clothing was pure courtier, the material thin and gauzy. He was finishing tying up a horse at the post by the side of the lane's entrance.

My hand was on my sword as I rocked towards him. There was no question of sneaking in my grand rig: the sword alone struck my boot with every step.

Too weak to fight.

'Everard,' I cried, seizing the advantage. His sword was out in an instant. Mine too. We adopted the *en garde* position and stood, measuring each other in the evening light.

He laughed – a brittle, quavering note. 'As you can see, Savage, I come as a gentleman. And I know how to fight like a gentleman. With honour.'

'Come to fight?' I shouted the words, hoping to attract attention. Though the street was dead, I knew people were watching. 'Come to fight me, Everard?'

He relaxed his stance, resting back on the ball of his foot. 'No.'

'Then why? Have you brought the document to me? Do you propose to tell me its contents? By God, man, what does it say?'

He slipped further into complacence. 'I have come for a book. I let your little whore take it. That it might not be found if your master's men searched my warehouse. I suppose you know it to be a cipher. Yet it is of no use to you without the key and the key is lost.'

'And you think to take it? By force?' I let him see my own stance waver. I winced, just enough to let him know that I was injured. Too much – a sigh or a cry of pain – would have been to reveal myself a player. Gregory Everard made a show of putting away his rapier. Its scabbard thudded against his own boot. I did the same, only partly feigning my confusion. Again, we stood and regarded one another. Windows above us opened, and people began leaning out, lighting the torches that stood ready on the plaster walls of their tenements. A fight between gentlemen was not a riotous assembly of plunderers, but a sight worth seeing.

'I come to do a fair trade. My book, which is of no earthly use to you, for what I have in my purse.' With slow, deliberate moves, he untied a purse from his belt and held it up. He had, I assumed, been to his ship, or raided the warehouse for his wealth. He poured coins out into a gloved hand. 'There is enough here to see you out of this place. Have my dead brother's home, if you will. It is a fine place. I shall not feel the want of it. Or the need.'

I let my eyes light up with greed but said nothing, gnawing on my bottom lip. I stepped closer. He smiled, and I made sure to keep my hand up, eying him warily. 'A fair trade?'

'You have the book?'

'I do. Yet none must know…'

'Back in your holes, you wretches!' he shouted up into the night, making me start. A few windows closed – not all. I moved closer and put out my hand to his opened palm. I had read him well enough. He meant to go through with the deal, undoubtedly stabbing me in the back when I turned away with my gains. The whisper of a smile twitched at the side of his mouth as my hand hovered over his.

And I jerked it. Hard and upwards, making a fist as it moved. I caught him under the chin, his head snapping back. As it did, my other hand caught him hard in the throat. Before he could react, I pulled free my own rapier and jabbed him in the chest. He fell backwards, landing on one hand, the other scrabbling at his own weapon. His purse and coins scattered. 'You might know how to fight like a gentleman,' I said. 'But I know how to fight like a dirty bastard.'

He made a mewling sound.

Pathetic.

I put the point of my rapier over his stomach. 'Wait,' he hissed. 'I'll tell you! I'll tell you everything. About the Scotch king! Cecil will–'

'Cecil will know, because I know, and I shall tell him.' I pressed down hard, the blade slicing through his clothing and flesh as easily as through butter. 'This madness ends with you, you lousy piece of shit.' He screamed, as I imagined his brother had done. Revenge did not motivate me. I was not thinking of the men that Gregory and Bartlet Everard had drawn to death through their plotting. I was not even angry at him stealing away Faith and forcing her into a night of terror.

I simply wanted to be able to sleep knowing that someone who threatened my family was no longer abroad in the streets.

Cries rang out from above me. Boos. I had not given them a fair fight. From below came another sound. Putting my sword to the dying man's throat, I leant in to hear his final words. My eyes widened, first in disbelief, and then in horror. He closed his mouth and I put a finger to his throat. Faith might have been the one with a head for numbers, but it was not difficult to count to zero.

Leaving his bleeding body at the foot of Shoe Lane, I collected up his treasury – more than I could make in a year, two, even from Cecil – untethered his horse and rode pell-mell for Richmond palace as that weak moon fought the gathering clouds to claim the soul of its mistress, the queen of England.

30

I was not shown to Cecil's chambers, but instead ordered to wait, to fret and cool my heels in servants' halls, galleries, and withdrawing chambers. Dripping wet (the clouds had made good on their threat), I had found it surprisingly easy to get into the great, many-towered palace, which stood like a stately sentinel over its portion of the Thames. Though there had been guards in forest-green-and-white liveries in tight packs surrounding the place, and more at the door to which I had ridden, they seemed quite willing to allow a man who gave a number and called himself a servant of the secretary inside. Their concern, it seemed to me, was in preventing folk from leaving.

Eventually someone brought a message from my master that I was to be taken to a closet room and offered refreshment. I followed, through the unfamiliar rooms of the place, expecting that I would have one of my secret meetings with the man himself. Evening at the palace seemed ripe for such a conference. It was deadly silent, with a queer, haunted feel. I had expected to find groups of ornamented ladies and gentlemen, of lords and barons and earls, busily moving to and fro, keeping up to date with the progress of the queen's illness. Yet they all seemed to have closeted themselves away – or perhaps were all standing hard by wherever the royal bedchamber might be.

'In here, sir.' The usher bowed me into a dark room, lit only by the gallery outside. It was tiny, I realised: truly a small closet, with only a canopied chair in the centre and a tall, unlit candelabrum in the corner by the door. Cecil was not present. I turned, to ask the usher, and found him closing me in. A hard *snick* followed, as blackness smothered me.

'Wait! What is this?'

I stumbled to the wooden door and felt for the metal ring, tugging on it. Nothing. Fear and panic fought one another, each wrestling for dominance in a giddy clamber up my throat. They made their joint victory felt in a strangled yelp. I did not like being confined. Even in prison, the rooms had been open enough to admit dozens of men. There was invariably some source of light in the London gaols, however meagre.

I closed my eyes, bringing even deeper darkness, and willed tranquillity. Slipping to the floor, as much as my boots allowed – my rapier had been confiscated on arrival – I gained the chair in the room's centre by touch and sat down beside it. It would not do to be caught sitting in a chair under a canopy of estate when he arrived. He would come. I removed my hat and cast it away, irritated by the maddening itch its lining caused on my shaven head.

And perhaps he will have you killed. You know too much. Knowledge is not power. It's death.

He would come.

I waited, unaware of the strange and terrible drama that was playing out in the palace of Richmond that night. I did not know that the world I knew, had always known, was passing, like an apple falling from a tree.

Time passed – I was unaware of how much. Hour melted into hour like molten black steel. Footsteps thundered by outside. Voices raised and fell. For a time, I thought I heard sobbing, although I could not tell whether it came from a man or woman.

Eventually, the lock clicked once more. A small figure was outlined in the doorway and he left it open, using the light to set the flame from a small lantern to the closet's candle-tree. I remained cross-legged on the floor whilst Cecil softly closed the door.

He blinked continually as he looked at me, his eyes pink and puffy. I rocked onto my backside and then stood as he moved to the centre of the chamber and, brushing down the back of his dark gown, he sat. 'It is done?' I asked.

'The queen died in her sleep several hours ago.' He said it without expression, seeming stunned, tired, unbelieving.

'And the king? The Privy Council has approved him?' Perhaps my tone was sharp, for he looked up.

'There is no Privy Council until our sovereign lord arrives to appoint one. The *Great* Council has approved his coming. The queen named him her successor by a clear gesture, sufficient in law. I shall hasten to him as soon as my public duties will permit.'

I swallowed, picturing the expression on King James' florid face when he learned the news. Would he reward the messenger or mock him? I looked into the shadows. 'Gregory Everard is dead, sir. As you wished.'

For the first time, he seemed to see me properly. 'And I see you have his purse.'

'Full of your gold, sir. He spoke to me before he died. Said there was a third person in this. One who guided him, and by him his brother in their plotting. The maker of the red cross plot. I trust he gave you the document?'

We stared at one another in that tiny room, he from his seated position and me standing. He was considering what I knew, and whether it was worth lying or dissembling. I saved him the trouble. 'It was you all along. This whole enterprise. The men of the red crosses. Gregory and Bartlet Everard. You set them all to work and then set me to stop them.'

To my astonishment, he grinned, blinking again. 'Sharp lad, Ned.'

I did not return his smile. Instead I said, 'why?'

He shrugged. 'Gregory Everard has been in my employ for years. Watching the news out of Scotland from the sailors. He came to me some months ago with claims that a Scot called Gowrie was attempting to sell a document prejudicial to the claim of our new king.'

'Did you know what it said?'

'Not until last night, no. In that I was quite honest. I had to have it, of course. And I do.' He reached under his black gown and produced the old leather pouch. 'Yet I would have had it sooner. Gregory Everard was willing to procure the document, but I thought it a waste to take it so easily.'

I made a snorting sound through my nostrils. 'Better to thwart a plot and show King James how necessary you are.'

He shrugged. 'A new reign means new servants of the crown. We must all show our worth. The king is alarmed by the plots of his subjects. One Mowbray came to London stirring up trouble some months ago and I returned him to his sovereign. Yet I fancy that showed only a little my skill in discovering intriguers.'

A blackened, tarred hand waved from the gate into Edinburgh.

He had not invited me to do so, but I sat down on the floor of the room. I was torn. At that moment I hated the shrunken little creature, hated his wiles, and especially hated the fact that he had made me a pawn in a game I still did not understand. Yet part of me admired his brain. And I could not fail to realise that he had probably just assured himself a place at the right hand of the incoming sovereign. 'But … why the red crosses?'

'Gregory bore an unnatural hatred for his fool of a brother. He offered to push Sir Bartlet into leading this plot. To encourage him then in his delusions. He, of course, thought the whole thing his own idea and quite real. Thus, the red cross plot, Sir Bartlet Everard its leader, was born. Born to secure this document and make wicked use of it.' He regarded his nails, frowning at something there and tutting. 'King James distrusts parliaments, Ned. Always has. I had had Gregory convince his brother to speak openly of the power of parliament often enough. It did not hurt to dress this little plot in parliamentary robes. And thus, I have shown our new king how a diligent servant might take the fangs from a member who grows overbold. And shown others who might one day sit in the house what a pretty pass such a fellow might come to.'

I shook my head, suddenly no longer caring about the reasoning behind his scheme. I wanted to know only my part in it. 'Why me? Why did you drag me into this?' Horror shot through me. 'Did you have me thrown in gaol with Ford.'

He did not answer that directly. 'You were to be a hero, Ned. I set Gregory to push his brother into making this plot, promising that his brother would hang for it and he would then inherit the family estates, be given wardship even of the traitor's son. That's all he wanted, you know – to have everything that his legitimate brother had. Yet a plot is only one thing. I needed a man to discover it, so that I might break it. An old stratagem of my father's friend Walsingham. Hatch a plot and then destroy it. Though I own this one very nearly got away from me.'

I could scarcely believe it. I suppose my disbelief must have shown.

'Yet I did not fully trust the bastard Gregory. Oh, not because he was base born, but because he was always so eager to destroy his brother. It is a cold creature who harbours such jealousies. And I was right. Our plan together was simple.' Cecil's tone became a little more animated, and I sensed he enjoyed laying out his wiles. 'He would secure the passage of Gowrie into England, feigning all along to be his brother's poor slave. Then he would procure the document and bring it to me, telling the fool Bartlet that it was lost to hold him in suspense, all the while encouraging him to acts of folly with his rabble.'

'But he wouldn't give it to you.'

'No, indeed.' An angry flicker of distaste wrinkled his pale brow. 'He claimed Gowrie had not made their appointment. That the document had *indeed* been lost. I did not know whether to believe him. And so a distrust grew between us. Not openly. I could not accuse him of trying to gull me or entirely break our arrangement. At best, if he spoke true, I had the red cross men and you on the trail. It was not until yesterday, when I knew time to be nearly spent, that I grew weary of his evasion. But I began to disbelieve him long since. These past weeks … I considered it possible he might even have somehow spirited the thing to her Maj – to the late queen, by some other buyer. I needed you then not as a hero to crush the plot. It had grown too hot for me. I needed you, truly, as an instrument in investigating it. I had lost control of my creature, and truly I feared the thing was indeed lost somewhere.' He sighed. 'So you see, Gregory Everard was my lapdog, and his brother his dupe. Yet oftentimes lapdogs grow greedy, pampered things, and seek ever more from their master. Gregory betrayed me. He had the damned thing all along. Killed Gowrie for it, and thought to cozen me, keeping it back until he might extract a better price.'

I touched the purse at my waist. 'I see he did.'

'But he did not live to enjoy it.' A warning note sounded. 'You see what might happen to those who are ungrateful for the chances given them?'

'I've been your puppet,' I said. 'Do you wish your gold back?'

'Keep it. You have earned it, Ned.'

I looked again into the shadows. Into the memories of travel, of gaol, of Raleigh and the Lady Arbella. My mouth tried. I folded my arms over my stubbly head so that it sat in the crook of my elbows. 'My God. My God. Raleigh and the Stuart woman. I … I wasn't investigating them. I was … *involving* them in the plot.'

Again, he gave that ghastly grin. 'My dear boy, you were saving them from it, if the new king wishes it. He trusts neither. Perhaps you noted that the men of the red cross visited both. Thus, Bartlet Everard's plot made both guilty, if King James wishes them guilty. And yet you found them innocent, and might testify to their innocence of any wrong, if King James wishes them innocent.'

'I'll do nothing.' I stood, stooping to retrieve my hat. 'I wish nothing to do with anything anymore.'

'Is that so? Tell me, how long do you think your new riches will last, Ned? A man of your tastes? A year?' He saw me falter. 'I know much about you.' A pause. 'Adam Norton.'

I sank again to the floor.

'Do you think I thought you some mushroom of the city sprung up in the night?' he asked. 'I know who you are. You have my sympathies. Do not be a fool. You can creep off and try to hide. You can resist me, Ned, and lose. Or you can play the role I designed for you. A hero. A trusted and assured servant of the crown who saved the honour and secured the succession of our new king. There will be rewards, I promise you. King James is open-handed to his friends, I believe. Especially the pretty young ones.'

'*My* friend died,' I said evenly, staring at him.

'Your friend was not supposed to be any part of anything. You asked no leave to involve any other man. Nor to put the fellow in danger. You chose to.'

He's got you there.

Stupidly, I rose and spat into a corner of the room. Cecil's brow darkened. 'As you like it. Get gone from my sight then, Savage. Take you to your hole by the Whitefriars. And when you get there, look upon your property, your stolen goods and chattels, and consider whether the man who has kept it all safe from routs and roils is worth spitting at.'

You know too much. Resist him and die or bend to him and live. And live well.

He had won and he knew it. I kept my hat before me and mumbled. 'I'm sorry, sir.' The words tasted like gall. 'The sudden learning of this matter, it has … troubled my mind. The death of the queen has upset me.'

'A fine player.' He shook his head, but the anger departed. Reminding him of Elizabeth's death acted like the tonic I had hoped it might.

'That … thing,' I jerked my chin at the black pouch, cradled in his lap. 'Is … is it true?'

'You know of its contents?'

Damn.

'Yes, sir.' I fished out Gregory's account book and passed it over. 'His cipher.'

'You are a code-breaker, now?' He did not ask questions, thankfully, but accepted the book. 'When my man gave him his cash and suit of clothes last night, he promised there were no copies, the bastard. You have read it, then.' I nodded. 'A tedious thing. False, of course.'

'Who … who wrote it?'

'I have hardly had time to make a study of it. I should judge it was Morton, the dead regent of Scotland. Probably he took a confession from the former regent, this earl of Mar, and had someone copy it and add in more. It was the trick the same fellow used in putting together the evidence against King James' mother. False tales attend on prince's births. Stories of switches, changelings, sudden deaths and infants hidden in warming pans. Yet, though it is trash, if it were to get out … I regret that the simple minded would believe it. Chaos would fall out.'

'Surely … they could just open up Edinburgh Castle and find no child's corpse hidden there?'

'Hmph. Morton was a wicked man. It would not surprise me if such a corpse was found, exactly as the confession states. A child dead of the plague used to lend truth to the account, hidden somewhere in the place. And in seeking to disprove it, in any case, we should make it seem all the more true.' He shrugged, before patting the document. 'Trash, as I said. And not even persuasive trash. But it is here in ink and paper. And if it is ever given voice and blown into men's ears, it shall become true enough. Slanders are dangerous things as long as people have ears to listen, tongues to repeat, and hands to reach for weapons.'

'You will destroy it?'

He rose from the chair, tucking the pouch and the book away. 'I regret I must leave you, Ned. Dawn will be breaking.' He yawned. 'And the proclamation is on its way to Whitehall, as must I be, that the people might celebrate their new king. I trust we are still friends?'

I clenched my jaw only for a second. 'Yes, sir.'

He clapped my elbow lightly. 'You may keep your riches. Enjoy them. I shall call on you if I need you. Is there anything else you would like? I fancy you deserve your own reward, not just that creature Gregory's.'

'One thing, perhaps, sir.'

He raised an eyebrow. 'Your true family's home at Norfield? I believe it could be done, with the king's grace.'

'No.' That had not even crossed my mind. 'There is a boy…' He frowned. 'A child, name of Dust, in the queen's chapel choir. He was stolen. I'd have him out.'

'There is no queen's choir. There is no queen.'

'All the same, I–'

'Take him, find him, do as you will with him.'

I could feel my features souring. Always, men, even men of wit, assumed that people like me were slaves to the disgusting and truly unnatural love of boys. 'It's not that, he's my friend's–'

'I said do as you will, Ned. I have weightier matters to attend to. You may leave when the palace is unlocked. Go forth, then. Make merry. We have a new king. And long may he reign.' Without another word, his busy little steps took him out of the chamber. He left the door open. I stood awhile in what had become my cosy little cell.

And then I crossed the threshold into King James's merry young England.

Epilogue

St Paul's Cross, March 1603

Forasmuch as it has pleased Almighty God to call to his mercy, out of this transitory life, our sovereign lady the high and mighty Princess Elizabeth, late queen of England, France and Ireland, by whose death and dissolution the imperial realms aforesaid are come absolutely, wholly and solely to the high and mighty Prince James, King of Scotland, who is lineally and lawfully descended from Margaret, daughter of the high and renowned Prince Henry the Seventh, King of England.

Cecil paused in his oration, clearing his throat before continuing. Not a sound of approbation or criticism rose from the assembled crowd. A small crowd, I saw – the booksellers' stalls were still shut up and no one seemed to want to be too near the covered pulpit. Faith and I stood well to the back of it, hand in hand. The paved ground was wet, and smelled it, and a smear of rain still hung in the air all around the great yard of St Paul's Cross. The secretary stood up on the stepped platform: a small black smudge at the centre of a rainbow of officials, nobles, lords spiritual and temporal. All had been arranged so hastily that they had not even time to have black suits made ready. Except for Cecil. I felt a tight squeeze of my hand as he droned on. He looked nervous, I thought – although he had already read the proclamation in Westminster.

'Let's go,' I said.

We parted from the small groups of people, who neither cried for Elizabeth or cheered for King James, but stood waiting and watchful, as Cecil began reciting something about 'our lives, lands, goods, friends and adherents, against all the force and practice that shall go about, by words or deed, to interrupt, contradict, or impugn the said King James's just claims.'

We drifted about the streets, watching the city wake. Doors and windows were opening cautiously, heads peeping about. From St Paul's behind us a cheer rose.

They've accepted it, then.

'What a way to start a new year. And on Lady Day. Queen

Elizabeth must have set her mind to it. And her watch. Making him wait until 1603.'

'It's a long way to come from Scotland,' Faith said. I smiled down at her. Having been dragged out of our house and forced to spend a night out of it, she seemed loath to be cooped up all day. I had expected tears for Elizabeth, sobbing and waiting. But she had spent her tears in joy when I told her of our plans for the day. 'Think something might happen to stop him?'

'No. He'll come.'

It had been said, proclaimed, cried publicly. James was declared king now, and whether he sat in London or Edinburgh, the power of those words had made it a true and unquestionable fact. She paused, and tucked a stray red strand back under her cap. 'That stuff in the thing I wrote out. Was it … was it real?'

I glared at her, releasing her hand and taking her by the shoulders. I could feel her bones through the thin material, and she scowled. 'You read it? You understood it?'

'I'm not an idiot.'

'You are if you repeat it. You heard what the man said: no one can now impugn King James's just claims.'

She shrugged, shaking free. 'But that account book said he was no king. A … a … just a base-born bastard playing at being a king. I understood it well enough.'

'That was a lie. A false slander. Made by an evil old man in evil old days. Forget it. We'll get rich under this new king, by God.' We resumed our strolling. The streets had grown busier, the news of the proclamation and the sense of safety and order it inspired spreading, as if by magic. People were pulling down chains. Here and there the very old were crying. Young men were darting about, straightening hats and meeting in groups, hope drawing grins across their faces.

I thought of Lockhart.

It would be a world made for young men now, a world with courts for a king, a queen, and a litter of princelings. No more dead ends for lads whose only choice had been to live under a chaste and decaying old woman. The new king, as unpleasant as he might be, would bring jobs and security for many. The king that Faith was worried might truly be a bastard playing at it. I laughed, not sure why.

'What is it?'

'Ah, nothing. The world is grown so topsy turvy, I no longer know if players take their acts from kings or if kings take their acts from players.' She frowned. Her aversion to theatricals had not dimmed.

'Which reminds me. Let's go and find your brother. You might start thinking of a new name. I'm a clean-living man. I cannot live with Dust.'

Author's Note

Elizabeth I reigned from 17th November 1558 and died on the 24th of March 1603. In the old-style calendar then in date, her death fell on the last day of the year 1602: Lady Day. Her death had been anticipated for some time, not least by her cousin James, king of Scots, and her principal secretary, Sir Robert Cecil. The pair had been in secret correspondence since the earl of Essex had fallen from grace and lost his head in 1601. The last weeks of Elizabeth's life are marvellously told in Leanda de Lisle's splendid *After Elizabeth: The Death of Elizabeth and the Coming of King James* (2006: Harper Collins). This book is a must read for those interested in the frantic and complex political machinations of the succession. For those interested in what came before, I would recommend Anne Somerset's *Elizabeth I* (1992: St Martin's Press) and Alison Weir's *Elizabeth the Queen* (2013: Random House). In terms of the queen's association with Essex and his subsequent, posthumous hold on the age's hearts and minds, readers might like my own nonfiction study, *Elizabeth and Essex: Power, Passion, and Politics* (2019: Sharpe Books).

Often, Queen Elizabeth's final weeks and months are treated with brevity by biographers, with the Essex affair marking the last important event of her long reign and the final couple of years instead focusing on increasingly lurid images of a Gothic spinster lurching about her palaces, smashing mirrors and stabbing at arrases, desperately trying to recapture youth by painting her face and body white. The stories of the mirrors exist in several sources, and her godson John Harington reports that she thrust a rusty sword about herself in fear. For the macabre coating of white lead, there is no contemporary source. With hindsight, we know that James VI became James I smoothly and with no trouble. But people at the time could not have known of Cecil's planning nor of his swift action (between her death at around 3am and dawn at 6am, he had called together a 'great council' and gained approval for the draft proclamation he had had ready to go). Other contenders for the throne included Lady Arbella Stuart, about whom Sarah Gristwood has written in her comprehensive study, *Arbella: England's Lost Queen* (1999: Bantam). The Grey sisters, Elizabeth's cousins, had tragic lives and their descendants were also candidates. Tracey Borman's *Elizabeth's*

Women: The Hidden Story of the Virgin Queen (2009: Jonathan Cape) provides an excellent analysis of their lives and posthumous importance.

In addition to de Lisle's study, a number of other nonfiction books were essential in writing this novel. For the succession itself, Francis Edwards's *The Succession, Bye and Main Plots of 1601-3* (2006: Four Courts Press) and Christopher Lee's *1603: A Turning Point in British History* (2014: St Martin's Press) were particularly good. From the former I discovered that prior to Elizabeth's death, 'seminaries' (that is 'secret agents') were dispatched to every country of England with the task of making James Stuart an acceptable prospect to provincial English folk. I based the unnamed balladeer on these men. His song comes from the archives of the University of Rochester's *The Camelot Project*, which digitises Arthurian texts and images. As ever in the early modern period, changes were rarely promoted as innovations, but as glorious rediscoveries of the classical or ancient past. The once and future king of Britain, therefore, provided fertile ground in pressing the idea that James' union of the crowns would not be a frightening new turn of events but a restoration of the old and rightful order of the island's governance. Susan Doran's 'Polemic and Prejudice: a Scottish King for an English Throne' in the edited collection *Doubtful and Dangerous: The Question of the Succession in Late Elizabethan England* (2016: Manchester University Press) is great, as are the other essays in the book.

Sir Robert Cecil, whom King James later ennobled as the earl of Salisbury, is for me one of the most interesting political figures of the entire early modern period. This is mainly because I find him surprisingly modern; he would fit neatly into an American political drama or a gangster film as easily as he would a Cold War spy thriller. Lacking the strict religious fanaticism of his father and the gung-ho, adventurous wiles of, say, Thomas Cromwell, Cecil is probably the first really modern statesman in English history. He was, as Leanda de Lisle points out in another of her books, *Tudors: The Family Story* (2013: Random House), corrupt. An enjoyable study of his career alongside that of his father can be found in David Loades's *The Cecils: Privilege and Power Behind the Throne* (2009: Bloomsbury Academic).

James VI of Scotland and I of England is an infuriating figure, partly because of his actions and beliefs, and partly because of the strange, contradictory nature of his personality, which could be as loving and generous as it was bullying, cowardly, imperious, and pacific. I thoroughly enjoyed John Matusiak's scholarly and often very funny *James I: Scotland's King of England* (2018: History Press Ltd) and Caroline Bingham's companion pieces, *James VI of Scotland* (1979: Weidenfeld & Nicolson) and *James I of England* (1981: Little Hampton). Bingham confronts the mysterious rumour of King James having been a 'changeling' head on, and in that she shares ground with Antonia Fraser, who notes the same rumours in her *Mary Queen of Scots* (1969: Weidenfeld & Nicolson). The story, which forms a major part of this novel, has very murky origins. It is alleged that at some point after his birth, the little James died and was substituted with another child, the whole affair being covered up and the corpse of the real James Stuart being hidden away in Edinburgh Castle. The rumour was given a burst of life (or, alternatively, was born entirely) with the discovery of bones hidden within the castle walls in the eighteenth century. Embroidery added a further frisson as it was variously claimed and written that those bones were wrapped in a length of cloth of gold, with 'JR' for James Rex sewn into it. Fraser has debunked this, noting the plain woollen cloth actually noted at the time and judging that the bones, which likely had nothing to do with the period of James VI's life, might have been those of the illicit offspring of a maid. Nevertheless, there exists a 'Mar family tradition', based probably on the similarity perceived between portraits of the adult James and members of the Erskine family, who were his childhood guardians and companions, that the king was indeed a changeling, being the secret son of the earl who died in 1572. It is a good story, but no more worth believing than similar tales that hold that Elizabeth died in childhood and was replaced with a boy from the village of Bisley.

What is certainly true is that James VI was involved in a bizarre affair involving the deaths of the earl of Gowrie and his brother (the previous earl having been executed) in 1600. This episode in Scottish history has puzzled historians for centuries, with all kinds of theories put forward. The king always claimed that he was lured to a tower in Gowrie House by the promise of buried treasure, only to find that the earl and his brother (with another man, later identified as Henderson and mysteriously pardoned) instead waiting to kidnap him. He shouted for help from a window and, in the ensuing confusion, his hunting party left the two men dead. It has been suggested that James, who was almost certainly bisexual with a preference for men, had tried to solicit sex, been rebuffed, and panicked, calling for the murder (and silence) of his putative lover. I do not think this is likely, but still find the king's own version of events unsatisfactory – and so I chose to use the event here. Andrew Lang's *James VI and the Gowrie Mystery* (1901: Longmans, Green & Co.) covers all the main events of the episode in a charming, clear way.

The issue of homosexuality looms large in the novel, and in terms of academic study of the period, it is a growing field. Early moderns did not have a conception of it as a sexuality; their chief interest was in sexual acts, not preferences. 'Buggery', therefore, was a crime, whether committed with a man or a woman. 'Sodomy' was a loose term which encompassed everything from anal sex to witchcraft to bestiality and werewolfery. Curiously, however, very few, if any, seem to have incurred the full force of the law's potential punishment – death by hanging. Obviously there were men who preferred men and women who preferred women in the period, as in all periods, but it seems that Elizabethans drew a censorious veil over people's sex lives, preferring innuendo and public shaming to keep people 'Godly', at least in terms of what they did between the sheets. Sex within marriage was encouraged, and couples encouraged to enjoy it, but outside marriage it was sin, and thus those who had sex but could not marry were inherently sinful. Strong male friendships were thus promoted as being better than illicit sex with women other than wives. As an introduction, I would recommend Bruce R. Smith's *Homosexual Desire in Shakespeare's England: A Cultural Poetics* (1994: University of Chicago Press), and Kenneth Borris and George S. Rousseau's *The Sciences of Homosexuality in Early Modern Europe* (2013: Routledge). The latter investigates the ways in which some early moderns attempted to understand and explain what they saw as a persistent phenomenon. Any number of books and articles are also widely available on the sexuality of the speaker of Shakespeare's *Sonnets*.

Ned Savage's public life involves a number of real figures. Ben Jonson is probably the most interesting. It was he who claimed that Elizabeth painted her nose red and was possessed of a membrane over her vagina that prevented intercourse; he also wrote some very good plays. David Riggs' *Ben Jonson: A Life* (1989: Harvard University Press) provides an enjoyable if Freudian take. Ian Donaldson's 2011 book of the same name (Oxford University Press) is more objective but just as enjoyable. A number of books on Shakespeare give perforce speculative accounts of his life, such as Katherine Duncan-Jones' provocative and interesting *Ungentle Shakespeare: Scenes from his Life* (2001: Arden Shakespeare), from which I drew the character of Sir William Dethick, Garter King of Arms (a very shady man indeed). Andrew Gurr's *Playgoing in Shakespeare's London* (2004: Cambridge University Press) is a must-read for how the Elizabethan and Jacobean theatres operated. For the ways in which England's most famous playwrights socialised, collaborated, worked together, and developed rivalries, see Stanley Wells' *Shakespeare & Co.* (2008: Vintage). What's probably more of interest to people though, is reading the plays – which are often available cheaply in e-book format.

Finally, I would like to thank those that have read this far. I hugely enjoyed writing this book and was sorry to see the end of Elizabeth, who is one of the most captivating figures in world history. However, those who came of age during her lifetime did not wake up on the 25th of March 1603 and see themselves, suddenly, as Jacobeans. Rather, the things we often associate with the Jacobean age – the theatre, malcontent young Englishmen, anxieties about the relationship between Scotland and England – had been around for quite some time, and some of the problems of Elizabeth's reign (such as the growing tetchiness of parliament, frustrated at having its prerogatives rolled back by degrees) were to burst into greater prominence after her death. I hope that Ned Savage will be around at least to see James's coronation…

If you enjoyed this book (or if you didn't), I would love to hear why. Please do let me know on Twitter @ScrutinEye or on Instagram @steven.veerapen.3 If you would consider leaving a review on Amazon or Goodreads, I'd be very grateful.

Printed in Great Britain
by Amazon